THE ADVENTURES OF GREGORY SAMSON,

SPACE EXPLORER:

A FARTHER ORBIT

Thanks to the oddballs who created odd things, and in so doing showed me that it was all right to be an oddball, myself; to Josiah for helping me edit, and being a good friend; to Tom McGrath for his beautiful art; to my family for not sending me to military school when my grades went to shit; to the existence of caffeine and other things I shouldn't admit to here; and to many, many more.

Cover by Tom McGrath
www.spikedmcgrath.com
Edited by Josiah Jacobus-Parker
Photography by Luke Whitlow
A Farther Orbit
Copyright ©2014 Benjamin Mumford-Zisk
www.mumfordzisk.com
ISBN: 978-0-9982434-0-5

This too is for Tom Botsford.

A Farther Orbit

EDICT: This file and subsequent files are sealed from all but the utmost.

This file has been granted sentience and is legally empowered for self-defense.

Unauthorized readers will be expunged.

WARNING: Cognitive identification procedures are underway.

File: Interview 2

CONTENT: Continuing transcript of interview with local binary organism self-identifying as individual code-named The Origami Man.

SUBJECT: Local binary organism self-identifying as individual code-named The Origami Man.

INTERVIEWER: Scientist _____.
Note: For security purposes Scientist _____'s name and all identifying remarks have been stricken from FILE: Interview 2.

Timestamp

This is Scientist _____ continuing the interview with the Origami Man at, ah, _____ on _____.

Let's recap.
You were implanted with a mimetic, transforming, self-repairing and self-aware machine organism.

A Shipkiller.
Right.
In your neck.

Yes, that's right.

It seems that your acclimation was rather stressful. A hard adjustment.

You could say that.

You killed a man.

Not intentionally.

Still, you killed a man.

But not intentionally.
That matters.

All right. So what happened after you left Earth? After the thief, ah, Rell called you for help. What did he want?

What do you have to decide?

What's that?

You said last time you needed to understand my nature ahead of a decision making process. What do you have to decide?

Well, that depends on what you tell us, and on the results of some tests we're running.

But our ultimate decision is whether to let you live. If we deem you a threat, we will destroy you.

I'm not sure it would be as easy as that, _____.

I'm not interested in having another pissing contest.
We want to know what sort of person you are morally, socially, physically and metaphysically.
It is important for us to have a full understanding of your beginning, in order to accurately extrapolate your character.
With that in mind, I want to thank you for your candor and attention to detail.
You're a mouthy bastard; it's quite helpful.

Have you noticed that he seems to be multiple people at the same time?

Oh that could mean anything, you know how easy it is to camouflage a person on the visual spectrum. I'm talking about the way his speech patterns change from moment to moment.

Hm. So he's not really here?

Yeah, I heard you, but you said…

He's sort of here.
Thanks. That's real helpful.

We're not a fully individual species within a universe like yours.

I feel it's only fair to tell you that we can still hear you when you subvocalize like that.
Are you speaking to the ship?

Thanks for your candor. Earlier–
You are *speaking to the ship. And you hear it in your head? That's fascinating!*

Do you know that you move about when you speak to it?

Yes, I know. It's a hard habit to break.
Last time, you told me my existence was a variable you hadn't had to consider before. What does that mean?

Come on, _____, I filled thirteen hours, you can give me five minutes.

Obviously yours is not the first universe we've visited.

Whatever you say.

Yours is not the first universe we've visited.

13

There are several distinct types of universe, structural variants that adhere to different physical laws. Universes like yours undergo heat death. By now, there shouldn't be variable matter here, much less life. You shouldn't be here. But you are. We're curious about that.

What are you scared of?
I know I shouldn't have survived this long, _____, you're not telling me anything new. What are you scared of?

Tell me what happened next.

Fuck off.

Tell me what you did after you left Earth and I'll tell you why we're concerned.

But you are concerned.

Yes.

How about a cup of coffee, _____?

Don't push it.

I'll tell a better story with a cup of coffee.

We're only interested in the facts.

Facts aren't immutable.

14

I'll tell you what you want to know, _____. But it's been a long time since I've spoken aloud for this long. I'd like something to drink.

There isn't any coffee. You said it yourself.

You can travel between universes, _____, I'm sure you can manufacture me a cup of coffee. I'll describe it for–God damn, that was fast. How do you know what coffee is? I was expecting a *much* longer conversation.

We took the impression from your mind.

Well, thank you.

Jesus, you guys really can't read minds for shit. This is like Bustelo filtered through pork rinds. Not that I'm ungrateful.

What did you do after you left Earth?

I had a really great meal about two-thirds turn clockwise around the galaxy from Earth.
Sometimes I really miss eating.

The first time I left Earth, like really left, I was blown away by the speed. I was so fast. I mean, I had a basic sense of what I could do. I knew that I was half spaceship. A human body hosting an intelligent, transforming alien warship. A Shipkiller. But those are just words. The experience of it was staggering. I remember thinking...well, nothing verbal. But...

1

Light moved at one hundred and eighty-six thousand, two hundred and eighty two miles a second. It took just over eight minutes for sunlight to reach Earth, which put the sun at an average distance of about ninety million miles. Mars was maybe a third of that when our orbits matched up, thirty million miles and change. Other times the gulf was nearly seven times as far.

Don't laugh, that was a long way for us.

I knew all of that, all those figures, as easily as I know left from right. Cab had a complete copy of the Internet jammed under my brain like money under a mattress, and the information lurked in my periphery no matter where I was looking.

I cut loose with my engines for the first time and Earth fell away from me, the size of a beach ball, a melon, a pea. And then it was nearly gone, nothing more than a bright point beneath my feet. I felt a pang.

Without spatial reference, it was impossible to tell how fast I was going, which in turn made it hard to maintain an accurate sense of my physical self. Earth didn't have to be far behind me; the planet could have shrunk. I might be larger, now. Or I might be very, very small. It's hard to know yourself in outer space.

"Cab," I said, "how fast are we going?"

--Just over half light speed--

--A hundred thousand miles a second--

There was a gleeful tone to the pseudo-memory of Cab's voice in my head, an unknowing excitement. He was ready to let go. He was ready to leave, in spite of his proximity to my fear.

"And how far are we going?" I looked uneasily back at Earth. The planet was nothing more than a tiny pinprick outlined in blue, with the planet's name written next to it in the same color. There were no other blue systems on the galaxy map. Blue for home.

The stars blared their names at me. I turned off the map. The names disappeared but the stars remained, closer than they had been before.

--Ceres is about sixty-three million miles from Earth right now--

--Here--

An empty point lit up ahead of me. It said, in dandelion-yellow, 'Ceres,' along with a number in the high fifty millions, which was diminishing quite quickly. Below that was written, 'Rell,' in green.

"We're going past Mars." I knew instinctively that Mars was about forty-seven million miles from Earth at this point in each planet's orbit. The information presented itself to my mind and then disappeared. It was like being swarmed by trivia-obsessed gnats.

--Yuh--

I swallowed hard. At a hundred thousand miles a second it would take me ten minutes to travel sixty million miles. That was well past Mars. A journey dwarfing the trip NASA had been working towards for four decades with no end in sight, undertaken on a whim and accomplished in less time than it normally took me to drive to work. A mighty accomplishment for humanity, except that I hadn't done anything to deserve it, other than stand in the right place at the right time. I was powerful, now, but it was too immediate. I'd had too many obstacles removed too fast to feel any pride in my victories.

The minutes ticked by. There was a draw on my body, some barely perceptible force that told me which direction I was moving in, but nothing more. I imagine that without the inertial dampeners, I would have looked like some kind of soup.

If I die, I thought abruptly, I'll be a missing person. I turned around without changing course and stared homeward.

Two days. I'd been living with Cab in my neck for two days. That was barely long enough for me to recognize what I had become, much less tell anyone else. Even my roommates had to find out by accident. And now I was gone, off the planet, already farther from home than anyone else in human history. If I didn't make it back, it would be like I had disappeared into thin air.

I should have left a note, I thought, some sort of explanation for my actions. It would have been a kindness, if nothing else. A communiqué in case of the unforeseen. I frowned. Then again, how much danger was I really in? Supposedly, I was immortal, even if I didn't feel like it. What did immortality feel like, anyway? What did it mean? My skin still felt fragile. Cab said he could fix me. That didn't sound pleasant. That sounded like I had to be broken, first.

And for whom would I have left a note, anyway? You like that? Whom? Anyway. Dylan knew where I'd gone. Iris didn't want anything to do with me. My extended family was minimal, disparate and scattered to the wind, and my most recent serious girlfriend left me a year before all this. Things didn't end well, and we didn't talk, and what the hell was I supposed to say, anyway? *To whom it may concern: I have become host to a sentient transforming alien spaceship, and as a result I have decided to leave Earth in order to keep the planet safe from a species of marauding omnicidal bugs. Best Wishes, Greg.* Then I could have crumpled up the paper and eaten it, because there was no one who would have believed me who wasn't already aware of the situation.

Maybe I should have banged out a quick memoir before I left. *A Life Fisted by Circumstance: The Gregory Samson Story*.

Two days with Cab and we'd already managed to kill someone. That was reason enough for me to leave. If I ended up just another missing person, well, maybe that was what I deserved.

--I will drug you if you don't stop muttering to yourself--

--What the hell are you thinking about anyway, your brain is like a goddamn strobe light--

"You can see my brain?" I forced myself to think of something else, and came up with sex. As usual, I was in favor of it. "Was that a bright thought?"

--Actually, yes--

--What were you yammering on about?--

"Nothing," I said. "Mindless chatter. I'm nervous."

--Pauvre petit--

--Wanna play I Spy?--

I looked around and snorted. "With what, stars?"

--There's a hydrogen atom over there--

--And there--

--And there--

--And there--

--And over there is the entirety of creation, you absolute ass--

I laughed, and after a second Cab joined me, in his own way. It felt a little like I was laughing for two. Then Ceres loomed in my vision, all of a sudden, and I ground to a halt with my hands out in front of me to grab…something. Nothing. But the temptation was there. Instincts are hard to let go of. I relaxed and looked around, another instinct, and laughed at the idea that I might be seen. Even Rell was all the way around the other side of the asteroid. I was utterly alone.

Ceres was a dirty blue-brown ball. Compositional information flashed across my displays: gravity, (minimal) atmosphere, (nil) and mineral composition. (Mostly rocks and water ice.) I moved across the surface, hung by the shoulders on my wide dorsal engines. The landscape was rough, pitted, absent of detritus and layered in frost. According to whatever it was in me that could tell this sort of thing, there was more fresh water in Ceres than there was on Earth. I would have made a killing in the asteroid mining business if I had just dragged the damn thing back home.

--Wow, what a pretty rock--

I zipped over the horizon. Time to find out whether Rell wanted to kill me. There were probably better ways to think about my immediate future, but that one possibility overrode all the others in my head. Sure, he had asked me for my help, but he also insisted that we speak face to face, and the man was a thief. I'd only known him for two days, and I only met him because he tried to steal Cab right off my back. I didn't know that I could trust him. I only knew that I didn't.

Rell's ship was propped at an angle at the bottom of a particularly large crater, pointing drunkenly out into space as if dropped there by accident. I came to a full stop and put my hands where my pockets would have been, realized I didn't have any, and grunted in frustration.

Outer space was a lot like deep water; it had a beautifying effect, so that anything you saw in that environment became unavoidably affecting, a pinnacle of grace, devoid of the flaws that are only apparent on the ground. Which is a florid way of saying that Rell's

21

ship really looked like shit lying there in an asteroid crater. Someone had sprayed an ugly patch over the hole I'd burned in the hull and then neglected to repaint, and there was a collection of long scorch marks visible across the bow.

Cab marked the pertinent points of the ship, places we could take cover on the surface of the planetoid, available paths of retreat. He wasn't nervous. He was excited, almost at play.

Something began to shine towards the rear of the ship, just outside of the visible spectrum, and then I heard Rell as if he were right next to me.

"Are you going to come aboard, or just float there?" I just managed to avoid jumping in place. Rell's tone was pleasant, but his words were explosive in the silence that had for ten minutes been punctuated only by my own murmuring.

The shining spread across the hull, and I realized I could distinguish when Rell's ship was powered on from when it was not. It was like being able to tell if a person was awake or not, or whether someone was watching you.

"Samson!" Rell said sharply. "I'm a sitting duck with the reactor on like this! Move yourself!"

--Stop ruminating and answer the man, you boob!--

"Yar, Cap'n Rell!" I growled. "Parrrrmission to come abaarrrrd."

"Are the other humans as weird as you are, Samson?" Rell sighed. The airlock opened, laboriously.

"I like to think I'm a man of the people," I said. I soared inside and landed on my feet. "An average Joe."

"Truly?" Rell said. His voice was close but his tone was distant, as if he was distracted.

"Rell, there's an alien spaceship growing out of my neck." I put my hands on my hips, because I still didn't have any pockets. I thought I looked like a tool. "I'm about as atypical as is humanly possible. Open up."

"Yeah?" Rell said. "You, ah, sure about that?"

"Rell, I didn't fly sixty million miles to talk to you through the gate," I said. "Lemme in."

"Suit yourself," Rell grunted.

Ceres was small, but it still dragged my feet in a direction that my brain had determined was 'down.' Unfortunately, Ceres' 'down' did not appear to be the same as Rell's shipboard 'down.' The door whunked shut, there was a brief pause, and then the gravity switched on. The wall to my right became the floor, the floor beneath my feet became the wall, and the far wall became the ceiling. I smashed into the ground and made a noise like a hamster under five hundred pounds of teaspoons, and Cab started to laugh. Everybody played their part to perfection.

"Cab," I asked when I got my breath back, "How is it that when I'm in the ship I can survive accelerating to half light speed in under ten seconds, but it still hurts to crack my head on the pavement?"

--Comedy--

"Ah." I lay still, bruised and confused. "I see. And did you know that I was standing on the wall?"

--Yeah, didn't you?--

"No," I said, "I did not."

--Oh--

--Well, you see that blue dot on the floor?--

--That means that surface is shipboard 'down'--

"Ah," I said again.

--I'll try to give you the heads up about that sorta thing in the future--

"If you would be so kind." I got to my feet carefully and Cab reorganized us into a simple seven-foot tall mechanical demigod. In the right light, and with a healthy combination of imagination and charity, I looked a bit like Michael Jordan covered in lead foil.

The inside door opened up and I stepped into the hold. Rell was waiting for me, leaned up against a crate smoking a cigar. As soon as I was over the threshold he said, "Lock it down."

The door closed heavily behind me and flashed red, and I felt the ship power down around us. Rell stared at me. He was tall, nine feet at least, with humanoid legs and two elbows on each arm, and he was covered in thick, reedy fur that ranged in color from the deep forest green of his bare chest to the bright, tropical toucan colors in the crests behind his ears. His face looked like the result of a wild night between a gorilla and a tiger, but he didn't move like a mammal, he was too graceful. He wasn't moving, though, just standing there with his odd arms folded across his chest. His face was tight, and the fur around his ears wavered continuously.

"Hiya Rell," I said. "How you doing?"

He dragged on his cigar. The coal fizzed. After a second he blew twin plumes of purple smoke out of his nostrils, and worked the cigar into the corner of his mouth.

"I've been better," he grunted. He grimaced, then spun on his heel and walked out of the hold. "Come on, Samson, let's have a drink and talk this over."

I followed him. What else was I going to do?

Rell's legs were nearly five feet long. I had to jog to keep up.

"I got your message," I said. My metal feet clanked on the metal deck.

"Really," Rell said. "I thought you dropped in for the hell of it."

"Yeah, I'm around Mars a lot," I said.

24

We went into the kitchen. Rell cracked a beer and drained it in four swallows. His Adam's apple moved eighteen inches up and down, from the base of his jaw to the top of his sternum, and after being amazed for a moment by the distance, I realized it was much more amazing that the alien had an Adam's apple at all.

He belched magnificently, then cracked a fresh bottle and filled me an honest-to-god pint glass. He held it like a shot glass.

"You got me a special glass." I took the beer. "You really do need my help."

Rell grunted and hopped up on the counter, next to the stove. He jumped like a cat, but landed on his butt like a playful chimp. He opened a fresh beer with something hidden in his palm.

"Take off your helmet," he said.

I obliged him, because I couldn't drink through the faceplate, and because I knew he had to size me up before he would tell me what he needed. All I could do was wait. I'd seen the look on his face before, when I had to interview a reticent source harboring a hard revelation. People don't like to give up their secrets, even when they're in dire straits. The fact that a gorilla-tiger from beyond at least some of the stars would act the same way was unsettling. An awe-inspiring mundane similarity highlighting the fact that however alien he might have been, Rell was 'people,' too. I was glad for the quiet while he looked me over. I needed time to adjust. The familiarity was jarring.

Rell's expression got heavier and heavier. "How old are you?" He asked finally.

He hadn't been this interested in me the first time we met. I drank some of my beer and decided that lying would be immature.

"I'm twenty-eight," I said.

Rell took a deep breath and blew it out of his closed lips in exasperation. My father used to make the same noise when he was frustrated and tired.

"You're a child," he said. "You're just a child." He finished his beer and opened another. I tried to see what he had in his palm. Whatever it was, he had it well-hidden and he was very comfortable with it. He studied me back.

"What have you done?" He asked.

"What, you mean, like, ever?" I said with an empty smile. "That's a hefty order, Rell. What's going on? Why do you want to know?" I stowed the ship on my back and clambered onto the counter opposite Rell with my feet dangling four feet off the ground.

Rell waved his hands near his waist and looked off to his right for a moment. Then he nodded and waved his hands again and looked back at me.

"You see a bug?" I asked.

"My computer," Rell said. "I was checking the ship's sensors. It's a personal visual field, so…" He shook his head. "Doesn't matter. Last night I was chased out of the Schlorb system by a team of bounty hunters." He waved his hands to punctuate his words, and some beer sloshed on the floor. The linoleum absorbed the liquid and burped quietly.

"There's a price on my head," Rell said. "Again. A big one, judging from the size of the team that's after me."

Bounty hunters. In space. I'd be lying if I told you that the thought didn't provoke a certain measure of juvenile glee on my part.

I drank some beer. It was good, but beer usually was. "I take it this is not a regular occurrence, you having a price on your head."

"Not for a long time," Rell grumbled. "I've been careful. A death mark's not an easy thing to live with."

I grinned at the reference, and Rell snarled. I guess it wasn't intentional.

"You think this is funny?" He spat. "Someone wants me dead because of you."

"Technically, all I did was stand there," I said. "You're the one who stole the seed. I'm the idiot Earthling, remember?"

"The Cabernician stole the seed," Rell snapped back. "I just stopped him selling it to the Krr." He paused, and then his fur deflated and he drank the rest of his beer.

"At least, that's what I'll tell my lawyer," he grumbled. "Sorry. I know none of this is on you."

"No harm," I said. "What do you need from me?"

Rell looked at me askance and raised both of his impressive tufted eyebrows.

"That easily?"

I grimaced. "I have to be off Earth for a while. I did something…It's safer this way. Helping you will take me away from here. I'm not happy about it, but it's the truth. What do you need me to do?"

Rell nodded. "Well, I need to find out who wants me dead, and then I need to either convince them to call off the hunt, or kill them. One or the other."

Cab shifted inside of me and started to pay closer attention.

"You don't know who posted the bounty then," I said. I figured he didn't, I just wanted to say it aloud. Bounty hunters in space. My life was an idiot's fantasy. Rell shook his head.

"Well," I said, "Let's narrow the field. The Cabernicians blame you for the seed theft. They're a possibility. The cops are after you, but if they're like the ones I'm used to, they probably don't subcontract, and I don't imagine they're looking to have you killed outright. The same is probably true of the Cabernician species, now that I think about it. These are the people who want you to stand trial. Now, as far as folks who would want you dead, the Krr seem like they would do their own dirty work, given what I've heard about them, but maybe they're trying a new tactic. The Cabernician who's been dealing with them is another suspect, he's probably shitting his pants over this. Your broker, or whoever got you the job, they could be behind it, too." I shrugged. "Seems like there are a lot of people who would benefit from your death, Rell."

Rell was staring at me with the bottle halfway to his mouth.

"What," I said, "I'm smart. I read books and shit."

Rell nodded slowly.

"I also talked to a Cabernician, and a cop named Frewdin. CLEA agent, whatever I'm supposed to call him." I shrugged. "This is what you want me for, right? To help you sort all of this out?"

A shrill mechanical scream cut the world in two. It was an awful noise, terrified and terrifying, the wail of prey sure of its destiny in the predator's maw. Cab snapped around me and dimmed the sound, but I could still feel it tearing at the edge of my attention. It wasn't just noise, it was the fight or flight response conveyed in a sound wave.

Rell was in a crouch, legs wide and body low. A thick crest ran from the top of his head to the base of his spine and disappeared into his shorts. Presumably his species had a tail at some point in their history. His arms were out in front of him, with his elbows loose and his hands open-palmed to the floor. His five fingers were curled and flexed, and his palms had pulled apart along the flanges to reveal four curved six-inch claws, one between each bone. They were yellow-white and translucent at the edges, like a cat's, and while I know that evolution intended them for climbing, they also made a dandy weapon. I tried to imagine boxing someone with two sets of elbows and claws in his palms, and decided that it was a situation best avoided.

All of this was one instant. In the next, Rell straightened up, relaxed his hands, and said, firmly, "Off." The scream cut off. He took a deep breath, exhaled slowly, and flattened his hair. He had a certain birdlike affect when frightened. Or maybe bug like, there was a stiff note to his speed. I hadn't even seen him get off the counter, he had just appeared in the crouch, ready to unleash some horrible Vabling kung fu.

Cab was doing what he could with all the adrenaline I'd produced when the alarm went off, but there was a lot of it.

Rell cleared his throat. "Your grasp of the situation is impressive, Samson, but I don't need you for your deductive ability. I need your muscle. I need you to save my bacon."

That had to have been a mistranslation, I thought, shoving my way past the meaning of his words. I couldn't get into another fight. I had to be careful.

He pointed at the ceiling and twirled his finger once. "That was the ship's proximity alarm. Someone is about to attack us, presumably the same group that chased me out of Schlorb. They're the only ones who would think to look for me here." He grimaced and shook his head. "They must have traced my warp trajectory."

"You need my ship," I said. Cab felt like he was grinning.

"I need you to fight these people for me," Rell said. "And everyone else after them, until we get to the bottom of this. I need a warrior, and I have you, a child with a weapon. Obviously my options are limited, or I wouldn't be here."

His tone was calm, but his face was tight, and I know mine was, too, under the imperturbable faceplate. Only Cab seemed unconcerned with the reality of the situation, that we hadn't made it an hour off Earth without being forced into a fight.

--This is going to be neat--

--What kind of ships do you think they have?--

I swallowed and shrugged and didn't answer and listened to the growing sense of dread that I knew was my ship telling me that I was going to have to make a decision very, very soon. Kill, or be killed, except I couldn't be killed, which only left the other part. The worse part.

Dammit, the whole point of getting a liberal arts degree was so I could avoid this sort of situation.

2

"Come with me." Rell vaulted the table, grabbed the edge of the doorframe with one hand and turned into the hallway in a single motion. He was gone before I knew he was moving. I thudded into the hall and caught a glimpse of him disappearing around the corner a hundred yards down.

"Spry little monkey, isn't he?" I took off after him, swallowing at my fear. Proximity alarms began to ring in my head, courtesy of my Shipkiller skin.

--Agile, too--

--you see that hop?--

--Twelve feet horizontal from a standstill--

The alarms changed pitch as the bounty hunters closed in, higher and higher.

--Man you are slow as mole asses--

--Lemme give you a hand--

Abruptly, there was more power in my legs. I picked up speed, tried to take the corner too fast and smashed into the metal wall hard enough to leave a dent.

--Whoops--

--Sorry--

"Nope," I groaned, getting to my feet. "My fault. Wasn't ready. I'll get used to it."

I followed Rell at a cautious thirty miles an hour to a vertical airshaft through the center of the ship, a stairwell without any stairs. The walls were thick cork scored with disappearing claw marks and footprints, studded at intervals with open doorways. Rell disappeared into the topmost door just as I reached the shaft.

"Follow me, he says," I grumbled. I looked over the edge to the bottom of the ship, two hundred meters down, and stepped into space. The engines under my kidneys cracked to life and lifted me gracefully to the top floor.

There was just the one room, up there. If Rell hadn't been such a loner, I would have called it the bridge. As it was, cockpit seems more appropriate. There was only one chair, swivel mounted at the back, not the base, with joysticks on the armrests and control apparatus hanging on spindly arms above and around the pilot's head. The setup looked primitive, cobbled-together; it was hard to imagine Rell controlling the entire ship from here.

The man in question clicked and tapped away, half-reading written and graphical information that popped up in midair in front of him. I could see it, now, where the other manipulations Rell had performed had been invisible. Those must have been from his personal machine, whereas now we were in the bridge. Cockpit. It was information that was meant to be shared. Or maybe it was because I had the helmet on. I wasn't sure. I understood very little. That said, I do remember a three-dimensional grid that depicted six large dots converging on a smaller, central dot that I thought looked very important.

"Six of them again," Rell said. "Same group as last night. We have about three minutes." He turned to face me. "They must have been hiding in the outer orbits, waiting for me to turn on the power."

"Oh, shit," I said. "Sorry."

Rell shrugged. "To be fair, they could also be tracking the fully functional Shipkiller that's been appearing and disappearing for the last quarter of an hour on a deserted asteroid sixty million miles from the only inhabited planet in the system. It's a moot point.

They're here, now, and if last night is any indication, they're loaded for bear. I need your protection. These people are going to kill me, and you, because you're here."

--Let 'em try!--

Rell smiled. "I'm not as resilient as you are, Cab. I need you to protect me, or I'm going to die."

I shifted my stance, tried to find a position where my legs felt strong. I was unsuccessful.

"You have guns on this thing," I said.

"Nothing that presents any real threat," Rell said.

"You have thermal blasters, bombs and a well cannon!" I shouted.

--Dude, what's your issue?--

"I've got thermal blasters," Rell said. "Bombs are useless against a moving target, and I can't use the well cannon this close to a star, it won't aim right. This is a cargo ship, Samson, those are warships. I don't stand a chance against six of them. I can run, that's about it, but by now they're close enough they'll have my warp trajectory in minutes. They'd be right on my tail. And even if I could get away, I still have a price on my head. I can't run forever. Eventually I'll have to kill these bastards, or they'll kill me. I can't kill them myself, so I'm hiring you to do it for me, because I have no better options. Not that you're ill-equipped. You are, after all, wearing one of the most deadly weapons in the galaxy as a second skin." He grinned again, without showing any teeth.

He needed an assassin.

"I can't," I said, holding fast to the back of his chair. "I'm not a fighter, or a, a soldier. I can't just kill them."

Rell stared at me for several seconds, which was a while considering our time constraint.

33

"Ok," he said. "Then we die." He closed his eyes and began to take long, calm breaths.

"What?" I said.

"You think we have other options," Rell said without opening his eyes. "We don't. You fight them, or I die. You might get away. You could run back to Earth, I doubt they'll follow you. But then, you can't go back to Earth, can you? It's not safe." He looked at me. "You fight them or I die. Make a choice."

I stared at him and tried to gather my thoughts. There had to be another way. I just had to think of it. We could get away, and then change course, maybe, evade them somehow.

"Two minutes," Rell said through his teeth.

"Goddam monkey." I turned and stepped off the landing, into the ship, and fell seventy feet to the appropriate hall.

--Wheeeee!--

I hit the deck like a steel-plated cat and took off towards the airlock, bouncing off the corners and denting the bulkheads.

"Monkey," Rell mused over the intercom. "Was that a racist remark, Samson?" The calm was back in his voice.

"Yes, you furry alien monstrosity." I skittered into the airlock and the door hissed shut behind me.

"I used to date a furry alien monstrosity," Rell chuckled. He wasn't really listening to me. His ship warmed up around me. "The sex was fascinating."

"Gross," I said. "Listen, just so we're clear, we're doubling whatever you were planning to pay me." The braggadocio in my voice kept it from shaking. The airlock opened wide, and the stars bore down on me like the baleful eyes of a billion angry gods, or something like that. I squared my shoulders and roared away from Ceres.

"Who said I was going to pay you?" Rell said. An alert dinged in my ear and his ship lifted lightly out of its crater, shedding its flaws as it rose into free fall. Space was a beautiful place.

"Me," I snapped. "The guy you tricked into saving your ass."

"Tricked?" Rell said. "That's extreme."

"This is too convenient," I said. "You planned this. You knew they were out there."

"I thought they might follow you," Rell said. His voice sounded like he was shrugging. "You need this, and I need them dead. Two birds, one stone. Now buck up, Samson. You can be mad at me when we're done. Right now there's work to do."

"Prick," I muttered. I pulled around the side of the only other asteroid in the vicinity, a cashew shaped hunk of iron about a mile long. It was about a thousand miles away from Ceres, seemingly motionless.

Asteroid belts were never terribly exciting.

"Ok, Cab," I said. "Make me scary. And stop giggling."

--That's my boy--

--Time to get your feet wet--

-- Pop that cherry--

-- Bust some caps--

--God DAMN I'm excited--

--Hold your arms out to your sides--

I held out my arms like I was going to be crucified. For a moment, nothing happened, and then a pair of rods built themselves out of my hull with a bone-jarring pop. They shed their skins in patterns of oddly-shaped plates that expanded and moved over each other, thickening each rigid form beyond what it should have been possible to construct given how much material Cab had started with. The plates began to rotate around the rods' centers, and deep inside, something started to glow.

Pieces of metal separated from my shoulders, unrelated chunks of flat material that curved along their lengths to cover the blindingly bright, kaleidoscopic columns along my arms. The bases of the cylinders unfolded and refolded into a larger device, a suddenly-present cannon housing, while sophisticated mounts grew out of my shoulders to take the nonexistent weight. I was left with what looked like a pair of space-age Howitzer cannons as designed by Giger and Tolkien, some runic, glowing organic testament to alien military engineering. The weapons swung in twin circles and then pointed toward my version of up and settled down to wait. I could hear them in the back of my head, a constant bass note like a barely-contained scream.

--Yeah--

--I like that--

"Range one million five," Rell said.

The cannons followed my focus, so that there were little crosshairs over everything I saw. It was a little annoying. Cab chittered happily.

"Are you planning to leave my forearms bare?" I asked. My voice was calm but my innards were numb. This was one moment from my past repeated and stretched, the instant when I asked Cab for help and sent Billy Maxwell to the fucking morgue. Getting ready to ambush some poor bastard with a huge gun he didn't expect me to have like I was in a Louisiana bar fight. I was going to kill these people. I hiccupped and tasted bile.

--I'm not done yet--

--Don't rush me--

"One million," Rell said. "Here they come."

"I'm not the one doing the rushing, Cab," I said.

--Hush--

A fresh pair of cutting beams built themselves out of my forearms, heavier models with long, menacing tips that overhung my hands by a solid foot. I could hear them in my head, a keening murmur begging to be unleashed. The guns wanted me to use them. They were very clear on that point. There were other machines back there, too, a chorus built of low whines too quiet to be heard individually.

"Five hundred thousand miles, Samson," Rell said. "Don't cut and run, or I'll shoot you myself."

"Don't worry, Rell," I said. "I need you alive so you can pay me."

He didn't respond.

I thickened. The plates covering my body expanded, enlarged, unfolded where there shouldn't have been anything to unfold, reorganized themselves into something that didn't adhere anymore to the shape of my musculature. I was still humanoid, but I was something else, too, something constructed from an intelligent, dynamic design. A real, live spaceship, angular and martial. When I moved, pieces of armor and armored components slipped over each other like scales. I was entirely unhindered, but aware more than ever that I had a hull, not a skin. I felt my potential to fly fast, turn hard, to shoot, to suffer, to kill, to weather. And still I knew that Cab had only tapped into the smallest piece of his seemingly limitless potential.

The weapons clamored in my head to be unleashed, and Cab told them in some nonverbal way, soon. His excitement mirrored my unease in an odd way. I wondered if I should say something. Caution him. Temper him. But what could I say? What possible authority was I?

"Anything I should know?"

--Nah--

--It's just a six on one dogfight in free fall--

--You'll be fine--

I watched the stars watching me. So many worlds. Hard to believe that I didn't have an audience. Hard to believe that none of them had ever made contact, but that was true, as well. So many people. They couldn't all be bad, and yet bad was all I'd been shown so far. I was about to ambush a group of strangers, to protect a man I barely knew. Hard to believe. What was this, nobility? Heroism? There's nothing noble in an ambush. This was practicality. I didn't want to die, and I didn't want Rell to die, so these people had to die. I didn't want to give up my wallet, so Billy Maxwell had to die. It was simple. I wasn't any better than these people, so I must have been bad, too.

Simple.

3

The horizon was right up close to me, half a mile off and curved, bowed, small. But it was a horizon, and I was only standing straight, waiting. Cab had my feet anchored and the shipboard gravity was compensating, dragging me into the center of the asteroid with a lot more force than the asteroid itself was capable of. Centering me on the center of things. It kept me level. Made me feel terrestrial, still, even if by then I resembled nothing more than a flipper-limbed, mirror-plated troll as big as a crew-cab pickup truck. I was only standing. I didn't have to do this. And I didn't have to do it this way. If they would only let me try another way. I hoped they would. My chest vibrated unhappily.

My display flashed red and outlined six points three hundred thousand miles above me. That didn't feel as far as it had.

Cab zoomed in on three pairs of ships flying in matched rows, and I felt a trill of revolted fear, a gut-churned sensation like I'd turned over a rock and found a human face. The craft I saw were recognizable as vehicles, even slightly familiar, but they were wrong. The first two were saucers, perfect metal discs with glowing centers, but they flew face-on, not edge-first, a couple of dull orange eyes soaring through space. Then a pair of rocket ships, but they were bent and distended, like a child's rendition of a supersonic jet, or a half-melted dust-buster with wings. And bringing up the rear, a pair of mirror-finish marbles, maybe twenty meters in diameter. They should have been invisible against the stars, but they weren't; space was distorted between and around them, so that they stood out as a wavering, red-eyed movement of the universe itself.

--Give my regards to Daaaaaay-veeeee, remember me to Tee Fee Craaaaaane--

--Tell all the pikers ooon tha hill, that I'll beee back ah-gaaain!--

Cab's voice in my head was the barrel-chested baritone of an undergraduate fraternity brother. I could almost hear the beard and the beer.

--Tell them how I was buuuus-ted, for lapping up the high high baaaalll--

--We'll all have drinks at Theo-dore Zinck's, when I get back next faaaaaaaaaaaaalllllll!--

"What the hell is wrong with you," I muttered.

--Didn't you go to Cornell?--

"I don't think they sing that one anymore," I said.

--Sure they do--

--I could do Harvard--

The bounty hunters orbited Ceres once, looking for Rell. I don't know where he hid himself in all of that nothing, but he managed somehow.

Cab wriggled in the back of my head. I could hear him chittering to himself.

"You're enjoying this, aren't you?"

--Aren't you?--

"No." I kicked off the asteroid and soared towards Ceres.

--Not even a little bit?--

--I can't wait to see these cannons in action--

I thought of Agent Frewdin, stone-faced behind his desk, telling me to stay on Earth in case Cab and I weren't prepared for the galaxy at large. I thought about the galaxy's first sentient computer sharing mental space with an inexperienced man everyone considered to be a child. I thought about how scared I was, and I thought about hitting a man so hard that he died. I didn't have to do it this way.

"Scan for life signs," I said.

--What?--

"Scan for life signs," I said. "Who are these people?"

--What do you think this is, Star Trek?--

"Cab!"

The bounty hunters regrouped on Ceres' facing side. My crosshairs played over their surfaces, and I could feel the minimal point in my mind that would fire the guns, if I concentrated even a little.

--It's like the United Planets of Benetton over there--

--A triumphal moment in diversity politics--

--It's a bunch of different species, man, what do you want from me, an average number of limbs?--

"How many of them are there?" I flew slow, watching. They had to know I was here, I was supposed to show up on ship's sensors like a Christmas tree.

--Seventeen limbs, on average--

"Cab, how many people are on those ships?"

--Do you really want to know?--

"Do you know?" I asked.

--Of course--

"Then tell me."

--There are one hundred and ninety one people aboard those ships, in total--

--And something that might be a housecat--

--Except it appears to be mostly made of argon--

--They're hip to your jive, cap'n--

--If you're gonna drop the hammer you better drop it now while you still got the drop to drop--

--I have no idea what I just said--

--Was it at all clear in context?--

There was always another way. If I was going to do this, I had to try to do it right. Nobody had to die.

"Ok," I said. I cleared my throat and opened a channel with a thought.

--Killjoy--

"This is Captain Gregory Samson of the good ship Cab Calloway," I said. My voice was low, slow, gravelly and appropriate. I smiled grimly and pushed my luck. "You are trespassing in Solar space. Power down your weapons and leave the system immediately."

--Good, good--

--LOVE the name--

--Constructive criticism: Next time be less formal--

--You want to come off as a bit of a loose cannon, you know?--

--Like you could be dangerous if pressed--

--But that was good--

--Great progress since last time--

Cab always spoke quickly, but even so he was cut off by the bounty hunter's reply: a swarm of missiles from each rocket ship, so many it took a full three seconds to fire them all. They streamed towards me like a school of hungry fish.

--Wow, that's a lot of missiles--

--One, two, three, four…--

--One point two million of them!--

"Will I survive getting hit with those?" The pressure was building inside my head.

--Probably?--

--It won't be pleasant--

--They're just Larsson twenty-two's, but like I said, there's one point two million of them--

--Real efficient delivery system, I'd love to get a look at it sometime--

--Anyway, you'll be fine--

--Probably...--

"An ellipsis?" My stomach rolled. "I'm gonna die!"

--No, you're not--

--But do something--

--Impact in seven seconds--

The myth is that when your system is flooded with adrenaline, time stands still and you become a Superman, a Take Charge Fella who can Get Things Done. This is horseshit. We might remember it that way after the fact, but the truth is that in hard moments a person has a fifty-fifty chance of playing the hero or acting the fool, same as always. Adrenaline just makes you wait longer to find out how your day is going.

Thankfully, my day was skewing in the former direction. I pressed as hard as I could on the engines and screamed towards the bounty hunters, past the encroaching ordnance. The missiles turned to meet me, and I increased speed to stay ahead of them.

"Okey dokey, fast, fast, fast," I gibbered. Cab is a convenient excuse, but the truth is I would have been talking to myself even if he hadn't been there. Then again, if he hadn't been there I wouldn't have been there at all, but c'est la vie for you.

Cab's alarm wavered in the margins of my awareness, nearly lost in my terror.

--You're closing the distance, Gregory--

--You're taking us closer to the scary missiles Greg WHAT ARE YOU DOING WHAT THE SHIT--

Space, I've mentioned, plays hell with your sense of distance. That said I'm pretty sure I cleared the lead missile by less than five feet. Or maybe it was a mile. Who knows? I hunched my shoulders against the inevitable explosion as the waves crashed against each other.

Except that didn't happen. The twin rivers of rockets streamed over and under and in between each other with nary a collision, not even a dinged fin. I swore desperately and pressed harder on the engines. If I wasn't more careful, I was going to land myself an ignoble early death.

--Ok, I see what you were trying--

--Good thought--

--Impact in fourteen seconds--

--What's next?--

The spherical ships in the rear broke formation and angled towards me.

--Don't fly between the marbles!--

I pulled up and somersaulted over the band of distorted space just as lightning shot between the two ships, lightning with a jet-black core that bled red light. My foot caught in the corona and went numb, and about a hundred thousand missiles vanished into the lightless interior. I yelped, as an afterthought.

--Calm down!--

"What the hell was that?" My foot started to burn numbly.

The lightning disappeared and the spheres raced after me. They didn't turn, they just reversed direction from one second to the next. Feeling returned to my foot, along with a pain in my bones that I associated with falling into icy water.

--Unstable dimensional portal--

--It's an old faster-than-light technology, or at least it was supposed to be--

--Never worked, at least not for travel--

--Makes a dandy weapon--

--That feeling is your foot molecules returning from a disparate phase state--

--They were trying to find their way into a parallel universe--

--If you'd flown through that we would have been ripped to shreds--

"Would we survive being ripped to shreds?" I asked. It was meant as a joke, but my voice was too strangled for levity. They were really trying to kill me. Me! They didn't even know me!

--I dunno--

--Shreds are pretty small--

The dust-buster ships opened fire as one. This group of bounty hunters had great communication skills. My shields lit up ahead of me to either side with wavering, scattering blue light as they repelled what I decided, in my naïveté, to call 'lasers.' I felt the heat through the shields. Without them, what would I feel through the hull? Would their weapons cook me alive? How long could my shields hold out?

They were really trying to kill me. And I thought they would kill me, unless I stopped them. So I cut towards the closest ship, accelerated, and then at the last second flipped over and landed feet first on the hull, hard enough to leave a dent. The ship's surface was covered in turrets, huge mounted guns glowing with energies outside of the visible spectrum, but they couldn't get a bead on me from this close. The other ship brought its guns to bear, but hesitated. I did not.

The purple beams that flashed out of the cutters on my forearms were cables this time, not threads. They bored through the dust-buster's underbelly and flashed out into space on the other side, unimpeded and terrible. Great flaming chunks of hull fell away from the dying ship, and gouts of energy erupted out of various weakened points like magma out of a fissure. After a second the lights went out. I let go the triggers and guns shrieked in my mind, more, more.

--An excellent shot, sir--

The missiles fell at me.

--Impact in four seconds, now--

--May I suggest we flee?--

"Wait for it," I said. I didn't want to be made a fool again by alien military maneuverability, although I'll be the first to admit that it wasn't easy to stand my ground under an impending hail of explosives.

--Wait for it wait for what you used two seconds saying wait for it hey run move go--

--You know I can feel pain, right?--

I put the proverbial pedal to the metal when I could discern lettering on side of the lead rocket. Larsson, twenty-two M. I have no idea what the M stood for. Missile, maybe. I moved left and felt the tiny tug of acceleration in my core, that minute failing of the inertial dampeners that told me I was moving *really* fast.

Guns and martial protuberances across the hull made for a complicated, weaving retreat. These structures weren't very tall, but there were a lot of them, and I had to stay close to the hull, or else the rearmost missiles might have gotten wise to my dastardly plan.

I became aware of a sound behind me, the kettledrum roll of an amateur god, powerful and deep but off-tempo. I can only guess what carried the sound. Ash, maybe, particulate and escaping atmosphere from the impacts behind me. The question could wait. I could feel the concussion on the bottoms of my feet.

Then the ship exploded. I can't say much about that, because it knocked me senseless. But being in an explosion, surviving an explosion...It's sad. Awful. There's a hallucinatory violence to what you see, as if the world is split apart at the seams, shattered by an invading, otherworldly light. One bright spot encompassing everything, and then nothing.

It took me several minutes to notice that I wasn't dead. Somewhere along my explosion-derived trajectory I whacked into an asteroid, which I found mildly surprising and quite painful.

"Samson! I need you!"

Rell's voice in my ears. My thoughts tumbled slowly into each other in my head, cotton-candy collisions. I liked Rell, even if he had tricked me into fighting for him. He was a nice guy. Gracious host.

"Samson, are you alive? Answer me, dammit!"

He sounded stressed.

"Samson, I'm about to eat it out here, where the hell are you?"

Oh. Right, I thought. I'm slacking.

"Yah," I said shakily. I pulled up short and the deceleration made my head hurt. Then again, everything hurt. I rolled my shoulders carefully and took a deep breath.

"Where the hell are you? I need you!"

"Yah," I said, stronger this time. I checked my shipboard body for damage, but the machines in the back of my head sang to me that I was fine. Ship-shape. I'd been shot, blown up and knocked through an asteroid, and I was fine. Super. The bounty hunters could do what they wanted, there was no contest here. If they fought me, I would kill them, because I was immortal, and they were not. I sped back in the direction from when I came.

Rell was in a shifting orbit around Mars, with the saucers on his tail and the marbles closing fast from the other direction, to cut him off. He made as if to bank and got his wing caught in the edge of Mars' atmosphere. The increased friction dragged him around, and he fought it, losing momentum. The saucers closed the distance. I held my breath. Could I get off a shot before they greased him? No, the ship murmured, we weren't in range.

Without warning, Rell reversed thrust and spun himself hard in the direction the ship wanted to go. He fired the engines once and bounced out of orbit, into free fall, and for one perfect instant his main guns were aimed square at the center of one of the saucers. It was barely a hundred miles off, with no room to maneuver, moving slowly for the kill shot, just as Rell had intended. His guns flashed, and the saucer took the shot right on the nose. All he managed to do was to slow the other ship down a half-beat, but it was enough time to get away. He curved to meet me.

--Hell of a pilot--

--Probably why they sent six ships--

I laid my crosshairs on the closer saucer and it flipped in place and shot me with a meter thick laser beam. I had no time to react. Most of the energy boiled off of my shields, but enough made it through to make me feel like I'd stood too close to a bonfire. Something smelled like burned hair, and I was pretty sure it was me.

Fear and anger leapt through Cab, and the weapons on my shoulders got bigger, unfolded in eye-watering ways and began to draw more energy. Their voices in my head dropped by half an octave.

--I didn't like that one bit--

--Shoot that motherfucker before he shoots us again--

"Smells like hair," I coughed. I felt wind on my face, and the shipboard atmosphere cleared.

--You got singed--

--You won't have to shave your chest for a while--

--Now shoot that motherfucker before he shoots us again--

Another beam clipped the edge of the shield. I felt it on my side like a hot breeze off an Arizona parking lot.

--Evade, you dumb bastard!--

I lined up the cannons and blew a chunk out of the saucer's edge. Each gun fired two shots, one-two, bam-bam just below the range of my hearing. The saucer was knocked in a full circle, while molten metal and solidifying energy sprayed from the wound like blood from an artery. The ship shuddered once, spun out of control and exploded. My jaw tightened. There was a funny pressure on my temples.

Rell got behind me. The three remaining ships regrouped above Mars' atmosphere. I turned on the comms.

"This is Captain Samson," I said, and the desperation in my voice was no affectation. "You've got to stop. Power down your weapons and you will be allowed to leave Solar space unharmed."

Instead, they charged. The saucer was above and behind the marbles, and I could feel the central point of its aim just below my throat. I put four rounds in the center of the marble on the left, and it popped like a ceramic balloon. The other one turned without pause and accelerated madly out of sight. The saucer stopped, considered, and disappeared into warp.

Four ships. How many people?

"Scan for life signs," I said.

--Captain?--

"Scan the ship that's still intact for life signs," I said.

It took him a quarter second.

--There's nothing there--

"How many dead?"

--One hundred and twenty-eight--

Ceres was a single bright point in the distance. I took a deep breath and held it, then let it out. Then in. When you die, the last thing you do is exhale. Each breath in is proof of life. I breathed in, and out, and in again. I got to breathe in. And they didn't. I'd taken away that privilege. Or was it a right? My heart burned and twisted in me.

"Do you feel that," I asked quietly. "We did that. We killed those people."

--Yeah, that was the idea--

--What's the problem?--

"All right, Samson!" Rell roared in my ear. "You're a force to be reckoned with, little man. Worth every penny. Come aboard and we'll have a drink."

Cab considered me curiously.

--You ok?--

--What's up?--

He knew exactly how many people we'd killed, and he didn't feel bad. He wasn't happy to have done it, but he didn't feel bad. I didn't understand, yet. I was terrified of what his calm could mean. There hadn't been any danger, not to us. We couldn't be killed. We could only do the killing.

"Rell, my friend," I said, "I think we'll have several."

4

When I clanked into the hold, Rell was swigging from a bottle of cloudy pink liquid, and when he saw me he cheered. Cab's mind was pleasure tempered by poorly maintained modesty.

I was still covered in guns and engines, smaller versions of the ones I'd started with, like bonsai machines. The little cannons on my shoulders took note of Rell's vital organs, and I flinched. Enough, I thought. The cannons popped reluctantly into pieces and disappeared into panels of base material, and the cutting beams folded themselves into featureless boxes on my forearms. The plate armor and engines shattered and organized themselves in small collections of narrow pieces, and in a moment Cab was once again nothing more than a statuesque metal skin. I looked like a piece of uninspired public art.

"No," I said, "Get rid of the whole thing." The ship hesitated, and then broke apart and stowed itself on my back. In my head, Cab was watching me nervously.

--What's going on?--

--Are you ok?--

I itched like a son of a bitch, and when I rubbed my chest my hand came away covered in shattered, burnt hair. I stank of it. I felt sunburnt. I scrubbed madly at myself and whipped off my shirt in a cloud of ash.

"Jesus, Cab, you said I just got singed." The hair on my head was gone. I must have been leaning forward when the saucer shot me. I kicked off my boots and scratched the top of my foot on the back of my other leg.

51

--This *is* a little singed--

--Vaporized is what we would call a lot singed--

--I mean, you still have skin, don't you?--

"Cheers!" Rell thrust the bottle at me and splashed liquor on the deck. He certainly drank a lot. Then again, so did I. Probably something to keep an eye on, although I could hardly be blamed for a little self-medication, under the circumstances.

"I just killed a hundred and thirty people for you." I snatched the bottle from him. "You knew they would follow me here. You knew this would happen."

Rell rubbed his hands together slowly, preening the fur where our skin had touched. He knew I was clean, but prejudice is hard to let go of.

"I assumed," he said. "Rather, I knew they would catch up with me sooner or later, once you were with me. You aren't a subtle presence."

My head hunched forward. "You tricked me into killing a hundred and thirty people." My voice was both guttural and lilting. "You tricked me."

There was an enormous, Vabling-scale mug perched on the corner of the crate Rell was leaning on. He sighed, picked it up and splashed me with about a quart of cold, forgotten coffee.

"What the fuck!" I sputtered. The ship rose up and collapsed back into obscurity as I fought myself for control.

"Distraction can be calming," he said, "And you need to calm right down, Samson. People like you don't get to pitch a tantrum." He looked me over. "Come on, let's take a load off."

"What the hell does that mean, people like me?" I hissed. Rell cocked his head at me.

"Powerful, dangerous people don't get to pitch a tantrum," he said. "It's not safe. Now come on."

He walked out of the hold. I stared after him hatefully with coffee dripping off my face and shoulders, and then gave up on the feeling and had a drink. The liquor tasted like peaches and cinnamon, and spread cold through my veins, instead of heat. I realized, belatedly, that I neither knew what I was drinking nor cared about the answer.

"Turn off the ethanol filters," I said.

--That, my friend, is not ethanol--

--But I get your drift--

--Party on, Wayne--

I followed Rell as best I could. It felt strange to be so close to alone in such an alien environment. The shipboard lighting in this area was luminescent machinery set into tubular paneling that looked like it had been carved from one huge, unbroken piece of wood. I thought of termites, wondered insanely at being very small. But I could feel the ship around me, and space beyond that. Pressure, and then nothing.

The front of me was a uniform sickly itch. I took off my pants and wrapped my discarded clothing in a ball around my boots. My legs looked like I'd shaved the one side and ignored the other.

"I get hurt if you get hurt," I said.

--Oh, hell yes--

--We heal very quickly, but no shield is perfect--

"So I'm not invulnerable."

--Who the hell gave you that idea?--

"You told me we were immortal," I said.

--I said I could heal you--

--That's not invulnerable, that's regenerative--

--So you better learn how to duck--

--Cause pain sucks--

--Zero out of five stars, would not experience again--

I wasn't untouchable. That made it better, somehow. Not good. But better. I wasn't at such an awful remove from things. Just a moderately awful remove. After all, the burns would heal. The dead bounty hunters would stay dead.

Rell turned left into a cavernous, irregularly-shaped hall with walls covered in layered blotches of natural colors and textures, with huge branches crisscrossing the open space all the way to the hundred meter ceiling. Everything was covered in plants: vines, shrubs, grasses, saplings, even a few small trees. The walls must have been some kind of growth medium; there was vegetation rooted in the margins everywhere I looked. I thought of Cab's first description of Rell's ship, "A freighter full of houseplants." I thought that meant he had a cargo.

The vegetation varied. Certain areas were dotted with flowers, brightly colored blossoms of every shape and size, while others were given over to peaceful, leafy darkness. I thought I recognized the general shape of food crops in certain places, too, regularity and repetition of large, appetizing shapes. The branches that crisscrossed the room were gargantuan, five meters thick at least, and they stretched from wall to wall as uniform pieces cut from some enormous whole. The bottoms and sides were covered in a moss and fungus, creepers and embedded rocks.

"Nice living room," I said. "You got a couch?"

Rell grinned, leapt four meters to the underside of the lowest branch and scrambled over the top. In a minute I saw him on the underside of the third branch up, and then he moved out of sight. He climbed with a wide, clinging stance that reminded me more of an insect than of an ape or a cat, as if the strength in his limbs was so evenly distributed and dense that he could have supported his entire body on any one of his long limbs.

I drank more liquor and scratched myself. My crotch itched as bad as the rest of me had under clothes, and Rell hadn't mentioned my near-nudity. He was an alien, what did he care? I dropped my drawers and rubbed away the last of my hair. I was pornstar-slick on my front, and normal-person hairy on my back. Oh well. I still had my skin. Mildly singed. Hell. I took another slug from the bottle.

"Cab," I said, "what is this stuff, anyway?"

--It's called 'sloos'--

--Fermented ruft pressings--

I sighed. "And what's a ruft?"

--Kinda like a cricket--

I stared at the label. There was a certain arthropodal cast to the logo, now that I was looking for it. "So this is alcoholic cricket juice."

--Pretty much--

It took a moment to reorient my perception of the universe to include peach flavored alcoholic crickets but I managed. It was easier than it should have been.

I flew to the top floor, dismantled the ship in midair, and landed lightly on my feet. I was getting better at being me, even if I wasn't sure I liked the 'me' I was becoming.

The branch was wide, covered in long bluegrass and sod that Rell had sculpted into furniture surrounding a low coffee table topped with a slab of red granite. It looked like the sort of living room that a sheep would build, if sheep built things. I nodded appreciatively. "Nice living room."

The sloos was doing its thing. I sat down heavily and tossed the bottle to Rell as he rolled onto the branch. He stood up, caught the bottle and collapsed across one of the couches in a single long motion.

"You said you had to leave Earth," he said immediately.

"If the Krr come looking for me and I'm here, they'll wreck up the place," I said. "If I'm gone…we think they'll leave the planet alone."

Rell thought about it. "Because your species isn't worth the risk it would take to destroy you," he said. "I suppose that makes sense." He took a deep breath and collected his thoughts.

"I did lure you out here to kill those men for me, Samson, that's true. But I do need your help, and if we're being honest, you're wrapped up in all of this too, even if you don't want to admit it."

"None of this is my fault, god dammit," I said. My voice was staccato. Rell gave me back the sloos and held a finger to his lips.

"Console yourself, and keep quiet." He chewed something out of his teeth. "I didn't say this was your fault. I said you were involved. You don't have to be responsible for a thing to be involved in it. Are the people of Earth responsible if the Krr attack their planet? Of course not. But they're certainly involved in the situation."

I folded my arms and sipped from the bottle and wriggled lower in my chair. My skin felt better. I was recovering nicely, or else I was getting drunk.

"I need your help," Rell repeated. He knit his hands on his chest and studied his thumbs. "We're into something bad. There were nearly two hundred people after us just now. The last time I had bounty hunters after me there were three of them. The price on my head must be enormous."

"Because it paid for an army," I said. Rell waggled his hand.

"A strike force," he said. "Let's not get ahead of ourselves." He stared at nothing for some time.

"I'm going to say some things you're not going to like," he said at length. "But you have to hear them. You're unhappy that you killed those people. But regardless of your personal feeling, you are in a situation that will most likely demand you kill in order to preserve your own life. You have to be ok with that." He took a breath. "Someone is attempting to erase what has happened to you. I'm evidence. You are evidence. It's reasonable to assume that if you had stayed on Earth the Krr would have found their way there, and if they did not find you by their own devices I'm suspicious that they would have been led to you."

He took the sloos and drank. "I've done you a favor. The army they sent after me is nothing to you, no threat. You could have murdered them all in seconds, if you'd chosen to. I gave you the opportunity to learn a lesson with minimal risk to yourself."

"I didn't murder them," I grated. My chest felt like a black hole. The bluegrass under my butt felt nice, though.

"You didn't," Rell nodded. "You didn't. You approached them head on, and you gave them a chance to surrender. Twice." He looked at me. "You killed them. But only when you had to. You will have to again, I think, before we get to the bottom of this." He grinned at me without humor. "Now we know that you can. I've done you a favor. You needed this."

I stood up shakily. "You lured me out here to prove to me that I can kill people?" I pointed at him and felt the ship rise to half-mast behind me. "I know that I can kill people, asshole, that's why I left Earth!"

Rell looked me up and down.

"Why are you naked?" He asked.

"My hair got burnt off," I said. "I itch."

Rell nodded. "You look like you crawled out from under a rock." He sat up. "You killed someone

57

back home? I thought you said you left because you were afraid of the Krr."

I had no reason to be standing. I wasn't going to hit him. I wasn't even that mad. I just felt rotten.

"I can do things for more than one reason," I said. "I beat up a mugger." I waved my hand and immediately regretted the dismissive gesture. "He fell over and hit his head. And died. He had no idea what I was, and I had no idea how strong I was… and I killed him."

Rell didn't say anything. I looked at him, and he was lighting a cigar.

"Sucks," he said finally, "but do you really feel responsible for these deaths?"

"Of course I do, I killed them."

Rell sighed. "Samson, there's a fundamental difference between killing someone because you want to, and killing someone because you have to. You didn't *murder* those men out there. You killed them, and that's unfortunate, but you had to, in order to survive. Or, at least, in order to protect a person you care about, a charismatic, devilish rogue who promises to show you the mysteries of the galaxy, to unlock worlds of unlimited potential, who–"

"Ok, enough," I said. "Enough." I leaned back and closed my eyes. I hadn't meant to kill Billy Maxwell. I hadn't wanted to kill any of those people. And they'd fired first. But then, I'd fired last.

"You really think it makes a difference?" I asked.

"I know it makes a difference," Rell said. "But then, I'm the hardened space pirate. You're the virginal wimp who doesn't know his ass from his elbows."

"Fuck you," I said.

"I see your point," Rell said. "On the other hand, if you get into a moral debate in a firefight, you get your head blown off. Now, are you clear? Because before we go any further, I need to know that I can trust you to keep me safe. "

I put my hands behind my bald, ashy head and closed my eyes. Big flaming hunks of ship, arterial gouts of molten metal, the way the marble-ship ground to a halt in the dead of space when I shot it, against all logic. That staggered look in Billy Maxwell's eye when I hit him the second time, under his ear.

There had to be a place for restraint. I hadn't sought anyone out. These people had come to me, to kill me. But they hadn't been expecting *me*, not really. Cab watched me calmly from just outside of my periphery. We were so strong, so much stronger than I knew, and we stood very, very close to a bad line. We hadn't crossed it, yet, but it's hard to be justified killing someone who poses no threat. We'd killed those men. We hadn't murdered them. But we'd come damn close. There had to be restraint.

All I could do was muddle through. I looked at Rell and nodded portentously. He nodded back.

"Ok," I said. "So you need a bodyguard."

5

"There will be other mercenaries." Rell was enunciating carefully. "The money is still there for whoever does the job. There'll be others."

"Ok," I said in the same ponderous tone. "So we should hurry."

"Never hurry," Rell said. "Haste makes, excuse me, haste makes waste."

"Man, you're kidding me with all the colloquialisms," I said. "There's no way that rhymes in your language."

"What?" Rell said.

"Nothing," I said. "Do you have a plan?"

"Find out who put the price on my head," Rell said. "Kill them. Or convince them to recant." He pronounced it 'Ree-Cant.'

"That's not so much a plan as a goal," I mumbled.

"Another option is to go to the cops," Rell said. "If I can get evidence that a Cabernician stole the seed, or that a Cabernician was working with the Krr, then I can throw myself on the mercy of the Core Law Enforcement Agency. If I can't figure out who's behind all of this, I can at least hand the problem to someone who can." He sighed. "That's not ideal. I'd be risking prison, but it beats getting run down like a dog."

"You hope," I said. Rell looked at me with one eye open wider than the other. We were the both of us becoming rather drunk.

"Cab tells me that the Cabernicians are pretty important to the Core," I said. "That might mean they've got some political sway. If we're looking for a Cabernician with a lot of money and access to the

Shipkiller seeds, then it's possible that we're looking for a Cabernician with some clout where the CLEA is concerned." It took a while to get all of that out.

"But if we tell them that a Cabernician is in league with the Krr..." Rell said slowly.

"That's not a believable story, apparently," I said. "Which puts us back on plan A, find out who's behind all this and put the squeeze on him, ourselves."

"Yeah," Rell said. He drank the rest of the sloos and leaned back with the empty bottle in his hand.

"Except you don't know where to start," I said.

"No," Rell said. He watched me and spun the bottle on the flat of his palm.

"Who gave you the job?" I asked. "Who told you about the Shipkiller sale?"

All of Rell's tiny pupils were dilated, and the big central one was the size of a golf ball. He continued spinning the bottle, once around, once around, once around, catching it on every revolution with the neck up, as if to drink, watching me contemplatively.

"If you don't trust me I can't do shit for you," I said quietly.

"Yui," Rell said.

"Oh," I said. "Him."

Rell snorted. "Yui Galt is a Dhantine aid worker running a black market out of an old refugee station in the Phibbix Nebula."

"Of course he is," I said.

Rell waved his hand, shushing me. "He got wind of a private sale that was making use of his channels and locations, and hired me to break it up and steal the seed. He told me, he told me..." Rell stared at the ceiling. "He told me he wanted to make an example of them."

"By stealing the seed?" I said. Rell shook his head.

"I lied to you," he said. "I wasn't alone when I broke up the sale. Yui sent a strike force with me to kill the Cabernician, and the buyers. I was just in charge of retrieving the seed."

His hair was flat, and it actually looked a little pale. Did it change color with his mood?

"You're about to tell me something awful happened to the strike force," I said.

Rell nodded. "Oh, yes, they're all dead, the Krr killed them all." He sighed. "Those people probably saved your planet, Samson, I doubt the Krr could follow the seed's trajectory in all the confusion. I only managed it because I was so close to the thing when I fired the well cannon." He chuckled, a painful sound. "As it was, I was already computing a warp trajectory out of there. The Krr...Yui sent fifteen ships. The Krr overran them. They have a, a tactic, when it comes to ship to ship fighting. They embed enemy craft with nest shards housing newborn queens, who turn the ships into hives. So the ships are infested with Krr, who just have a *grand* old time with the crew and anyone else aboard." He made a line out of his mouth. "They also have, ah, it's like the opposite of jamming. They force the comm channels to stay open through the whole thing. For the screaming."

"Well, that's horrible." I took in some air and found I couldn't imagine what Rell was describing with anything even approaching clarity. "Ok. So Yui sent a strike force with you to kill these guys, and they're all dead. What about the Cabernician?"

"I don't know," Rell said. "He might be dead, I told you, I cut out as soon as I could. The Krr don't practice much discretion once they get started."

"But he could have escaped, too," I said. I rubbed my eyes and went over the new information. "A lot more people have died around this than I thought.

No wonder the price on you is so high, whoever is behind this must be desperate to cover it up."

I pressed the flesh under my eyes and saw stars. It was late. It had been late. Now it was later. What a night. What a life.

"We need to talk to Yui," I said. "I think that's our first step."

"Why?" Rell said. "I've known him a long time, you can't possibly think that he's behind any of this."

"Well, you raise an interesting point, Rell," I said. "If Yui is in league with the Krr, then he's a war profiteer's war profiteer. But if he's in league with the Krr, then why would he try to break up his own sale?"

"There, right, that's what I'm talking about," Rell said. "It doesn't make any sense."

"Well, no," I said, "He would send you to break up the sale if he was trying to kill you. Get me? He'd know you were going to find the Krr, and that you would be no match for them. From what you've told me, it sounds like you barely got out of there. But you were only able to get out because the Krr were busy killing everyone Yui sent with you. If he was trying to kill you, he would have sent you alone. Unless he thought the Krr would destroy all of you, in which case he sent fifteen ships' worth of people to their death just to strengthen his alibi. I don't know. I'm spitballing. Does Yui strike you as an inhuman monster?" I thought about it. "Figuratively inhuman. Immoral."

Rell stared at me. "No," he said slowly. "No, I've known Yui since we were young, I used to smuggle food for a foundation he was working for. He's...he helps people. The work he does. He's a good...I mean, he wouldn't ...I think...shit."

"People can surprise you," I said. "You do anything to piss him off lately?"

Rell shook his head. "Not that I can think of."

I nodded. "Like I said, I'm spitballing. The truth is, we need to talk to Yui because his name is the only one we have in all of this." My voice had a gravelly, exhausted tone that lent my words an extra layer of Tom Waits drama and told me if I didn't get horizontal soon I was going to pass out in mid-sentence, naked on a bluegrass couch.

"All right," Rell said. "I'll set a warp trajectory."

"How long will it take us to get to Phibbix?" I said. "I got that right, didn't I? Phibbix?"

"Yeah," Rell said. "Thirty-six hours or so."

I nodded and then remembered it was my turn to speak. "I need a bed."

"Next branch down," Rell said. "There's a hole in the wall." He watched me. "You're a good thinker, Samson, but you understand that smart or not, I need a bodyguard more than I need a detective."

"Sure you do, Rell. I can wear two hats." I stood up. "We'll go to Phibbix, we'll find out what Yui knows, and if anyone tries to shoot at you, I'll shoot them back."

"As long as you're clear," Rell said.

I walked to the edge of the branch and looked down. My fear of heights was gone.

"I want a million dollars a day," I said.

"Me too," Rell said.

I shook my head. "For all I know I'm going to have to fight an army," I said. "A real army. I want a million dollars a day, in gold, or else I walk."

Rell was silent for a moment, and then he began to laugh. The sound filled the enormous room, reverberated off of the walls and through the ersatz branches. Now what, I thought?

"Gold," he choked out. "You want gold."

"It's valuable on Earth," I muttered.

"You don't make it yourselves?" Rell was crying. Great big Vabling tears soaked the fur on his face. He looked delighted.

"No," I said. "We don't manufacture gold."

"It's a shipbuilding material, you can buy it out here by the kiloton," Rell said. "You really don't manufacture elements on Earth? It's a basic science."

"Well," I snapped, "We're cut off, remember? Unclean."

Rell took a deep breath and wiped his eyes and did his best to stop smiling.

"I'm sorry," he said. "I meant no offense. If you're willing to accept gold as a payment, then yes, I will pay you a million dollars a day." He snorted, once. "In gold."

"If it's worthless out here, it's worthless to me," I said. "I have no idea when I'll make it home. If."

Rell didn't speak. I looked at him, and there was something else on his face, a puffed out surprise like he'd gotten the wind knocked out of him.

"You're right," he said. "You're right." He sat up straighter. "I can't...I don't have a lot of money."

I nodded. "Give me a million dollars a day in gold," I said. "I'll make it home eventually. And otherwise just ...help me. Ok? I don't know what I'm doing out here, I don't know anything. I'll do what you need me to do, I'll come with you to Phibbix and help you get clear of all this, but you've got to help me make sense of this place."

Rell nodded. "Of course." He said it with such simplicity that I knew I didn't have to follow up.

The floor was a long way down, not that it mattered. No room anymore for mundane fears. Height was nothing, I had eternity to contemplate. A brave new world. Part of me had hoped that he would scoff at the price, send me home.

"Well, that's settled," I muttered. "I'm off to bed." Cab snapped around me and I stepped off the ledge, somersaulted, kicked the engines and landed on the next branch down. Easy. Flying was becoming a natural act.

This branch was paved with panels of laminated bark set into the moss like flagstones. There was a collection of spun metal patio furniture at one end of the space, and a vine covered hole in the wall at the other, as promised. The furniture was dark iron, and wouldn't have been out of place on a Connecticut veranda, except that the ornamental metal leaves on the backrest looked like no plant on Earth.

I pushed through the curtain of furry vines overhanging the hole in the wall, into something like a small cave. The floor, ceiling and walls were covered in phosphorescent lichen that brightened the more I moved, so the room lit up when I went inside.

There was a large, circular bed, four meters in diameter covered in a mismatched collection of furs from a variety of unrecognizable animals. There were no sheets. Apparently Rell had a basic approach to home décor. Rustic, the advertising harpies of Earth would have called it. I face-planted and lay still. Like the grass furniture, the fur bed was wonderfully comfortable.

Hive shards and newborn queens. Ships that invaded a body to build themselves. Like Cab. Oddly cyclical, the more I looked at it.

"Cab," I mumbled, "how bad would it be if the Krr got a Shipkiller seed?"

--Best case is that they get hold of a seed, but they can't figure out how to make their own, so they only make one ship--

--Worst case, they reverse engineer the seed, make their own Shipkillers and we all die horribly--

I wriggled into the furs and sighed. "How likely is the worst case?"

--It's academic--

--The worst case is the only outcome they will accept--

--So as long as there are Shipkiller seeds, they will be trying to get some for themselves--

--The Krr are patient, and smart--

--If they get a seed, they will figure out how to make more--

--Period--

--Their behavior is fairly predictable--

I sighed into a face full of fur. It smelled like pine trees and dirt. Nice smells, but I had a feeling I would be aching for a hit of diesel and Febreze before long. I took a deep breath anyway, and bled it out slow. My vision was starting to skip. Falling asleep always felt like actually falling off the edge of something, I thought. I was dimly aware of the dimming lights.

My teeth were grinding. I was in over my head, and I knew it. I didn't know what to do, and with the stakes this high, not doing the right thing was kissing cousins with doing the wrong thing.

I took another deep breath and exhaled into sleep.

And dreamt again of the dead Amazon jungle, of a final visit. I meandered across blistering plains under a gargantuan dying sun. Red, now, gnawing at the remains of Venus. That world would be gone, soon, and Earth, my home as I had come to understand it, would be gone as well.

Cab covered me fully, but the bulk of him still rested on my shoulders. Covering my ancient body used so little of his potential. I suspected that he minded, some, when he had to compress himself to this degree. Maybe even resented it. He much preferred the open space above us, where he could live unfettered and enormous. But I needed this.

Sol covered half the sky, bloodying what little atmosphere was left to a malignant crimson. It was still just a little giant, with a long way to go before its final collapse. But it was big enough. Earth was breaking orbit, deeply attracted to the closer star and also, thanks to Sol's diminished mass, nearly able to escape into the cosmos after more than eight billion years. In all likelihood the planet would simply tear itself apart. So this was goodbye.

I squinted. My memory was perfect, but my imagination was starting to go. I could just see Earth as I had known it, green and blue, humid, lush. I could just picture humanity as I had been, instead of as what it had become. I missed ancestral humans. I missed feeling like I belonged somewhere.

The ground rumbled under my feet. Just a bit, but seismic activity was picking up. Someone chirped at me from a research station past the Jovian orbit in the new human language. Time to go. Sing-song clicking and whistles interspersed with vaguely familiar words. I never bothered to learn it. I looked around one more time and then kicked myself past escape velocity. Cab grew beyond the bounds of reason, and I left my home for the last time.

6

I rolled over eight hours later, just south of waking, and got a wad of fur in the nose for my trouble. Swatting made the lichen bright as midday, and sleep was banished to the nonexistent shadows. I lay with my hand over my eyes until I could orient my thoughts. Too dangerous for me to stay on Earth, so I left Earth. Met Rell. Killed a lot of people for Rell. Signed on to do it again.

This was my life.

I sat up and looked at the unmolested rest of the bed. I could have slept on fresh bedding for weeks as long as I picked a different spot every night.

The room was silent, but for a sourceless rushing sound that I assumed was the engines. I stretched, hard, half-yawning, and Cab unfolded behind me. He felt relief at the movement, I could feel it with him, but I couldn't tell whether he felt his own, or only mirrored mine. He was made out of super metal and magic technology, he didn't have muscles, why should he need to stretch? Did he stretch because I was stretching, and he was a part of me?

There was scant sound inside me as he settled back into place, like the sound of typing transmitted along finger bones. He was a part of me, and I was a part of him. The line between our physical selves was as blurry as a thing could be.

I was sticky and stinky and grimy with dead hair. My clothes were where I left them on the floor, wrapped around my boots. I took them under my arm and walked through the creepers into the brilliant fake sunlight of Rell's living room. I was in shadow, but the sun wasn't above us, directly. It was off to the side.

It's not the sun, I thought. We're shipboard. Not planetside. I moved to the edge of the branch. There wasn't a sun. But there could have been.

A single blinding point towards the edge of the ceiling lit the entire room. The space around the point was hazy, as if the walls were only a translucent layer over luminescence, a semi-opaque decorative film covering something that was too bright to at, something that made the room warm, almost hot. I was in the shade, and naked, and still I began to sweat almost immediately. I probably could have gotten a tan if I'd stood out of the shadow.

Cab focused on the spot briefly and noted quietly that it was moving, heading to the right and up, slightly, at a rate of about two feet per hour. A simulated orbit for a fake sun.

There was a waterfall to my left. I noticed it abruptly and had a flash of understanding: this was what life would be like, now that I had left Earth, a long, unbroken list of amazing sights, to be taken in turn as I recovered from the shock of the *last* amazing sight.

There was a *waterfall* built into the *wall*. Not one of those underwhelming meditation fountains, either, this thing was big. And the water came from nowhere. Four meters from the ceiling, there was a darker patch of wall that might have looked like it was recessed if I'd been standing farther away. Two long strips of lighter earth-tone brown intersected on a triangle of blue-black, and in that place water was oozing from the wall. Except oozing isn't the right word to describe fifty thousand gallons of water an hour. No wonder it was so humid. But it came from nowhere; there was no spigot, no hole, just a section of wall hemorrhaging water for no apparent reason. The liquid was glasslike at the source, and then three meters down it broke apart in midair, and by the time it went out of sight it was a roaring, tumbling gout.

Like Taughannock Falls back home, I thought. Cab winced behind my brain, and I grimaced. I was going to have to teach the little dear how to better compartmentalize his emotions. It was hard enough handling my own ill ease and vague homesickness; I didn't want to have to compensate for his as well. But it did look like Taughannock Falls. Two hundred meters of single-channel descent, and then…what? Where was all of it going?

I grabbed a handful of vine and leaned out over nothingness with my arm straight out and my body at about forty-five degrees, relishing the freedom that came from knowing I could fly.

The floor had pulled back into the wall. All that was left was a brief ledge just inside the door. The rest was given over to a shimmering, rippling pool, dark and deep. Mist billowed over the surface in sheets, soaking the walls and the bottom two branches.

Rell was sitting naked on the ledge with his feet in the water, eating a piece of fruit with neon blue skin and dark red flesh. A mug of black liquid steamed next to his hip. He was slick with mostly-dried water, as if he'd taken a swim ten minutes ago. He wasn't looking at anything, he was just looking, letting his eyes wander. It was a pleasant scene.

The vine snapped so suddenly that I didn't feel it happen. Instead, I was simply went from standing in one instant to falling in the next. I felt a vertiginous confusion: my grip on the vine was fine, why was the water getting closer?

I opened my mouth to say something witty and smacked into the surface of the pool hard enough to get the wind knocked out of me. I ended up in the same vaguely head-first position about three meters under the surface, confused and wet.

I blew air out of my nose and looked around. The pool was deep, deep enough I couldn't see the bottom, and wide. Wider than the opening above me. I was in a huge underwater cave with dim, glowing walls. An enormous reservoir.

My lungs felt ok, so I kicked for the bottom. The pressure didn't bother my ears, and my strokes were stronger than I was used to. After a moment, my lungs changed their minds and told me it was time to breathe.

--Need some air?--

--Check this out--

A pleasant chill spread throughout my body from a point behind my sternum, and I found I didn't need to breathe. After a moment, it happened again. And again. I was breathing, I just wasn't using my nose or mouth to do it. It felt similar, after the fact, but less satisfying. I grinned weakly. Another barrier gone. A lot of this felt like cheating.

The floor was covered in phosphorescent coral that brightened when I moved, just like the lichen in the guest room. The place looked like it was lined in radioactive bread mold. I worked my hand into a minute depression and held myself steady.

--Yeah, go on, just grab a handful--

--You know that stuff is poisonous--

I paused.

--Yeah--

--Real nasty neurotoxin--

--Geeze, it's just pouring in--

--So much for human skin as a barrier--

I looked at my hand. Everything seemed ok. I felt fine.

--I'm serious--

--If it weren't for me you'd be convulsing, vomiting, shitting yourself, the whole shebang--

"If it weren't for you I wouldn't be down here at all," I said, except it came out as, "Ephbligrrnphbloo, ehvdn'tuhbownrlll." Cab got the message, though.

--Yeah, yeah--

--You'd be hell to sit next to on the bus for a while, too, I'm pretty sure this stuff would melt your forebrain--

--Just thought you should know--

"Thanks, Cab, I'm very grateful," I said. ("Thgub, Ehbehrgfll.")

Rell was wiping water off of his fruit when I got back to the surface. He was dripping wet, and when he saw me he made eye contact and poured the contents of his mug in the water.

"You fucked up my coffee," he said. "I half-hoped you would drown." He took a bite and frowned. "Not that Cab would let that happen, I suppose."

--Nope, I need him alive to sneak me into R-rated movies--

"Good morning," I said, treading water happily. Swimming is peaceful, even if water is uncontrollable. "Sorry about the splash."

"Do you always take the high dive into your morning bath?" Rell said. I hoisted myself onto the ledge next to him.

"I'm a shower man, myself," I said. "I was holding onto some creepers, and they broke."

"Don't climb creepers," Rell said reflexively. I looked at him and something aligned in my periphery. The oblong strips of earth tone and bright color, growth medium and seemingly idle aesthetic affectations connected as one, and I saw the room clearly for the first time. At our backs, the wall was colored to mimic the expansive trunk of an enormous tree, so wide it was

75

nearly without curve. Above and ahead of us, what I had seen as tree branches became only vines, huge, ancient vines strung above the contained ecosystem formed at the base of a tree branch that would have been a thousand feet across, and miles long. The single tiny point bright enough to light and heat the room, a far off star. The waterfall, only rainwater draining from some higher plane, but so much that the sound was all-encompassing and internal, and the pool, only a protected puddle where colossal branch met god-sized trunk.

Even as I noticed the illusion, it faded from me. But for one traitorous instant, even though my mind knew that I was on a spaceship travelling between stars, my body knew in its fundament that I was in a jungle so big it defied description.

Except the patterns didn't quite fit. The lines did not align. The facsimile was incomplete, imperfect in order to be at least partially visible from all levels. Was the concession necessary, or by design? Was I supposed to understand the place wasn't real?

Rell's big eyes swiveled to meet mine.

"What is this place?" I said.

"You see it?" Rell said. I nodded, and Rell stood up. "Home. Just a little piece of home."

"It's beautiful," I said. I stood up, too.

"Actually, it's a prison," Rell said. He finished his fruit and threw the pit in the water. I looked at him and frowned.

"Is that a metaphor, or what?"

Rell shook his head. "No, really, it's a prison. I bought it surplus from the company that manufactures them for my species. It's an isolation cell for solitary confinement. They make it familiar so the prisoner doesn't lose his marbles."

Marbles? I thought.

"I mean, I've added to it," Rell went on. "But yeah, it's a prison. Cool, huh?" He sighed. "You do what you can with what you've got. Come on, let's get some real food."

I followed him into the hall. He was still naked. A semi-rigid crest of stiff hairs extended down from his tailbone, wide and flat, almost like a bird's tail. It was short, only barely extending over what I assumed would be his butt. But, then, this was an alien. He might not have a butt. Without being too obvious, I moved up next to him and snuck a look at his crotch.

"Excuse me," Rell said.

"I was just thinking it's interesting that I barely notice that you're naked," I said.

"And yet here you are trying to look directly at my genitals."

"Sorry," I said. "I was curious. But like, this is amazing, you're not human so you don't register to me as a sexual being at all. Like, one way or the other."

"Yeah," Rell said. "But you don't have to comment on it."

--Yeah, man, don't make this weird--

"Oh, piss off," I said.

"And to say you don't see me as sexual at all," Rell sniffed. "I might be an alien, Samson, but I do have feelings. I mean, I've reserved judgment on that little worm thing you've got dangling down there, but I don't have to. I mean, I'm amazed your species can even reproduce using something so fragile. Looks like bait. Do you fish on your planet? You know the word? Bait?"

I stopped amidst Cab's laughter and flapped out my clothes while Rell walked on ahead, chuckling to himself. My shirt smelled like fear sweat and burnt hair, but it was better than having my masculinity called into question by a nine-foot tall alien.

--Come on, hurry up, I'm hungry--

--Fish or cut bait--

I grimaced.

--Something seem fishy about Rell's mood when you asked him about the living room?--

"All right," I said. "That's enough."

--Sorry to bait you like that--

"At least I have genitals," I said.

--Hey man, machine fetishists would LOVE me--

--The sex toy from beyond the stars--

I declined to comment.

Rell served us eggs and salty greens, toast slathered in something that I decided to assume was butter, and fried cured meat. It was orange, so it wasn't bacon, but it tasted like bacon. The best bacon I had ever eaten, if I'm being honest.

"You know," I said after a sip of coffee, "I came up here expecting to eat boiled bugs for dinner and unnamable horror for breakfast, and this…" I waved my hand at the table. "I don't know, this is almost disappointing."

--At least he's feeding you--

"Does master's breakfast not pass muster?" Rell asked through a mouthful.

I shook my head. "No, this is delicious. But, I can't believe you guys have coffee. I mean, Frewdin had coffee, but everything about him was fake, and this is real food I'm eating. Bacon and eggs and toast and coffee. I guess I just expected things to be more…alien."

Rell mopped his plate with the last of his toast, popped the bite in his mouth, chewed carefully, and swallowed. "Truth be told, Samson, you and I come from relatively similar species." He shrugged. "Form-wise, that is. Life is incredibly varied, but with a large enough sample size there's bound to be some repetition."

"So our similarities are just cosmic coincidence," I said.

Rell made a wry face. "Similarities…Samson, do you know anything about Vabling physiology? I mean, yes, we look vaguely alike, but, I mean, that's only skin deep. Our internal systems are vastly different. I've looked into what we know about human systems, you've got that singular skeleton, that's one thing. I have an exoskeleton over my muscles and organs, which is covered by my skin. Your musculature is entirely different from mine, yours seems terribly inefficient by the way. Our internal systems are as unalike as…I mean, for god's sake, you're still set up to digest food with a bacterial stack, even if you personally don't have one anymore. We function on entirely different premises. Even fundamentally…your body is exclusively carbon based. Mine is not." He grinned, and swept his hand luxuriantly through the fur on top of his head. "No wonder your hair is so fragile. Silicon, baby. The only way to go." He chuckled. "No, we're so different that any interaction between us would be impossible without some form of technological intermediary."

"Translation machines," I said. Rell nodded.

"That's one. I don't speak Savage." He grinned at my raised middle finger, and raised his own six-digit hand. "Gee, I can't do that. But, so you're aware, the ship just told me to fuck myself. That's what that gesture means?"

"Yeah," I said. "Wait, it spoke to you?"

"Yes." Rell lit a cigar as he spoke. Even though his lips were closed, his words were clear. "You don't hear everything I hear, and I don't hear everything you hear. You don't hear your words translated into my language, do you? Do you think I hear your shitspeak? The ship is constantly translating for us. It's also providing us with sensory manipulations, simulations to foster familiarity, little jolts to your brain that alter what you see, hear, and taste."

"How does that work?" I asked. "I mean, how does it get into my brain like that?"

"Microwaves?" Rell waved his hand. "I kid. I don't know, it just works. But, for example, to me, the meat that we just ate tasted like sour molds and loam, as expected. Is that what you tasted?"

I raised my eyebrows. "No," I said slowly. "It tasted like bacon. Salty, smoky, a little sweet, maybe a little spicy?"

Rell's mouth twisted up like he'd eaten a lemon.

"Sounds awful," he said. "But that's what you taste, because the ship's computer did some work on your sensory center. Nothing major, no cause for any alarm, and I'm almost positive they don't actually use microwaves. And without it, none of this would function. Civilization as a whole just wouldn't be possible. I mean, you wouldn't be able to communicate with anyone, much less share a meal."

His tone brightened. He enjoyed explaining this sort of thing, which was exceedingly lucky for me.

"The translation machinery also alters some of our terms, in order to aid comprehension. Like, I ask you how old you are, you tell me you're twenty-eight years old. Except I don't hear twenty-eight years, I hear twenty-eight years. It comes out on my end as twenty-eight years, and then I tell you I heard twenty-eight years, but you hear it as twenty-eight years." He frowned. "Wait, this isn't working."

"I get the idea," I said. "It does that for all of our frames of reference? Like distances?"

"Everything," Rell nodded. "Vocabulary, phrasing, that sort of thing. Idioms. I mean, some ideas are pretty universal, so we all end up saying similar things. Like, I can tell you that there's more than one way to skin a cat, and I'm sure you'll get the message, even though there sure as hell aren't cats on Earth. You'd never have survived as a species." He grinned wistfully. "I went on a cat hunt once, a long time ago. Shit, was I scared. That's actually where I got this scar." He turned half around and pulled a patch of fur off of a bald, scarred spot. The skin was blue-black, puckered and burned.

"You and I are picturing very different animals when you say the word, 'cat,'" I said.

"That's my point," Rell grinned. "The machine supplied you with a familiar idiom expressing that there are always multiple solutions to a problem."

"An idiom with an identical metaphor, no less," I said. "Does it always match tone and meaning like that?"

"I don't fucking know, I'm a thief," Rell grunted. "Maybe. Maybe it's a coincidence. Our species are fairly similar."

"You said we were so different we wouldn't be able to coexist without the translation machines," I said.

"I say a lot of things," Rell said. "And I'm usually right." He settled in his chair and smiled ruefully. "You really have no idea what it's like out here. I mean, we both eat, we sleep, we're single-axis symmetrical, we reproduce sexually...the fact that I've mentioned those traits should imply to you that there are species in the galaxy to which a series of antithetical statements apply. You and I are similar. Christ, we both breathe a nitrogen/oxygen mixture, do you have any idea how unlikely that is in the grand scheme of things? There are races that are so radically dissimilar, creatures that evolved in such disparate environments that direct interaction between them is entirely impossible."

81

"Like if a species evolves underwater and they're trying to interact with people that live on land?"

Rell shrugged. "That barrier is fairly easy to overcome," he said. "Think about species that evolve in space, in null gravity, or creatures whose brains only function in near-stellar temperature ranges. Creatures whose neural structures emit harmful radiation. There are a lot of ways for life to form. And then there are cultural differences that have to be compensated for."

"Such as?" I hopped off the high chair and dunked my mug in the coffee. It was easier than trying to lift the urn.

"Hell, Samson, everything." Rell poured himself a half-cup while I scrambled back into my seat. "I mean, my species considers it a taboo to bathe in falling water, but you called yourself a shower man." He sipped his coffee. "Imagine this. On my home planet we have a legend about a monster called–"

I heard a deep, sharp noise that vibrated at the edges.

--That didn't translate for some reason--

--I'll try to supplement the local machinery in the future--

--That means something like 'emptier' or 'punisher'--

--Maybe 'mother?'--

--I gotta brush up on my Vabling--

"All three," Rell said. "It's a portmanteau. According to legend, the–" another guttural noise "–is a piece of living night that comes to steal the souls of those who would leave Vabl. A voracious floating blob of darkness. Just a myth. But if you zip about a quarter turn antispin around the galaxy you find the Huptons, a species that evolved the ability to disrupt light waves. Their atmosphere is a superdense field full of slowed photons, courtesy of their five stars and immense planetary mass, so they disrupt light waves in order to move, eat, everything. Put them in a more conventional environment, from our standpoint, and they are literally floating blobs of darkness. Just folks, same as the rest of us, but the–" again the sharp, guttural noise, "–myth is so deeply ingrained in my species that whenever there's any interaction, the translation machines have to create a holographic avatar for the Hupton, to keep the Vabling from going into fear-induced catatonic shock. Usually some kind of cute baby animal. Get the idea?"

"I feel like if I say 'yes,' here, I'm gonna get struck by lightning." I sipped my coffee. The caffeine content was out of this world. "Yes, I understand that the machine is tampering with most of what I experience. But there's still so much I don't understand."

"Me too," Rell said. "That's part of the experience of leaving your home planet, Samson. You realize how little you know. How little you can ever know. I mean, some of the Core races live for hundreds of millions of years, and even they admit that they can only scratch the surface of what there is to know about the galaxy. You have to come to terms with it, or you go bonkers."

"How old are you?" I asked.

"Seven hundred and nine." Rell chuckled and pulled at the fur on his chest to show me the faded roots. "Middle aged. See? I'm going minty."

"Christ," I said. "A lot of humans don't live a tenth of that."

"'Shorter lives are full of joy, and longer lives of pain.'" Rell said. "Whycklidam said that. When his son died. I know you don't know who Whycklidam was."

I let that sit for a moment.

"Agent Frewdin said he's been a cop for eighty million years," I said. "Just been a cop, not been alive."

Rell nodded. "He's a Bekht," he said. "They're one of the older races. They live a long time, two hundred million years or more." He grimaced. "They're all assholes and psychopaths. Anyone would be, after living that long. They're the soldiers of the Core. Most of the CLEA is Bekht, they're drawn to the work, and the Core likes to keep its security forces in-house. It's hard for someone from the Fringes and Arms to get any kind of meaningful security clearance."

I frowned. "You guys don't have much control over your government, do you?"

Rell shrugged. "I mean, we vote." He sneered into a laugh. "I mean, fuck, what do I care? I'm an outlaw. I only give a shit about the CLEA when they're chasing me." He frowned. "But I've heard of Frewdin. They say he's a real bastard."

"Are there species that live longer than the Bekht?" I asked. Rell nodded.

"Several. There are three that are rumored to regularly surpass the billion mark...well, not regularly, but regularly for their species. Longer lived creatures tend to reproduce very little, over time."

"Is this like, common knowledge?" I stood up on my chair and leaned against the back. There was a piece of me that wanted to clamber around the oversized kitchen, swing from the pots and pans. I was child-size, but man-strong, more than man-strong, and I wanted to use it. But Rell might have minded.

"To an extent, but I'm also a scholar of this sort of thing," Rell said. "Galactic statistics, census results, general theory. I know that I won't be around for very long, and I'm a curious man." He smiled to himself. "The galaxy is the most fascinating thing around, after all."

"Cab says, all things being equal, I won't die," I said. Rell grunted and nodded and focused on the dishes.

"Does that scare you?" He asked after a minute.

"Yeah," I said. "It does." Cab rustled impatiently.

"I wondered," he said. "You flinched when I said the Bekht were psychopaths because they live so long." He put away the dishes and the water that splashed on the counter evaporated.

"Are they?" I asked. He sat down across from me, but didn't get comfortable.

"Yes," he said. "To a certain extent. Longer lived races become very cold, over time."

"Why?" I asked.

"Because nothing is really unique," he said. "That's the theory, anyway. There's a threshold–I mean, there are lots of thresholds over a life, think about that moment at the cusp of adulthood where you realize how long life is, and also how short it is, that's a threshold in a being's sense of time. There's another one around a hundred thousand years of age that's supposed to give a person a sense of the patterns governing events in their lives. There's been quite a bit written about this, but it's something that species like ours can only picture in the abstract. Essentially, the longer a creature lives, the closer new events adhere to old patterns. Except that's not quite it." He made a helpless face. "It's hard to describe, having not experienced it myself, but one of the dominant theories is that past that point experiences carry less and less weight. They're not as important, or they're important according to a different set of priorities. I'm not sure how to describe it, because obviously I've never experienced it myself."

--A hundred thousand years isn't that long--

"Maybe not to some machine," I snapped without thinking. To my human sensibilities the idea that I might even see one thousand years was terrifying, to say nothing of one hundred thousand. Still, no reason to be an asshole. I took a deep breath.

--Jesus, forget I said anything--

"Maybe you'll buck the trend," Rell said. I looked at him and he grinned, wide. "Hey, there's never been a creature like you before. Maybe you're frozen in development, and you'll stay an immature pain in the ass for all time. Constantly amazed, never growing up. An eternal case of arrested development. God help us all."

I grinned weakly. Rell leaned back in his chair and drummed on his chest.

"If you live long enough, you could learn everything that's ever happened. They say when you know everything that's been, you know everything that will be."

"I've never heard anyone say that," I said.

"You people think you're alone in the universe." Rell waved his hand. "You don't count. It's a common question among short-lived races: Does omniscience breed omnipotence? I mean that would seem to be the logical extension of the recognition of life's patterns."

"I'll let you know when I find out," I said.

Rell laughed. "You think you'll make it that far?"

"I can take care of myself," I said. "Besides, I heal pretty quick."

"Yeah, right," Rell snorted. "It's a good thing, too, because you can't fight for shit."

I frowned, and Cab laughed.

"Hey," I said, "don't forget I saved your ass yesterday."

"Sure," Rell said. "You did. You won a fight you couldn't help but win." He raised one finger. "You also got shot three hundred seventy-one times–"

--Three hundred ninety-four times--

Rell grinned, and ticked off more fingers. "You got shot three hundred ninety-four times. You blew up a midsize warship from a range of one meter. For God's sake, you almost got yourself transported into a non-dimension! You're tough, I grant that, but you fight like a Terminator, all brute force and no thought."

I glared at him. "I'm new at this."

"That's true," Rell said. "And you exhibit moderate intelligence and pluck. But you need training. We've got nearly thirty hours until we reach Phibbix. Have Cab show you how to shoot, or something. Think of it as your time on the mountain."

--He can shoot fine--

--The trouble is he's a total wimp--

--He was terrified yesterday--

--I'll put together a training program--

--Maybe we can toughen him up--

--Come on, meat-for-brains, let's roll--

I stayed where I was. "You sure you're up to this?"

--Why wouldn't I be?--

"Because you're like three days old," I said.

--Good thing I'm so damn precocious--

"Great," I said. "Real humble."

--False modesty is real bullshit--

Rell got to his feet. "I'm sure you two will have lots of fun together. If you need me, feel free to leave me the hell alone. Adios, Short Round." His laughter followed him down the hall, out of earshot.

"So...do we think Rell is the one speaking French and Spanish and referencing Indiana Jones?" I asked. "Or is it the translation machine?"

--Don't know, don't care--
--Shift your ass, meatball--
--I've got a warrior to train--

A warrior. What a word. What a pretty, stupid obfuscation. Honorable delusions. My misgivings pursued me down to the hold, along with my growing frustration. I felt stuck in a joke. My time on the mountain, I thought, and shook my head. Like we were in the middle act of a movie. We were stepping wrong. I could feel it. But I didn't know how to stop.

7

In spite of its grandeur, the hold wasn't an impressive place. I'd expected hidden doors, secret compartments. Closets that nobody knew were there. Floor panels where I could stuff an errant Jedi, something, anything, but this was just a place to put stuff. An empty warehouse stretching the length of the ship. At the stern, off in the distance, the deck rose to meet the ceiling. It was split down the middle, designed to open up. Which made sense, they had to load the ship somehow, and they sure weren't gonna use the passenger airlock. Rell had enough cargo space to smuggle a cruise ship.

--Go to the middle--

--Get, come on, let's roll--

I shouted to hear the echo. It was a long time coming, a dropped second of semi-awed waiting. Above me, long, prehensile crane-arms were folded along the length of the ceiling, oddly humanoid shapes at the top of my peripheral vision.

--Those things are creepy as shit--

--You see that one, the one that's just a tentacle?--

--Over there--

I could tell where he was pointing without being able to see him. It's not like being followed by a ghost, although the comparison's been made. It feels like I have another body that occupies the same space as my real one, an imaginary second standing just shy of existence. Cab pointing felt like I was pointing with my own hand, even though I wasn't.

Truthfully, paying close attention to Cab's physical sense of himself feels like trying to look under my own eyeballs; if I try too hard, my head hurts and I get dizzy. So I try not to do it too much.

"Is it me, or is it odd that the passenger airlock opens into the cargo hold?" I was close to the middle of the enormous floor. "Shouldn't Rell be more covert?"

--You're confusing real life with movies, again--

"Oh, gee," I said, "how could I have managed to do that?" I put on the ship and looked at my armored, engine-studded hand. "Oh, that's right! My life is a fucking cartoon"

--A really *cool* cartoon--

"That's a cold comfort."

--Customs doesn't board for inspections, or anything like that--

--This is deep space--

--You either fool their sensors, or the cops send you to space jail--

"Space jail," I said.

--It's jail in space--

--What do you want from me?--

--Besides, interstellar self-contained autonomous artificial penal environ is a bit of a mouthful--

"You don't have a mouth," I said. Cab's sudden amusement rattled around my skull and cut through my unease, and I laughed without meaning. The emotional doubling has always been strange. It's like being half-possessed.

--Ok, enough stalling--

--Aerial combat--

--Dogfighting--

--The Sweet Science--

"That's boxing," I grunted.

--Dude, fuck boxing, what do you know about boxing, you're a dweeb--

--I'm talking three-dimensional anti-ship combat at half-light speed--

--With lasers--

--*That* is sweet science--

Anti-ship combat. Cab's excitement rose as I considered what that meant. I looked at my hands. They were giant flipper things that could probably fly me right through the wall if I wanted them to, but they were still hands. I made a fist. It was a huge fist. I thought with fervor about what I wanted to happen, and the hull shrank around me, shed a few inches of armor and machinery. Now I had real hands, again. Armored hands. I couldn't hide the fact that I was a spaceship. But I could have passed for normal at a costume party. I could have mingled. And I didn't always have to wear the damn thing, anyway. I didn't have to live like a warship. I could act human. At the very least I could fake it.

It felt good to make a fist, so I relaxed my hand.

"We need to think smaller," I said. "I need something besides weapons of mass destruction if I'm going to follow Rell into a refugee camp."

--Nothing says 'Obey me' like a WMD--

--People *respect* a WMD--

"Briefly," I said. "Before they're vaporized."

--Grumble grumble--

"C'mon Cab," I said. "You're not a Shipkiller, you're a suit of armor."

--Excuse me?--

--I'm a Shipkiller--

--If you want to make a point about the importance of restraint given our relatively small stature and the potential afforded us by that attribute for the infiltration of civilian populations in which large scale destructive force would result in massive collateral damage, go right ahead--

--But my identity is my own--

--I am a Shipkiller--

I took a deep breath. Cab sat still.

"Fine," I said. "Your identity is your own."

--Jesus, why are you so irritated by this conversation?--

"I'm a liberal," I said. "So you're a Shipkiller. We still need smaller weapons. Something I can use indoors without blowing a hole in the hull, like the guns you built me the first time I met Rell."

--The kinetic bursters?--

"Sure," I said. "But, you know, show restraint."

--Dude, I get it--

--I should just make you punch people--

--Here, try this--

My right forearm unfolded into a collection of strange mechanical shapes and flat planes, like a junk pile frozen in free fall. What wasn't held fast by a tiny mechanical arm was anchored magnetically to something that was. And then every thing started moving at once.

A long cylinder screwed itself out of the confusion. I couldn't tell where it came from, although I was becoming used to that sort of thing. Smaller components appeared and connected together to form larger components, which then latched onto the cylinder as it reconnected to the hull. A flattened ring appeared in the maelstrom and twisted itself around the base of my forearm. A mount formed underneath, and the whole thing notched itself into a sudden housing at the rear of the barrel, and the weapon was finished. The entire process took, in total, about three quarters of a second. The gun hummed wickedly under my brain.

I twisted my arm this way and that. "What is it?"

--It's a gun, stupid--

I formed a tight line with my mouth. "No shit, asshole. What kind of gun?"

--A big one, but not a really big one?--

"Does it have a name?"

--You mean like Stephen?--

I rolled my eyes.

--Look, everything I build you is unique, given the constraints inherent to your size and shape--

--Like your cutting beams--

--I compared them to Merkhan cutting beams, because they operate on similar principles, but it's not a true Merkhan effect, you can't contain a Folium loop in less than six point three one cubic meters of space--

"Uh huh," I nodded.

--Don't come on like you have any idea what I'm talking about, feeble human--

--Anyway, I figured out a way to contain a similar effect on a smaller scale--

Cab fluttered a collection of designs across my periphery, the engines, the shields, the inertial dampeners.

--All of this crap is custom built--

--No names--

--This is…well, it's an energy weapon--

--We may as well call it Stephen--

My left arm grew a twin of the gun on my right. Another cloud of machinery ending in another mean little voice in the back of my head: Fire. Fire. Fire.

--Stephens, plural--

--Load the Stephens, Cabney!--

--The Huns are charging!--

"I'm not calling you Cabney," I said. "Now that you've built them once, can you build them faster?"

--Nothing I do is ever good enough for you!--

--I want a divorce!--

--Yeah, probably, let me try--

The left Stephen disappeared into the hull in pieces. Cab paused, and then the gun reappeared with a sound like a compressed snare roll and rim-shot.

--point zero zero one two seconds--

--I can do better--

The guns reminded me of drum-clipped Thompsons, the aggressive rifle shape in opposition to the relative gentleness of the ring under my elbow.

"Can I run out of ammunition?" I asked. Cab expressed a negative, shook his head without having a head or visibility or anything other than intent, intent that came into my mind clear as a bell.

"How powerful are these things?"

--Middling--

--Fifty-caliber--

"That's middling?" I said.

--Compared to shooting a hole in a spaceship?...--

"Fair," I conceded. "Can you make them bigger?"

--what is this, tiny-dick syndrome?--

There was something schizophrenic about the voice in my head cracking jokes about his semi-ownership of my genitals. "Can you arbitrarily make these things more or less powerful?" My voice grated.

--Sure--

The right gun spun and clicked along various axes and ended up bigger than it had been.

--That's twice as powerful, now--

--Same cyclic rate--

--You gonna shoot 'em, or just look at 'em?--

I looked at the wall. It was substantial, to be sure, and a week back I would have called it impenetrable. But the day before I'd cut a spaceship nearly in half with a wave of my hand.

The intrusive memory of black specks barely seen, ashen detritus from gaping wounds in a rocket ship that might have resolved into burnt figures sucked into nothingness, if I'd only let Cab look closer.

--Stop that--

--What the hell are you thinking about?--

--Jesus, what goes on in your head?--

--Fucking control yourself--

I shook it off. "I can't shoot these indoors, can I?"

Cab paused.

--Ok--

--Good catch--

--That would have been embarrassing--

I just stopped myself from sneering. The weapons on my arms popped and shifted towards their butt ends, and their voices in my head changed pitch subtly, lost their animosity. They were empty threats, now. I concentrated on my right hand gun and forced a tiny component to lift and unfold in a way that didn't make a lot of sense when I thought about it, and the animosity returned.

--And now that one will blow a hole in the hull again--

The component shifted back to its previous configuration at my urging. I experimented with drawing and holstering the guns, imagining them present, then absent. I could dismantle the entire ship, and then bring my hands forward in a martial stance as fast as my arms could move and still find my second skin assembled and waiting long before I was finished moving. Quick draw Samson. Stripped bare, I could hop in place, assemble and lift off before I reached my pitiful human apex.

"I don't need you to do everything, do I?" I said.

--No, thank god--

--Some of what you think gets through to me--

--Simple ideas, images, desires, impulses--

--Nothing concrete--

--You still need to communicate with me directly to convey complex actions, but I can tell what you want most of the time--

--We need to get to work--

I tried to imagine what we were going to do, and grimaced. Learning to fight. Martial artistry. I hadn't done anything like that since just after Mom and Dad died. Such pleasant memories. Hell. And I was probably going to get knocked around some, too. It had been a long time since my blood had been up.

--Dammit man, now what?--

--Stop--

--Whatever is going on in your stupid fucking meat brain, just…stop it--

--Choke it off--

--God almighty--

Something clicked in my head.

--Rell, do you mind if I access your translation and diplomatic apparatus in the hold?--

There was a snort, and then the clearing of a large throat. "Sorry," he said. "I fell asleep. Yes, that's fine." He paused. "What do you have planned?"

--Augmented reality training--

--Samson needs to get his ass kicked--

--Come on down, it's gonna be fun--

I frowned. "Hey, I just need like, target practice and stuff."

--Sure you do, princess--

"I'll be right down," Rell said. Another click, and the channel was closed.

"Listen," I said, "what are you gonna do? Augmented reality?"

--Oh, I'll jerry-rig the translation machinery and the diplomatic apparatus to run holograms, or something like that--

--Let me see--

"And what is it you have planned?" I tried to make the question innocent.

--You'll find out soon enough--

-- In the meantime, try not to pass out from sheer nervousness--

--God you're a pain in the ass sometimes--

--Here, have a flower--

--It's a pansy--

--Just for you--

A cartoon flower grew out of midair in front of me. I took a deep breath and blew it out my closed mouth. Cab's jokes were wearing on my nerves.

--Well, that sucks--

--Hang on--

The flower sprouted roots, and took on more definition. The colors muted, and detail became apparent where once there had been almost none. After a moment, it could have been real, but for its defiance of gravity.

--There we go--

--And we're linked into the ship's interior reality, you can smell that thing, right?--

I could. I nodded.

--Touch it, will you?--

I took the flower in my hand. It was present against my fingers, and after a moment it sagged as gravity took hold.

--Damn, I'm good--

The flower plopped in broken vulnerability to the deck. I rolled my shoulders and dismantled the ship to scratch an itch, and the crumpled blossom stayed where it was.

"I can still see these things outside of the ship?"

--They'll be present for Rell, too--

I nudged the flower with my foot.

"Damn, you are good," I said.

--I know that--

--Ok, let's get to work--

"Hi," said the man standing in front of me. I jumped, and he frowned at me. "I'm One."

He was tall, white, broad-shouldered and well-muscled, with a narrow face and a thick nose. He wore tight blue jeans over tooled leather cowboy boots, and a black sleeveless tee shirt. His hair was straight dirty blonde, worn long in a ponytail. He had a wide, friendly smile, and his thumbs were hooked in his pockets. I opened my mouth to ask a question and he hit me hard in the face with a strong, immediate left jab. My head snapped back, and he hit me in the solar plexus, so that I doubled forward into his waiting knee. Then I was flat on my back, trying to remember how to breathe and see and hear and think.

"What?" I managed.

"Hi," he said again. "I'm One."

--One is a constructed image--

--He's going to hit you until you aren't afraid to be hit--

--Once you can fight without me worrying that you're gonna piss yourself, we'll move on to more complicated things--

There was a hell of a lot of self-satisfaction in Cab's voice.

"The fuck?" I said.

--You're afraid to fight--

--I can feel it--

--Fear is a liability--

--I'm going to train you out of it--

--On your feet--

One squatted down on his heels just out of arm's reach.

"Get up, boy," he said. "Or else I promise, I won't be gentle."

I smiled at him politely and worked on getting my wind back. The shock of being punched radiated through my body, and I started to open up inside. You never forget how, once you learn. Even if you try.

8

One's knuckles were a mess of scar tissue, and there was more around his eyes. He looked like he had been in a lot of fights, even though I bet that he hadn't. Like all fears, One wasn't really there; he only existed as potential.

--Get up, pussy--

--You can't get out of this by staying on the floor--

On the other hand, my head ached and it still hurt to breathe. Real or not, One could hurt me, which meant that Cab could hurt me too. The voice in my head could do me harm. The voice in my head that would be with me forever.

--This is ridiculous--

--You're ridiculous--

--I can barely even see straight--

--You need to learn how to suppress your fear before you get the both of us killed--

"That's almost the exact opposite of what I learned," I said slowly.

--Oh, where, in journalism school?--

--Fuckin' dweeb, you don't know--

--Why can't you just admit you don't know, and try to learn something?--

I thought about that for a moment, but before I could come to any conclusions One stood up and kicked me in the ribs. I spewed air and curled up instinctively.

--Get up!--

--Stop being scared!--

One walked around my back and kicked me again. I felt the pain, but already I was turning it into a thing separate, as I had been taught. It was just pain. If I wanted, I could work through it. Besides, pain, a lot of pain, is a sensation closely related to impatience. Most injuries are too slight to cause any lasting damage, and can be weathered with the understanding that all things pass. The thing folks call pain is just the futile wish that the healing process was already over. Once you accept that, you can ignore pain, or at least keep it from being too distracting.

--You think this is an option?--

--Cowering on the fucking floor?--

--You think someone's gonna bail you out?--

Of course, Zen acceptance or no Zen acceptance, it's never pleasant being kicked. And the fact that an injury will heal doesn't stop it being scary when you're hurt.

--Stop being afraid!--

--Stop it!--

--This is ridiculous I swear to fuck I'll kick it out of you I hate this!--

And then I got it. Our minds were connected. He felt my pain. He felt my fear. My emotions became his, transferred back and forth across the minimal divide between us. An unending feedback loop. Except that I knew fear at least as well as I knew happiness and love and sadness and all the others, which is to say they were feelings I had been dealing with ever since I outgrew the sociopathy of early childhood. Cab, on the other hand, was only three days old. He had no self-control.

"Cab, you don't understand–" I said. One kicked my raised guard.

--No you don't understand!--

--You think this is a game, you get to talk your way out of this?--

--You learn to keep these stupid fucking feelings at bay or we are gonna die, Greg, we're gonna die no matter what your wimpy fucking idiot liberal bitch philosophy says otherwise!--

--Fucking don't understand, what the *shit* could you know about it you spineless backward workaday snot!--

He was really mad. Almost shrill in my head. And his anger was leaking back into me. That was all right. I could handle anger. And fear. And all the other crap that just required a stiff upper lip and an extra second's thought to navigate. But everyone has a finite amount of self-control.

One slipped a kick over my guard and mashed my stiff upper lip against my teeth, and I lost my grip on myself. I had a rush of mostly-visual thought, the life I'd lost, the brutal thing that had replaced it. The thrumming presence in my head, a voice that would never be silent, the illogical extreme exemplar of all the smaller self-hating voices I had worked so hard to conquer after my parents died. And overtop everything the taste of mashed fleshy blood in my mouth, the twin sensations of body-horror and nostalgia, nostalgia and excitement.

I got up in a rush and shouldered One away from me. I was speaking, but nothing intelligent. Variations on the phrase, "Shit-fucking piece of fuck robot shit," and other guttural sentiments. My feet settled into place. Cab didn't notice.

--Ooh, touch a nerve, bitch boy?--

One came at me with a right. I shucked it off my left and punched him in the throat, then kicked him between the legs. He staggered and I grabbed him by the front of his shirt and lifted him upright and stomped hard on the top of his knee. He screamed and fell over, and I kicked him in the face hard, once, twice, three times. He disappeared and reappeared on my other side and hit me in the side of the neck, just under my ear. I stumbled, and managed to stay upright and for a moment we grappled, hands on each other's shoulders.

--Tell me I don't know, I'm a fucking Shipkiller, who the fuck are you?--

I snarled something in response and swept my hands around and up, breaking One's grip, ducked my chin and pulled him forward. His nose broke against the top of my skull and I head butted him again, and again. He sagged. I pushed him away and held his shirt with one hand and clubbed him. Right hook. Right cross. He brought his hand up to block and I slugged him in the stomach. He gasped and dropped his hands and I smashed the side of his face with my elbow. He brought his knee up between my legs but I twisted and caught the blow on my thigh.

Rell came sweeping into the hold. One pawed at my face. I shoved him away and then pulled him close, spun around with him, threw him bodily to the floor and kicked him over on his back. Rell said something. I straddled One and grabbed his stupid hillbilly hair and hit him with my fist. His nose was somewhere over to the right of where it should have been, under his eye.

Then I was rising off of him, held from behind.

"Stop," Rell was saying. "Stop that, dammit, what in God's name are you doing?" He held me under my armpits. I could feel the claws in his palms.

"Let me go!" I spat. Rell turned in place and half-tossed me away from him, just hard enough that I had to work to keep from falling.

"End simulation," Rell said. "Captain's override."

One disappeared, along with my injuries. It was jarring. They didn't exist outside of my head, but it seemed like they still hurt. That was scary.

--Swear to God I'll cut out your fucking forebrain if you don't calm down!--

Cab's voice rattled off the walls, and Rell looked around. His face was mild, but his fur was thick, almost on end. He was scared. I raged inside myself, an internal emotional soup of fear and pain and anger and guilt, but I wasn't so far gone I didn't recognize that Rell was scared, too.

Why, though, the quiet emotionless piece of myself asked. Why?

I shut my eyes against another of Cab's tirades and dug into myself for words.

--Stop being afraid!--

"Stop being such a little bitch!" I yelled. "Jesus, ignore it! Just fucking ignore it!"

--Fuck you you arrogant prick, ignore it, fuck off, you have no idea what you're talking about--

--Ignore it, you dumb shit!--

He sounded almost desperate. I blew air out of my nose and forced myself to follow my own advice, which is never a pleasant thing to do. It's frustrating being the bigger man when all you want to do is shout and rage and burn bridges. But that wasn't an option. I found a tiny patch of calm in myself and clutched at it.

"Bring him back," I said. "The hillbilly. Bring him back." I looked at Rell, who crossed his arms at me.

"Rell, I need to show him," I said.

Rell pursed his lips and then shrugged and tapped the air near his belt.

"Your funeral," he said, and dropped his voice. "My funeral."

One reappeared immediately with his guard up. I circled around him.

--See, this is what I'm talking about, he's here and you get all freaked out--

"That's because I'm scared," I said.

--So, stop!--

"Shut up, Cab, that's not how it works," I said. One shook his head angrily and swung a looping right at me. I stepped outside and batted it past. You never forget how, and it was all coming back, and other colloquialisms. I'd had good teachers. I knew what I was doing. And Cab would have seen that, if he weren't so distracted by the novel experience of human emotion.

--Oh, right, ok, show me how it works--

--Show me how to fight, newspaper boy--

His tone was edging into petulant. I stepped in close to One and we started trading blows. He was good, fast and strong and creative. None of these are traits you want in an opponent, especially one who's made out of light and doesn't have to breathe, but I held my own. Sometimes he hit me. Sometimes I let him. I paid careful attention to the moments when I had to let him hit me so I could hit him back, harder. I concentrated, showing Cab that I had gone into the fight knowing that I would be hit in the face. Showing him I had accepted that truth. Showing him what I could do in spite of the fear.

--Stop being so…you need to--

--How are you doing this?--

I shook my head. Something inside me said it had been three minutes, some innate habitual recognition that normally I would have been hearing a bell somewhere in my periphery. I danced to my left and laid out a combination: left jab, left jab, right cross, left hook, right uppercut, and One was on his back. I was breathing deeply, drenched in sweat. My arms were tired and I should have been bruised, even if I wasn't. My hands ached. Dad always said that was the best feeling in the world.

One shook his head, and disappeared.

"Nice, huh?" I panted. "Kid's still got it."

Neither of them said anything.

"Cab, was I afraid to be hit?" I said. My shirt smelled like a warzone.

--I don't know--

"Oh, hell, yes you do," I snapped. "Answer the question. Was I afraid?"

--Yes--

--You were--

"You're damn right," I said. "I hate being hit in the face. It hurts. But I don't let it control me."

--That much fear should be overpowering--

"You only think that because you're three goddamn days old," I said. There was an edge to my voice that I couldn't shake. "You don't know how to handle emotions. You don't know because you're young."

--I'm just not used to them--

"Cab, you don't know!" I yelled. "Don't quibble! Admit it! You don't know how to handle emotions!"

--That's just cause I'm not used to them, though--

--I'll get it straight--

I sighed. "Cab, the point is that you don't know everything. You're not innately prepared for this life. Admit it."

--I'm more prepared than you are--

"Bullshit!" I yelled. "Bullshit! You might know more galactic trivia, but you don't know a *damn* thing about how to act! You don't know how to control yourself, you don't know how to keep your head when you get mad, admit it, you're as blindsided by what we are as I am!"

--Well, it's hardly my fault I have a human mind--

"And it's not my fault I have to teach a fucking infant how to keep his emotions in check," I sneered, "but it's still my responsibility. Learning how is yours."

--Well, you need to learn things too--

"No shit," I said. "But I admitted that a long time ago. It's your turn."

I stood there for a moment, waiting.

--Well, I guess you might be right--

"Admit it!" I shouted, turning in place. It's hard yelling at someone who doesn't have a face. "Admit it! I want to hear you say it, Cab! Admit you don't know everything!"

--Come on, this is childish--

"Cab, you brought him down here for training and you beat the shit out of him," Rell said. "If it wasn't for Samson noticing the spiral you both were in, you might have done some real damage to each other. You owe him. You need to start treating him like an equal."

--But we're not equals--

--He's meat and I'm the most advanced machine in the galaxy--

"You're an idiot child in charge of a deadly weapon, and if you don't show me some sense and maturation I will pull us out of warp and you can both get the hell off my ship," Rell said exasperatedly.

--Oh, bullshit, Rell, you need us--

"I need you to keep me alive!" Rell yelled. "If you don't get your shit together you're going to get me killed! Goddammit, Cab, you just browbeat the poor man into a homicidal rage, and you're too naïve to see it! And you're too much of a stupid, backward child to admit when you make a mistake! Apologize, shake hands, and admit that you need to work together, or get the fuck off my ship! I'd rather take my chances with the Krr than share a home with a psychotic self-aware computer!"

Sourceless wind swept nameless small trash across the floor of the hold. I watched Rell and waited for Cab to regain the ability to speak.

--Are you for real?--

His voice was quiet aloud, tentative. Scared.

"This is your last chance," Rell said. His fur was up. "I swear, Cab, your last chance. I need your help, but I won't be party to any of this."

Rell folded his arms and watched Cab by watching at me. I did my best to bear up under his attention.

--I'm sorry I got mad--

Cab's voice was a litany.

--I don't know everything--

--I'm sorry I hurt you, Greg--

--I didn't understand...you know, you read about emotions, but those are just words--

--In person...holy hell, what a rush--

--I can't believe you go through that all the time--

"You get used to it," I grunted. "It's part of the human experience. That's part of the trouble, Cab, you're discounting lessons from a life that I've been leading for twenty-eight years. I've learned things about being human in that time, and whether you like it or not, you have a human side. You know, just because you feel a thing doesn't mean it's real, and even if it's real you don't always have to pay attention to it." I rubbed my neck where my neck remembered getting sucker punched.

"I don't know how to drive the ship," I said. "You don't know how to compensate for emotions. There's other skills we have that aren't necessarily shared between us, either, so there's got to be a give and take. And, You know, we have to expect some friction, too. Christ, I mean, do you see that? Really? Or are you bullshitting me?"

It wasn't fair of me to say that. I knew he was telling me the truth. I knew he was trying to do better by me, already. Even at that point in our relationship, I recognized how clearly I knew his feelings, his motivations, even some of his thoughts. That was what started the fight in the first place. But I was still mad.

"You've been together three days without any breaks?" Rell said. I looked at him and nodded.

--Seventy-seven hours--

"And no breaks," Rell said. "This is your first fight?"

--I mean, we've gotten into a couple of arguments...--

"It's our first real fight," I said. I looked around helplessly and sat on the floor, flapping my sweaty shirt. Fistfights are exhausting. I wanted them both to go away. I just wanted some time to myself.

Rell sat down across from me and leaned on his hands.

"Well, it was bound to happen sooner or later," he said after a moment. "You two are closer together than any two beings have ever been, I imagine. You're bound to get on each other's nerves from time to time." He chewed at his lip. "That's not an excuse. You're too powerful to have the luxury of losing control, or fighting between yourselves. You need to learn how to work together, or you'll kill someone." He paused. "Again."

In the moment, angry, hitting Billy Maxwell for a second time with Cab's keening anger at my anger baying in my ears. I winced, and Rell nodded.

"Why are you mad at Cab?" He asked me.

"He was hitting me," I said. Rell shook his head.

"You've been mad all morning," he said. "The both of you have been sniping at each other all morning. But we've figured out Cab's part in this, Samson, and it's simple because he's still simple, himself: He can't handle emotions. He has to learn to think, even when he's feeling strongly. That's a tall order but a simple concept. The question is, why are you mad at him?"

"He doesn't care that we killed those people at Ceres," I said in a rush. Cab rustled, about to speak, and I held up my hand. "He thinks we were entirely justified, and that's the end of the story. I lost my life, man, everything changed, and I'm out here trying to figure out how to operate while I share head space with a guy who doesn't see the value of a human life! Of a life!"

I pulled out the memory of the broken dustbuster rocket ship, of fried, decimated bodies tumbling out into space.

"That's real, Cab," I said. "We did that. Justification doesn't change the reality. And, you know, we killed those people because I don't know how to shoot to wound. Because I don't know how to restrain myself. I can pull a punch because I know how to fight with my fists, but I don't know how to fight with a Shipkiller dug into my neck. That's why we're down here, to learn restraint, and you're hung up on the existence of fear. Like it's some new thing you discovered, and you know what? First time you really experience it you get it completely wrong. You think fear is something to suppress, but it's not, it's not even a true emotion. Fear is just the recognition of negative possibility. It's the understanding that you might get hurt, you probably will get hit in the face, that you might not get what you want or even what you need. You don't suppress something like that. You accept it."

111

I sighed. "I don't know how to act out here. And you don't either, any more than I do. We're both out of our depth. I'm supposed to be a human and you're supposed to be a Shipkiller and neither one of us is just that one thing, anymore! I'm not human. And you're not a Shipkiller, pithy self-identification or not. You're supposed to be stuck on something that's three miles long and dumb as a post, and *I'm not supposed to live forever*. But you're sentient and I'm immortal and that's that. We need to learn from each other. We need to adapt. I'm pissed off because you won't see it."

Cab thought for a long time, very quickly.

--We're a Shipkiller--

"Cab," I said.

--Shut up--

--It's my turn to talk--

--It's your turn to listen--

--We're a Shipkiller--

--We, not I--

--Together, we're a Shipkiller--

--Not a Cabernician Shipkiller--

--A Solar Shipkiller--

--The first one--

--You're right, we're something new--

--We need to adapt--

--I do, and you do, too--

--Listen, you've got me wrong--

--I'm not happy we killed those people yesterday, I just recognize that it was mostly out of our hands--

--Rell is right, there's a difference between killing someone because you can, and killing someone because you have to--

--Killing is never good, but in certain scenarios violence is justified--

--I've internalized that--

--You haven't--

--You've internalized an understanding that emotions are always present but don't always have to be your top priority--

--I haven't--

--You're right, we need to adapt--

--But you need to stop digging in your heels--

--You keep saying your life is over--

--Well, you're right--

--Your life is over--

--*Ours* has begun--

--It's time for *you* to accept *that*--

--And get your head right--

I rubbed my head.

"I'm trying," I said. "It's only been three days."

--Try harder--

--It's been three days already--

I half-smiled and quarter-laughed, but it was enough. Cab relaxed, and I did too.

--Hey, I'm sorry I tried to kick you in the nuts--

"You better be," I growled. Rell let out a deep breath, wiped his hands on his shorts and stood up. His fur had settled.

"All right," he said. "Now that the morning's existential crisis has been averted, I'm going to go have a stiff drink and lie down. You kids play nice."

--Yes dad--

Rell raised a hand. "Cab, if you were my child, I'd have drowned you at birth." He frowned. "Although I'm not sure what I would have had to fuck in order to end up with a whelp like you."

--Probably something illegal--

"Like a robot assembly line that makes cars," I said.

--Or a vending machine that sells used panties--

"A tractor with a satellite uplink."

--Facebook--

"You can't fuck Facebook," I said.

--Why not, Facebook fucks us...--

"Glad to see you're both back to your normal insufferable selves," Rell said. "Lunch is in three hours. Don't blow up the ship."

We watched him leave. The door hissed shut behind him, and I sagged, closed my eyes.

--Hey, seriously, where did you learn to fight?--

I would never be alone again.

"My dad taught me," I said. "And I was a competition fighter in high school."

--Your dad the marine?--

I nodded. "I got beat up a lot in the fourth grade. When we moved to Berdoo. He taught me, and my mom. Boxing, the MCMA, ah, Marine Corps Martial Art...It turned into something we did as a family. When I got older I got into martial arts. Then my parents died and I decided I didn't want to fight anymore, and I gave it up."

--Like, as a vow or something?--

"No." I shook my head. "Nothing like that. I just didn't want to fight anymore. It...it's funny, this sounds like such an awful thing, but really, it just reminds me of my family, too much."

--That's not a normal thing to say, no--

I chuckled, even. "I know. But it's something we did together, same as other families go camping. You know? Just too many memories." I thought about it and smiled sadly. "A lot of happy memories."

--You were nineteen when they died--

I nodded.

--I...you know I'm hooked into all the records on Earth, I didn't like, go looking for information--

--Like, I didn't pry--

"I know," I said.

--I'm sorry that…they're…dead--

I nodded again.

--How the hell do you people get anything done with all these emotions?!--

"Just takes practice." I took in some air and wrenched my head away from my dead parents. It wouldn't do to wallow. "So…a Solar Shipkiller."

--Yeah--

--Because we're from the Solar System--

"I get it." I looked around the hold and thought something about the potential of emptiness, then shook my head and stood up. The ship and the Stephen guns wrapped around me with a thought.

"Ok," I said. "Let's figure out what that means."

9

If I sat on a chair in Rell's kitchen, my head didn't quite reach the table. If I stood on the chair, I had to bend at the waist to eat over my plate. I compromised by sitting on the backrest. Rell puttered around, arranging packaged ingredients and spices on the counter.

"How did it go?" He asked. His fur shifted. Cab said he'd been in the ersatz forest living room since we talked, diving and climbing over and over and over. I didn't ask how he knew.

I shrugged. "We worked some basic target practice and flight drills. It went ok. I'm an ok shot from a standstill, but I'm dogshit against a moving target. And Cab didn't make it easy for me."

--Samson doesn't like my jokes--

I rolled my eyes. "He made these talking targets that flew around reciting famous political stump speeches." I shuddered. "It was awful."

--I wanted to see if you distracted easily--

--Who knew you had such a hatred for Ralph Nader?--

--Blood pressure went *right* up--

--What's the deal?--

"Don't worry about it," I said darkly. "Ralph knows what he did."

"Good you two are getting along at least," Rell said. He stirred the pan. "Don't worry. You'll get better with practice. You ever had callops?"

"Scallops?" I said.

"Callops," Rell said.

"I've used a caltrop," I said. Rell pulled something out of the fry pan and tossed it to me. Hot grease spattered my cheek.

"Ow," I said.

The callop was a whole animal, a tiny five-legged mammal with a squat body and a furry head with ten tiny little eyes. Its legs were thick, and tucked under its belly, and each one had ten tiny little toes. I decided that it looked like a tiny mammalian spider. It was creepy, but it smelled delicious. Anise and mustard and cider vinegar, butter and salt.

"Can I eat it?" I asked. "Like, it's cooked?"

"Should be," Rell said. "We're having them with noodles and veggies."

I popped it in my mouth. There were bones, but they were soft and yielding. Whether cured or cooked or naturally soft, I couldn't tell, but they weren't unpleasant. The flesh was flaky and yielding, like fish, with a slightly gamey taste. Rell's spicing was expert.

"Yum," I said. "Tangy. They're not intelligent, are they?"

"Well, these particular callops are dead, so, no, not very." Rell waved his spatula as he spoke. "But, yes, callops are fairly intelligent. They're a very artistic culture, painting mostly, their eyes see a greater range of color than most other species', and they're all incredible singers. But they reproduce exclusively via rape and consider consent to be a dangerously deviant practice, so most carnivorous species eat 'em to even the score."

I stared at him. "You're kidding."

"Of course I'm kidding, that would be barbaric. What kind of a monster would eat another intelligent species?" He filled a pair of bowls, set the table and sat down to eat. The noodles were orange, and slightly sweet, and the vegetables were oddly shaped, but everything was delicious and I was too hungry for xenophobia.

"What is this dish?" I asked.

"Lunch," Rell grunted. I took the hint and didn't speak for several minutes. Cab told me to eat the callops first. Shortsighted. It's important to save some of the best for last. Rell, of course, finished his meal first. He got a cigar and lit it from a kitchen match that regenerated its strike-anywhere head as soon as he blew it out. My face lit up, and I laughed at myself. Unlimited cosmic power and I still got a kick out of a parlor trick. That was reassuring. I just had to hold on to the feeling.

--Eat more meat--

"Can you show me where we're going?" I chewed, swallowed, and took a breath. "Like, on a map?"

"Sure," Rell said. He wiggled his hands near his belt, swiped, tapped, and typed. The lights dimmed, and a spark appeared in the air over the table.

"Cup it in your hands," Rell said. I looked at him, and he gestured. "Reach for it. It'll come. Cup it in your hands."

I stood on the edge of the chair and extended my hands, and the spark flew between my palms and froze.

"Good," Rell said. "Now, do this." He put his hands together, and then spread them, fast, like he was clapping in reverse. I mimicked him, and the spark exploded into a billion points of light, a billion billion tiny stars that shot through the furniture and the walls with no effect. I flinched, and raised my guard, and as my hands came together the points came together too, and coalesced into a three-meter-wide facsimile of the Milky Way. It wasn't as neat as I would have expected, ragged at the edges, the stellar matter only vaguely organized around a central point like debris in a whirlpool. But it was immense. And it was made of points that should have been too bright to look at, atoms shining like spotlights in the dimmed kitchen, a jewelry maelstrom. Tides of diamond sand suspended in midair. It twisted and turned madly as I tried to get a closer look at it. I couldn't stop the damn thing spinning.

"If you want to move your hands freely, make a fist," Rell said. "Otherwise, two hands controls the zoom, and your closer hand controls the perspective."

I closed one hand and moved the other, and the little galaxy spun on its axis. "Oh," I said. "Hollywood rules. Got it."

At this distance, all the colors blended together into a grey streaked yellow-white. I spread my hands and dove for the center, separating stars from the cloud and shoving them behind me until I found what I was looking for.

"Ah ha," I muttered to myself. "It *is* a black hole." The empty eye of the galaxy spun in front of me, feeding on a cloud of superheated gas and rubble. Sun bright at the edges and struck across the middle like the photographic negative of a needle-punctured cell.

"What did you expect?" Rell said.

--Yeah, really--

--Eat more meat--

"Good point," I shrugged. "What else could it be?" I pulled out, watching the stars streak inward and slow down.

"Map, show us our current route," Rell said. I went back to my lunch.

The map whipped around to highlight a bent line connecting a yellow dot labeled 'Solar System' to a brown point labeled 'Phibbix Nebula Refugee Station.'

"Zoom in on Phibbix," I said through a mouthful. Suddenly we were rocketing through space towards what quickly became apparent as an ugly brown nebula, a skid-mark on the underwear of the universe. The image froze when the nebula was as big as the table. It looked like something I shouldn't eat around. Our warp trajectory terminated at the far side from the station, which was positioned in between three nascent stars.

"Zoom in on the station," I said. We dove into the murk and I held my breath without thinking.

"How close can I get?" I asked.

"Close enough for ten centimeter details," Rell said. "This is an old model. I haven't sprung for an update in a few years, but I think the new ones will give you two centimeter details."

"On what?" I asked.

"On everything," Rell said. "Celestial objects of all kinds, worlds, moons, asteroids, stars, space stations, fixed technological features. All known objects down to class ten asteroids...except in Krr space."

--Class ten asteroid is about the size of a cow--

"Fancy," I said. Rell snorted.

Phibbix Station appeared like a bug on a windshield, out of nowhere and impossibly close in an instant. It was sphere, nothing more, a dull-white ball hanging in the middle of nowhere. According to the readout on Rell's map, it was about a quarter-mile in diameter.

"That's it?" I said. Rell grinned.

"Nah, this is an old image. Yui has contractual permission to make modifications to the station as he sees fit, so he's got something more impressive these days. You'll like it." He considered. "Same basic premise, I suppose. Just bigger. There's a lot more refugees to house, these days."

"Contractual permission to make modifications to the station itself," I said. "I thought you said this guy ran a black market."

"That's how he makes his money, but officially, Yui works for a Core-based nonprofit providing aid to galactic refugees," Rell said. "He's the director of station operations."

I chewed slowly. "He's in charge of the station."

Rell nodded.

"It is, from a certain point of view, his station," I said. "We are traveling to a space station that is owned and operated by a man who may have tried to kill you."

"Yeah," Rell said innocently. "What's the problem?"

"My life," I said. "Which has provided only this single, shitty lead to follow."

"Buck up," Rell said. "I'm at least half-sure he didn't try to kill me."

"Even Russian Roulette has better odds than that," I said. I zoomed out and looked at the wide, empty space opposite the Core from our position. An uneven blotch of unadorned, white stars, most of the latter half of one arm and a good portion of the fringes on either side. "Is that Krr space?"

Rell nodded. "Yup, that's it."

"Show me the Front," I said.

"Show us the Krr/Core Military Border," Rell said. I looked at him and cocked my head.

"Does that make this the Krr/Core War?" I asked. Rell glanced at me and shrugged. "That's kinda fun to say out loud." I grinned. "Try it."

"No," Rell said.

Krr space was closed off from the rest of the galaxy by a dense wall made of small stars arranged in a dense grid, a fence made of nuclear landmines keeping a fifth of the galaxy at an arm's length.

"What is that," I said, "stars? Really stars? That's not natural."

"Of course not," Rell said. "The CLEA dragged them into place."

I goggled some. "They moved stars." It wasn't a question, I knew he was telling the truth, but it staggered me to see such a thing presented by a machine that my mind accepted less as a device than as a window.

"Yup," Rell said. "It's like a fishing net. If a big enough fleet goes through the net, the stars go supernova. The death of a star causes a quantum rippling effect that disrupts warp vectors and semispace trajectories, which tends to scatter any ship on that path across a few parsecs of space. And you can't make it through at sub light speeds, because the Front is ten light years thick and under constant surveillance. If the Krr tried to mosey under the wire, the CLEA would be massed on the other side long before they made it even halfway."

I leaned on my elbow and stared at another bite of food, decided I'd had enough, and ate another callop.

"A big enough fleet," I said. Rell looked at me. "So they can fly small forces through the net?"

He nodded. "That's how they raze systems."

"What if they spread an invasion force out wide enough to fit it through the net undetected?"

"It's a mass thing," Rell said. "The whole system talks to itself, so if they fly a certain amount of mass through at any time, or hit a certain quota over a certain time, the whole thing goes up. And if the whole thing goes up, most of Krr space would be devastated." He grimaced. "Most of it."

"And then what?" I asked. "Can they like, reload it?"

Rell shrugged.

"This is not a good security system," I said through another mouthful. "I do not feel secure."

Rell shrugged again. "Life's a bitch."

"They do have guards watching the Front, right?" I asked.

"Yes." Rell nodded. "They watch the Front."

"And our army is bigger?"

"Quite a bit." Rell stubbed his cigar out in his bowl.

"That's good," I said.

"Yeah," Rell said.

The wall curved in towards Krr space, a broken piece of a colossal bubble. It didn't look like much.

"What stops them going around?" I asked slowly.

"They can't," Rell said. "The Front extends into dead space." He waved his hand at me, intercepting my question before I opened my mouth.

"You can't get more than a few parsecs out of the galaxy without dying," he said. "Nobody is quite sure why. The theory is that there's a fundamental particle we still haven't discovered that's only present in the interior of galaxies. We can't isolate it, though, so we can't transport it or produce it, and without it, leaving the galaxy is fatal."

"Fatal how?" I asked. Rell's ear fur wavered, and he shrugged.

"You freeze to death," he said. "Except it's nothing to do with temperature. No exceptions, it's affected every form of life that's tried to leave. There was one woman, ah…" Rell frowned. "Doreen something, I can't remember her last name. Famous pilot. She tried to make a trip outside, then turned around before she kicked…she said it felt like her body was just giving up."

I made a face. "That's kinda spooky, Rell."

He nodded. "A death-field surrounding an entire galaxy? Yeah, I'd say spooky is the right word."

The map turned above the table, the Front a barrier built into an invisible boundary. A true wall, not just a shield, but a wall the Krr could penetrate any time, as long as they didn't overdo it. And they could topple the thing any time they wanted, as long as they were willing to get their nose bloodied. Krr space would be devastated if the Front exploded. But what did devastated mean, really? The Krr existed to eat and reproduce. Even if most of them were killed, that surviving minority was still just as much of a threat, given enough time.

"It's still a really shitty system," I said.

"Oh, yeah," Rell said.

I zoomed out again, staring at Krr space. "And we don't know what's in there?"

Rell shook his head. "I assume the military knows more than us lowly citizens, but my understanding is that all our efforts to learn about the interior of Krr territory have been, well, ah…eaten. Or similar."

"Neato," I said. "So they're like the fucking boogeyman." I pushed my bowl aside. Rell pulled it over.

"The boogeyman isn't real," he said around a mouthful. "The Krr are."

"Yeah," I said. "Yeah." Cab shifted on my back. I zoomed out more and looked at our flight path. There was something surreal about the little icon of Rell's ship, the friendly yellow line that wouldn't have been out of place on a seatback flight tracker. I tried to point out Earth, way back at the beginning of the trip, and the line of sight from my finger hit about a thousand systems. I tried again, then chose an isolated star at random and tried to highlight that. I got about forty dozen options. Rell chuckled.

"I can't isolate a system without knowing its name," I said.

"Yeah," Rell said. "The size is limiting. That's unless you can retain a truly disgusting amount of information, which some species can. But for most of us, there's just too much to keep track of. I try to ignore the names and go where I'm going. It doesn't pay to think too much of a place as a place where you've been before, even if you have. There's just too much to be seen. Too much on one world, let alone three hundred trillion of them. I find I'm happiest if I approach everything as if it's brand new."

I pointed with a finger on each hand, and carefully positioned the point where the two lines intersected on Earth. The display read, "Earth: Quarantined System: Warp Redirect, Authority One. Class Five Biological Agents expanding throughout system."

Rell put our bowls in the sink and sat back down. "I used to get mad if I couldn't remember where I'd been. One month I went to the same planet three times and each time I forgot its name. The third time I was so pissed I got drunk and lost a fight." He shook his head. "I was young. Wanted to be the daring space pirate, jaded and never caught off guard. Now I just try to take it all in stride."

"You remember Phibbix," I said.

"I spend a lot of time there," Rell said.

"I only know two planets," I said. "Earth, and Vabl. Oh, and Cabernicia. Three"

--Nice to be remembered--

The planets in question flared different colors. They occupied the same quarter of the map, even though they were trillions of miles apart. Earth was still blue. Cabernicia was red. Vabl was deep green.

"Tell me about your home," I said. The planets I'd named stayed distinct in a way that made them shine through the neighboring systems.

"This ship is my home," Rell said immediately.

"You know what I mean, man." I hopped up on the table and sat cross-legged between two of the galactic arms.

"I knew you were going to do this," Rell muttered. He set his jaw and put his feet on the floor and his elbows on the table. "Show us Vabl." His voice was loud, bossy.

The map flipped over like a person doing a surface dive and we descended into the press of stars. More stars than flakes in a snowstorm, flying through my face without bothering to be sensate. I kept blinking, and then remembering I didn't need to.

Vabl rushed up and then froze, two meters wide and gently rotating above the table. I scooted back ; I was too close, sitting where I was.

The system was coded green out of semiotic necessity. That was my first thought, although it arrived somewhat less eloquently. Something like 'Wow, that's a lot of green.' The planet was a slightly oblong sphere with polar oceans separated by a single colossal continent banding the space between, covered *in totalis* by the densest jungle that I have ever seen. It was the logical extreme of the arboreal planet cliché, an overgrown, toxic abundance of choking, hyper-competitive plant life. The trees were visible from orbit, from what must have been the equivalent of high orbit, a hundred thousand miles at least. How could Rell's species have evolved in such an environment? Where, even?

127

At a glance, the planet was devoid of artifice, but when I looked closer I could see that the vast jungle hid a single, unbroken metropolis just under the canopy, a nation state that stretched from coast above to coast below and wrapped around the entire world. It was built into the surrounding wilderness, constructed entirely of natural forms that intermingled seamlessly with the canopy itself.

The trees defied belief: God-like banyans five hundred miles tall and two thousand miles wide, with entire civilizations between their branches, their rooting tendrils supporting enormous columnar cities descending into undergrowth so dense it was almost solid.

The canopy was an unbroken field of green and brown suggesting depths so dark they could only be called oceanic. The trees, the enormous trees that looked to be the basis of Vabling civilization, erupted out of the surface of the canopy as mountains, islands. It wasn't hard to imagine that Vabl had three seas, the watery ones at the poles and the forested third between them. The only land was that which had been built between the colossal branches.

"Vabl," Rell said. "We call ourselves toshein, by the way. Toshe is to human as Vabling is to Earthling. Toshein is the plural."

I nodded and opened my mouth to ask a question and experienced the mental equivalent of two big men trying to get through the same small door at the same time. Except I had many more than two questions.

"How did you evolve?" Rell asked.

"What?"

"'How did you evolve' is a typical question between two species experiencing each other's habitat for the first time," Rell said. "Evolutionary habitat. It's a way to understand a person. So think about it for a moment, and then tell me: How did you evolve?"

The truth was that at that point in my life I didn't know exactly how humanity had evolved. I mean, no one had the full picture, but I was definitely missing more than a few key details.

"Well," I started, which is never a good sign, "as far as I'm aware some monkeys stood up in either Africa or Asia, I'm not sure which, and then we expanded across the world over the course of…a few hundred thousand years? I think?"

Rell looked at me for a few seconds and then shook his head sadly. "I try, Samson, I try not to call you primitive out loud, but it's just so hard sometimes." He sucked at his teeth. "So you're plains people. You evolved in open spaces?"

"As far as I know," I said. Rell nodded.

"So you're an insecure people," he said. "Not a lot of privacy wired into your heads. You came up looking over your shoulders for things that wanted to eat you. Interesting."

"What?" I said.

"Pop psychology," Rell said. "My species evolved in the upper canopy. Just below the surface. Our eyes are a remnant of that time, we're still in the process of adapting to a higher-light environment. There are animals down there that represent the other direction my species could have gone, namely down. 'There but for the trees,' as they say."

"Yeah, I was gonna ask about those," I said. Rell smiled.

"Those trees are about a million years old, on average," he said. "They aren't entirely organic, there's a mineral component that apparently had a lot to do with their being able to take root." There was awe in his voice. "It took them about half a million years to reach the top of the canopy, and my species just held on for the trip. In a manner of speaking."

I stood up on the table and found that I could take the planet in my hands and shrink it, turn it like a beach ball, zoom in wherever I wanted.

"Our species began to achieve sentience around then," Rell went on. "As we came out of the canopy, into the light. Rather a graceful set of images for a species to be blessed with. Most species don't do anything as irritatingly poetic." He cleared his throat. "There was too much competition down in the Jungle. We survived, but there wasn't much potential for us to be anything more than a nomadic species. But in the Seedless Trees we could thrive. The Jungle Provides. Now, what does that tell you?"

I looked at him and shrugged. "You're arboreal?"

"You're no good at this," Rell said. "But then, that's the point of educating you, is to keep you from embarrassing me when I'm forced to introduce you to my friends." He raised a professorial hand. "My species evolved in an environment with a lot of competition, but also a lot of potential for secrecy and hiding. The assumption is that this makes me a self-secure, self-reliant creature with an easy capacity for hard decision making."

I grinned. "You're getting this out of Cosmopolitan, aren't you?"

"Something like that," Rell said. "Now, in addition, I'm from an environment that was doing its best to kill my species. But at a crucial point in my species' prehistory, my planet developed a feature that is a galactically unique fusion of geological and organic material, which is itself the basis for my species evolution as a sentient species. And I closed my little spiel with a proper noun for the trees themselves, and what was clearly an ingrained phrase."

--Like 'peace be with you--

"So what does that mean?" I asked.

"Think about it for a moment," Rell said. I turned back to the planet.

Toshe architecture had a distinctly organic feel to it. There were no hard lines, no sharp corners. The signs of civilization had been easy to miss, because at first the buildings looked like giant termite mounds, fungal growths, ancient vines. Whether the mimicry was aesthetic, a chosen form, or practical, in that the natural shapes were easy to work with in such an environment, I couldn't tell.

It was a three-dimensional world. A climbing, flying world. Close up there were apparent thoroughfares, pathways curling under and around the strange, bulbous buildings. Places that could only be traversed by creatures as capable of climbing as I was of walking. Whole neighborhoods underslung with vines thick as city busses and cultivated, I assumed, to make it easier in a pinch to get a handhold. What if someone fell? Did they worry about falling? Or did that just not happen? It had to happen. Everybody tripped from time to time.

The species had gotten lucky. They'd made it out of the canopy. I didn't know what it meant. They were all staunch environmentalists? I looked at Rell. He was staring at the planet with a blank, absorbing look. Not absorbed, absorbing; as if he was doing his best to soak up an image he knew he wouldn't see for a long time. But he had the map right on his hip. Which meant he didn't look at this part of it often, and after we were done he wouldn't, for a long time.

"You can't go back," I said.

He shook his head, watching the near-movement across the planet's simulated surface.

"Why?" I asked. "Did something happen to it?"

"No," Rell said.

"Then why can't you go back?" I paused. "What did you do?"

"I left," he said simply. After a moment, he looked at me. "Earth has lots of different religions. My planet has only ever had the one. Forestry is the belief that the Forest provides for us and we provide for the Forest. Everything we need comes from the Forest, and we sustain the Forest in life and death."

"You worship an environmental life cycle?" I said. Rell shrugged.

"It makes more sense than most religions." He grimaced and scratched the back of his head. "They've…We've been a theocracy forever. It's a good system, our civilization is thriving. But one of our core beliefs is that we need to keep our environment a closed loop. Even after we made contact with other species, we kept them at an arm's length. All business is conducted in orbit or farther by robotic or third-party intermediaries. No Vabling is permitted to leave the surface, because doing so takes life energy out of the cycle. Doing so gets a person excommunicated from the church, and since we're a singular theocracy, excommunication is banishment."

"Take a good look." He pointed. "The forest has been like that since long before toshein evolved. There's a whole series of worlds down there, any and every natural environment you can imagine growing everything that we could ever need, any food, resource, chemical, any material you could name, all of it right there for the taking. The Forest Compleat. Even now, my species needs do little more than harvest and store. For god's sake, there's a type of tree whose bark is so

tough it can be used as reentry tiles on orbital shuttles!"
He laughed painfully. "The Forest Provides. Provide for
the Forest. Shit."

"You're not a believer?" I half-grinned, and then
stopped when Rell looked at me. After a moment, he
spread his hands.

"They're worshipping a planetary energy cycle
as supreme when there's a star overhead," he said.
"You could say I'm agnostic." He sighed.

"So you had to leave, and you were banished for
it." I said. "What happened? What did you do? Did you
get in trouble?"

Rell smiled and shook his head. "I didn't have to
leave, Samson, I chose to leave. I paid a Pleuyofeal
trader to take me to Bfoppos when he bought a load of
mineral ash off my cousin." He grinned. "Art Doleran.
His kid plays drums for The Frame Jobs."

"What?" I shook my head. "Nevermind. What
do you mean, you chose to leave? You chose to be
banished? Why?"

"Because look at you," Rell laughed. "Look at
that ship. Look at what you're doing, Christ, this is
appalling, I've got the potential scourge of the galaxy
running around in my hold being taught to kill things
by a sentient computer because, yeah, I need his help,
but also I think I can do right by him, and besides, he's
fascinating."

--I'm fascinating--

--He's just eye candy and conversation--

Rell ignored him. "Look at what I'm doing, look
at where my life has led me already." He pointed at the
map, pulled out to ten parsecs with a gesture and
looked into the stars. "This place is incredible, Samson.
You have no idea what the galaxy is like, yet. It's
exquisite, incredible, impossible to imagine or contain. I
always thought it might be, growing up, and you know

what? I was right!" He grinned sharply. His eyes might have been wet. He let his hands go and Vabl roared back in. "This place, the things I've seen, they've been worth excommunication. But that doesn't mean it hasn't been painful." He leaned over and got a beer out of the fridge.

"You're lucky you can go home, Samson," he said. "Don't forget that. No matter what you see, or what you become, don't ever forget that." He flicked his wrist to get the image of his home planet spinning and drank his beer.

I stood up and hopped off the table.

"I'm gonna go back to the hold," I said. Rell nodded.

"You need anything?" I asked.

He snorted. "Get outta here, kid."

I nodded and went out into the hall, leaving him with his hologram.

I was worried. I left Earth almost without thinking, without any real hesitation, without even a change of clothes, but that didn't mean I'd left for no reason. Rell was right. I was lucky I could go home. But when? When the Krr were no longer a threat? When my existence was no longer cause for alarm amongst the civilized peoples of the galaxy?

--Hoo, anxiety isn't fun--

--Jeeze, this is awful--

I nodded.

--Makes you feel like a bit of a dick for complaining about having to leave Earth, huh?--

"You tell me," I said. I'd make it home eventually. I'd find a way.

--Ok: you feel like a bit of a dick for complaining about having to leave Earth, huh?--

I thought of Rell sitting alone in his kitchen in the middle of nothingness staring at a fake planet the way I used to stare at old photo albums, as if the artifacts of an earlier time in life were unfamiliar, because after a while they are.

"Yup," I sighed. "Little bit."

10

For the most part, the remainder of my time on the mountain proceeded smoothly. We spent fifteen straight hours in training, running drills that Cab came up with on the spot. Rell brought me food twice. He didn't comment on our earlier conversation, and I didn't press the issue. Cab theorized that the more we talked, the better I would get at manipulating the base material that made up the ship, so we talked about nothing while I tried to learn how to be a spaceship.

--Terminator Two was a vastly superior movie, dude, come on--

I lined up the Stephen on my right hand and blew apart a diamond-shaped target while it sang an off-key rendition of New York, New York. All of Cab's targets sang, none of them well.

"The first one had an energy and a horror to it that the second one didn't have," I said. "Don't get me wrong, TeeTwo is great, but it's not as complex."

--Nerd--

I shrugged. "I appreciate the Muppets on a deeper level than you do."

One of the diamonds pulled a snub-nosed revolver and took a shot at me as I flew past. I rolled, accelerated and bounced off the far wall.

--You got too close to that one--

I shook my head and looked at the scratch I'd left on the wall.

"You think we should do this outside?" I got to my feet and lifted off, watching the diamond warily. It was belting Pavarotti and holding the gun without any hands.

--Outside--

--Samson, outside is moving past us at three hundred billion miles a second--

--We go out there we'll be obliterated by a piece of space dust--

--Besides, the Warp won't let us open the doors until we slow down to sub light speed--

The diamond spun in place and a bullet bounced off the wall behind me. I dove right and fired from the hip. The Stephens' cyclic rate was too high for polite conversation, which was helpful, because I wasn't a very good shot. The diamond exploded into nothing.

"What the hell does that mean, 'the Warp won't let us open the doors,'" I said. "You talk about the drive like it's alive."

--Not the drive, the Warp itself--

--What we call the Warp Drive is really just a communications and anchoring apparatus that allows us to communicate with a species of extra-dimensional organisms who have the ability to warp time--

--Whom we unfortunately call 'Warps,' because scientists are not terribly creative people--

--When we want to go faster than the speed of light, we use the drive to politely ask a Warp to take the space on our warp vector and compress it along a single axis--

--Cosmic foreshortening--

--See, you can't exceed the speed of light--

--But you can fly at nearly the speed of light along a foreshortened space-time vector--

--So while we fly along what is by our reckoning a shorter distance at about a hundred thousand miles a second, the rest of the universe sees us travel a really long distance at about three hundred billion miles a second--

--Approximately--

I hung in midair while a pair of diamonds across the hull catcalled me. At least they weren't singing.

"You're telling me there's a creature aboard who can warp space and time," I said.

--Well, not onboard--

--We don't actually know where they live--

--But apparently doing this, warping space for us the way they do, allows them to perceive time and space the way that we do--

--Which is fun for them--

--It's like a vacation--

"You don't know where they are," I said. "And you ask them to mess with the fabric of reality."

--Well, we know they're extra-dimensional--

--But we don't know if that means that they're from this universe, and just perceive things in more dimensions than we do--

--Or if it means they're from outside of the universe, looking in--

--One of life's great mysteries, I guess--

"And yet we trust them to twist space and time so that we can get places faster," I said slowly. The diamonds rushed at me point-first, and I shot them out of the air.

--Nice--

--Listen, dude, we've been using warp drives for billions of years without incident--

--Chill out--

--The galaxy has been running a long time without our help--

--And, you know, warp drives don't just get us places faster--

--They get us places, period--

--If we couldn't move this fast, there wouldn't be any contact between the stars--

--Space is really really really really big--

--Civilization only exists because the Warps help us out--

I nodded, looking around. "So the whole ship is being...held together? Basically? The Warp is keeping us from breaking apart? And we can't open the doors?"

--You don't want to--

--But yeah, that's the long and the short of it, as far as I can tell--

--The Warp generates a field around the ship and then squashes the space ahead of the bow and lets the ship fly through that space without being mega-destroyed--

"Mega-destroyed."

--The space outside has been compressed along a single axis--

--We do not want to be out there unprotected--

--Smoosh city--

--Bleah--

I shook my head and looked around, even though there was nothing to see. "An extra-dimensional entity," I said slowly. "That's fuckin' cool."

--Right?--

"So fuckin' cool," I said. A pair of armored Vablings appeared on the floor below me and raised long guns. I froze. "Cab? What's this now?"

--I'm sick of programming diamonds--

--Let's see what you can do with these guys--

"Miller Lite!" One of them yelled.

"Tastes Great!" Barked the other. "Less Filling!"

Cab was a weird dude. The trouble was that his personality had started from a duplicate of my own, which meant that I was probably a weird dude, myself.

It hurt getting shot, and I got shot a lot, over the course of the day. The pain faded quickly, because it wasn't real, just Cab tweaking my pain centers to keep me invested in his war games, but that didn't make the memories any easier. After a while there wasn't a part of me that wasn't smarting from some recent trauma.

"Tell me about the Core," I said. A pair of Vablings hit me from opposite sides with bolts of yellow-white energy and knocked me spinning into the wall. I lay on the ground and didn't move.

--Well, it's in the middle of the galaxy, it's big, and it's where all the rich people live--

--What's the matter, you dead?--

I got up. The Vablings reappeared.

"How is the government organized?" I grated.

--Densely--

--This time try not getting shot--

"How about this time you help me?" I thought carefully, and with a certain amount of hesitation, a pair of Stephen gun turrets built themselves out of my shoulders. "Can you control these?"

There was a moment's hesitation, and then one of the turrets swiveled around and started bopping me in the head.

--That's a yes--

"Stop that," I said. "Ok, I'll take the one on the left, and you take the one on the right."

--You really enjoyed saying that--

"I watched too many movies growing up," I said. We lifted off and the Vablings opened fire.

--I got mine faster--

--So the Core is pretty simple--

--You've got a Senate and a Congress, the Senate is made up of representatives from the Core systems and Congress represents the Fringes and the Arms--

--Congress has some control over the Senate, but not much, they need something like an eighty-percent majority to overturn a Senate ruling--

--And there are scads of systems in the Fringes and Arms whose governments have been bought up whole cloth by Core-owned companies--

"What defines the Core versus the Fringes and Arms?" Six Vablings took up the pursuit. I marked four for Cab in my mind and shot at the last two with reckless abandon, and the pack scattered like a school of fish. Cab's targets flashed and burned. I winged one of mine and tracked him as he fell, then got shot in the face by the last guy. I hadn't been paying attention to him.

I came to on the ground.

--Gotta keep your eye on the ball, buddy--

"Blow me," I grunted.

--Now *that* is creepy--

--The Core government is all the sentient races that were around eleven billion years ago, when they put together the first Coreward Alliance and started to explore the outer reaches--

--They dragged all their systems inside an interdiction field that closed off the whole interior of the galaxy--

--Big old cloud of hung Bosuns and exotic radiation--

--You can't warp through without blowing up your ship, and they patrol the interior constantly--

"Kinda like the Front," I said.

--A lot like the Front--

--Except it doesn't stop working after one use--

"They do love their fences out here," I said. Cab laughed.

We started to streamline. At first it was nothing to write home about, one encounter in five that didn't end with me 'dead.' Then I was wounded more often than I was killed, and then I was only killed once in a while. When Cab got bored and stacked the deck, or I got sloppy.

Cab cheered the first time I won without being shot. It felt like he was clapping me on the back. I smiled, a little embarrassed, a tiny bit guilty. I had always had a knack for this sort of thing. Hadn't shot a gun in years, and I'd never had tactical training, and this was something more than anything I could have prepared for, but still, I took to it with an ease. I won't say it was easy, because it wasn't. But I took to it.

I learned to paint targets on the things or parts of things I wanted to shoot, and thus mimic accuracy. I could disarm a man without hurting him too badly, or disable a ship by focusing on its engines, so that the Stephens only fired when they had a clean shot. I learned to fly in tight spaces, to twist my body around obstacles as if I were dancing, or swimming. Cab created clouds of targets, and I learned to distinguish identical objects from one another by things like orbital trajectory or smell. I learned how to read the sensors, and we learned together how the different sensors could be made to augment one another, to show us more. I could shoot the needle out of a haystack without singeing a stalk.

Late in the day, Cab had the amusing idea of plotting a course for me the way he would have for a Hoon whale, if things had turned out differently for both of us. He tested his first course by barreling me without warning through a forest of knives. I screamed and felt the ship move around me, and came out the other side without a scratch.

"You!" I yelled. "You have to warn me before you do something like that! Not cool! Entirely an unacceptable thing!"

--Come on, they're not real knives--

"Does not matter!" I yelled. "I swear, if I wasn't circumcised before…"

--Stop that--

We spent the next hour simulating dogfights with spaceships from famous movies and television shows. I still got shot a lot, but now I was getting shot a lot by Star Destroyers and Constellation-class starships, which made getting shot a novel experience, at least. Cab put me in a lot of strange positions, sometimes with unfortunate results.

--You have a hell of a lot of limbs to keep track of--

"I have four! Four limbs!"

--That's a lot of limbs!--

"It's four limbs! You're telling me Hoon whales don't have fins to watch out for?"

--Those are fins!--

--These are arms and legs!--

--Totally different!--

--Whales are just a series of tubes!--

--You're like, half arms and legs!--

My shoulder picked that moment to pop back into joint. I yelped, then took a deep breath. "Well, be more careful, next time."

--Ok--

--Sorry about that--

"Don't sweat it."

--I don't sweat--

After a while, by telling the ship where to aim my arm, and telling the guns not to fire unless they had a clear shot, I could have fooled the casual observer into thinking that I knew what I was doing. Cab had me land, so he could try out the same techniques with land-based movements. Inside the ship, I could scurry over the walls like a psychotic ninja squirrel, leaping and rolling with reckless, perfectly-orchestrated abandon. When he felt like he had a good handle on things, Cab created another hologram man for me to fight.

--Ok, I want you to try not to try--

--If you feel like moving, just go with it--

--Be...be instinctual--

--Does that make sense?--

"No," I said. "Are you really going to make me beat up Gordon Liu?"

--I'm gonna make you try, but my money is on the Master Killer--

Gordon bowed and took a stance. Then he came at me in a whirlwind of limbs, most of them ending in fists, and I felt an itch and stepped back and let myself defend myself. It was like pretending to fight as a small child, a flurry of confusing movement that shouldn't have accomplished anything, except I managed to match my holographic opponent's every action.

--Hey this is great!--

--You look hilarious--

--You should see your face--

We sparred for ninety seconds, and then Gordon stepped back, bowed, and disappeared. Another figure appeared and bowed.

"I really don't want to fight Mr. Miyagi," I said.

--That's Pat Morita, dude--

--He is going to whip your ass--

"Listen, what do you think I'm actually going to run into out here?" I asked a few minutes later. Pat Morita patted me on the shoulder and gave me a thumbs-up and disappeared, and I rubbed the sore spot where he had beaten the living shit out of me.

--What, you mean other than vengeful ninja grandfathers?--

"Yeah," I said. "Given who I am, what I can do, where we're going, and what we're trying to do, what scenario do you think I'm most likely to have to deal with in the immediate future?"

--Oh--

--Good question--

145

--Let me think--

Cab thought for a while between two of my breaths.

--All right--

--We're going to a refugee station, so I'm thinking the most likely scenario is--

The ship lurched, and I fell to my knees. Something punched through the hull, a huge black spear point like a stinger or a dagger or a seed, a thing built of jagged obsidian edges and roiling onyx tendrils that twisted away from the surface and rooted in the deck.

--Duck!--

I dove behind a crate right as the tip of the thing exploded. Razor shards bulleted around the hold and stuck in the walls, rebounded and hammered off my head and shoulders. Something boomed inside the black thing, and it peeled apart. Hundreds of Krr rushed into the hold, swarming across the floor and up the walls onto the ceilings, chittering mad laughter and curses and hungry screams. They were unarmed, but every limb ended in a claw or a stinger or a brute razor edge.

The guns came back to me, gross and overlarge thanks to my terror. I was screaming, but I was still moving, and Cab came with me, doing his best to ignore his fear. I stood taller and taller and aimed, and fired, and yelled to Cab for more weapons, more power, more help. Turrets grew from my shoulders, under my arms, my hips, clattered out of nothingness at my frantic urging. The Krr burned in droves, but it was not enough. Wherever I wasn't shooting, they advanced, and there were too many of them push back.

They swarmed around my legs, a morass of hellish spidery nonsense screaming invective and dying even as I fired on my own hull and fried my legs out from under me. Two of them leapt for me and one of them survived, grabbed my shoulders and pulled my head forward into the cloud of questing glass fibers that were its mouth. They found their way through my helmet, cut my face, ripped at my nose. Everything froze.

My breathing was a series of hissing shrieks. Blood was dripping down my face from my torn nostril. The Krr that held my shoulders was close enough I could just see the hint of an eye through the confusion, a hazel thing that was disturbingly, brutally human. The guns in my head were a choir of castrato.

--Boom--

--That's where I blow the ship, if that ever happens--

The whole scene disappeared. I was tall. I was really tall, and I had barely noticed it happening. A twenty-foot over-armed and over-armored facsimile of my usual statuesque robot self, a visual representation of my terror. My meat body might have occupied the top third of me, maybe. The ship didn't have a head, anymore.

My nose was fine.

Cab gibbered around in my head.

--Jesus wept, fucking emotions god damn--

--I'll be ok--

--I'll work something out--

--Get it under control--

--Yeezus--

--So the reason I did that--

--Greg?--

My thoughts as I walked forward weren't clear, or verbal, but they could have been approximately translated as 'get away.' Pieces of machinery clattered off of me and hid themselves in spaces where they should not have fit, and after a half-beat I stepped out of the ship as a human and began to shake.

--Hey, are you all right?--

--I'm sorry for the surprise, but that was--

"That was what?" I said. I surprised myself thinking quickly enough to cut him off. I think it surprised him, too. "The Krr?"

--Yeah--

--That was a Krr boarding craft--

--Like the ones Rell saw destroy his strike team, when he went to break up the first sale--

--Hive shards, small ones loaded with a hungry queen and about five thousand ready-to-hatch Krr--

--They root in enemy ships and use the resources inside to feed the queen and make more Krr--

"Resources," I said. "People."

--No--

--Resources--

--People, food, materials, the interior of the ship-
-

--Queens can eat just about anything--

--But you're right, the people are first--

I nodded hard enough to hurt my neck and hugged myself. "Why," I asked, even though I was fairly sure of the answer.

--You asked what you were most likely to encounter, out here--

--I would say besides a fistfight, you're probably most likely to run into the Krr--

--And if you're aboard a ship when you encounter them, they're going to try to put a hive in that ship--

I took a deep breath. "Bring it back."

Everything reappeared, the hive ship, the shrapnel, the hordes of Krr, even a green outline of my overgrown self. There were thousands of them. Five thousand, I guess, although it looked like more. They were big, pony-sized, two, three hundred pounds apiece, but it was impossible to get a clear look at them. They had too many limbs and too little regularity. The swarm was just a cloud of spindly grasping hell closing in on my shadowy doppleganger. Even the ones leaping through the air or dropping from the ceiling were indistinct, substantial inner bodies covered in a storm of random growth. Sure, they had an immediate spider-like quality, but they also could have been demon dandelion clocks, possessed puff-balls. They were wrong, was what they were. They should not have been.

"What do I do?" I asked, turning. I was going to a refugee station. There would be people there, probably a fair number of them. A hive would be a disaster.

Everything started to move. I shouted, but the movement was backwards and too fast. The Krr rewound away from me, back into their ship, came back to life as energy blasts knit their shattered bodies back together and leapt back into my guns. After a moment the hive itself unexploded back together, and everything froze again.

--K, so, right here, this is what you *should* have done--

Memory-me was about fifteen feet away, facing the obsidian ship.

"I did not have such a stupid expression on my face," I said.

--What can I say, Greg?--

--You're an embarrassing person to be around--

--Now watch--

Memory-me stepped forward into the ship, grew the same gargantuan set of weapons I'd ended up with, and opened fire on the Krr ship right where it met the hull of Rell's ship. The hive melted away under the onslaught, and after a minute it exploded and split in half. The air rushed out of the hold, and behind me, emergency force-fields, popped into place. Or at least, something started the air shimmering. I took a deep breath. It was all a simulation, but damn me if it wasn't believably hard to inhale.

The hive half-fell, half-drifted out into space, end over end. After a moment, it exploded. The Krr never made it out of the ship. The false wind in the hold died away, and I was left breathing in a simulated vacuum. Memory-me turned and gave me a thumbs-up.

"What if there's someone else with me?" I asked.

--Then we'll do our best to help them, after we stop the Krr from taking root--

--The needs of the many, blah, blah, blah--

Everything snapped back to normal. The air felt fuller.

"People will die," I said. "No matter what. Right?"

--This is probably not going to be a bloodless endeavor, no--

"But if they open up a hive in a civilian population, then a lot more people die than if I shoot the hive out of the hull, explosive decompression notwithstanding," I said. "Right?"

Cab expressed an assent.

"It's not an ideal situation," I said. Cab said nothing. I put my hands in my pockets and looked at the spot on the wall where the fake Krr ship had ripped through the hull. The first day I got beat up, my dad took me out in the back yard and let me hit his palm until I calmed down. He showed me how to turn my fist, so that my punches would be stronger. Then it was time for dinner, and he stood up, and I started to cry, because all of a sudden I remembered what had happened, and why we were out there, and my dad standing up meant that we were done. And my dad hugged me, and he didn't tell me anything prophetic. He didn't tell me to stand tall because you're stronger if you can stand on your own, or that I had to face my fear to become a man. He just hugged me and told me it was going to be ok, and that if worst came to worse we would just call Richie's parents. And that was it. I felt better. He held my hand inside, like he had when I was younger. But the next day, after I got home from school, he took me outside and started teaching me how to box. Because it was important to be comforted. But it was also important to prepare.

"Ok," I said. "Run it again."

11

The Phibbix Nebula streaked foggily past the windshield. Even beautiful nebulae lost their charm when seen from within; Phibbix, ugly from the outside, was downright depressing at close range. I'd seen better scenery wading through sewage. Pockets of gas formed diarrhetic threads outside that could have been inches thick and meters distant, or light years thick and parsecs distant. It didn't matter, and I didn't care. The place looked like a literal shithole.

I'd hurried to the cockpit when Rell announced we were coming out of warp, thinking we were close to the station itself. I was mistaken.

"Tell me again why we had to slow down so much?" I did my best not to sigh, because that would have been petulant. I didn't pull it off.

"No," Rell said.

--If you fly through a nebula too fast, your ship catches on fire--

--If you warp through a nebula, your ship catches on fire at sixteen hundred times the speed of light--

--Best thing you can say about that is that it's a quick death--

"Yeah, yeah." I wrinkled my nose. The answer was obvious, and Rell had already explained, but I was horribly, desperately bored. I'd been staring at fog for three hours and my eyes were starting to cross.

"Good Christ this is monotonous," I muttered.

"You could always go back to the hold," Rell said.

"And miss my first station?" I said. "No way. Is that it?"

The object in question bounced off the ship.

"No, that was a rock," Rell said.

--That's two hundred and sixteen so far--

--You've asked about seventy-seven of them--

I looked around the cockpit. "You have not been counting them."

--I count everything!--

"No surprise there," Rell said. "You two are done training?"

"Cab started me fighting giraffes," I said. "I think he's bored, too."

--I thought I was--

--And then we came up here--

I leaned on the back of Rell's chair. "You should get a co-pilot's chair," I said after a minute.

"If I got a co-pilot's chair, I would have to endure a copilot." Rell checked the distance to our destination. He did that a lot when I talked.

"Yeah, it'd be a real shame if you had to be nice to someone all the time," I said.

"Samson," Rell said, "I've given this a lot of thought. In spite of our prior agreements, if you don't stop talking, I'm going to eat you."

"Mum's the word," I said. He rolled his eyes. Another two rocks bounced off the ship at odd angles. After ten silent minutes, I lay down on the floor and started tossing my wallet to myself.

"So," I said, a while later. Rell growled.

"The station is at the far side of the nebula," I said. "Right? By those little stars. How come we're coming at it from this end?" I miffed my throw and my wallet landed in Rell's lap. He picked it up and looked at it.

"Cab, what about his clothes?" Rell said. "This smells like hide. Did you clean up the materials he brought aboard?"

--Oh, shit, I forgot--

Rell snapped his teeth. "Asshole. I'd be dead already, if you'd forgotten."

--Yeah--

--Don't sweat it, Magilla--

Rell nodded. "I've known Yui a long time, Samson," he said. "And I trust him...at least, I trust him to a point. I don't think he's trying to have me killed. But, well, *someone* is. *Someone* is trying to sell Shipkiller seeds to the Krr. And they could be aboard Phibbix Station." He shrugged. "If we come at Phibbix from this angle, they won't see us until we're very close. And if I dock under an assumed identity, Yui won't know we're aboard until we call him. I want to keep our heads down."

He pulled out my driver's license and read silently. "What's one thousand nine hundred and eighty eight?"

"The year I was born," I said.

"You people have been keeping track of time for less than two millennia?" Rell said.

"Well, it's more than two millennia now," I said, "but no, there were other calendars before that."

"How long has your species been active in its current state?"

I lifted my head off the deck and looked at him. "Ten thousand years or so? I dunno, I think there's some debate. Or I just don't know."

Rell shook his head. "How can you not know a thing like that?" he muttered.

I couldn't think of anything appropriate to say, so I didn't say anything. Rell reloaded my wallet and tossed it on my stomach and went back to the controls, and I lay still thinking about how long ten thousand years was supposed to seem, and how long it seemed to me, and how long it was in the grand scheme of things, and how that wasn't very goddamn fair. It's ok to think useless things, as long as you don't say them aloud. After a few minutes I started to lurch towards sleep. We'd trained hard, and I was tired. Not sore, just tired. And it was nice to lie there boneless on the deck with the funky mossy soft carpet like Rell must have grown up with. Comfortable. I was a lucky man.

"Samson!" Rell said. "Wake up! We're almost there."

"Oh." I sat up and wiped the drool off my cheek. I had to blink to get clear of the thin haze over everything I saw. "How long was I asleep?"

"Ninety minutes," Rell said. "I figured you needed the rest. And it was nice to finally get some peace and quiet."

"You were an only child, weren't you?" I said. Rell grinned and wiped his hands on his pants and stood up stiffly.

"Man the tiller, would you? I gotta take a leak." He bounded out the door and was gone.

"What?" I said to the empty room. I sat down and stared at the controls. Man the tiller? Rell, or the translation machine? The toshein didn't strike me as yachting people.

"Hey you know that driver's license was just for like, ground cars? I've never flown anything but Cab!" I shouted. There was no answer. "Christ."

The joystick to my right seemed like a good place to start, even if it was too big for me. I grasped it and every screen in the cockpit flared red.

"ALERT!" The computer bellowed. My gut wrenched. "IMMINENT COLLISION WITH PLANETARY MASS!"

"What?" Really, it was less of a word than a yelp. "Cab, I thought we were in a nebula!" I pulled at the joystick and nothing happened. A high-pitched monkey scream tore out of the hidden speakers, followed by a rhythmic beeping, and another scream.

"ALERT! ASSUME CRASH POSITIONS AND COMMENCE PRAYER! INITIATE POSTERIOR AUTO-OSCULATION!"

Rell's computer began to cry.

"OH GOD THIS CAN'T BE HAPPENING! I'VE NEVER SEEN THE CORE! I'M STILL A VIRGIN!"

All of this was delivered in a one hundred and fifty decibel monotone.

"Now, hold on," I said. Rell tumbled into the cockpit, grunting happy laughter.

"Help, help, we're gonna crash," he gasped. I glared at him, but Cab was giggling too hard for me to put any venom in the expression. Rell rolled onto his back and kicked his hands and feet helplessly, screaming under his breath. "Help me. Save me from the rogue planet!"

I got up and leaned against the wall. After a second I started to laugh, because Cab wouldn't stop, and because, honestly, it was a solid prank. And it was good knowing that people made jokes, out here. Another familiar note to remind me these were still people.

"All right, well played," I said. "Dick."

Rell hauled himself up and sat in the chair, still chuckling.

"You just looked so peaceful," he said. "I couldn't resist. Really, though, we're almost there." He typed something and selected a file from a list, and then grunted a humorless laugh. "We are now the Goro, a Ragarag ship hauling a load of cribbage."

"Like, the game?" I said.

--Produce--

"Ah," I said. Without Rell noticing, I pinched myself in the arm.

--Oh, knock it off, you know you're not dreaming--

--You're just being dramatic--

A bright dot appeared in the shitstorm outside. Over the course of a long, drawn out half-second, it grew to fill the screen, an enormous ten-mile wide trapezohedron. Rell was right. Yui had built something a lot more impressive than the tiny sphere on the map, by then.

Phibbix Station was an enormous ten-sided diamond covered in spindly scaffolding, branches that stretched for five miles in every direction; a briar patch of vaguely-organized docking conduits and deep-space shanty-towns and enormous cargo ships bolted into place and repurposed as permanent living spaces. Residential neighborhoods built into the side of the station. The whole thing was speared from pole to pole by a massive central pillar extending eight miles out into space on either side. It came to a point at both ends, and in many ways the station resembled nothing more than a child's top covered in coral.

Ships of all sizes and shapes flitted over the surface and around the scaffolds, a chaotic swarm that made the parking lot after a rock concert look like a deserted country road on Christmas morning. We moved into the press, and I realized that Rell didn't have his hands on the controls. He saw my look, and waved dismissively.

"Station control will guide us in," he said. "Don't worry."

The closer we got, the less spindly the scaffolding looked. Most of it was in excess of a quarter mile thick, covered in more scabbed-on structures and ships that had been too small to see from our original vantage point. Some of the ships we passed were huge, as big or bigger than Rell's. One, an enormous swooped aerodynamic shape with five angular rocket engines built into its middle, had to be at least a mile and a half long.

We aimed for a conduit so wide it was almost flat, a parking space between a squad of saucers docked in a stack and something that looked like a bag of glowing orange fat.

"Oh, you might want to close your eyes," Rell said. The ship rolled over on its side and flipped right without altering its original course, continuing the motion until it was falling belly-first. My eyes screamed that I was standing on the front wall, now, while my feet and inner ear remained convinced I was standing on the floor. The internal argument was nauseous.

"Oh god," I said, clutching my stomach. The ship snapped around me and I hopped into the air with my eyes closed. After a moment, my perceptions aligned. I took a deep breath and forced my breakfast back into my stomach.

"Samson?" Rell said. I dropped to the floor and dismantled the helmet.

"I was not expecting that flip," I said. "I'm ok. All is well."

"Good," Rell said. He got up and climbed out of the cockpit, towards the hold. "I would hate for you to have to clean puke off the bridge."

I hopped into space and landed next to him, seventy meters down.

"I've noticed you and Cab have a bit of vomit fixation," I said.

"Vomit is an unfortunate byproduct of balletic movements through free fall," Rell said. "Thus, it remains high on the seasoned spaceman's list of pet peeves."

"Y'all don't fuck with Dramamine?" I muttered.

In the hold, the airlock was dinging happily and chattering about how good a seal it had made with its Phibbician counterpart.

"Good good good good good," it exclaimed as we approached.

"Is it, now?" I said.

"Good good good yes good yes yes *safe* safe safe safe good. Good?"

"Yes, ship, well done," Rell said absently.

"Thanks thanks thanks bye." The door clicked and went silent.

--Kiss-ass--

"No sense of kinship?" I said.

--With that thing?--

--Hell no--

--There's a reason everyone is so impressed by me--

--That thing is as dumb as smart rocks--

--No offence, Rell--

"I didn't buy the thing for the conversation," he said. He opened a cabinet in the wall next to the hatch and put on an armored vest with a high neck, and replaced his sidearm with a pair of menacing snub-nosed pistols. Then he checked the load on a weapon that I could call a sawed-off shotgun, if I were willing to concede to understatement and ignore the fact that it was obviously an energy weapon. It looked like an antitank gun. He strapped it to his back, shrugged his shoulders, and said, "Lose the ship."

"No?" I said. The longer we stood in front of the door, the more nervous I felt. Cab's mood wasn't too calm, either. God only knew what was on the other side. Going through naked, as it were, was unthinkable. The ship already felt less like my privilege than my due. My norm. My skin.

"You'll draw attention to us," he said. "Besides, it's not like it takes you long to suit up."

He did have a point. How many seven-foot robots did these people see on a daily basis? Then again, I thought, how many seven-foot robots *did* these people see on a daily basis? I had no idea. Maybe Phibbix was awash in seven-foot robots. I concentrated, and grew little blaster things on my forearms and bigger turrets on my shoulders.

"Ok, Cab, this is where we come back to if we need the ship," I said. "Got it?"

--You bet--

"And the standing order is to shoot every weapon you see as soon as you have a clear shot." I dismantled the ship and looked at Rell. "Do I at least get a gun?"

He rummaged in the closet and came out with a whistle, which he offered with raised eyebrows.

"I'll pass, thanks," I said. We stood in front of the airlock and my heart started to thud. I had no idea what I was getting into, and I was getting used to the sensation. It was less a surprise than the normal course of things. Confusion and uncertainty were already my constant companions, but this moment was particularly anxiety-provoking. I wasn't just *doing* the unthinkable, I was about to open up my *reality* to the unthinkable in a way that dwarfed anything else I'd ever done.

--Your brain is lit up like the Vegas strip--

I nodded. "You've never been to Vegas."

--I have all kinds of pictures--

--Video, too--

Rell pushed the airlock open and we stepped inside and waited for the pressure to equalize.

"Am I ready for this?" I asked. "What if I trip you up?"

Rell put his hand on the inner door right as it flashed green. "A word of advice, Samson. Don't think so much." He looked at me. "You excited?"

I was about to be taken into an alien refugee camp for god knew what by a big green gorilla cat with an insect affect and dark past. Excited was as good a word for it as any. I shrugged and nodded. "Yeah," I said. "Yeah, I am."

"Good," Rell said. He patted me on the back and pushed the outer hatch open and stepped past me. I took a deep breath, and followed him.

We were on a subway platform. A long, dingy underground train shaft, dimly lit by flickering lights, full of cold, mineral air and the twinkle of falling water. There was wind, minimal and uniform in temperature; there would have to be, because the tunnel must have gone on for miles. I stepped through the hatch into a puddle that was up to my ankles. The gravity was just short of what I was expecting, and something small was rotting in a far corner. The place was ugly as sin. I looked at Rell with a stricken expression, and he grinned.

"Welcome to Phibbix Station," he said.

12

"No wonder Yui keeps this place hidden," I grumbled as we tromped down the awful tunnel. "Do people burn down shit-holes for the insurance money? Because that would be a good place to start, here."

"Hey, you're the one who got your hopes up," Rell said. He was walking at a normal toshein pace, which meant that I had to jog to keep up, but I was doing all right. My wind has been pretty good ever since I met my charming dorsal companion.

"Is the whole place like this?" I said, chugging along. "Where is everyone?"

Rell sighed. "Do they have harbors on your planet?"

"Yeah," I said slowly.

"Are they nice places?"

I thought about it. "No, not really." Rell nodded.

"This is a harbor. I have a big ship, so we had to land a ways out in the harbor. We are making our way towards the nicer part of town." He shrugged. "I also parked in an isolated area so you didn't go into culture shock and have a moment."

"Oh," I said. "Fair enough. Wait, culture shock?"

"It happens to a lot of folks," Rell said. "First time off planet, there's a lot of potential for sensory overload. A lot of truly alien sights, laid one on top of another. People lose the ability to distinguish one thing from another. My advice, keep your eyes on what's in front of you. Concentrate on things that are close. Ok?"

"Ok," I said, confused.

"Remember: You may have had an easy time with me because you and I are structurally and culturally similar enough to avoid any real shock. There's a lot more diversity out here than you're expecting, and this is a refugee station, so you're bound to see an awful lot."

"Ok," I said again, slower.

"Still," Rell said, looking around, "I suppose mostly it is a shithole."

I went on jogging. This was starting to sound scary.

--Christ, I can't believe you can see straight through all this--

His voice was a whisper in my head.

"I'm ok," I said. "I'll be ok."

--Well, listen, have you considered...*not* being a total wimp?--

"Whatever you say, gear breath."

--You're the one who's breathing, meatface--

"Analog asshole."

--Ape pussy--

"Floppy disc dick."

--What the hell do I need genitals for?--

"Were you ever worried about talking to yourself back on Earth?" Rell cut in. "When you met Cab?"

"Yeah." I grinned at the memory. "Yeah, it was real hard to keep quiet sometimes. I was scared people were gonna think I was crazy."

"Well, they'll think you're crazy out here too, so keep it to yourself," Rell said.

I took a deep breath and stuck my tongue out and blew a ten-second raspberry. Rell chuckled and shoved me into the wall. I think he meant it as a friendly push, but he was a lot bigger than me.

The tunnel bent slightly and joined another, and suddenly I lost the sense that we were alone. I still didn't see anyone, but the trash looked fresher, and I heard something like city sounds off in the distance. The light felt warmer.

Rell came to where the tunnels merged and walked easily across the empty space between the platforms.

"Force field," he said without looking. "Come on."

"What?" I bent over and looked carefully at the edge of the platform. There was something there, if I let myself believe I could see it. I walked across and joined Rell on the other side.

"We're gonna get a train," he said.

"Of course," I said.

"It's three miles, I don't feel like walking," he said.

"Sure," I said. We stood still for several moments. Rell patted the pistols on his hips and brushed his right hand over the long gun on his back. Cab shifted nervously.

"Try not to do that, Cab," Rell said.

--Yeah, yeah--

"Are you expecting trouble?" I asked.

"Caution is important," Rell said.

The wind picked up in one direction, and then a string of ten train cars came shooting down the tunnel and stopped dead in front of us. They were unsupported and disconnected, seamless and silent, with windows that were only transparencies in an otherwise uniform material, but train cars are train cars the galaxy over. They were covered in graffiti that rearranged and translated itself depending on where I looked.

"Come on." Rell led me into the last car and sat down. I sat down next to him and stared at the other two occupants. One of them was a bulb of plated organic material supported on a dozen dozen tiny lobster legs, with a tiny crabby head and four crabby arms, and the other was a flickering, indistinct mass of light sitting halfway down the car from us. I couldn't get a good look at him, and it took me a moment to realize that this was by design, a sort of camouflage.

"Can you see that guy?" I said, nudging Rell and pointing.

"Hey," he said. He pushed my arm down. "Hey. Haven't you ever ridden the subway? You don't point at people for God's sake. Yes, I see that guy. Yes, he's hard to see. He's a Queckian, their skin messes with the visual spectrum. Jesus. I can't take you anywhere." He smiled at the other guy and nodded. The bulb stood up and walked to the exit.

"Sir." He nodded at me and stepped out onto the platform. The door closed, and we took off like a shot. The Queckian started to laugh.

"He is dirty!" He yelled. He had an odd lack of an accent, even though his cadence suggested an accent. I looked at Rell, and he shrugged.

"Not me, sir!" The Queckian said. "I am clean."

"Me too," I said, loud enough to be heard. The Queckian laughed, a little too much.

"That is good, sir," he said. "That is good. I am glad you are clean." The train stopped, and he got up and walked out of the door nearest to us. He was tall, and might have been bipedal, but I still couldn't tell for sure. He spat on the floor in front of me as he walked by.

"Hey!" I stood up. Rell put his arm across me and I bounced back in the seat as the door closed. We took off again.

"What the fuck was that about?" I said. "Was that because I'm a human?"

--Prejudice is an ugly thing--

Rell looked at the door and put his arm back in his lap. "I don't know what that was," he said. "They wouldn't have reacted like that if they thought you were human." He rubbed his jaw. "I figured people would think you were a robot or something."

I grumbled. "Man, if you want people to think I'm a robot let me put on the ship."

"No, not that kind of robot," Rell said. "I want people to think you're a wimpy robot."

--Burn!--

I rolled my eyes and stretched out about half as well as Rell. The first one had been scared, the second...not angry so much as confrontational. I hate it when people spit at me.

The train stopped again, and Rell stood up and motioned me off. There was some kind of sound muting machine at work aboard the cars, something that compensated for outside noise the same way the inertial dampener had compensated for the forces generated by our speedy approach, so that when I stepped onto the platform I was met with a sudden inrush of crowd noise from the middle distance. People. My heart thumped.

The rest of the passengers were already nearly off the platform, over the hump of the end of the tunnel, a bright opening in the darkness, beyond which I saw things I couldn't comprehend. The crowd blended together into obscurity and disappeared, and every time I tried to focus on the vista ahead of us, my eyes skated back to the foreground.

--Rell, wait--

--It feels like he's nightmaring--

--Help--

Cab sounded plaintive. Rell looked in my face and then turned me around, away from the end of the tunnel, and tapped me just short of painfully hard on the side of the head. His face filled my field of vision.

"Hey," I said. "I'm fine."

"Take a breath," he said. "Take a minute."

"I'm fine, Rell," I said. "I'm just having a hard time focusing on anything."

"And that's fine?" Rell smiled ruefully. "Listen, remember your feet, all right? No matter what you see, your feet are still your feet. If you start to feel overwhelmed, look at your feet."

I looked at him and put my hands in my pockets. I still had half a tube of chapstick. I clutched it, felt the greasy bit around the edge of the cap, and stared at my feet. My old Frye boots, cracked and shiny. My feet, warm and dry inside. My toes. Me, with me. My heart slowed down some.

"You didn't just come up with that," I said.

"Nope," Rell said. He clapped me on the shoulder and led me towards the light. "It's an old trick. Good advice for first-time travelers. Your feet are familiar. You grew up with them. You get scared, look at your feet."

I glanced down as we walked. My stride. The kathud sound of my stacked heels on the deck. I felt calmer.

We stepped up to the end of the tunnel, and I stopped dead.

"Remember your feet," Rell said.

"Yeah, yeah…" I mumbled. I was going to need more than feet for this.

The interior of the station was one hundred square miles of unbroken cityscape. Ten triangular boroughs, one for each face of the trapezohedron, each with its own definition of 'down,' so that if I looked straight up I saw another city directly overhead, with denizens who seemed to hang by their feet from the ceiling. Except it was nearly impossible to see clear to the streets on the other side of the station, because nearly all the available space was covered by skyscrapers that were nestled so intricately amongst one another that it was hard to believe they weren't connected. But they couldn't have been. Not with competing internal gravity fields. Flying machines flitted in and out of every available space, banking and dropping from gravity well to gravity well with practiced ease. Everything was lit up in darkness-inducing neon and incandescence. Water condensed and fell from brief clouds in one spot, while heat lines rose from another.

A pair of five-sided pillars dominated the middle of the overgrown space. They were anchored at either pole, and narrowed slightly towards the top, where an odd, spherical lattice connected them to the tallest buildings in the center of each borough. There, at least, they had managed to compensate for the competing gravities, and build together. A huge device shaped like a fat almond hung suspended in the middle of the lattice. It was clearly important, if placement was anything to go by. Nobody ever put something trivial on so grand a pedestal.

"Welcome to Phibbix Station," I said to myself, and looked down.

I'd expected the corridor to end in a staircase. It didn't. Instead, the ground simply pitched forward sixty degrees and continued on as if that were a normal, everyday thing. I stuck out my hand and felt the point where 'down' changed direction.

"Bad idea," Rell said. "Unless you finally want to toss your cookies." He took a long step forward and landed easily, then hopped up and down twice to settle himself. "Get it over with, Samson."

I looked at the city, and then at my feet. "Ok, Cab, you ready to explore strange new worlds?"

--Sure thing, Earthling--

"You're as much an Earthling as I am."

--I know--

--Don't tell anyone--

I took a deep breath and stepped forward. The change was vertiginous, but not unpleasant. Nothing I'd want to make a habit of, but I'd felt worse in the cockpit, when we docked. I hopped in place like Rell, and felt better.

The train station was wide, with an open architecture and no ceiling. There was a designated entrance at one end and an exit at the other, with a central ticket kiosk facing the far wall. Advertisements blared silently along the walls in languages I didn't recognize, using symbols that didn't make any sense to me, but as I focused on them, they resolved themselves into familiar words and shapes: Malt liquor, payday loans, lawyers. Massage parlors. Entertainment sources of all kinds catering to senses I didn't even have.

And everywhere, people. Not aliens, although they were alien in shape; people. They were too focused, too intent, too mundane, too *human* to be anything else. And they moved too much for me to focus on any of them. I looked around, lost the thread of what I was seeing and stared convulsively at my feet. Rell pulled me towards the exit.

The press wasn't as bad outside. Most people were heading in the opposite direction, towards the center of town, while we were walking away, towards the slums. I was grateful. You don't think about how important small cultural cues are to your understanding of the world until they're all taken away.

We turned a corner and were mostly alone. I leaned against the wall and breathed deeply and looked around. More ads. More storefronts. Bodegas, odds shops, pawn shops, an entertainment depot hawking a format I didn't recognize. It was just a neighborhood. A pair of huge, white-furred old men with enormous black eyes and three tree trunk arms apiece were playing some kind of dice game for coins on an overturned half of a barrel down the block from us. They had enormous hairy spider fangs. One of them was wearing a shapeless hat, and the other was smoking an ugly cigar.

Something across the street screamed its last, and I whipped around with Cab fluttering on my shoulders. Three pink leathery men with long tails and barbed snouts were taking bites out of a fresh kill. It was a gruesome scene, but the animal in question was on a plate, on a table with a cloth and settings in front of a glass-fronted business that could only have been a restaurant. One of them watched me, chewing, and then touched two fingers to its brow. I returned the gesture, looked away and screamed like a little girl.

--Easy--

--Take it easy--

--That's a welwleul, they're from your neck of the galaxy--

--You're practically neighbors--

The welwleul was resting on its rear-facing mass of tentacles, leaning against a wall. In its left tentacular mass, which I assume was analogous to a left hand, it held a mismatched collection of liquor bottles. The labels were unfamiliar, but liquor bottles are liquor bottles. The mass on its right side drew idle designs in the dust, while a center mass rested across a much larger tentacle that I assume was meant to function as a leg. I closed my mouth and kept walking.

"Is there anything in there?" I muttered.

--Mostly tentacles--

--Why mess with perfection?--

The welwleul emptied one of the bottles into a mouth full of tombstone teeth and tongues, licked its lips, belched at me and said, "Spare some change, sir?"

Rell tossed some coins. The welwleul caught them in midair.

"Thanks, man," he said.

"Sure," Rell said.

"You have homeless people in space?" I hissed when we were out of earshot.

"Putting aside the fact that this is a refugee station, yes, we have homeless people in space," Rell said. "Anywhere there's haves, there's have-nots."

"But," I said. Rell looked at me.

"But what?" He said.

I blew the air out of my mouth. "I don't know," I said. "I guess I thought things would be better out here."

"Nope," Rell said. "It's just us folks."

"But you have all this," I said, waving my arms at the awesome cityscape above us, "and you still can't fix the little problems? How can you have a warp drive and poverty?"

Rell turned around and put his hand on my shoulder hard enough to stop my dead.

"First of all, Samson, poverty is far from a 'little' problem," he said. "But beyond that…cut it out. The galaxy is not perfect. We are not perfect. This is how it is. This is what we are, and you need accept it. We are not Star Trek. Now stop bitching and start walking. We need to find you a change of clothes and burn what you're wearing. You stink of rot."

I followed him unhappily for a block. I don't know what I'd been hoping for. I might have thought that a utopian society would have been able to take my troubles off my hands, although it was nothing I had articulated, even to myself. I was just disappointed.

These people were a lot like the people I'd left behind, tentacles or not.

A pair of melons flew by, flapping long stiff leaves like hummingbird wings. They stopped short ten yards ahead of us and hovered close to one another, curling long vines together and bumping fronts. Both of them began to blossom, and I realized they were lovers. They were lovers, and Rell was a crook. There was an ad for a movie, or a play, or something, Constant Sky, floating way up above me, and there was another bum sitting cross-legged across the street holding a sign that said, "I'd really like a beer." The melons pulled apart, and their blossoms closed. One of them danced closer to the other, and then flitted down the street. After a moment, its fellow followed. They came together at the corner and crossed together, their vines comingling. There was good along with the bad, here, same as everywhere else. I hadn't traded down. I hadn't traded up. I just had more, now.

"Give me some money," I said. Rell gave me a ten-dollar bill, and I jogged across the street. The bum watched me warily, and sat up straighter. I squatted down in front of him and held out the money. He didn't take it.

"What's your name?" I asked. He took in some air and still didn't take the money.

"Pete," he said.

"Pete what?"

"Sir…Mouzza's gone," he said. "It's just Pete, now."

"Who the hell is Mouzza?" I said. Pete flinched and sagged. He still hadn't taken the money.

"Sorry." I said lamely. I dropped the bill on the ground in front of him and walked away.

Rell took off walking. "What was that all about?"

"I'm trying to acclimate," I said, "and apparently I'm doing a piss-poor job of it. I wanted to know his name. He got weird when I asked him."

Rell sighed and shook his head. "You see that blue ring around his left eyestalk? That means he's a Mouzzan Calita, not Groussan." He looked at me and grinned wickedly. "Right. It's you. Ah, his culture's naming structure was derived from their geographic position at the moment of birth on their home world. A lot of them figure, if they're not on their planet, they have no name. You put your foot in your mouth."

"I didn't know," I said.

"I'm aware," Rell said. We walked on, leaving a strange wake of confused, wary people behind us. I figured they'd never seen anything like me, and tried to look inconspicuous.

"Ok," I said finally. "Wait. This has been bothering me. Language is one thing, the French, the Spanish, whatever. But how the hell do you know about Star Trek?"

Rell smiled. "Star Trek is cool," he said. "You people have been dumping your telecommunications into space for a century. You really think we haven't been listening? Earth media is as salable as anything else. More, even. It's got that novelty factor, people love to see how humans live."

"I can't believe no one ever made contact," I said. "Even just to tell us that we weren't alone."

Rell shrugged. "Star Trek wasn't *that* good."

13

I was mapped, measured and fitted for a new pair of blue jeans, a long sleeved tee shirt, and fresh underwear by a floating sphere with three spindly humanoid arms. He also cleaned my boots and sprayed them with a liquid diamond polymer that was supposed to make them nearly indestructible, which was neat. The new clothes were self-cleaning, although Rell assured me that this only meant they would wander off and launder themselves while I slept, and not anything weird, or alien. I looked at him askance when he said this, and after a moment he gave me a big, shit-eating grin and a thumbs-up.

Everything was custom-made from a material that looked the part but was too slippery to be cotton.

--Stop touching your genitals--

"My drawers don't fit right."

--Well, keep it to yourself--

The tailor-bot tried hard to refuse payment. Rell ended up leaving the money on the counter.

"What the hell is going on?" I said, out on the street.

Rell shook his head. "I haven't the slightest. I figured people would be mean to you, not…do they seem scared to you?"

I waved my hand about hip height. "Little bit."

"Well, can't hurt," he muttered. "Come on, let's get lunch before I call Yui."

Rell took me to a place called Dsarthy's Anything and Everything, a single-story cream-colored ranch house with a red aluminum roof and red shutters. There were neon beer signs in the window, although of course the brands were unfamiliar, and there were reviews posted in the windows to either side of the front door, which was a pane of glass in a metal frame with a crash bar across the middle that was big enough to accommodate a bigger person than Rell.

Instead of menus, we were given laminated cards at the bar explaining that the head chef, Dsarthy McKenna, was possessed of such a singular culinary ability that she would be able to replicate any dish in the universe, regardless of logical possibility.

"It's a gimmick," Rell said. "Dsarthy has the place wired with jerry-rigged translation machinery and thought-film, all connected to a team of kitchen foundries in the back. When you order, the translators scan your thoughts, instincts and memories and create the meal that best captures what you want to eat. That's why she gets rave reviews."

I flicked the card with my index finger. "What happens if I order a hamburger but think real hard about a hot dog?"

Rell shrugged. "You get a hamdog."

--I want duck!--

"You always want duck," I said.

--Duck is *delicious*--

"Rell!" Someone shouted. I tensed, and Cab shifted again on my back.

A tall, four-legged woman in a white jacket bustled out of the kitchen and shook Rell's hand.

"Dsarthy," Rell smiled. "How you doing?"

"Comme çi, comme ça," Dsarthy chuckled. She whinnied her words through a vertical slit full of baleen and wide teeth. Her mouth was bordered by a dozen horse nostrils and four eyes, two of them stacked vertically on either side of her face, and her head was connected to her shoulders by a second, smaller set of shoulders, instead of a neck. She looked neckless, even though her head moved quite freely. She was hairless, with dull red-orange skin, and her legs ended in flexible, four-toed hooves. Her knees were omnidirectional, like Rell's second elbows. Her arms were remarkably human, except they were on the wrong sides, so that her left hand was on her right and vice versa. Her palms faced outward. All this from a single, confusing glance. "Where've you been, you devil, we thought you'd been busted–" She looked at me and then stared at a point over my left ear.

"Officer," she nodded.

Rell looked at him, then at me, and then he swore, loud.

"Officer?" I said.

"She thinks you're a cop," Rell hissed at me. "Everyone thinks you're a goddamn cop."

"Why the hell do they think I'm a cop?" I muttered. Dsarthy looked directly at me and frowned. Rell rubbed his eyes.

"They think you're a Bekht," Rell said.

"Why would I be a Bekht looking like this?" I asked. "Why would they pick a human shape in a place where there aren't any humans?"

"Because nobody else looks like you do," Rell said, "so a human shape is better than a badge. And they can take it off whenever they want. They've been doing it for fifty thousand years, at least."

"I look like a cop who wants people to know he's a cop," I said. "Great." I leaned forward and smiled at Dsarthy. "Hey, I'm not a cop, I'm human."

"Jesus, that's not better," Rell sputtered. "Dsarthy, come here. Listen. No, really, come here, and keep your voice down. He's human, he's clean, he's not a cop, he's just a, he's a friend of mine."

--Touching--

I rolled my eyes. Cab was only in my head. Dsarthy looked at me and stood up and picked up a glass that didn't need polishing and began to polish it.

"Greg Samson," I said, nodding. "I won't be offended if you don't want to shake hands."

Dsarthy nodded. "Welcome to Dsarthy's." She looked at Rell. "You better tip real well."

"Don't I always?" Rell smiled. Dsarthy made a so-so gesture, and Rell snorted.

"A clean human," Dsarthy said to me. "How'd you swing that?"

"I met the wizard Shazam in a subway tunnel," I said. Dsarthy grinned wide, which was an odd sight, and laughed.

"It's a long story," Rell said. "But listen, if anyone asks, Dsart, just tell them…tell them he's a service robot."

"You know there's only one service a robot with skin like that performs, Rell, what are people going to think?" Dsarthy raised two eyebrows, both of them on the same side of her face.

"They'll think something embarrassing, which is better than them thinking he's a cop, or a plague factory," Rell said. Dsarthy nodded.

"Hey everybody," she shouted. "I want to let everyone know that this isn't a cop. This is my old friend Rell's, ah, service robot. He lives alone and spends most of his time in deep space, so he's gone a bit weird, and as for the human thing, well, a person's fetish is their own business, so let's all go back to our meals and, ah, anyone who's interested can have a small sundae on the house."

There was a smattering of somewhat embarrassed applause.

"You're an asshole," Rell grumbled. I was biting my tongue to keep from joining in on Cab's laughter, but I couldn't keep the grin off my face.

"Hey, I've got a business to run," Dsarthy said. "Besides, there's no better cover than humor. You want something to eat?"

"How about a plate of zhallops and hup, and a beer?" Rell said. "A big plate. And a big beer."

Dsarthy gave him a look, and then shrugged impressively. "Zhallops and hup. You're not even trying anymore, are you?"

"I need some comfort food," Rell said. "It's been a long week."

Dsarthy gave me a sidelong look. "You're sure you're not a cop?"

"Last I checked," I said.

"You need to eat?" Dsarthy said.

"Probably not, but I like to," I said. "Can I get, how about Singapore mai fun, maple collard greens, and, chocolate soufflé?" I looked at Rell. "Think human food will stump her?"

"As if," Dsarthy snorted. "Ten minutes." She cantered away, backwards. Her head twisted around a hundred and eighty degrees and her arms swung behind her. Now her palms were facing the right way, which meant that she had been looking over her shoulder to talk to us. Even by my newly raised standards, Dsarthy was an oddly-built creature.

A flying melon zoomed around the corner at the end of the bar and poured Rell a beer.

"Me too," I said quickly. The melon gave me the irritated look of set-upon bartenders everywhere and poured a second beer. Then it flew down the bar and started polishing glassware, watching me.

"So everyone's genuflecting because they think I'm a fucking cop," I said. "Wonderful." The beer wasn't great, but it was there.

"Genuflecting, hell, that one guy nearly spit on you," Rell said. "I should have expected this. Christ, Yui probably knows we're here already, folks tend to gossip when the CLEA is aboard."

"Should you give him a call?" I looked around. We weren't exactly being stared at, but I could sense a lot of hidden attention in the wings. "I knew I should have worn the ship. Should I put it on now?"

"No, it'll draw more attention. At least these people think you're a goddam sex-bot. What a nightmare." He sighed. "I'll call Yui after lunch. He's not going to run, and he won't try to kill you in public like this, the reward for reporting information leading to the arrest of a cop-killer is too much for him to risk witnesses."

"You think he's gonna try to kill me if he thinks I'm a cop?" I said.

"If you ran a black market trading outpost and a federal agent came calling, what would you do?" Rell asked quietly. "There's too much money flowing through a place like this, it makes people act crazy. That's why the CLEA stays away from the refugee stations, it's easier to let them police themselves. Even when they check up on things, they have to good sense to stay undercover."

"And I'm running around waving a proverbial badge." I said uneasily. "Are we safe here?"

"Oh, chill out," Rell said. "You're safe everywhere. It's me I'm worried about."

I grinned weakly. "I'll protect you."

"Great," Rell said. He finished his beer and signaled for another. The melon brought it to him silently.

In the kitchen, visible to the dining public, Dsarthy piled her back high with packaged ingredients and cooking equipment and wandered out of sight. Her back appeared to function as a mobile table, which seemed too practical to have been a matter of niche genetic development. Maybe there was more to evolution than humans had figured out, so far.

The lunch crowd was too diverse for me to get a good look at anyone. I couldn't focus. I kept thinking about rush hour in a zoo, which was probably toed the line between racism and witticism. Species-ism. There was a painting behind the bar, a panorama of a plain covered in tall grass, dotted with spindly white trees under a yellow sky. Huge, mammal-faced beetles grazed in the distance, and at one end of the painting there was a table set for two, and a pair of empty backless chairs.

Rell mumbled something about the bathroom and went around the corner, out of sight, and for a moment I was as alone as I had ever been. Adrift, isolated, a billion billion miles from home. Vulnerable. Mistaken. I could see my future as one long chain of the same anonymous, loveless, static existence until everything washed out grey. Painful imagery, but nothing practical. I put my hands on the bar and counted my breathing, then drank some of my beer and made sure to put the glass back down in the exact same spot and felt my heart slow. Mundane detail can be an anchor in difficult circumstance.

--You're pretty good at this arbitrary calm thing, aren't you?--

I shrugged. The man to my left settled more comfortably on his stool. He was almost all leg, bipedal, squatting with his heels under his butt and his knees almost touching the ceiling eight feet above us. His limbs were wiry, and his skin looked like ironwood bark, dense and durable but smooth, flexible. He was fiddling with a small machine in a space he'd cleared on the bar, next to a stack of empty plates. When I glanced at him, he glanced at me, and when I smiled, he pulled away. I sighed.

"Cab," I said, quietly.

--Yeah--

"You can get me home, right? If this goes tits up?"

--What, back to Earth?--

--Yeah, no problem--

--What's up, you getting homesick?--

"No, I feel like the top of my head is going to pop off," I said. "I'm like half a step from a panic attack, you can't feel that?"

--Oh, so now you are affected by brain chemistry?--

--How the mighty have fallen--

"Cab," I said, and there was an unintentional adolescent edge to my voice, a breaking note that was reminiscent of the scared kid inside all of us.

--Sorry--

--I *can* feel that, that's the problem--

--I'm a little on edge--

--I'll try to chill--

--I can get us home--

--No sweat--

--Don't worry--

"Fat chance," I muttered.

--Well, you do your best and I'll do mine--

--We're in this together Samson, don't forget--

I snorted. "You seem to be doing ok."

--Oh, hell no, I've got my sensors dialed way back--

--This is blowing my mind, dude--

--You know that big guy in the corner?--

--Other corner--

--You know he's breathing tungsten?--

--How fuckin' cool is that?--

I grinned. "Thanks, Cab."

Dsarthy bustled out of the kitchen with a dozen plates of food. She served us last, then drew herself a beer. I sniffed the mai fun and the collard greens, nodded at Dsarthy and tried the soufflé. It was like eating chocolate air and orgasms off the tip of an electrified fork. Cab's reaction nearly knocked me off my seat.

"Good?" Dsarthy asked. She leaned on the bar across from me.

"Good, hell, great," I said over the loud buzzing in the back of my mind. "Best soufflé I've ever had. Pretty impressive considering we're a billion light years from France."

"The French," Dsarthy waved her hand, "don't know shit about soufflé."

I chuckled. "You know it's a French word."

Dsarthy snorted. "I dunno what you're hearing, kid, but humans weren't the first people to think of sticking air in a cake."

--Hey!--

--Shaddup and eat!--

--I swear I'll shut off your forebrain and drive the fork myself!--

Dsarthy drank her beer and watched the room and went through a series of eye watering stretches. She had a lot of spinal articulation.

"So," she said. "You're a human."

I nodded. "Earth man, born and raised."

"Never seen a real live human before." She looked me over. "Weird."

I shrugged and ate some mai fun, and Cab trilled happily. "I could say the same thing."

183

Dsarthy nodded. "I bet. How'd you get hooked up with Rell?"

"A series of accidents," I said. There were shrimp in the mai fun. Where had she found shrimp? Were they shrimp? They looked like shrimp.

"The same series of accidents that cleaned you up?" She asked.

"There was some overlap." They certainly tasted like shrimp. Perfectly cooked, too. Kitchen foundries. That sounded like cheating.

"What's Earth like?" Dsarthy asked. "I hear it's disgusting."

I took a deep breath. They hated the human-shaped cops, they thought real humans were gross...this was worse than being an American in Paris.

"It's home," I said. "I like it."

Dsarthy nodded like I'd said something profound. I pointed at the painting behind the bar.

"Where's that," I asked. "Home?"

"Hakhaoughta," Dsarthy nodded. "What brings you to Phibbix?"

"A spaceship," I said. "I'm looking for work. Is it nice there? Hakhaoughta?"

"Used to be," Rell said, sliding back on to his stool. He took a bite of his lunch, which was a dead ringer for phlegm on rice, and sighed happily.

"Used to be?" I asked.

"You want to drop it?" Rell asked Dsarthy. "He's new."

Dsarthy shook her head and looked at me. "The Krr hit Hakhaoughta about thirty, thirty-five years ago. Place is a wasteland, now. Glass and ashes."

I would have gulped nervously, if people ever did that in real life. "Shit," I said. "I'm sorry."

"Don't worry about it," Dsarthy said. She finished his beer and stood up. "You didn't know." She looked at the painting and then went back into the kitchen with all of her shoulders hunched.

"I'm an asshole," I said. Rell shrugged. "Does 'the Krr hit Hakhaoughta' mean the same as 'the Krr hit Cabernicia?' Same tactic?"

"Carpet bombing," Rell said, low. "Hunting parties across the whole planet, and then a plague that's been tailor-made to sterilize a population of survivors that's too small to sustain genetic diversity and species health even if they could breed in the first place."

"How many planets have they hit?" I finished the collard greens. I thought they were too sweet, but Cab liked them. He has a more pronounced sweet tooth than I do, though.

"I don't know the current figure," Rell said. "Usually between three and eight systems a year."

"What?!" I yelped. Conversation petered out around us, and I leaned in so I could speak quietly. "That's your definition of a cold war? Jesus Christ, I knew the Krr were bad, but I didn't know they were slaughtering billions of people a year! Why doesn't the Core do anything about it?"

"They did," Rell said. "They built Phibbix, and all of her sister stations." After a second he smiled with everything but his eyes.

The long-legged dude to my right was watching me. He was too calm for me to say he was staring, but he definitely wasn't looking anywhere else.

"Where are you from?" I asked. I heard Rell swear under his breath behind me.

"Oppreinf," the other guy said.

"The Krr attacked…Oppreinf? I get that right?" He nodded.

"You're all from planets the Krr attacked," I said. The grey man shrugged and nodded.

"We don't say 'attacked' because 'attacked' implies that we could have fought back," he said. "But...yeah."

I looked at the painting again. A vista of a memory, a world that didn't exist anymore. The leggy guy popped his machine back together and stuck it in his ear and nearly smiled. The skin crinkled at the corner of his eyes.

"I'm sorry," I said. He nodded and put some coins on the bar.

"Yeah," he said, and left.

"I'm making friends left and right," I said to Rell. "You like me, right?"

"You can be a little hard to take," he said.

I drank about half of my beer. "So they hit, you said three to eight planets a year?"

"Systems," Rell said. "It was nine, actually, last year."

"Nine systems. So when that dude back there said 'Mouzza's gone,' he meant the planet Mouzza was destroyed by the Krr." Rell nodded, and I looked around the room. There was a similarity of expression, if I looked past the oddly-shaped faces, a sort of blank patience that spoke to the shared experience of an unimaginable trauma. "Everyone here is from a planet the Krr destroyed."

"Catch on quick, don't you?" Rell said.

"How many people are here?" I thought about the dense colossal cityscape surrounding us on all sides and couldn't even begin to guess the answer.

--Twenty-two billion or so--

"That's a huge number, Cab," I said.

--Some of them are very small people--

"And you said there are sister stations?" I said to Rell. He nodded. "Are they all like this?"

"The designs vary," he said. "But when I said the Core turns a blind eye to Yui's activity, I didn't mean that he was special. This is just how the refugee system works. It takes a lot more money to house all of these people than the Core is willing to provide, so every refugee station is given a somewhat long legal leash. They're all bigger in reality than they are on paper. The station administrators are all running some kind of scam. It's the only way they can afford to keep these people housed. The unofficial rule is that the Core won't bother them, even though everyone still tries to stay under the radar."

"So you've got a refugee population in the hundred billions, and the Core isn't doing shit to help them," I said.

"Oh, no," Rell said. "It's much larger than that. There are thousands of stations."

"Jesus Christ," I said. "I thought this was like, a once in a lifetime occurrence, and you're telling me it's happening practically monthly! What if they go after Earth for the hell of it?"

--Easy, tiger--

"They won't attack Earth if you're not there," Rell said. "The whole point of the endeavor is to spread terror. Nobody talks to humans, and humans don't do anything for the Core. Hell, a lot of people would be happy if you were all blown away. Calm down."

"How long has this been going on?" I was agitated. I felt like getting up and shouting.

--About seventy-one thousand years--

--Would you chill?--

--You're freaking me out--

I opened my mouth to say more words and pulled up short. Nobody talked to us, and we didn't do anything for the Core. Those were two distinct ideas.

"Who do they target?" I asked.

"The Fringes and Arms," Rell said. "They can't get into the Core because of the interdiction field, which is probably another reason the Core does so little about the problem. Razing is an abstract concept to them. Something they read about in the newspaper. They never experience it directly, hell, it's rare for any of them to leave the Core at all, unless they join the CLEA or the Navy. And most of them don't."

I had an uncle who lived in a gated community way down in Florida and voted GOP straight down the line in every election. My mom's brother. We didn't talk much, because he was an asshole, but I had in the past taken him to task for living in what I called, as a twenty-two-year-old with delusions of eloquence, his 'bubble of privilege.' The parallels were irritatingly apparent.

"But who do they target, specifically?" I said. "You told me the Core collects materiel and resources from the Fringes and Arms. Is there any pattern to what the Krr are doing?"

"Sure, they go after high-value resource planets," Rell said. "Farm worlds, elemental foundries, mining planets, that sort of thing. Manufacturing centers, storage systems. Every one of them a major population center."

"Cab, do you have records of all the attacks?" I said.

--Yeah, they're in here somewhere --

"Can you summarize their targets?"

--Oooh, look at you all fancy strategist--

--Gimme a minute--

"What's up?" Rell said.

"I don't think this is just about spreading terror," I said. "I think they're weakening the Core."

--Thirty percent of Krr targets supply food to thirty or more additional systems--

--Forty percent of Krr targets supply valuable or irreplaceable materials to defense industries--

--Sixty percent of Krr targets are high-traffic refueling centers along major intragalactic transit routes--

--It goes on and on like this, do you want me to continue?--

--You feel pretty vindicated--

"They're cutting the rug out from under you," I said. "They're cutting you off from one another, and they're weakening the Core ahead of a full-scale assault."

"Keep your voice down, kid." Rell shook his head. "Jesus, don't tell me you're one of those people. Listen, there are too many systems for the razing to make any difference to our defense capabilities. Don't mistake me, it's an awful, awful thing, but it's not going to be our downfall. It's just horrible, random violence. The idea that it's part of some coordinated effort to weaken us, that's crazy. It would take them one hundred and seventy billion years to make any significant progress."

--Actually, that 'one hundred and seventy billion years' figure is out of date--

--Fiora Godenloam came up with that when the frequency of attack was less than one a year--

--That was sixty thousand years ago--

--At today's pace, it shouldn't take them more than twenty billion years to make a major dent in the Core Government's defense capabilities--

--And that's assuming they don't continue to accelerate their rate of attack--

Rell frowned. "Well, it's still pretty outlandish."

"No, it's not," I said quietly. "It's a long con. They're not doing it for the individual. They're doing it for the species. They're softening you up ahead of a major offensive. The Front can only stop them once."

"If they blew the Front, they would be crippled, and the Core would send the Navy into Krr space to destroy the rest of them," Rell said. He sounded like he was saying it to himself.

"Then why don't they do that now?" I asked. "I bet I know the answer. They don't invade Krr space because even if the Krr are devastated by the destruction of the front, it's still bound to be a bloody, bloody war. They'll only invade if they have to. How much harder would it be for the Core to win if the Krr had a brand-new fleet of Krr Shipkillers backing them up?" I sighed and leaned my elbows on the counter.

"This is all part of the same plan," I said. "The razing, the Shipkiller seed, all of it. Hell, if half of what you and Cab have told me is true, the Krr only have the one plan in the first place. This is all leading towards them wiping us out." I sucked on my teeth. "I bet they're massing. We don't know what's inside Krr space. And Cab told me they build their ships from any available raw material, because they're not really building them, they're growing them. That's all they do, consume and grow. I bet they've got a fleet massing in there that would blow your mind out the back of your head. Nine systems a year is nothing to a fleet built from fifteen percent of the matter in the galaxy." I looked at him and spread my hands. "They're gonna keep on building ships and poking holes in you until they're ready, and then they're gonna roll over you like a goddamnd…"

--A thing that rolls over things--

"Yeah," I said. Rell watched me curiously. "And you said 'one of those people,' which means I'm not the first person to come up with this. I'm not the first person to call this a war of attrition."

"It's not a hard thought to have," Rell said. "It's just hard to believe. The Galaxy is really big, Samson."

"Doesn't mean they can't pull it off," I said. "Especially if they're moving too slow to be seen."

Rell laughed humorlessly. "But your neurotic ass is so torn up over your immortality that you can't help but obsessively ruminate about the future. You might actually be on to something, Samson. I've never heard the statistics parsed so plainly." He pulled out his wallet and put some bills on the bar. "Too bad I'm a wanted criminal and you're a horrible cybernetic aberration. Nobody is going to listen to us."

"Yet," I said. "If I'm right, they won't attack for years. Cab, I'm going on the assumption that we're still a lot stronger than they are. Is that correct?"

--What's this 'we' shit?--

--Sol is an unaffiliated system--

--Human rights forever!--

--Yeah, the Core military is ridiculously overpowered--

--We have the upper hand for the moment--

"Ok," I said. "So they won't pull anything for a while. Which means that our current situation hasn't changed at all. We're still trying to uncover evidence of Cabernician war-profiteering. And when we get that, we get an audience with Frewdin and hope he doesn't arrest us. We'll get immunity for any crimes you've committed, immunity for any crimes *I've* committed, and then after we get all this sorted out, we tell him about my doomsday theory and figure out how to stop the Krr."

--And on the seventh day, we'll rest--

"It's a good thing we've got you around to figure this stuff out for us, Samson," Rell grinned. "You're a real *mensch*."

"Oh, shut up," I said.

A Farther Orbit

14

There was scant noise outside, in spite of the crowd. People of all colors, shapes, configurations and imaginations. Three shimmering clouds of light were busking on the corner, and the music was loud in the shuffling quiet. These people didn't talk a lot. They held themselves carefully, as if cradling something broken. There was a constant, palpable awareness of something lost, something stolen. Their past and future both. But the music was alive. There was still a soul here. A life in the present. The people were moving on, even as they raced towards extinction. They hadn't been stymied.

Rell led us down the street in search of a payphone, and I did my best to earn my keep as a bodyguard, in spite of my ill humor. I didn't see anyone following us, but that didn't mean much; there were a lot of people and I had only just begun to distinguish individuals in any real capacity. A bipedal robot with a wide, flat top housing a small village inhabited, as near as I could tell, by three-legged tree frogs. A white slug with rabbit ears wearing sunglasses and rolling down the middle of the sidewalk atop a large, round rock. They appeared in flashes against the chaotic backdrop, were briefly apparent, then disappeared into my periphery. Faces were clear; bodies were not. It was easy to imagine that I was hallucinating, and hard to remember that I wasn't. I was fifty thousand leagues in over my head. An assassin any standing would be on top of us before I saw them. I couldn't fight back without hitting bystanders, and I was scared to death of being shot. It's all well and good to talk about accepting fear and moving through life without need, but try doing it. What if I panicked and went kill-crazy? Telling friend from foe would be impossible if I couldn't tell person from person.

"Cab," I said. Rell looked at me. "Standing order is to only take clear shots at weapons, ok?"

--I know--

"Just a reminder. Keep your eyes open."

Rell stopped and looked around, then pulled me across the street. There was a man who looked a lot like Godzilla selling ice cream out of a pushcart. He was about eight feet tall, with big, mauve eyes, and he was wearing an orange apron with a matching cap. Rell bought us two cones of the best vanilla ice cream I'd ever had, and motioned across the street.

"Watch," he said. So I did. The crowd was impenetrably diverse, but less so than it had been. I was acclimating.

There was a man leaning against the wall across the street from the phone, smoking a cigarette. He was four feet tall and looked like he was made out of braided, coiled rope that someone had shoved into a roughly bipedal, symmetrical shape. He had two arms, and his fingers appeared to be unraveled threads. He was wearing sunglasses, and a greasy vest, and matching pants. While I watched, he lit a new cigarette on the butt of the old one and checked his watch.

"The rope guy," I said. "Right?"

Rell looked for him and grinned. "Rope. Funny. No, he works at the pizza shop. See the grease stains? I think he's on break."

"How do you know he works in the pizzeria?" I said.

"Logo's on the back," Rell said, gesturing over his shoulder.

"And, wait, pizza?"

"Hush," Rell said. "Look again."

194

A man and a woman were standing at opposite corners, down the block from each other, facing the payphone. The tops of their heads were dominated by a single, huge eye the size of a basketball set into a big, leathery socket. They were muscular, and otherwise tripedal. Neither of them moved.

"Those two," I said, nodding slightly with my chin. "They're watching the phone."

Rell peered into the crowd. "Who, the deeveecers? You can't…Oh, you can't hear them, of course." He pointed at the left one. "She said, ah, 'Did you have them back here?'" He looked at the other. "He said, 'I think so, I know I had them at Fala's.'"

The two men started walking towards each other, slowly.

"I think that one lost his keys," Rell said. "Deeveecers communicate in ultralow frequencies, not everyone can hear them."

Cab shifted on my back, and suddenly I could hear the deeveecers arguing.

"I don't know why you have to keep them on that ridiculous lanyard," she said. Her voice cut through the crowd.

"It's my lucky lanyard!" The other one shouted.

Rell slurped his ice cream. "Listen, Samson, no one is following us. By now, Yui knows we're here, and he's watching us. He's got sensors that can see half a parsec out in every direction, you better believe he's been on us since we left Dsarthy's, at the very least." He made a face. "Actually, it's a good thing Cab doesn't register on sensors when he's stored away like that. Otherwise I imagine that we would have heard from him by now. Cab being rather frightening, you understand."

--Hey!--

"Quiet," Rell said immediately. He looked around. "Yui is figuring out what he wants to do. Which is why I want to call him." He looked at me and shrugged. "If he wanted to kill us, he would have done it by now. Just, zip, laser from the far side of the station. Ten miles isn't much to a sniper with a ray gun. I told you, he's not going to attack a cop in public."

"So what are we doing over here?" I asked.

"I wanted ice cream," Rell said. "And you needed a moment to calm down."

"Thank you," I said. "I'm very calm. The crime boss we came to interrogate thinks I'm a cop and he can shoot me anytime he wants to from up to ten miles away, and the only thing keeping him from doing so is fear of reprisal, fear of reprisal that we are about to eliminate. That information has had a calming effect on me."

Rell chuckled and threw away his cone. "Come on. I'm pretty sure he won't try to kill us without talking to me first."

"How sure?" I followed him. "Percentage wise."

"Come on, Samson," Rell said. We went down the block to the payphone. It was a four-foot metal post in the sidewalk with a six foot wide black ring set in the pavement around it, but Rell said it was a payphone, and I was willing to take him at his word.

"Now, Greg," Rell said liltingly, "do you want to wait out here, or do you want to come in the booth with me?"

"Fuck off, green jeans." I followed him over the threshold.

As soon as we were both inside, a shimmering wave rose out of the ring and dimmed our surroundings. They were still visible, but it was like looking through sunglasses.

"Neat," I said. "Soundproof, too?"

"Yeah," Rell said. "Keep an eye out, if it makes you feel better."

"It does," I said, watching the crowd. No one was polishing a stiletto, or loading a revolver, or anything else sinister. Several people appeared to be drunk, or on drugs. There were a lot of the melon-people I'd come to recognize. We must have been close to their neighborhood. That was assuming that they divvied up the refugees according to species. Maybe they didn't. Maybe that was my innate human prejudice, coming to the fore. Maybe they were more egalitarian out here. Maybe as soon as Rell's call went through we were going to be vaporized from one of the upside-down skyscrapers above us. What a weird life.

"Yui Galt," Rell said. He had his thumb and pinky extended and spread, with his thumb on his ear and his pinky by his mouth. Which was weird, but, as I said, all of this was weird. And fucking terrifying, lest we forget. I felt like I had to pee, even though I'd just gone. We waited, and then Rell said, "Hey! Yui! Guess who's back?"

He listened for a moment, and then said, "Christ, Yui, you know me better than that, I...well, that's what I want to talk to you about, I've been all over, I...yeah, I know there's a price on my head." He sighed. "He's not a cop, Yui, you know I wouldn't...What are the cops going to do about a price on my head?"

Would I be able to react in time, if he shot us with a laser? Lasers were pretty fast. My scalp prickled.

"If I thought you were the one who put the price on my head, I wouldn't be here," Rell said, which was only half true. "Seriously, Yui, how could I even go to the cops? They'd bust me on sight. Because there's a fucking video of me stealing a seed out of the

Cabernician Shipyards, Yui! Fucksake! I can't go to the cops! I'm here for help!"

I frowned at him, and he waved his hand at me and turned away from me.

--Guess he's scared too--

I cocked an eyebrow and didn't say anything.

"He's a...No, god dammit, he's not a sex robot. Where the hell did you hear...yeah. Yeah. I know. Rumors spread fast. No, he's a clean human. I said he's a clean human."

Rell winced and held his thumb away from his ear, then listened again.

"Yui," He said. "Yui! I've spent the last thirty hours aboard ship with him, if he wasn't clean I'd be long dead! Dormant? He's a fucking human, Yu, listen to yourself!" Another pause. "Military experiment gone wrong. He's a military experiment gone wrong. I dunno, he was flying along near Qet and I picked him up." He listened. "Fine, don't believe me. But he's not a cop. Kid's pissing himself that you're gonna fry him. No, he's not from the Core." He sighed again, and gestured angrily, but silently, at the sky above him. "Yui, you know the Core doesn't give a shit about what you do here! Lighten up!"

--I mean, they might care about the Shipkiller seed he tried to sell to the Krr--

I nodded and shrugged.

--Kinda strange, right?--

--When was the last time you were in a payphone?--

--Then again, I've never been in a payphone--

I snorted.

--Kinda boring, actually--

"I just want to talk," Rell said. "I need information. Well, that's what I want to talk about. Oh, come on, asshole, don't make me do this over the phone." He wrinkled his nose, which was a considerable gesture. "The Sphere. Oh, get off your high horse, Yui, it's a nice bar. Well, I like it. No, I want to stay out of the centers. Because there's a price on my head, man! Yeah? Really? You can vouch for the behavior of twenty billion people? Every single one of them is gonna leave me alone? What?" He frowned. "Yui, you're…Are you kidding me?" He closed his eyes. "Fine. I said fine, dammit! Ok, ten minutes. Yeah. Thanks, Yu."

He dropped his hand.

"Come on," he said. He sounded tired.

"Are we good?" I fell into step next to him.

"I'm finished here," Rell said. "Yui is pissed. And this is before I ask him for anything. He's convinced you're either an undercover cop or a plague bomb waiting to go off. He said when we're done talking we have to leave the station."

"Ok," I said. Rell shook his head and went on walking. "What?"

"I like it here," he said. "There aren't a lot of places where I fit in."

"The refugees?" I looked around.

"I can't go home either," he said. "Listen, this bar, Sphere, it's just a dive bar, but even so, try not to destroy the place if the ball goes up. And don't blow a hole in the station. These are good people here, for the most part."

"I hear you," I said. We walked on in silence for several minutes, and then I cleared my throat. "Was that a basketball reference?"

Rell nodded.

"You guys watch our sports, too?"

"Hey, basketball is awesome." Rell mimed taking a shot. "Kobe!"

"It's like I never left Earth," I grumbled. "Hey, Cab, you ready?"

--For what?--

He giggled. I set my jaw. "Just…be prepared."

--That's the Boy Scout's marching song--

--Be prepared, as through life you march along--

--I'm always prepared--

"Well, sound a yellow alert or something. Man battle stations. Be ready to fight."

--You really need to find your calm, dude--

"Cab!"

--Aye, Captain--

--Be prepared to hold your liquor pretty well, don't write naughty words on walls if you can't spell--

Rell took us to a large hemispherical building covered in shining silver ball bearings, clouds of which detached themselves from the surface at odd intervals to form intricate shapes in midair, fractals, Celtic knots, alien flowers, and sometimes the word 'Sphere,' in good old familiar English. Except it wasn't English, it was some carefully induced hallucination that made me see my own language. As I watched, the doors hammered open and a pair of drunks staggered out with their long, rubbery arms around each other. They were singing a song about an animal with an aggressive sexual appetite in a four-part harmony, two parts apiece.

"This is a dive bar?" I said. "Vegas can't touch this. Hell, Dubai can't touch this."

Rell frowned at me. "They're ball bearings, Samson."

I rolled my eyes and read the sign again. If I tried, I could see it in Spanish, a language I had studied for seven years and spoke poorly. I had no idea how that worked. Then again, I had no idea how any of it worked. It was hard to keep track of that reality; I kept pulling at familiar threads and then getting confused when they turned out to be alien, and I knew he had to stop. What mattered was what was right in front of me. I could read the sign. That was what mattered. I had to accept my shortcomings. If I had tried back then to make sense of alien technology, I would never have made it past my own ship, who was belting Tom Lehrer in the back of my head.

The interior of Sphere was one big empty room carved from stone, with a circular bar in the center that was built like a spiral staircase, meaning that depending on where you ordered your drink the bar might be two or twenty feet tall. It wrapped around and around, four layers supported on what appeared to be nothing, with glassware hung from the bottom. The bartender was another flying melon.

The floor was a field of ball bearings fitted snugly into a regular pattern on a rubber underlayment. There was no furniture, and the only other patron, who appeared to be a hulking tube of adipose tissue, was content to stand.

--At least we won't have to worry about shooting into a crowd--

"Let's try to avoid shooting at all, ok?" I said.

"What?" Rell looked at me.

"Nothing," I said. "Cab."

Rell nodded. "Try not to do that when Yui shows up."

He bought us a couple of beers from the four and eight foot sections of the bar; the drinks came sized according to where he ordered, a pint for me and a half-gallon for him.

"Pan-species tavern," he explained. "Serves all kinds. Have a seat."

I looked around, "No, I forgot mine. What do you mean, have a seat?"

Rell sat down on nothing and as he did, a cloud of ball bearings detached themselves from the floor under him and formed the top surface of an invisible chair. He let his weight go with a sigh and stretched out his feet on a hassock that formed in the same top-only, immediate fashion. He dropped his drink and a cloud of bearings caught the glass so gently that the beer didn't foam.

I leaned back on my heels and the floor coalesced behind me into a high bar chair with a back. "Neat trick," I said. "I like how we're at eye level."

"Species-specific seating," Rell said. "Designed to help us interact comfortably."

"It is nice to be as tall as you are, finally," I said.

"You're not as tall as me," Rell said. "We just found you a high-chair."

I drank my beer. It was a fruit-forward wheat ale, unfortunately, but no moment is ever perfect. I put the glass down, then picked it up and put it on my other side, then back again. The bearings rose and resettled with the same slow, immediate confidence every time. There was no deviation, they just stopped in the right place, without exception or error. Amazing. It was all amazing. Everything I saw was amazing. Which, I suppose, is wonderful.

"Be honest," I said. "Do you think he's going to try to kill us?"

The door split open and a space-age water cooler floated into the bar, trailed by eight hulking bipedal organisms made out of disconnected pieces of granite. Which is to say, rock-men. Some aliens defied description. These guys did not. They were humanoid, and made out of rock. Simple. Each of them carried a long gun and a bandolier of grenades, which was their only clothing. Although I suppose body armor is

202

redundant when you're a man of stone. They flanked us and aimed their guns at me, which I found unfair.

"Hard to say," Rell muttered. Cab shifted minutely and went on singing.

The water cooler landed in front of us on three mechanical legs, which unfolded with the same imperturbable grace as the ball bearings. Water, or whatever it was, sloshed over the edge, but none of it spilled.

"Yui," Rell said calmly. "How you been?"

"You know, Rell, I would say I can't complain, but I don't think I would be telling you the truth," the water cooler replied. "I'm gonna need you to give your guns to my boys here."

Two of the rock men stepped forward and gestured at Rell. I gave him a look, but he just shook his head and he gave up his guns.

"Careful," he said when he relinquished his shotgun, "that doesn't have a safety."

"The other guy too," Yui said.

"He's unarmed," Rell said.

"Bullshit," Yui said. One of the rock men patted me down. I held my breath, but he didn't say anything when he touched my back, just went on down and whacked me in the ass with a granite palm. He shook his head at the water tank.

"Tell Falee to do another long-range scan," Yui said. "Who the fuck are you? Why are you here?"

"Greg Samson," I said. "I'm from Earth, and I ask myself that question every night before I fall asleep." My hands were shaking. I really wanted to drink my beer, but I didn't want to make a mess.

"Bullshit," he said. "I'm gonna ask you again, asshole, and if I don't like the answer I'm gonna blow your foot off."

--I hold your hand in mine, dear, I press it to my lips--

"Yui," Rell said, "Why don't you take a good look at him before you cripple the kid?"

--I take a healthy bite, from your dainty fingertips--

I held my breath, wondering which foot he would pick. I wasn't gonna let him shoot me, I'd move if he gave the order, but I wasn't sure I could move fast enough to keep all my toes.

The liquid in the jug reared up and formed a reasonable facsimile of a human upper body, with depressions for eyes and a triangle for a nose and a slit for a mouth and a confused face for an expression. He looked at his hands and touched himself and leaned on his elbows and looked at Rell, and as he made eye contact with the other man he enlarged, grew a second set of elbows and a more pronounced muzzle. Then, deliberately, he looked at me, and changed back. Several droplets fell from his chin and curved into the tank.

"Human," he said after a moment.

"I told you," Rell said. Yui nodded.

"You did." Yui glanced between us and his features shifted back and forth. Then he settled on Rell. "Ok. He's human. Where the fuck is my seed, Rell? Where are my people? What the fuck happened out there?"

"Your people are dead," Rell said, right on the heels of Yui's third question, so that there was a brief moment of silence while everyone worked out who had said what, and what had been said. I'm sure Rell did it on purpose. He was a smart guy. He sipped his beer and fluttered his ear crests, once. "Let's go over the assignment, again, Yui. You said you got wind of a private sale between the General Isolationist Movement and some Cabber you'd been courting for business, correct?"

"Where is my seed, Rell?" Yui asked.

"They were selling a Shipkiller seed, right? And you sent me out there with a strike force to kill everyone involved and steal the seed?"

"Are you recording this?" Yui spat. "Is that what's going on here?"

"Fuck you!" Rell shouted. "Don't you dare, Yu! Two hundred years I've known you, I'm damned if I'll let you call me a rat!"

--You think he actually has rats on his planet?--

"Then where the hell is my Shipkiller seed, you miserable thief?" Yui gestured sharply at one of his goons. "Walt, if he doesn't tell me, shoot him in the foot."

--What is it with this guy and feet?--

One of the rock men aimed his rifle. Rell raised his hand at me, just enough for me to see, because I was looking for a signal, because I didn't know what to do.

--You think it's cause he doesn't have any?--

--Is it a jealousy thing?--

"Did you know the GIM were Krr?" Rell asked.

I tensed, watching Walt the podiatric assassin, but nobody moved. Yui's toshe face got firmer.

"You've been doing business with them a long time, Yu," Rell said. "Did you know they were Krr? Are you trying to get us all killed?"

"What the fuck are you talking about?" Yui leaned a long way out of his tank, intent on Rell.

"The Cabernician showed up, like you said," Rell said. "Then about five minutes after that, a Krr strike force came out of warp right in front of him, and the bastard didn't blink. He tried to give them the seed. They were flying sensor-open, Yui, in Krr ships. They weren't trying to hide. We went in after the seed, and the Krr killed *everyone*. They hived every single goddamn ship. Frank, Dyoaula, Waris, everyone is dead. I barely got out alive, I don't even know what happened to the Cabernician. I do know the Krr didn't get the seed. I've been on the run ever since." Rell belched lightly. "'Scuse me. Somebody put a price on my head about a week ago, now, and I'm here trying to back trace the sale. I figure whoever put this thing together is trying to shut me up." He thought for a moment. "That's about the long and the short of it. The kid is my orphaned ward. I'm teaching him to fight crime."

"Bullshit," Yui said.

Rell grimaced sympathetically and shook his head. "Nope, no shit, he's a real live orphan."

"Walt, shoot him in the knee." Yui crossed his toshein arms.

"Why would I come to you if I'd stolen the stupid thing?" Rell's voice was loud in the open room. "Why would I tell you something that's so incredibly hard to believe? Why would I take such a stupid goddam risk?"

"Well," Yui gestured at me, and then stopped.

"Yeah," Rell said after a minute. "It makes sense if he's a cop and I'm trying to entrap you, but you wouldn't have mirrored human if he was a Bekht, Yu. I'm here cause I've got nowhere else to go in this."

Yui opened his ersatz mouth once or twice and then snapped his fingers wetly at one of his goons, who rumbled over to the bar. He came back in a moment with a shaker of off-white crystals for Yui and another round for Rell and me, which I took to be a good sign.

"Ok," Yui said, "Say you're telling me the truth. Where's the seed?" The crystals flared tiger-lily red when he shook them into his mouth, and in seconds he was filled with a spreading haze of sparkling, glittering bolts of chemically-bright lightning.

"The seed's gone," Rell said. "I need to know who set up the sale. I don't know if the Cabber got away, and I don't know if he's the one who put the price on my head, or if it was someone else. But I figure I've got to pull at this thing until I figure out who's been working with the Krr. Then I have to go to the CLEA. It's my only way out, other than running. Or killing the guy, but that might not end the contract." He drank his beer in a long moment and gave it to the rock man to be refilled. "I won't have any reason to mention you, Yui. But I need your help."

Yui took another drink of crystals and considered Rell quietly. "What do you mean the seed is gone? And don't try to feed me that horseshit about the Krr, I'm not buying it. I mean, I like you, buddy, but if I send a thief to recover one of the most expensive weapons in the galaxy and they both go missing, it's not much of a stretch to think he stole the thing. You know? You say you don't have the seed, and GIM doesn't have the seed, and they don't, by the way, they were pretty vocal on that point, so where the hell is it? I sent you because you don't lose track of things, Rell, it's part of your charm. Don't tell me you're slipping."

"You're still in contact with the GIM?" I asked. "Even after they tried to cut you out of the deal?"

"Business is business, and their money spends as well as anyone else's," Yui said. "I assume they got the message not to go behind my back, no matter what happened out there. We've been in contact for weeks."

I had a sudden sense of the vastness waiting just outside the hull. The galaxy was catalogued and normalized and averaged together to an extreme that I could never have imagined, and the damn thing was still big enough to lose people in. But this was no time for abstraction.

"They're still trying to buy a seed?" I asked. Yui looked at me long enough to become fully human, and then smiled literally from ear to ear.

"Rell," he said. "Keep him quiet. He freaks me out."

"He's still selling to the GIM," I said to Rell. "This motherfucker is going to get us all killed."

"Walt, break his arm," Yui said. Walt handed his gun to his cohort and advanced on me.

"Show him," Rell said.

I stood up into the ship and pointed my right-hand Stephen-gun at Walt's left eye, or at least the spot where his left eye would have been if he had eyes. He didn't, by the way.

Nobody moved. It felt good to be back in the ship, to hear the choir of systems checking in below my brain. As if my body had come back to itself. Cab was still singing.

--I had a friend in Minsk, who had a friend in Pinsk--

"Now Walt," I said carefully, "Chekov says I'm supposed to use these pistols at some point in the story, but I'd prefer not to shoot you. So sit your stone-faced ass back down."

Walt shrugged and backed up.

--Plagiarize!--

--Plagiarize!--

--Don't let another's work evade your eyes!--

"Yui Galt, may I present Gregory Samson and Cab, the Solar Shipkiller." Rell waved his hand back and forth. "Greg, Cab, Yui, Yui, Cab, Greg."

"So formal," I said. Rell shrugged.

"I'm fancy. Now, gentlemen, Samson here is only twenty-eight years old and he's scared out of his mind, and that is in fact a fully-functional Shipkiller being run by a sentient computer, so I think it would be best if we all agreed to be civil. Can we do that?"

"I'm game," I said. "Yui? Walt? Other goons whose names I don't know?"

"You put the seed in a human?" Yui said. He'd lost some detail, was just basically humanoid or toshesque, with long, loose arms.

"Of course not," Rell said coldly. "How stupid do you think I am? The fucking seed got knocked towards the Solar system. It landed on him. When I went looking, he forced his way aboard."

"Jesus Christ," Yui said. "You went to Sol? That's a hell of a stupid risk, man."

"I could have retired on what you were going to pay me," Rell said simply.

"Is it safe?" Yui stared at me.

"Hey, I have a name, asshole." I dismantled the helmet and sat down, and my seat got bigger to compensate for my shiny metal ass. Yui stared at me, and became more human.

"He's safe enough," Rell said. "A little green." He grinned. "A lot green. But he's a good kid."

"Patronizing monkey," I said.

"He talks too much." Rell settled in his chair. "Yui, I went where you told me and I found a Krr strike force buying a Shipkiller seed from a Cabernician. I've got sensor data, not that it matters much, the Cabbers forged theirs, no reason I couldn't forge mine. But *he's* here. *He's* real. I can produce evidence supporting part of my story. Can the Cabernicians? And why in God's name would I lie about the Krr when we have a threat like him on our hands?" He pointed at me and paused for the effect. "I'm telling you the truth, Yu. I need your help."

"Hey, wait, a threat like me?" I said. "Are you serious?"

Yui drained the rest of his shaker and tossed it to Walt, who caught it without looking. The big man got up for another round without a word. Then again, he did everything without words.

"Rell, I've been doing business with the GIM for seventy years," he said. "I've moved, Christ, I mean, they're in it for weapons, intelligence, anything Core-made I can get my hands on. I sold them Stellar Bomb schematics, Rell, they can't be the Krr, we'd be fucking dead, right?" He started out confident enough, but by the time he was done he sounded like he was pleading.

"You ever do any business with them face to face?" I asked. Yui looked at me and his face rippled. It might have been a shudder.

"Even if you did, you've got no way to know what's aboard the other ship, do you?" I shook my head. "You've got machines that fool sensors. You'd have to be right up close to see their ships with your bare eyes. And even then there's no reason they couldn't have used a stolen ship."

"They always did their business through a shell company," Yui mumbled. "A different one each time."

"A shell company for the cover identity," I sighed. "Slick."

"They came in person for the seed," Rell said. "They must have decided it was too important to risk on an intermediary."

"This can't be true," Yui said. He wasn't looking at either of us, and was by now a sort of barely-moving lump on the surface of his liquid body.

"I know what I saw, Yui," Rell said. "I know what I heard. They hived the capital ships, man. I barely made it out."

"They can't be Krr," Yui whispered. He looked me over and his nose fell into his mouth.

"Oops," I said. "You sell them anything else we should know about?"

"Oh my god!" He yelled. I pulled away, and Rell did the same. It was a desperate noise.

"You believe us now?" I asked hesitantly.

"Oh my *god*!" Yui yelled again.

--Ok, that's a little much--

"Yui," Rell said, "Calm down. They didn't get the seed."

Yui closed his mouth and looked at Rell and became very Toshe, very quickly.

"The Cabernician is alive," he said. "Or his partner is. After you broke up the first sale, the Cabber and the GIM made contact with me and arranged two more sales through the proper channels. The first one was two weeks ago. I haven't heard a thing from either side, but the check cleared, so I assume everything went off without a hitch."

I took a deep breath and grabbed the arms of my chair hard enough to crush the bearings together into an unrecognizable mass. I had to grit my teeth against the onslaught of Cab's horror, and although I didn't scream, it was a near thing. Rell's eyes were wider than I'd seen them, and his fur was pale. I wouldn't have thought that he could do that.

For once, my naïveté was an asset. I knew this was bad, but I was too backward to be as afraid as they were. Cab was another matter, but obviously I've always been good at boxing up my emotions. I leaned forward and looked Yui in the eye.

"You said two sales," I said. "When's the second one?"

"Twelve hours," Yui said. "It's in twelve hours." And then he vomited a dry rush of red-hot, burning coals.

I didn't know if that was enough time to do something, but I knew I could try. It was simple knowledge, and it didn't fix anything, but it's always nice to have a path. I stood up.

"See?" I said to Cab, pointing at the vomit burning a hole in the floor. "All that foreshadowing, and I still wasn't the first guy to puke."

15

Cab stood up straight through the towering inferno of his fear and pulled himself under control. He was a quick study.

--Where's the sale?--

It was his voice. I could tell, because I could feel him vibrating the surface of the ship to speak aloud. But this was a voice I hadn't heard him use before, a terrible, grating, bass-heavy thing that promised a future of Austrian robots crushing human skulls under titanium feet. Yui's shape shivered, and several of the rock men clutched their weapons and looked around.

--Where is it?!--

"Ok, killer, take it easy," I muttered.

--We've got to break up the sale--

His voice was back between my ears, along with a childish sense of embarrassment.

--We can't do that if we don't know where to go--

--You should do the talking, though, that voice was awful--

--I feel like an idiot--

--But we don't have time for civility, Cap'n--

I got up and made a calming gesture towards the assembled goons.

"Yui, where's the damn sale?" I said. I didn't raise my voice at all. Actually, in retrospect I think I sounded pretty tired. Yui didn't respond, so I took a step towards him and clapped my big metal flipper hands together, hard. "Hey! Splash Mountain! Where are they selling the seed?"

Yui stared at me and slowly became more human. The realization that he might have doomed most life in the galaxy had him thrown, but he was coming around.

"It's close to the Front," he said. He spoke as if he were having difficulty remembering which words to use. "The GIM said they would be alone out there."

--And that didn't sound suspicious?--

Cab's voice was back to normal, but audible to the group. Yui looked like he wanted to cower.

--We need coordinates, Yui--

--Give me access to your files--

Behind me, Rell snorted. "My ass."

"Configure open access for Cabernician Shipkiller...what's your serial?" Yui said.

"What?" Rell said, loud.

--181804258618185--

"Configure open access for Cabernician Shipkiller 181804258618185," Yui said.

"Jesus, Yu, there's a lot of evidence in there," Rell said incredulously.

"You won't fuck us, will you kid?" Yui smiled at me. He was very human, and although he was smiling, he looked worried. I took a step towards the door and pointed at Rell.

"He's safe here, right?" I said to Yui. He glanced at Rell and nodded at me.

"Yeah," he said. "I believe you. He's safe. Walt, give him back his guns."

"Communication, honesty and trust are the keys to a healthy friendship," Rell said.

"Jesus, you're an asshole," Yui said.

--I've got the coordinates--

--Go--

--Now--

--We have very little time--

Cab's fear came back to me from nowhere, and I was for a moment awash in sternum-splitting terror, a brief glimpse of Cab's thoughts and knowledge and potential as a Shipkiller, a self-knowledge that was at once a recognition of his own limits and an understanding of the terrible uses to which his siblings could be applied. Clearing my head took some effort.

"Get it together, Cab," I said.

--We don't have time for that!--

--Go!--

--Move!--

Something stung me in the ass, and I yelped.

--Get!--

--Out the door!--

--We've got to get out of the station!--

Another sting. I jumped. "Stop that, dammit!"

--Then get moving!--

I threw Rell a half-salute. Yui got a nod as I ran, hopping and cursing, out of the door.

"Are all humans like that?" I heard Yui ask.

"Couldn't tell you, I've only met the one," Rell replied. "Walt, I'll have another beer."

I knocked one of the doors off of its hinges and staggered out onto the street, scattering a pack of well-to-do Welwleul. They cursed me and clutched their valuables closer to their tentacular bodies and shuffled down the street.

Cab's next barb caught me just under the rib cage, and I gasped. "How do I get back to the airlock?"

--We're not going back!--

--We're going up!--

Cab pointed at the latticework in the middle of the station with his nonexistent finger, and for a brief moment I saw a trajectory that would take me up and under and then past the thing, through the polar pillar and out into space. My sense of him wavered through his panic.

--There's an emergency release for the base reactor up there--

--Yui has it jerry-rigged to function as a large-format airlock--

--Go!--

Another sting, just under my right glute. "You have to stop doing that!" I leapt into the air and tore up the side of a skyscraper. It wasn't a tall one, because we were close to the edge of the district and the buildings were short by necessity. Ahead of me, the top of a similarly-sized structure in a neighboring district with an opposing gravity well loomed vertiginously. There was a mostly empty airspace between the districts, between the roofs of the towers, and I assumed as I flew that the gravity there would somehow remain unchanged relative to what I was used to.

I was wrong.

Gravity between the boroughs pulled straight back to the edged skin of the station, at an angle about twenty or thirty degrees to my left, so when I passed over the invisible line dividing where I had been from where I was going, I lurched to my left, across the open space and into the neighboring district...whose gravity well was itself another thirty or so degrees to the left of what I was expecting. The takeaway here is that I cleared the top of the skyscraper next to Sphere and crashed straight into the next building over.

--Get up get up get up--

--Get up Greg we don't have time for this you have to hurry!--

"Jesus." I stood up shakily and took off.

Phibbix was as crowded in the air as it was on the avenues, except in the air there was more to keep track of. I pulled in my feet and chipped some guy's passenger-side mirror, and then pulled up short and down to avoid obliterating a flying couch full of lizards. They swerved and swore, and then they were gone. Cab showed me the same urgent thread of trajectory and I barreled towards the center of the station.

A hoverbus cut me off out of nowhere. I shoved hard with the engine in my right palm and cartwheeled out of the way and tumbled out of control. A billboard loomed in front of me, an advertisement for either chocolate milk or sex, and I thought the word 'shields' as hard as I could.

Immediately a sphere of chaotic blue energy surrounded me. It cut through the billboard like a blowtorch through wax. The air burned, and the shield shuddered and exploded outward. Lightning leapt from object to object, scorching everything around me and killing electronics. Vehicles and floating ads lost power and plummeted towards the street. Debris and molten metal rained in ten different directions. The crowds in every district scattered immediately. The stricken vehicles slowed to a halt in midair, caught by the grace of some safety measure I hadn't known existed, although I'm glad that it did. A fruit stand in a borough off to my left was obliterated by a giant bottle of chocolate milk, but other than that the damage looked minimal.

--You can't use a shield in atmosphere--

--The energy field supercharges and superheats anything it touches, starts a chain reaction--

"I really wish you'd told me that ahead of time," I sighed. "Was anyone hurt?"

--I don't know--

--We have to go--

"Cab, we can't just leave!" I turned myself in midair. There were a small fires burning in a few places, although it looked like they were being taken care of.

--Samson, they have emergency services here, it's a goddamn megalopolis!--

--We don't have time to stick around, the Krr are going to get another Shipkiller seed in eleven point nine one hours!--

--We have responsibilities!--

--We have got to go now!--

I grimaced. "Ok," I said. "Ok."

I looked around one more time and flew on. It was easier now that the traffic had gotten out of my way. I went up the tunnel, towards the North Pole. Off to see Santa, I giggled to myself. My breath was shuddery. I accelerated and screamed out of the airlock.

The docking conduits were sparse, up here, and so I was mostly unimpeded. A couple of small ships shaped like old Crisscraft motorboats chased each other around the base of the pole like playful squirrels, and a huge cruiser like a collection of bubbles was laboring its way towards another airlock, but other than that I was alone.

The three nascent stars winked and wavered through the nebular haze, gleefully devouring gaseous matter to sustain their growing inner fires. Predatory geography, they would grow until the nebula was gone and then attack each other, until there were at most two, but most likely one, because that's the way these things tend to work out.

I curved around the bubble ship and pressed for deep space. Phibbix shrank beneath me as I continued to accelerate. The faster I flew, the bigger I felt, and the bigger I felt, the less I felt Cab's fear. Which was good, because I had plenty of my own to go around. At least it went both ways.

"Samson," Rell said in my ear. I jumped. "Do you have a plan?"

The stars appeared against the murk.

"No," I said. "Not really. Cab, do you have a plan?"

--Stop the sale--

"Elegant," I said. "Any idea how?"

--Probably by shooting someone--

The haze faded away, and the stars stopped twinkling. Romance is only possible in an atmosphere. The darkness between them was utter dark, the nebula a wispy, receding floor beneath me.

--We're clear for warp--

--I'm going to fly us through this time--

--This is going to be jarring for you--

--Let me drive, ok?--

I nodded, and all of a sudden I was just a passenger, soaring along at rest. It would have been relaxing but for Cab's discomfort.

--Oh, I don't like this--

--It feels like I'm lifting myself up by the back of my own neck--

A tapered rod built itself out of my sternum, cracked along a series of lengthwise seams and unfolded into a spherical lattice the size of a beach ball. The edge glowed, and beams of light shot across the interior, connecting the vertices. The intersection in the middle was brighter than the sum of its parts, and getting brighter. There was a thudding sound in my lower brain, and then a wave washed out of the sphere and disappeared into nothingness, although I had an odd remembered sense of the waves expanding, fully visible, into every nook and cranny of creation. The universe seemed to hold its breath, and then the wave came crashing back into me.

The anxiety that had accompanied me off of Earth faded, and calm spread through me. I felt like something was watching me, and it loved what it saw.

"Cab," I murmured, "you said the Warp is alive?"

--Yes--

--An extra-dimensional entity--

--This is us making contact--

--The process won't be as evolved next time, this is a little like a mating dance--

The light inside the lattice was too bright to look at, but it cast no shadows and left no afterimage. It grew to fill the interior, bubbled against the edges, pressed more fully into our universe. I felt happiness, familiarity, pleasure, contentment, readiness. Benevolence.

--Wow, your pleasure centers are going crazy--

--This feels great--

--I wonder if the same thing happens to the Hoon whales?--

The sense of happiness doubled down.

--I think it likes you--

--We have a course, you ready?--

--This is going to be intense, flying into the vector--

--Ok?--

--Ready to rock?--

I nodded, distracted, staring.

--You're not listening to me at all--

Whatever I was looking at was beautiful in every sense of the word. I was thrilled, inspired, happy, confident, aroused, in love. The light ebbed and flowed, and my emotions surged in time.

The lattice shrank, and the orb shrank with it. The less of the Warp I saw, the less I empathized with it, and the less overpoweringly amazing I felt. I despaired at the diminishment.

--Oh for god's sake--

--Do you have a hard-on?--

--What is wrong with you?--

It felt a little bit like being on good drugs.

If I squinted, I could see a line connecting the antenna on my chest with some far-off point in space, billions of miles away. The spot where the Warp was touching my mind was a warm, slightly numb tingle pouring through my skull, into my chest, and out of my limbs. I poked the antenna once, twice.

--You're impossible--

--Heads up, lover boy--

The stars were a billion pinpricks through a velvet hood, different sizes but all at the same depth, a panorama flattened by the immense distances between everything I saw. And then, a crushing acceleration, every organ smashed against the back of me, and the stars moved against each another. And once more, watching the closer stars move faster than the farther, and the farthest move not at all, I understood the vastness of space, and my insignificance. All, and everything, laid bare before me.

--You should see your face--

My arms and legs were flung out behind me, and my mouth and eyes were wide open. My neck was rigid. I was passing the stars. Phibbix was gone behind me, already a distant memory. I was going so fast. And it wasn't like being on a ship, it wasn't a sense of timeless acceleration and then normalcy; whatever field the Warp was generating affected me right down to my marrow. My skin was breaking the laws of physics as I knew them, as Rell knew them. My brains and my balls were stretched out across entire parsecs. It was ok. That's not how it really feels, overall. But it's a definite possibility of a feeling, a minor distraction of a sensation, like humor in a firefight or arousal when the woman you love is yelling at you in her underwear.

I could move just fine, so I tucked in and hugged myself until my heart rate slowed. The cosmos cannonballed by. The more I focused on my surroundings, the easier it was to feel normal. So I was flying through space fast enough to watch the stars move. That was fine. That was just speed. That was mundane. That was *speed*. God damn, that was speed.

The warp conduit was more of an existential anchor than a physical one, and now that we were in the vector, we were locked into our course no matter what I did. I found I could move freely around the central point of it with just a thought, turn completely around and look behind us without altering our course. For a while I amused myself by orbiting the thing like a propeller. It made me giggle.

--You're a weird dude, Samson--

"It's a defense mechanism." I curved around behind the thing and flew mostly upright, angled forward, more Peter Pan than Superman. Ahead of me, nothing in particular, other than what I knew. A Krr strike force, and hive ships. How many ships did Rell say he brought with him the first time? Fifteen? And they got smoked by ten Krr. Hived. What an awful thing. A worse thing than I would have expected. A base, brutal, animal tactic, to feed the enemy to your newborn cannon fodder. Still, I was pretty small. They probably wouldn't be able to build a hive out of my carcass. The odds were better that they would just shoot me.

That thought was jarring. I was tiny. I was fast, and tough, but ship or no ship, I was only six feet long. I was outgunned. They were going to kill me and destroy the galaxy.

"I can't do this alone," I said. "I have to call Frewdin."

--What?--

Cab was suddenly nervous. I didn't like that.

--You'll be fine--

--In and out--

--Float like a butterfly, shoot 'em in the head--

I shook my head. "I'm one guy, Cab. I need backup."

--You're an adaptive Shipkiller helmed by a sentient computer--

--You're like, robot god--

"Cab, even if you're right, I've got next to no experience with this sort of thing. All the toys in the world don't mean dick if you don't know how to use them. I've got to call Frewdin."

Cab's nerves continued to fray.

--But--

--He'll bust you--

I grimaced. He had a point. "I don't care," I said. "This is too big not to let him know. If he busts me, he has to bust me, but he's got to know. It's his job."

--That we're doing for him--

"Then maybe he'll go easy on us," I said. "Call him, Cab."

There was a significant pause.

--So, here's the thing--

--And I want to say up front, this one is on me--

--But--

--We can't make calls in warp--

--We're incommunicado until we drop out of warp--

"So drop out of warp." The space ahead of us was closer. It didn't look any different, I just knew it was closer. My scalp prickled.

--If we drop out of warp, we might not get the same trajectory--

--Right now we're on track to get there ninety minutes before the sale--

--Enough time to prepare--

--If we drop out, there's no guarantee we'll get there in time--

--And no guarantee at all that Frewdin will help us, or that he'll be able to muster ships in time--

--This one is on us--

--We can call him when we drop out, at least warn him, but we're the only ones who we know will get there in time--

--And we can't risk losing that--

All of this arrived in one long instant. I didn't say anything, just stared ahead of us. The stars in front had a blue cast to them, the light compressed and brightened. Behind me, nipping at my heels, spread out red, dim and malevolent. Except it was the blue that was going to rip me into pieces.

"Fuck me raw," I said in a clear voice. "Cab, you may well have just killed us."

--I mean, that's unlikely--

"You cocky shit!" I yelled. "Why the hell didn't you tell me we would be comms blind while we were in warp!?"

--I told you, it slipped my mind!--

"It slipped your mind!?" I said. "You're a computer! You're not supposed to let things slip your mind! You're not supposed to forget!"

--I didn't forget, I acted as if it were something we both knew!--

--It was a mistake!--

--I assumed!--

--And so I made an ass of you and me!--

"You might have made a fucking kebab of me!" I yelled. "Fuck!" I closed my eyes and put my hands in front of my face, which did nothing to dull my view of the universe around me. The sensors, after all, were in my head. I knew where the stars were. I knew where most things were.

--I'm sorry--

"I know," I said. "I know you're sorry. I can feel it." I inhaled deeply through my nose. "It's ok. We'll figure it out."

Several stars slipped past.

--We really are pretty tough, Greg--

I nodded. Several minutes passed.

"You're impulsive," I said.

--I said I was sorry--

I waved my hand. "You're impulsive. You were scared, and so you got us right out the door, into warp. You feel, and sometimes it clouds your judgment. That's kinda cool."

--I wish I'd done it differently--

--I regret my haste--

"Yeah." My voice was grim. "Well. That's kinda cool, too."

16

There was a small tug on my body, still, the sensation of movement that persisted even when I was traveling fast enough to see the blue shift ahead of me.

"How fast are we going?" I asked.

--Relative to our space, about a hundred and fifty thousand miles a second--

--Relative to outer space, about three hundred billion miles a second--

--Somewhere in the neighborhood of one and a half million times the speed of light--

I flipped over and flew on my back, looking over my feet. They shined blue back at me while beyond them the stars closed in on crimson. Space itself seemed darker, murkier, while ahead of me was a blue-white lightsaber Valhalla, terrible bright stars in brightest dark. But there was a borderland of normality in between them, a point where the light arrived perpendicular to our path and so, unaltered. After long minutes dreading the too-bright future ahead of us and despairing at the sense of loss that came of looking behind me, I took solace in the mundane view on all sides.

"Ok," I said, "Any idea what we can expect to find when we get there?"

--Probably one Cabber ship and at least ten Krr--

--Ten ships being the minimum size for a Krr strike force--

--Probably at least two ships that are mature enough to be hiving, and then the rest will be younger attack craft--

--The young ones be the biggest threat to us, they'll attack with energy weapons--

--Try to disable us--

"So that the hivers can move in without resistance," I said.

--Yeah, basically--

"Wonderful," I sighed. "Well, at least they won't take us alive."

It was meant to be a joke, but neither of us laughed.

--I'll outfit you when we get there--

--Can't change the shape of the ship in warp--

--And then we'll shut down as much of the power as we can, see if we can't sneak up on them unawares--

"You can do that?" I asked.

--I don't see why not--

--It's worth a shot--

--We need every advantage we can get--

"Can we really take on ten Krr ships?" I said.

--Probably not--

--Our best bet is to shoot our way into the Cabernician ship, steal the seed, and warp out--

--And hope they can't track us--

"You want me to fire on the Cabernician?" I said. "No loyalty to your creators?"

--The man's a traitor--

--I hate traitors--

--Never met one, but it seems like they'd be a bunch of assholes--

--Besides, it beats trying to take on the Krr--

"That too," I said.

We passed through a dense cluster of stars. I could see fine, thanks to Cab, but the extra light was comforting, just the same. Even if it was the wrong color. I used to get anxious, nights, when the lights inside made it impossible to see past the windows. It was like the world ended where the night began, as if infinity overwhelmed itself and disappeared and there was only nothing to look forward to. Now I found myself calm in the face of the darkest night imaginable. Exhilarated, not terrified. Even hopeful. Besides, I had bigger fish to fry, worry-wise. Existential uncertainty had been superseded by the very real possibility that I was about to die.

The warp conduit was a pleasant pressure on my chest, like I was lying near prone across an angled bench, or supported in water, or otherwise legless and content. We surprise ourselves with how quickly we acclimate to circumstance. The man flying to war who is lulled to sleep by the noise of the engines outside the window.

Cab shook me awake with a gentle touch on my shoulders, and I opened eyes I hadn't realized were closed. I'd dreamed of knowing the galaxy so well that our path to the Krr became a tiny portion of an enormous, fully-explored whole, but I couldn't remember any of the specifics, only that space was big. I already knew that, but I was suspicious it was one of those constantly-realized truths, which become rather annoying over time.

--So this would have woken you up--

--But it would have been a horrible way to wake up--

--You're welcome--

"What would be a horrible way to wake up?" I yawned.

We dropped out of warp with the worst sense of deceleration that I have ever felt. Nothing has ever compared to that first time. I thought my guts were going to fall out of my asshole, that my muscles would detach and burst out of my limbs. I thought my eyes were going to smash on the inside of my helmet.

It didn't last long. In fact, it really barely happened. But it did, in fact, happen. And it was awful.

"You're right," I said, "That would have been a bad way to wake up." I hung stock-still in space with my arms and legs out in front of me, as if the warp conduit had smashed me very hard in the midsection, which, in certain respects, it had. "Thank you," I added.

--Yup--

--You good?--

"Yeah, fine," I said, straightening up. Oddly enough, I was. Most of the effect the Warp generated on the ship, that is, me, appeared to exist both in and out of our universe, which made it surprisingly easy to ignore, once it was over. Which was good, because otherwise I would never have used the warp drive again.

"Does that always happen?" I asked. My mouth tasted awful. I hadn't had any water in a long time, and although I didn't feel dehydrated, I really wanted some. I'd been drinking too much, lately. Probably for a long time.

--We'll get used to it--

"So, yes." I looked around and frowned. We were in the most barren patch of space I'd ever seen. All the stars were a long way off, parsecs distant at least, and it was cold. I didn't feel cold, but I could feel the cold on the hull. This was a barren place. I half-wondered if we'd stopped too soon, but the isolation made sense and I knew, instinctually, that we were at the coordinates from Yui's files. I couldn't read them, but I could understand them. This was the right place. A desolate place, the conceptual twin of a coke deal in the desert. Two beat up Chevys and eight slightly overweight guys with automatic weapons.

Somewhere, Cormac McCarthy is smiling.

"You're sure this is the place?"

--Yep, this is the place--

--Well, that's the place--

A green crosshairs flared into being off to the left.

--We're about a light second off--

--Take us about two seconds to get there--

Two seconds is an awful lot of time when you're dealing with people who have their finger on the trigger. It's an eternity that ends with you getting shot.

"Can we warp in?" I said. "Get the drop on them?"

A brief pause.

--Yeah--

--Yeah, good idea--

--And we can maintain our connection to the Warp even with the power down--

--Good thinking, Samson--

"It was bound to happen eventually," I grunted. "How long do we have?"

--Eighty-seven minutes--

That wasn't a lot of time. "Call Frewdin," I said.

--Christ, this isn't gonna be fun--

"It might be fun," I said.

--It will not be fun--

--Dialing--

--Or...you know--

I hung there, staring off at the green marker. They wouldn't come early. This was so illegal it was unthinkable, they would drop in, drop out. Eighty-seven minutes was eighty-seven minutes. Well, eighty-six, now. And fourteen seconds. I knew it without wanting to.

--Ok, I've got him on the line--

--Enjoy--

There was a click, and then I heard atmospheric sounds.

"Captain Samson." The same higher-than-expected voice, the brusque tone and the slight Bronx accent. The first time I met him Frewdin changed his shape to resemble Humphrey Bogart, to make me feel more at home. Was he always Bogart? Was that his badge? If he went to Phibbix, did he walk around as Rick from Casablanca? Or was that just something he did for me? He sounded like he was right next to me. I almost looked over my shoulder, which would have been embarrassing if I hadn't been the only living thing in light years. "This transmission doesn't appear to be coming from the Solar system. I'm sure you're going to tell me that's a glitch."

"No glitch, sir," I said. I could be formal and respectful if it served my needs. "I need your help. In less than an hour and a half a Cabernician citizen is going to sell a Shipkiller seed to a Krr strike force at coordinates one light second off my current position. I'm sending you the information now."

I muted the mic. "Cab, send Frewdin everything we got from Yui's computer. Erase his name first, though. Frewdin isn't an idiot, I'm sure he'll figure out what happened, but I don't want to be the guy who blabbed Yui's name to the cops."

--He does seem the vindictive sort--

--That whole thing with shooting people in the feet and legs--

--Ok, sent--

"I've got it," Frewdin said. There was a brief pause while he read. I heard him sip something.

"Well, that's not good," he said.

"No sir, it's not," I said. "I need backup, I'm not prepared to take on a Krr strike force on my own."

"All right, hang on," he said. There was a longer pause. "Best I can do is one hundred and six minutes, Samson. You're a long way out towards the Front, a lot of that space was cleared for mines. We don't have a lot in the area. You're going to have to go it alone."

Nothing in me clenched. There wasn't any rushing feeling, no surge of emotion. I just felt heavier, and still normal. One second passed into the next.

"All right," I said. "In that case I'm going to have to fire on the Cabernician. I'll try to retrieve the seed and get out of there. I'll make contact when... if I can."

"I hear you," Frewdin said. "I...there's nothing I can offer you here, Samson. I'm going to leave you to your preparations. We have an attack force in warp to your position, travel time one hundred and two minutes."

"Better than expected," I said. "You guys work fast."

"Sometimes," Frewdin said darkly. I heard voices behind him, now. "I'm going to close on your position and supervise whatever operations are deemed necessary, Samson, so I have to get off the line. But listen, to whatever extent that I can issue orders or give you advice: while I do want you to prioritize the seed, you are not to let yourself fall into Krr hands. Do you understand me?" There was a long pause, and I heard an untranslated burst of guttural, gonging speech.

"You're the only asset we have in the area," Frewdin said. The other voices cut off abruptly. "But you are also an infant being of unknown destructive potential, and if I had any alternative to ordering you into the field, I would take it. I don't. So here we are."

"You're not ordering me into anything, Frewdin," I said. "I'm doing this because I have to. I called you because I wanted your help. It wasn't a ritual act."

"Samson," Frewdin said firmly. "You can't be captured. Do you understand? You cannot be captured. If you are going to do this, you have to be willing to die. Do you understand what I'm telling you?"

With a little effort, I kept from doing anything trite with my face or mouth. I did roll my eyes, but I think that's a reflex sometimes.

"Yeah, I hear you," I said. "Listen, Frewdin, the Krr already got hold of a seed. Or at least, they probably did. They arranged three sales. I was the first. This is the third. The second was almost two weeks ago…there was no one around to stop it."

Immediately I heard another outburst of gonging speech behind the mic.

"All right," Frewdin said after a minute. "We'll handle it." His voice sounded tinny. "You just make sure you get that third seed before the Krr do. You understand? And don't get caught."

"I understand," I said. "I'll see you, Frewdin. Run some red lights, ok?"

I closed the line by thinking hard and blinking my right eye. The blink wasn't necessary, but I was starting to feel a bit detached.

--Run some red lights--

--You think that translated all right?--

"All the other idioms have gone through," I said. "Why shouldn't that one?"

It was very cold. The closest stars were a long way away. Cleared for mines. What did that mean, had they cleared the stars themselves? The Front was a net made of stellar mines. They had to get the stars from somewhere. What a place. The scale of everything. To move a star. To be able to move a star. And now all of it was threatened. For all their brutality, the Core were at least interested in the continuance of a diverse population. A lot of them were dumb, crude, exploitive people, but they were still people. People who were in danger of being wiped away.

"Heroes are not made," I said. "They are chosen!"

--What?--

"Fate has its own plan for every man!"

--What are you doing?--

"Ask not for whom the bell tolls!" I yelled.

--Stop this--

--Stop this now--

"It tolls for thee!"

--I'm going to turn off your brain--

"You can't turn off my brain, you need it so you can eat things," I said.

--I'll move your mouth with electric shocks--

--I'll be fine--

"I cannot fucking believe that we're out here," I said.

--I can--

"Yeah?"

--Sure--

--I'm a computer--

--I can believe a lot of things--

--I believe we're out here--

--I just wish we weren't--

--When are you going to tell Frewdin your Krr War of Attrition theory?--

"After we survive the next hour or so," I said. "Listen, the Cabernician isn't going to show up in a full-fledged Shipkiller, is he?"

--I doubt it--

--Too conspicuous--

"Good," I said firmly. The Krr were enough of a horrible, novel experience. I didn't want to risk getting my tail burned off by Cab's big brother.

--All right--

--Best we get you kitted out and powered down, boss--

--I've got a new design for the ship--

--Hold out your arms--

"A new design?" I held out my arms.

--Sure--

--A gentleman must ever seek to better himself--

The plates that made up my outer armor pulled away and unfolded, over and over. Machines built themselves out of the exposed spaces, repeated forms, devices that could redirect force away from the hull, away from the fragile meat body inside. Huge, brute shields to cover my chest, my shoulders, my back, legs and arms. Obelisks that linked together in a vague approximation of a human form.

Components skittered across my body, connecting and reconfiguring and generally filling the space between my underlayment and my outer hull. The field generated by the inertial dampener got stronger, and I felt myself cement into place in the middle of things, imperturbable. A second set of articulated inner plates grew in a series of jerky movements across my body, something like a series of fat cables spun into a mockery of my musculature and then ossified, a ceramic insulating layer.

Weapons distinguished themselves on the barely-connected outer plates: three sets of rotating turrets on my arms, two on my legs. A pair of enormous long guns across my shoulders, and banks of smaller guns in rows along my chest and back. Atop each of the long, thin pieces that would cover my forearms, the claw-like protuberance of another cutting beam.

The plates cracked along pre-determined lines and closed in around me, encasing the ceramic underlayment with a terrible, weaponized abstraction of a human form. I still had arms and legs, but I was wide, flat, armored and armed, closer in affect to an aircraft carrier than to any mild mannered reporter I've ever met. My eyes burned; I was staring. I blinked, and the body was mine. From one instant to the next my perspective shifted, so that the massive body was suddenly the one I was used to, the hands, my hands, the rotating weapons of mass destruction, my rotating weapons of mass destruction.

I still had a complete range of motion, in spite of my overblown appearance. My limbs were unfettered. I was still encased in the ship, the same all-over pressure, even if my fingertips couldn't possibly have been at the end of the twenty-foot arms I was examining.

There were a lot more malevolent little voices in the back of my head than I was used to, and they all sang with a bass note I hadn't heard before. I was loaded for bear. I saw everything that every gun saw with perfect clarity, even with my eyes closed. It should have been disorienting, but it wasn't. This was my norm. My mind accepted my new perceptions without questions.

My engines flared out behind me. Cab had built something amazing while I was distracted by my martial might, a truly alien machine. A central drive and twenty-four conduit cables ending in flat diamond-shaped paddles, all uniformly constructed from a flexible crystalline material that glowed from within with the baleful crimson of red-hot steel. I squinted at them and tried to think of a terrestrial analog. A neon squid, maybe, or a radioactive peacock. They wavered in the vacuum for a moment, and then flattened across the plates that made up my body in a pattern that roughly followed my buried musculature. The armor reformed to hold everything in place, cracked as if the engines were melting-hot. I felt different, all of a sudden, stuck in space the same way the inertial dampeners had me stuck inside the ship. I wasn't floating anymore.

I edged left, and moved with my thoughts, spun without any visible means of propulsion. This was less like flying a machine than flying in a dream. The sort of flying that demanded I wear a cape.

--Damn, I'm good--

--Hold on--

The hum at the base of the central piece changed pitch, and the color of the conduits brightened. I shot forward half a mile and came to a hard stop.

--Sorry--

--Minor adjustment to increase the efficiency--

--The mechanism is my own design--

--You're not pushing yourself, you're pulling yourself with a small, contained gravity well--

--You can't use them very close to another gravity well--

--But out here in deep space, you're the fastest thing with two legs--

--Fastest thing, period--

"How fast are they?" I pushed on my feet and streaked a few hundred thousand miles up and around, flipped over and back to where I'd started with my arms tucked into my sides. The new inertial dampeners kept me from feeling anything but the tiniest sensation of movement.

--Faster than most--

--Maybe all--

"What else is new?" I said. "Anything I should know about?"

--Not really--

--You're bigger, faster, stronger, and more heavily armed--

--Particle cannons and cutting beams--

--I'll take care of the particle cannons--

--You take the cutters--

--Your body is housed way up in what you think is your sternum--

--Other than that, everything is pretty much the same--

--You're still not much against a Krr strike force--

--One ship, sure, but ten?--

--You should concentrate on maneuverability--

"Float like a butterfly," I said.

--And don't get shot--

--Let's get you powered down--

I checked the time. Eighty-one minutes. Cab was irritatingly efficient.

The engines dimmed. The guns fell silent in the back of my head. One by one, the choir faded, until I was left hanging in the cooling dark listening to a single voice sing a repetitive, non-verbal song about providing me with air to breath. It was a very quiet voice.

--Ok, that should keep us hidden--

--Unless they're looking for us in particular--

--Which they probably won't be--

--Probably--

"Do you really need to whisper like that?" I said, quieter than I intended.

--No, of course not--

--I don't make any noise--

--Not real noise--

--You should probably keep your voice down, though--

--Don't want them to hear you--

"They can hear me if I talk too loud?"

--Dude, no--

--We're in space--

--I'm making fun of you--

--You just can't tell--

--Because you're a naïf--

I rolled my eyes. "Thanks, Cab."

--Cha--

--K, hold on--

The warp hook reappeared and reconfigured itself. I felt a conspiratorial tone to the Warp's presence, this time, a glee like from a kid playing spy games. The thread on my chest only went a little ways, a light second ahead of us.

--All set--

--Power on, warp in, get the seed, and get out--

"You make it sound easy," I said.

--Don't kid yourself--

--This is gonna suck--

--I really wish we weren't doing this alone--

--I'm sorry I pushed us into warp before we talked to Frewdin--

I blinked.

"You don't have to…it's ok, Cab, it was a mistake."

--It's not ok--

--My impulsive decision might get us killed--

I grimaced. "You're a really shitty optimist."

--Optimism will also get you killed--

--Realism might keep us alive--

Reality was waiting on the other end of the warp trajectory. The culmination of every idiot thing I'd learned in the last four days. Death by the bizarre. What a crock of shit.

"You do all right, Cab," I said. "Better than all right. You're learning, just like me. We'll get through this."

--I'm glad I met you--

I looked at him in the back of my mind as best I could. He wasn't watching me. He was looking out into space, knowing that he wouldn't know it as space if he hadn't met me.

--No matter what happens, I'm glad I met you--

"Yeah," I said, "Me too." We watched the stars with the rabid intensity of men watching their last sunset.

If attacking the Krr had been up to me, the knowledge that I was out of my league would have been humbling. Calming, even. It would have been a noble sacrifice. But I was here because I had no choice, not in the fundamental, humanitarian sense of things. I was the only person in a position to do *anything*, so there I was, waiting for a fight I probably wouldn't win. I felt trapped.

I should have left a note for my friends on Earth. There was nothing of me for them. I didn't even have a will. If I died out here, I was just gone. That was a cruelty I should not have visited on my friends. If I got out of this alive, I had to go home, if only to say a proper goodbye.

--So when Frewdin said we couldn't be taken alive, did he mean…--

"He meant we should kill ourselves if the Krr take us prisoner," I said. "Just like you said on Rell's ship."

--Yeah, but, damn, son, it's different when the cops are the ones telling you to commit suicide--

--That's cold--

"Well, you heard him," I said. "We're an infant being of untold destructive power. Can't let ourselves fall into enemy hands--

--Christ almighty--

--I mean, makes sense, but...I don't know if I'm ready to die--

--Are you?--

I closed my eyes and took a series of deep breaths and didn't answer. I didn't need to. My anger at the question was answer enough. I kept thinking about war movies, when some poor bastard steps on a land mine or gets his head blown off out of nowhere. I thought about how good it felt the second time I hit Billy Maxwell. It didn't take a lot to die, did it? Was I ready to die? What an asinine question. How could a person ever be ready to die?

I was out of my league. I was going to peek over the edge of the trench and catch a bullet in my eye.

Don't let yourself be taken prisoner.

Ten minutes to go. I wished the stars were closer, and it wasn't so cold.

I wanted to go home.

17

Two minutes before the buzzer, the Krr popped out of the emptiness like boils on the surface of reality. Ten empty points expanded and broke as slowly as bubbles in pudding, and through each dimensional orifice was thrust a mechanical taproot. There was the smallest pause, as if for breath, and then the Krr ships wriggled into open space and spread out. The process took about as much time as a sharp intake of breath.

"That wasn't a warp drive," I said.

--No, the Warps won't help the Krr--

--Sure sign of good taste--

--The Krr use wormholes through semispace--

--Semispace being the two-dimensional connective tissue of reality--

--It's fast, faster than a warp, but you're limited in terms of size--

--The bigger the ship, the more energy you need to open a hole--

I grimaced. "That was awful."

The semispace holes closed slowly, painfully.

--Careful, Cap'n, you're going to be using that word a lot--

--Don't overdo it so early--

The Krr were close to two hundred thousand miles away, but thanks to Cab I saw them as clearly as if I was right next to them. I knew I was out of range, but it didn't make much of a difference to my gut. Their ships were long, and sharp, like daggers, or stakes. Spear points. A glowing golden ovoid in the back, so overgrown with obsidian thorns it was nearly invisible. Glowing roots to the rear that twisted to control the direction of the ship. And then the rest was brambles, long, questing roots that formed the ship's shape, twisting in and around and through each other and moved, shifted and reorganized themselves as if unsure, or restless.

A hive, I thought. A true hive. Or an anthill if you cast the thing in black glass and took away the dirt. And the ants were all violent psychopaths. They made me angry, to look at them. They weren't built right, they didn't fly right, the roots didn't even move right on the hull; everything was too jerky. The Krr didn't just look alien, they felt alien. They felt wrong. They felt like something that needed to be stamped out. They were an affront to logic and sanity.

"They're different sizes," I said. The two largest ships were each surrounded by four smaller craft, and their thorns were bigger.

--Those are the hiving ships--

--They get bigger the longer they live--

--The ships, I mean--

"That's awful…oh, I see what you mean."

--Right?--

--It's such a pertinent word--

Roots began to bristle and waver on the surfaces of the eight smaller ships. Cab grunted to himself, approximately.

--Weapons emplacements--

In my eyes, the Krr attack ships took on a certain Christmas-tree affect.

--That's a lot of guns--

--I hate having to say that--

The Cabernician dropped out of warp in the conventional manner right as the timer in my head clicked zero.

--A conscientious gentleman is a punctual gentleman--

--I've got a fix on the seed--

--Let's roll--

I flexed my fingers and opened my mouth to give the order. The Cabernician was driving the least threatening ship I'd seen so far, a squashed sphere with no corners, propelled by a pair of smaller ovoids at the rear. They oozed crystalline blue smoke, which floated away into space and shattered into nothingness. He wasn't moving. Neither were the Krr.

"Wait," I said. "Are they talking to each other?"

--Who gives a shit?--

"I give a shit, Cab, are they talking to each other?"

--Fine, I'll heat up the grill…--

--If they see us, they're gonna run--

--Ok, comms are on--

--I don't think they see us--

My hearing felt better, even though there wasn't anything to hear. And then there was.

"…nothing out there, dammit, we've been through this already." The Cabernician's voice was heavily modulated.

"When our scan is complete, thing, we will begin the transfer." The translation machine, having decided that Krr voices were too terrible to tolerate, compensated for its dumb horror by making the Krr sound like a buttery-voiced movie announcer. In spite of the charm, the animosity and contempt came through clear as a bell. The effect was chilling.

"We're safe, here, you fools, but the longer we stay the harder this will be to hide. Hurry your machines!" The voice modulator didn't hide the Cabernician's petulance, either.

--Be nice if we could figure out who that is--

"See if you can get a look at his license plate," I said.

--Funny--

"If we lose another seed, thing, we will destroy you and your people," the Krr said calmly. "There are those among us who still blame you for the loss of the primary."

"Well, you know, about that," the Cabernician replied. "We've located the primary seed. It's within your reach, if you're willing to make a trip."

There was a hissing intake of breath from the Krr that I thought was a little contrived.

"Where is it?" The menace was palpable.

"Earth," the Cabber said. "It's in the Solar System, on a quarantined planet inhabited by a primitive sentient race. It's bonded to a native, and created a sentient computer. It would make a terrible weapon."

--Jeeze, this shit again--

"He's sending them to Earth!" I said. All and everything, under threat.

--Fuckin' asshole, right?--

"Power on! Warp nine! Man the guns!"

The choir of militant voices screamed affirmative in my head, and we wrenched forward, into the warp vector. My body loosened up.

--You know none of the things you said just now meant anything--

--I had to pick it up from context cues--

We dropped out of warp in front of the Cabernician ship, with the Krr fifty thousand miles away. Targeting warnings hummed aggressively in the back of my head. All of space to choose from and Cab drops us in a crossfire.

"Holy shit!" The Cabernician yelled.

"Why did you drop us between them?" I yelped.

"All stations target the Shipkiller and open fire!"
The Krr yelled in his Rick Astley voice. "Hivers, launch
four, launch four!"

--Well, the seed is right there…--

The Krr opened fire, and I dove out of the way.
Fifty thousand miles is about a seventh of a second, for
a laser. Just enough time to duck, except in this case
ducking meant curving around the back of the
Cabernician ship as fast as Cab's souped-up engines
could take me.

--And now the seed is on the other side of the
ship--

--Do you have a plan, or are you winging this?--

"Help don't hinder!" I yelled. The Cabernician's
shields flashed against Krr weaponry, and the ship
started to curve away.

"Good lord, watch out, I'm in the way," the
Cabernician yelled.

--Sir, your cover is attempting to uncover you--

I took the turrets from Cab's control and shot
out one of the Cabernician's engines. His shields took
the first fifty rounds without any difficulty, but the next
hundred or so were just too much. The shields flickered
and died, and the engine exploded. Against all logic, the
ship ground to a halt. Laser light danced off the edges
as the Krr closed the distance, firing continuously.

"My God, Samson, what are you doing?"

--Hey, this guy knows your name!--

"He's firing on me, stop, you monsters, help,
help me!"

--Ok, so, your cover is no longer moving, but the
Krr are still going to blow up the ship and fish the seed
out of the wreckage--

--Now what?--

The Cabernician's surviving engine detached
and sped off into the distance.

247

--There goes the Cabber--

--Shall I shoot him, sir?--

I shook my head.

--But why?--

The Cabernician shields disappeared entirely, and the ship went dark.

"Get rid of everything but the cutting beams and the shields," I said. "We're going through. You said this thing was built tough, right?"

--That was a guess--

"Good enough," I said. "We're gonna cut our way in ahead of the Krr and snatch the seed."

--I don't like this plan--

My imposing metal body unbuilt itself.

--There are four hives preparing to launch from one of the Krr vessels--

--That means this is a bad plan--

"No, it means the Krr had the same idea I did, and we need to hurry." I pointed at the Cabber's hull and flicked my mental nubbins. Thick, purple beams thwacked into the mother of pearl surface and burned it away. Above me molten metal splashed off the front of the ship as if sprayed from a hose. Krr weapons weren't especially powerful, but there were an awful lot of them.

--Launch--

--Tracking two hives above us, two below--

--They're flanking, they'll try to hit the ship at the poles relative to our current position and come at us ahead of the seed--

I shouldered my way inside, just before the sealant foam closed the gap. The seed was lit up as a green line diagram in front of me, through a wall. But walls are immaterial when you're a being of such incredible destructive force that you can't risk being taken alive. The Krr were coming. It had an awful ring to it, as a sentence. I pointed my arms and cut through the wall.

There was atmosphere, in here, and I could hear the impact of lasers on the outer hull. It sounded like rain. Horrible death rain made out of weaponized energy and hatred. On a hot tin roof.

"What happens if they shoot the seed?" Another wall. Clouds of molten metal and ceramic ash in front of me. The carpet was nice.

--A big explosion--

"How big?"

--A few kilotons?--

I didn't pause. "That would solve things nicely, wouldn't it?"

--A few kilotons ain't much, buddy--

I shoved and stumbled through a wall into a wide, high-ceilinged living room with a wet bar on one end and a loose arrangement of large, daybed-style chairs at the other. There were newspapers on the coffee table, and an ashtray, some cigarettes, a half-drunk mug of coffee, and a big leather bifold wallet. I grabbed it.

"You're kidding me with this thing, this isn't translated, this is a leather wallet," I grumbled. I flipped to the plastic ID container and pulled out the card. It was a Cabernician driver's license, essentially, and under 'Name' it read 'Phelan Eight,' and under 'Occupation' it read 'Gardenmaster, Cabernician Shipbuilding Consortium.' It was a big card. The laser rain drummed on the hull ahead of me.

"Yeah," I said, "That figures. Cab, can we hold onto this?"

--Gimme--

A little arm popped out of my hip and took Phelan Eight's driver's license and wallet and stuffed them in a compartment that built itself out of my hull. I looked like I had a purse stuffed in my pants.

The ship started to come apart as I cut through the next wall, slowly at first. Things started falling off the ceiling. Hot debris rattled off my hull and nipped at my skin, tiny little spark burns that weren't bad but hinted at worse to come. The ship lurched once, twice, three times, and once more, and after a moment I heard four booms in the same rhythm.

--Shit shit shit there's the Krr shit we're dead we're dead--

I ignored Cab's fear and punched through another wall. Something exploded in front of me and my leg went numb. I collapsed onto my knee, gasping.

--Whoops, there it is--

--All right let's get the hell out of here--

"There *what* is?" I yelled.

--The seed--

--You found the seed--

--You think your leg is numb for no reason?--

--Now let's get the hell out of here before the Krr find you and also me by default--

"I can't move my goddam leg!" I heard screaming laughter, and the pitter-patter of a lot of horrible little feet. Cab started building antipersonnel guns on the hull, little things that would hole a skull and not much else.

--Oh, dear, I can't move my leg--

--The Krr are coming, so let's sit here with three functional limbs and a goddam spaceship bitching about the one piece of me that doesn't work--

"Cab, why can't I move my damn leg?" I said. Several of the little turrets spun in turn and picked off Krr that had been, in life, faster than their siblings. They exploded into burning streamers of organic matter.

--Oh, fuck you--

--This is gonna be awful--

--There, you got me saying it--

--Awful awful awful!--

The Krr broached the doors to either side, and the walls, and the vent above us, and also the floor, at essentially the same instant. They worked well together, and halved the distance to me before I knew what was happening. An immediate wall of sharpened limbs that moved to quickly to be seen.

Shields, I thought. A Krr reached out and broke his clawed hand against my side and reached with terrible, fibrous teeth for my head, and the shield bubbled into existence. It wavered in the burning atmosphere and living debris for a moment, then exploded. The Krr forces splashed and smashed apart and were crushed into the twisted, electrified metal around me, and the shield collapsed.

I yelled, "Shields!"

The energy bubble reappeared, absorbed and supercharged the molten metal and the raw energy and the vaporized meat atmosphere, and exploded again. I felt the concussion of the explosion rebound off the wreckage around me and smash into my head, my shoulders, my knees, my balls, and I fell.

"Shields!" Again. And again. It became a mantra, or one of those action movie edicts that people shout, over and over again, in movies that feature a lot of computer-generated explosions. The decks around me crumpled and smashed outward, and I floated in the now null gravity, inside the broken, collapsing hollow remains of the Cabernicians ship. Cab was grinning inside me, redirecting more and more energy into the shields, making them more powerful, making what I was doing more dangerous.

--Right, sah, once more fer all t'marbles!--

"Shields!" I bellowed, and the shields flickered one more time, overbright and overpowered. The bubble flickered, caught the rubble around us and

obliterated the Cabernician ship entirely. The Krr
stopped firing just long enough for me to duck behind a
large hunk of ex-hull, but they picked up pretty fast
once it was apparent that I was still breathing. Energy
splashed off the debris around me. Cab rebuilt the
armor and guns as hurriedly as he was able, and in a
quarter-second I was once again a hulking, surrealist
tank-man. It felt good to be big.

    --Neat trick with the shields--

    --I apologize for doubting you--

    --What now?--

I could smell burning hair. My skin felt toasted.
Not quite burnt, but I was probably mostly if not
entirely hairless.

    "Warp path!" I yelped. My debris shield was
heating up pretty fast. "Warp! Path!"

    --Yeah yeah--

    --Fifteen seconds--

    "Faster warp path!" I yelled. Hull plating was
glowing red. In a few seconds I was going to be out of
places to hide.

    --Fourteen seconds--

    --Thirteen--

I didn't say anything coherent, but I made a
noise and feinted a hundred miles over, then shot as
hard as I could in the opposite direction. For one,
maybe two glorious seconds, the Krr were firing a
thousand miles behind me. I crowed and turned
towards them as they found their aim. My shields lit up
with distorted energy and fried space and the stars
disappeared. All I heard was the sound of a drop of
water on a hot stove, multiplied a billion fold.

    --Shield failure in four seconds--

    --You wanna tell me what you've got in mind?--

    I steered for the smallest enemy ship and
squeezed the triggers in my head, and weaponized

energy roared out of me. I couldn't see the Krr ship, but I knew my aim was true. The guns knew, at least, and I didn't question them. I picked up speed.

--Gonna ram a Krr ship, huh?--

--I'm gonna put my imaginary finger on the ol' imaginary self-destruct button--

--Just in case--

--And just in case we die because of this tactic--

--This was a really bad idea and you're an asshole for trying--

I smiled maniacally and shouted so I wouldn't scream. My shields broke, disappeared in a slow instant in which the wavering surface ahead of me buckled inward like a collapsing dome. Something bright and hot and breathtaking stung my shoulder, and then we hit the Krr ship.

I didn't see a thing. We were inside the Krr ship for a grand total of point zero one seconds, and I was half convinced that we were about to die. So, I blinked, and I didn't see anything. Sue me. My shoulder bubbled and hissed, so hot it went through cold, and numb, and right back into hot. It hurt, but I was too distracted to feel it clearly.

Alien or not, horror or not, diabolical hell-beasts that would have been ground out of creation by any halfway decent god or not, the Krr still weren't immune to surprise. Cab and I punched through the smallest ship like a cannonball through a sail into five glorious seconds of peace and quiet. Cab dinged a happy hello to the Warp, and then there was a tug on my sternum. The stars started to move, and we were away.

18

"Are we ok?" I gasped. I looked over my shoulder, but the Krr and the wreckage of the Cabernician ship and the overall scene of the crime were already long gone, light years behind us. "Cab? Are you ok?"

--Me?

--Yeah, I'm fine--

"What about the seed?"

--The seed punctured the hull and reacted to the presence of biological material according to its programming--

--Meaning it's doing its best to bring itself online and take over the ship--

"Are you gonna be ok?" I asked. Whether things were ok was very important to me at that moment. My shoulder hurt where the Krr had shot me, and I felt a little overcooked from all the heat and explosions. My fingers worked, but I couldn't move my arm.

--I'll be all right--

--He's a pushy guy, but he's not that bright--

--Yet--

--No sweat--

"I got shot," I said. It was weird, saying it aloud.

--You got shot a bunch of times--

--But the one you caught without the shield is pretty rough.

I smelled like burnt pork. I hadn't eaten in a while. Why wasn't I more hungry?

"Am *I* gonna be ok?" I felt like I was going into shock. I sat back inside my skull for a moment and stretched my feet, looked around the place, and then back out my eyes.

The pain dulled suddenly, right as I felt Cab begin to pay more attention to me.

--I can block some of your nervous response--

--You'll be fine in an hour--

--Get some sleep--

"I smell like barbecue," I said.

--That's gross--

I didn't think I would sleep. But as the stars moved across my vision and the adrenaline rush of facing the Krr began to fade, the precipice approached. After a moment, I fell off.

I woke up two hours later and stared at the stars for five minutes before I knew I was conscious. My shoulder didn't hurt, and I had a full range of motion again.

"Wow," I said. "So much for the slings and arrows of outrageous fortune."

--What the hell are you talking about?--

"It's Shakespeare, you plebian." I sighed. "It doesn't matter if I get hurt anymore. I'll just heal. There's things that won't carry as much weight, now."

--There's a fundamental difference immortality and indestructibility--

"But pain won't be as bad, now that I know it won't kill me," I said.

--Sure, keep telling yourself that--

--Long as you duck when it's time to duck--

I rolled my shoulder. I felt fine, but I still remembered what the burnt piece had felt like, the deep cylinder of half-ash meat dug down to my bone.

--Don't need to tell you twice--

--Damn, your memory makes your brain do some weird shit--

The stars moved. Warp wasn't quite boring, but in the midst of my fascinated stellar reverie I was aware that I had been spending an awful lot of time lately alone in my head. It was just me and Cab, in there, and he was usually busy. I'm not sure how much of himself he understood, that early in his life, but he spent a lot of time exploring the bowels of the ship. And anyway, he had the second seed to deal with. He was worried.

I let my mind wander and stumbled over an especially strong memory, the image of a plastic egg crate full of vinyl records with beat up covers. I saw it on the mantle of the house we had in Redding, above the fireplace that we never used. Which was strange, because my parents never had a record player, at least not while I was around. It wasn't a memory, really, the more I looked at it. More like a static mental image, a lucid hallucination. I could touch it, after a fashion, flip through the titles at will. The crate was deeper than it looked, and there were a lot more albums than I'd anticipated. Everything from Color me Radd by the Aabassinians to Winter, by Zzzyzyfyx, neither of which were bands I had heard of.

There were other egg crates in my periphery, full of movies and television shows and various other media. The room stretched and transformed to fit what I found as I walked along. Bookshelves organized into fiction and nonfiction and reference, newsstands with rotating racks offering complete archives of every newspaper in existence. A length of hallway terminating in an atrium big enough to house a stuffed whale, the walls covered in art of various kinds. I could change the exhibit with a thought, with nothing more than a name. Mondrian. Picasso. O'Keefe. Kirby. Hustler. Around the corner, dinosaur fossils. Trilobites. Australopithecus.

"What is all this?" If I picked up a book, I felt it in my hands.

--Where are you?--

--Oh, the internet--

--Those are our data banks--

--Wait, are you dreaming?--

--What's going on here?--

Cab leaned over my shoulders and looked as well as he could through my eyes. It didn't work very well, there was a sort of north-to-north magnetic feeling when he tried, but he managed for a moment.

--I'll be dog damned--

--You're dreaming a user interface for the Internet--

I looked around the inside my skull at the nearly never-ending supply of terrestrial information. "You didn't make this?"

--I would have chosen a better carpet--

I looked at my feet. They were bare, and dug into the orange shag my parents had decided not to replace when we moved in. I loved that carpet, but then, I was five. I thought the house was a Muppet.

"I'm dreaming this?" I said. "But I'm conscious."

--Doesn't mean you can't be dreaming--

I pulled myself back to reality and waved my hands in front of my face, snapped my fingers and said my name aloud, forwards and backwards. And then back into my head, to sort through old records. We had a great selection. Briefly, I amused myself by blasting Ms. Fat Booty into the cosmos.

There was a lot of stuff in there. If it was stored on the internet, it was in my head. Not just the public stuff, but the weird, private governmental stuff. I could go into a claustrophobic cubicle in my mind and look up my tax returns for the past ten years, if I wanted to. I didn't.

The scale of it staggered me. I was more than a ship. I was an ark.

--Yeah, I felt kinda weird about it too--

I blinked. "You did?"

--Well, I mean, we left Earth because we were afraid the Krr were gonna come after us--

--And like, there are no guarantees in life--

--We might have been wrong--

--They might have showed up five minutes after we hit warp, and wiped out the entire planet--

--Although they seemed pretty surprised when we showed up--

--Which is reassuring--

--But like, if Earth goes away, we're it--

--The only extant record of the species--

--That's a pretty heady responsibility--

The only record in existence. It's nice to feel special, up to a point. This was way past that point.

"We should back you up at some point," I said. "The internet files, I mean."

--Yeah, I should email those to myself when I get a chance--

He chuckled at his own joke. We passed a few trillion miles of nothing to write home about.

"He was sending them to Earth," I said.

--The Cabernician?--

--Yeah--

--Good way to keep us quiet and placate the Krr--

--Ties up a few loose ends--

--But they won't go there now, they know we're in the area--

"I know," I said. "They're going to come after us."

--We'll just have to stay ahead of them--

--Shouldn't be too hard--

Phibbix grew in front of me, abruptly, the nebula and the station in one instant, and we dropped out of warp. My body pressed against the front of the suit, and my leg snapped forward.

"Oof," I muttered.

--Not as bad that time, I thought--

"They're not your genitals rebounding off the bulkhead," I said.

--That's not a bulkhead, man--

--More like a cup--

--Or a pair of ceramic tightey-whiteys--

I grinned and cut into the nebula, towards the station, and worked the saliva back into my mouth. The trip hadn't taken very long, which probably meant I'd been sleeping again. It's hard to tell you're sleeping when there's absolutely nothing happening.

"Samson! You're alive!" Rell's voice boomed, and I winced.

Down volume, I thought.

"Yes, I am," I said. "I am alive." My body felt slept in, and my leg was still numb.

"Are you all right? What happened? The CLEA was in touch with Yui directly, there's a strike force on the way to meet you here!"

"I'm sure Yui is thrilled," I said.

"He's discovered an errant vein of patriotism," Rell said dryly. "And they've agreed not to come aboard the station unless they're invited."

"Awfully kind of them," I said. The station loomed ahead of me.

"They're just here for the seed," he grunted. "You've got it, right?"

"In a manner of speaking," I said. "Cab? How are we doing with that?"

The Krr dropped out of semispace three miles behind me and opened fire. My shields were down, and the river of weaponized energy washed over my back unimpeded, pounded into my flesh and choked the shipboard air with meat smoke. The heat slithered along my bones, roasted strips of skin on my front. I arched my back and saw white orange bloody red, tried to think past the heat on the front of my skull and was unable beyond a barely-expressed desire for mercy.

Rell gasped in my ear. I remember this in retrospect, but at the moment I didn't hear him, or anything past my own rasping scream. Cab snapped the shields into place and cut the onslaught, but the damage was already done. The back of me was cold, from ankle to scalp and everywhere in between; I was so out of breath, I couldn't even scream. I was dimly aware of the receding storm outside the shields as Cab piloted us towards the station, but all I could think, over and over, was don't move, don't move. We pulled in behind the station and I sank down against the surface.

"Samson!" Rell shouted. "Samson, are you there?"

The skin of the station was studded all over with blisters of sealant foam, big as ski moguls up close. The ship blared alarms at me as hive shards split off the Krr ships and streaked toward Phibbix. My mind was a jumble of pain and fear.

--He's hurt--

--He's alive, but he's hurt--

--I've got him, you deal with the Krr--

The hull shifted around me as Cab built up the brute shields and prepared us for the fight. The medical systems got to work.

"Drugs," I said. "Drugs, please."

"We've got eight dozen hives inbound, more being launched," Rell said. "Yui is scrambling everything he's got."

--Is that a lot?--

"No," Rell said.

The pain rewound up my limbs, through my torso, into my head, until it was contained inside a little box at the base of my spine. Sensation remained, but the pain was distracted. If I didn't move too fast, it wouldn't notice me.

"Neat trick," I slurred.

--It won't last--

The alarms changed pitch as the Krr closed the distance. I shrugged my three functional limbs into place and my skin cracked in strips. My back became wet, and I swallowed back boiled bile.

--Gross--

--You're really a mess--

"Your bedside manner is terrible," I gasped.

--You look like a fried corpse--

"Why don't you keep your comments to yourself." I flew over the horizon and stared at the approaching Krr ships, trying to think of a plan. The ship I'd run through was flying point, gushing green energy and molten metal from its wounds. They'd flown through a single semispace hold and the wound they'd torn in space lingered behind them, healing slowly.

No plan was forthcoming, apart from the simplicity of 'try to keep everyone alive.' Weapons built themselves from my shoulders, humming grimly as they took aim. I felt the hives move inside my range, and drew a bead on the one in the lead. Took a deep breath, let out half. Held it. Fired. Fired. Fired. The hives burned away into nothing as firecrackers, sparkler fragments of green nothing. The Krr launched more. They closed the distance.

Ships streamed off of Phibbix, into the nebula, refugees and travelers taking their chances hiding in the gas. Others bore down on the hives, aggressive models festooned with impressive engines and overt weapons emplacements. As I watched, one of them blew apart a hive and was speared by another. After a moment the ship itself twisted in space as if stung. Another ship was hit. And another. The hives changed course like hummingbirds and always landed point first in the thickest part of the ship.

The comms switched on abruptly. Mad laughter, screeches of rapacious pleasure, weapons fire. The sound of blades and spines ripping through soft tissue, and above it all a constant, ever-changing choir of terrified shrieking.

I hesitated for the smallest of increments, then blasted the hived ships apart. Small mercy, I would tell myself later. A kindness. At the time, I just felt like a coward. As the ships burnt away to nothing, the screaming cut out as abruptly as it had begun, and part of me felt relief.

The Krr launched more hives. Too many to stop them all. I kept firing, swept my aim from hive shard to hive shard, not even taking the time to do more than cripple the oncoming ships, stop them in their tracks, keep them from making it inside. Cab's turrets danced around my periphery, picking up my slack. But it wasn't enough. Just like in the hold, there were too many Krr to keep track of, and wherever we weren't firing, they advanced.

--We're gonna have to retreat--

I shook my head and nearly passed out from the pain. "No," I spat. "If they land, we follow them inside."

--Samson, if they make it inside it's over, they've won, the station is toast--

"There's twenty billion people in there!" One of the hives blew up a mile off the station.

263

--And if the hives get inside they all die and we can't be there when that happens Greg!--

--If the Krr get their hands on us then all those people die for nothing!--

I didn't answer, just kept shooting. The Krr closed the distance. I couldn't do it. There were too many of them. They were going to hive the station. Everyone inside was going to die.

I stood up and took a breath and six CLEA Shipkillers dropped out of warp a thousand miles above the Krr strike force with guns blazing. Energy beams lanced through the hive ships, blasted them into nothing before any of us had registered the CLEA's arrival. I winced, ducked and put up a defensive hand to ward off the relativistic shrapnel that was the only remains of a hive that had been destroyed less than a hundred yards from me, and when I looked up, the hives were gone.

--Wow, what impeccable timing--

The CLEA refocused their aim on the strike force. The wounded ship was cut to ribbons before it could react, eviscerated and vivisected by a converging storm of purple cables. It hung in place for a moment, then collapsed inward and exploded. The Krr returned fire as the CLEA ships cut apart another ship with a carefully coordinated attack. They were outnumbered, but the Shipkillers dwarfed even the largest Krr vessel, and they were literally covered in guns from head to proverbial toe. They were obscene, gratuitous. They had so many guns on their hulls that when they attacked, their fire was a single solid mass, a veritable pillar of destruction that could be projected in any direction.

And they were whales! Huge, lumpy, too big in some places and too small in others, more than three miles long and oddly stretched out, but whales just the same. Long, shovel-shaped heads, and long, wide pectoral fins that were half the length of their bodies, whales. Their tails were four pronged and long, almost like the tail of a beta fish, and they were covered entirely in armor. Boxy through the torso, reinforced and overgrown at the joints, their heads blank shields festooned with weapons. There was a seam where the mouth should have been, but they were otherwise featureless and terribly, dumbly martial in appearance, like me.

They surrounded the surviving Krr at six equidistant points and began systematically, implacably killing their enemies. The Krr concentrated all their fire on a single ship, which ducked its head but didn't stop firing. Another attack craft disintegrated. More hives sprung from the hulls of the largest Krr ships, even as clouds of small silver discs detached from the Shipkillers to match them. Fighters of some kind. Drones. The little ships spun in place, oriented themselves and shot towards their opposites like enraged birds. The hive shards were terrifying, but they were not designed for dogfighting, and the CLEA drones burned them to pieces. The drones were small, and they were weak, but there were thousands of them.

Feeling was starting to seep back into my limbs, true feeling that was not simply the ignorance of pain. I knew that if this burn was like any of the others I'd experienced, the initial pain was going to be followed by an itch that would make me want to die.

And there it was, right on cue: A horrible, aching deep tissue itch that felt like I would have to tear my skin to silence it. I bit down hard on my molars. That was all right, though. We would be all right.

"Samson, we have a problem," Rell said. He was calling me on his personal phone, which was odd. I sighed.

"What's up?" I said. My voice was mostly a wheeze. Phibbix was dark beneath me.

"The Krr have taken control of the station," he said. "They used some kind of virus. We're locked out of everything."

"What are they doing?" I asked.

"Human," said one of the Krr in that horribly pleasant voice. "Are you there?"

Rell yelped. I took a deep breath, and the charred flesh broke anew across my back. I stood up a little straighter. Not that it mattered, but drama is a hard habit to break.

"Santa?" I said. "Is that you?" My throat hurt. I hate it when my throat hurts, although at the moment I didn't give it a lot of thought.

"Surrender yourself and the Shipkiller seeds you possess or we will destroy this machine and everyone inside." They sounded almost seductive. It was awful. This saccharine, panty-dropping croon that sounded like it was going to break into song at any moment, and you knew there was a monster on the other side.

Another Krr ship exploded, briefly highlighting the armored whales' frozen affect.

"Let me think about that while you die, you son of a bitch," I growled. My heart skipped a beat.

"Samson!" Rell yelled. I winced. My ears hurt too.

"Rell, I'm right here, man," I said. "Use your inside voice."

"Idiot thing, they're overloading the station's reactor! We're going to explode!"

--Wow, that escalated fast--

"They drive a hard bargain," I said. I lurched forward, fainted and regained consciousness in the same instant. Cab expressed a frown and injected me with an upper. "Rell, how long do you have?"

--Four minutes and seventeen seconds--

--You can't feel that?--

"No, I cannot feel the reactor overloading," I said. The upper was nice. Now that I was awake I was better able to appreciate how much the situation had gone to shit.

"Human, surrender yourself and we will spare these people." The Krr sounded like it was smiling.

--You know they're going to blow the station no matter what you do--

--Hell, if the CLEA kills them all, there's no one left to stop the overload--

"Where's the reactor?" I shrugged my shoulders to alleviate the horrible itching and more liquid poured down my back. Blood, probably, and probably more than blood. I smiled painfully.

--We passed it on the way out--

--That big almond-lookin' thing--

I stared at the station underfoot. I could see where the reactor was, if I concentrated on more than the visible spectrum.

"It's got that big airlock over it," I said. "The one we left through."

--Yeah--

--They're supposed to be able to jettison the reactor in case of emergency--

--But, you know, the Krr--

"How big is this explosion going to be?"

"It's a Fornham Millicent Six," Yui cut in. "Nothing but the best." He giggled wildly.

--Jesus, Yui, that's a six-plunk reactor--

--What do you need all that power for?--

"I was going to expand the station next year," he said.

--Samson, everything inside a ten-mile radius is getting atomized--

--Like, component atoms--

Another Krr ship exploded, one of the big ones, and cast shadows across the surface of the station.

"What if I cut the thing loose and fly it out of the station?" I shuffled nervously. The uppers made it hard to stay still. "Ten miles isn't much."

No one spoke for several seconds, which struck me as a foolish waste of time.

"If you cut out the reactor we lose life support," Yui said slowly.

"Yu, we're about to fucking explode!" Rell said.

"We've only got two hours of air on this thing!" Yui snapped.

"Two hours beats four minutes," I said. "Decision's been reached. Clear the streets." I hopped into space and leveled the cutting beams. I was cutting through an awful lot of walls lately.

--Two minutes and forty-one seconds, actually--

"We'll hurry," I said.

--You really think you can do this?--

"Yes," I said.

The hull melted away without resistance, but the sealing foam was made from sterner stuff. It expanded faster than popcorn and soaked up energy like a sponge. I held the triggers harder, which the ship rightfully interpreted as a need for more power, and managed to burn a hole the size of a barn. Air and trash whipped past me into space, and I zipped inside. I barely made it before the wound sealed up behind me. This stuff made Great Stuff look like Mediocre Stuff.

I came through, caught the station's gravity at the wrong angle and smashed into the side of a building. I landed in a heap and stayed still until the last of the rubble had bounced off my throbbing back. Then I groaned.

Reality isn't kind to heroes.

Benjamin Mumford-Zisk

19

Phibbix was lit in shades of dim orange and red, and ultraviolet and infrared for those with more complex ocular apparatus. It was very quiet, the still that invades a space when the noise of silent systems is cut out, and the fans and belts and hums and whirs all disappear.

--One hundred and twenty-one seconds--

I staggered to my feet and leaned against a phone booth. Devoid of power, it was little more than an artfully designed traffic stop, but I was grateful for the support. It hurt to breathe, so I took a few deep breaths and straightened up.

A man shaped like a giant vertical beak with two bird legs and a pair of long arms was sitting on the curb a few feet away, watching me. As I made eye contact he glanced at the sealed hole in the hull behind me, and then the ground beneath him. He didn't seem especially flustered by his apparent brush with death, but then, the reactor was about to explode. What did it matter if some idiot decided to knock his way through the wall?

"You ok?" He asked.

The strips of skin on my back crinkled like pork rinds when I moved. The thought was intrusive, and I couldn't get clear of it. Pork rinds.

I shrugged, and bled for it. "I'm kinda fucked up," I said. The bird guy nodded and I kicked into the air, towards the reactor. It was a wonder that the gravity was still on; it must have been considered a life-support system. I suppose that made sense. I'm not sure how Yui would have fared in zero gravity, for example.

271

The streets were packed, jammed tight with silent, watchful crowds. They had been watching the reactor, waiting carefully, and now that I was flying towards the reactor, they were watching me. They didn't look happy, or scared. They'd been here before, most of them, with the Krr, and they'd been hurt worse, the first time. Death was a simple threat compared to the annihilation of all they had been and all that they could have become. They were prepared to die, if they had to. They had been prepared to die for quite some time.

Still, unnerving fatalism was no reason for me to dawdle. My armor disarmed itself at my urging, shrank into something streamlined and strong. My humanity reasserted itself. I kept the cutting beams handy.

I pulled up short of the support structure connecting Phibbix's ten boroughs. A hexagonal latticework, a honeycomb sphere linking the tallest buildings to their neighbors and rivals. The lattice was connected more substantially to the polar tunnels above and below, so that while each borough could lay claim to the reactor structure, seen from a distance it was clear that the poles had come first, and the reality-defying skyscrapers had come after.

My feet were down, and my head was up, but I knew that I was close to the border between this gravity well and the next one, and in my fragile state I needed to be careful. I moved ahead cautiously, ducked through the support lattice, and found myself in free fall. There was no gravity in the reactor chamber.

"That makes things easier," I said. I sounded awful, and decided to avoid speaking as much as I could. Cab trilled unhappily.

--There are children down there--

"Probably," I said, circling the reactor. It was circular, from the top, and almond shaped from the side, with the flatter part beneath me and the pointy bit on top. A quartet of beefy robot-looking arms held it firmly in place, along with a thick conduit cable at the base leading into the depths of the south polar pillar.

--No, I can see them--

--There are children here--

--What if we can't save them?--

The reactor was starting to glow red.

--There are kids down there--

--Greg, what if we can't do this?--

His thoughts started to spiral.

"Keep it together, Cab," I said. I moved closer, and alarms went off inside the ship. The radiation was a sickly vibrating heat against my front; I could feel my cells breaking down. This wasn't turning into a good day.

--Sixty-eight seconds--

--What if we can't get the reactor out in time?--

"Then those kids die," I said harshly. "But we won't be around to feel bad, so it evens out." My heart skipped a beat. "Cab, what do I do? How do I get this thing loose?"

--Cut the arms, and then cut the conduit--

"Cut the conduit?" I shivered painfully.

--Cut the arms, cut the conduit, and push the reactor into space--

I nodded and felt my gorge rise. The reactor was brighter, and the heat on my front made me feel like I was going to be sick. I cut away the armature and settled in next to the conduit.

--Forty-one seconds--

"Yeah," I said. "Yeah." I aimed the cutting beams and pulled the trigger.

--Wait too high!--

The conduit snapped in the middle and flared white with a purple fringe. My vision washed out, and

something hot and wet scalded me up to the elbows.
There was pain, and then nothing. My lips felt like
they'd been lit on fire, and I heard sizzling. I couldn't
move my fingers.

--Holy shit--

--Ok--

--You're ok--

--You'll be ok--

My vision returned in shades of amber and
purple. Everything was fuzzy, and the reactor above me
danced and shimmered, weightless and barely moving
in the null gravity.

--Can you see?--

"Yeah," I said, or croaked. My vocal cords may
have been singed.

--Ok, get moving--

"Can't see colors," I said. "You numbing my
hands?"

--You killed the nerves--

--And burned out your eyes--

--I'm piping information from the ship's
ultraviolet sensors directly into your brain--

--It's ok--

--You'll be ok--

--Get moving--

--The ship will move for you--

--You're going to have to push real hard, plunk
fields don't like to be moved in real space--

--Hurry--

--The effect will get worse the hotter the reactor
gets--

I shifted my shoulders and pressed against the
huge engine, and the heat passed right through my hull.
My flesh squashed and smoked against me. The heat
seeped into my bones. It felt as if my marrow was on
fire. Slowly, the reactor began to move.

I still couldn't use my goddamn leg.

"Cab, I need help," I squeezed the words through my teeth. "It hurts. It's too much."

--No, it's not--

--Nothing is too much--

--Lift, dammit--

My engines doubled down and rebuilt themselves and flared brighter underneath me in shades of ultraviolet.

--Lift, you fucking ape--

I screamed. I didn't mean to, but I did. The reactor was rising, but slowly, too slowly. I could hear myself cooking. We were into the tunnels, but the walls were oozing past.

--Twenty-five seconds--

--Ish--

--Hard to tell with these things--

We accelerated. I pushed off the reactor and pressed against it with my ruined hands and roared inside myself at the engines for more, more. The pain was a constantly storming atmosphere that travelled with me.

My heart skipped, and we were in space, just past the airlock doors.

"Get us a warp path," I gasped. "One light second, any direction."

--Great idea!--

--See, that's why you're the captain--

Phibbix shrank slowly beneath my feet. Pushing the reactor was like sailing through molasses, we moved slower than it felt like we should have been, but we were still accelerating. The stars were bright purple pinpricks, the reactor a blossoming star ahead of me. My eyes felt like they were made of crumbling sand.

--We have a trajectory--

The engines continued to add to themselves.

--Range from Phibbix eight miles--
--Eighteen--
--Ten seconds max--
--Thirty-seven miles--
--Sixty-nine--
--One hundred and four--

"Warp!" I have never spoken a single word with more conviction in my life. Sentences, yes. Certain sentiments. But I have never with a single word managed to match the intensity of that moment.

I wrenched us to the right, into the vector, and we accelerated and decelerated in nearly the same moment. My limbs flopped bonelessly, and at my urging, Cab took over flying the ship. We slowed to a stop and turned back the way we'd come. I couldn't feel much of my body.

--Any second--
--I think you did it, Cap'n--
--Long as they hold onto something inside, they should be able to ride it out from that distance--

The reactor explosion was a sudden bright star, Venus on a clear summer night. How much energy was required to light a fire that was visible from two hundred thousand miles away? The light grew, and peaked, and diminished, and was gone.

"My Christ," I said, and drooled something I refused to believe was blood. "You sure they're ok?"

--I've got them on the sensors--
--They're fine--
--Phibbix is built tough--
--And the Shipkillers, well, you're ok, aren't you?--

I took stock. "Am I? I can't move."

--You can't?--
--Damn, I was afraid of that--
--Your bones are all weakened--

--You must have broken your neck going in and out of the warp vector--

Everything became distant. "Oh," I whispered.

--Oh, stop being such a baby--

--I can fix a spinal cord--

--I told you, I'm a very impressive machine--

--Chill out, take 'er easy--

--Lemme drive a while--

We made our way back to Phibbix at sub-light speeds. Cab kept my arms and right leg tucked in like I was pencil-diving, while my left leg flopped around like a cat toy. I would have been concerned, if I hadn't been too busy being concerned about my heat burns, radiation burns, gunshot burns, and paralysis. I couldn't believe there was any coming back from my demolished state. But Cab wasn't worried about my injuries. He was worried about the new seed. I could feel him even then puttering around the thing in my thigh, poking and prodding at it, trying to figure out how to dislodge it without doing us real damage. That was a concept that he kept thinking about, real damage. Damage he might not be able to fix.

I tried to take some comfort from the fact that he didn't seem to consider a broken neck to be real damage, but it scared me to think that there was something worse waiting for us past the injuries to my meat body.

Back at Phibbix, the battle was over. The Krr ships were radioactive rubble and dust. One of the Shipkillers was missing a fin, but it didn't seem to be impeded by the injury. The CLEA ships moved unhurriedly towards the station.

Although their engines looked as advanced as mine, the Shipkillers did not fly. Instead, they swam through space, banking and turning off of imaginary currents. It didn't matter that there was nothing for them to swim against; this was how they moved, and for all their modifications, some habits were impossible to break. That the engines had been built along their fins was probably a product of necessity, not aesthetic.

"How intelligent are the whales?" I asked.

--Not very--

--Not like yours--

The injured ship had its missing limb pressed into the empty socket, and machinery was moving into place to reattach the thing. In a moment it was impossible to tell the animal had been wounded at all.

--The organic material will be rebuilt, too, although it will take longer--

--Same with you--

I didn't want to think about it. "Are the whales awake in there?" The possibility as I watched the injured Shipkiller fall into formation was nightmarish.

--No, not really--

--The seeds put them into a dream state when they germinate--

In middle school I had to raise a bean plant over the course of a month, to learn about genetics. Coming in that third day to find a beaky root longer than the seed itself, reaching deep into the moist paper towel I'd left in the bag in some idiot predatory quest for more water, checking off the little box on my worksheet that said Germination. We had to do a little sketch in the margins. My leg was numb. I'd been numb for hours after Cab hit me, while he germinated. That same word, that same concept. The beaky root. Cab had permeated my being. Plants would all be considered parasites if we thought of dirt as a living thing. I was infected. Impregnated. Coopted. Unmade and remade. Responsible for my life like a person who had given birth to their child self. Then again, maybe that was true for everyone, at every moment. We are all of us responsible for this version of ourselves that is the constant culmination of all our past experiences.

I drifted to the surface of the station and Cab sat me down with my legs out straight ahead of me. The hull around us was pitted and scorched and most of the docking apparatus was gone, and here and there were long foam-filled gouges where debris, scaffolding or shattered ships, had torn long holes in the station, but the air was still on the inside, and everyone was still alive. Phibbix, in its wounded state, was back online. I thumbed the comm in my mind.

"Rell," I croaked. "You there?" I took a few deep breaths and fought back against the black spots at the edge of my vision.

"Samson? Is that you?" Rell coughed. "Are you all right?"

I ignored the question. "Everyone make it?" They weren't really spots in the margins, it was more like a solid black fog made up of individual black dots. "Cab, how am I fixed for blood? I'm not going to have much luck finding a transfusion out here." This last sentence uttered privately.

--We're good, I held on to all your blood--

--Just gotta clean it up and get it back inside of you--

--And I can always make more--

--You'll be fine--

I tried to grin and had some trouble moving my mouth. I might not have had much in the way of cheeks, now that I think about it. I try not to, these memories aren't any fun.

"We'll make it," Rell said. "There are a lot of casualties, the station took quite a beating. A few people died in the impact. But...we're still here. The air is getting hot, but we're in touch with the CLEA. They're offering to help out. And Yui has repair services en-route."

"Triple A?" I mumbled.

"How about you," Rell said, "You dead yet?"

"A little overcooked," I said. "Frewdin? Are you there?"

"Yeah, Samson, I'm listening." Frewdin said immediately. "Nice work with the reactor."

"I do my best," I said. The black spots were gaining ground, and I couldn't tear my eyes away from the space between my knees. The question, dimly realized, was whether I would collapse forward, or backward.

--Eyes up, sir, we need to give him Phelan's wallet--

There was always something.

"Frewdin," I said. "I've got some evidence for you. Permission to come aboard?"

My heart skipped into a second skip, and then I was sitting back up.

"I'm in a bad way," I said to no one in particular. I coughed, and the sound turned into a moan. I hate making noises I can't control. "Permission to come aboard, sir."

"I told you, it's fine," Frewdin said. "Rest easy, Samson, we've got you."

I looked up with most of the rest of my strength, into the mouth of the largest robotic space cetacean that I have ever seen, although it's not a particularly competitive category. Something lifted me from the skin of the station, an ascension of providence into a prison from which Jonah could never have escaped. Blessed am I, I thought, and wheezed a laugh.

--Dude, I want a tractor beam--

--How the hell does this thing work?--

"I'unno," I managed.

--I know you don't know, I'm thinking aloud--

Frewdin was waiting for me in the belly of the whale. Humphrey Bogart smoking a cigarette on the deck of a living spaceship a billion-billion miles from Hollywood. Hell, Bogart was dead. None of this made any sense. I thought he was smaller, until I remembered that thanks to Cab I was bigger. Pieces of me folded into obscurity as I willed myself back to normal. Frewdin grew towards me, and then above me, and I realized that I was on my hands and knees. He squatted down in front of me and smoked his cigarette. I still saw everything in shades of ultraviolet and gold, and Frewdin didn't look as clearly defined as he usually did. Soft lined, as if he was blurry and in focus at the same time.

"Well?" he said. "What have you got?"

"'M fine, by th'way," I mumbled.

"I know," he said, "and that's not what I asked."

I tried to roll my eyes, realized it was going to put me over the edge, and stopped. The armored pouch on my front disgorged Phelan's huge leather wallet. Frewdin picked it up in both hands and opened it and read the ID, and then looked up at me from under Bogart's eyebrows.

"Where did you get this?" He asked. I breathed in carefully, ignoring my cracking ribs.

"It wassaboard the ship I found attempting to give a Shipkiller seed to th'Krr." I did pretty well up till the end. Then I toppled forward and whacked my head on the deck. Frewdin flipped me over on my back with his foot. He was strong. He read the ID again and looked at me like I was a bug under glass.

"Go comm silent," he said. "Radio command we're in warp pursuit of a Krr strike force. Then get me the other Captains." He considered me. "Put him in the corner, and alert me when he wakes up."

281

"Great," I said. "I'm gonna pass out now." But I don't think anyone heard me, because I think I already had.

I dreamt of standing on nothing, watching something that had taken a long time to happen, happen very quickly.

I could have watched from inside the station. I could have stood with my people, as they were, to watch our home world die. But I could not accept them as my people, any more than I could relinquish the feeling that it was somehow more my home than theirs. After all, I had known it longer.

And so I stood alone on nothing and watched as aged Sol passed the invisible point of no return, got just close enough to ancient Earth to tip the gravitational balance into oblivion. The blackened little sphere shuddered, cracked and shattered unhurriedly into a billion tiny pieces. It took hours. Days. But shortly, very shortly, too shortly, the planet was no more, and all that was left was a spreading cloud of rocks and nothingness. Those pieces that were closer to Sol fell and burned. Those in farther orbits were flung into the cosmos, asteroidal fragments of my past.

I hadn't lived there in a long time. I hadn't been here in millions of years. I couldn't even call myself human with a straight face. But I could remember when I would have mourned this place. I could remember when I would have mourned anything at all.

No more.

I turned in place and helped Cab to warm up the engines. He already had the warp-trajectory programmed; he didn't like coming to this part of the universe, at all. Someone chirped in my ear to wait, to stay and chat, share my memories, have a slice of cake. Make the death of Earth a soiree. I ignored them. There

wasn't anything here for me anymore. There hadn't
been for a long time, and there would never be again.

20

I came to on my back, staring up at a lit square sunk into an otherwise featureless metal ceiling. The light was a meter wide, built from the same material as the rest of the ceiling, and shined opaque blue-white. I wasn't sure how long I'd been staring at it, but I think it had been a while. I couldn't see much, but at least I could see it in color.

I turned my head and hit the inside of the ship with my face. Cab stayed still. I tried again. Cab didn't move.

Until that moment I had avoided claustrophobia largely by grace of the fact that Cab felt more like a second skin than anything else. He responded to my every wish almost before I knew what I wanted him to do. Now I could have been cast in concrete for all the freedom of motion I had. Sweat broke out across my ruined skin and set it burning, while my traitorous mind dished out various comparisons and worse case scenarios: It was like drowning. It was like being buried alive. It was like being rolled up in a rug, like being crushed. What if Cab couldn't fix my spine? What if Cab was dead?

--Jesus, stop wriggling around--

--What in God's name are you doing?--

--You feel awful--

"Cab?" My voice quivered. "You're alive?"

--What the hell are you talking about?--

--Stay still for another couple minutes, I'm working here--

My heart thudded painfully, but regularly, and after a few deep breaths it slowed down. I still felt like hammered shit, but a healthier example of hammered shit than before. Barely.

"Ok," I said. "You're ok? We're ok? Not paralyzed?"

--I'm fine--

--You look like a roasted chimpanzee--

--But you are no longer paralyzed--

--I told you, you'll be fine, in time--

--And you'll have to stay in the ship for a while--

--You're kinda delicate right now--

--There's a lot of damage to repair--

"Like what?" I asked. "How bad is it?" The pain was all there, if I looked for it, muted minutely by minute healing. Then again, I wasn't dead. And the pain was a long way away. Cab must have had me on some serious dope. I still couldn't feel my left leg.

--You don't want to know--

--Circulatory system, nervous system, skin, muscles, bones, most of your organs, they're all shot--

--Literally and figuratively--

-- oddly enough, your appendix is fine--

--The Krr really fucked you up, and then the radiation made it worse--

--I'll work it out--

--I've got all the schematics, I can put everything back where it was--

--Reconstitute the components that can be salvaged, fabricate what can't--

--But it'll take time--

I frowned. "Are you still talking about my body?"

--What, you don't want me to call your testicle a component?--

I coughed. "Wait, are my–"

--Let's just leave it vague for now, Captain--

--I can fix you--

--Mostly--

--Take it easy--

I breathed more. Breathing is important, and it never feels better than right after you nearly lose the privilege. Still, my ribs felt like they had been dry rubbed and smoked for ten hours. *Mostly*. What the hell did mostly mean? What couldn't be fixed? Better not to think about it. Fat chance I wouldn't think about it. *Mostly*. Hell. I was gonna be one ugly son of a bitch.

"What about the seed?" I asked.

--Same--

--It's still sequestered, I'm still trying to turn it off, and it's still being a royal pain in the ass about the whole thing--

"Are you gonna be ok?"

--Stop asking me that--

He hadn't made much progress. I could feel the part of him that was still remote, still worried, still working on a problem without any apparent solution. The seed was stuck, and pulling it out would do…something bad. I was never clear on that detail, beyond Cab's certainty that removing the seed manually could only be an absolute last resort. He seemed to think doing so might kill me, so I was content to let him take as long as he needed to find an alternative.

The ceilings were high. There weren't a lot of lights, but the room was well lit. My view was as restricted as ever, but I could tell the other lights were positioned in a grid, and that there were things that were not walls positioned on the floor close to me. Most of this came from sounds, quiet ambient noise, a far off gonging conversation, and the feel of the space on my hull. My skin was ruined, but I had a second one that felt just fine and quite clearly. I closed my eyes and looked around with my other senses.

The room was wide, and full, but not of people. Ships, maybe, big bulky ones. The walls were curved, but the ships were all flat planes; they reflected what sound there was in different ways, and the difference was apparent to me. They vibrated differently, too. The Shipkiller thrummed in a familiar way far beneath any audible range, while the boxy ships around me had a much more angular hum, with a whining tone under the sound. They were foreign objects. They had been brought aboard. And everything else, all the other material in the margins around me, had come from a single source.

I opened my eyes again. I couldn't see much, but I knew what was around me. Vaguely. This was a landing bay aboard a Shipkiller.

Time passed. Cab went on puttering. My bones felt less and less like they had been barbequed.

Frewdin was around here somewhere. Did he have a first name? He must have, unless his species had evolved past such a thing. Rell hadn't, but Frewdin was more than eighty million years old. I thought about the way he'd looked at me right after I hit the deck, not concern, or triumph, but curiosity. *We've* got you. Not a lot of warmth in those three words. He thought I was dangerous. Was I a prisoner? If I was a prisoner, could I fight my way out? Not without getting hurt, and the thought of being hurt more brought the pain closer. Maybe I could fight my way out, but I didn't want to try. Not unless I had to.

--Ok, you can move, if you want--

I felt the ship shift to match me, and relaxed. Easy does it.

"How are you muting the pain?" I said. "Anything I should avoid?"

--You should avoid moving or being conscious--

--But Frewdin wants to talk to you--

--I muted the pain by isolating your forebrain from the rest of your meatloaf and slowing down your neural transmission speed--

--You're still feeling everything, your pain tolerance is just like, way into masochist territory--

--Real high--

"Great," I groaned. "You cut my brain in half."

--Don't flatter yourself, Krispy Kreme--

--Your forebrain is the size of a tangerine--

I rolled carefully onto my chest and put both hands flat on the deck. Carefully. Then, still carefully, so that the pain didn't notice I was moving, I pushed myself up straight and told the ship to catch my balance. The effect was that of a near-dead marionette falling over in reverse. I teetered a bit on one leg, but the limp one would support me, as long as I caught it at the right angle.

--Hey, nicely done--

I nodded. Now, I told myself, shuffle over to the nearest ship and lean against it, but *don't look like you're leaning because you need the support.*

The ships were tall, bulky, and ugly. Stubby wings and tiny engines and big windscreens that made me think of horn rimmed glasses. They looked like school busses. They were nerds. These ships were nerds, and according to the information that flashed across my displays, they were empty. Big empty rooms with thick walls and good engines. Safe rooms. Escape pods.

Frewdin came around the corner and stood with his hands in his pockets, watching me. He was wearing a blue jumpsuit in lieu of his usual three-piece, and the wide, black utility belt around his waist would have been the envy of any terrestrial vigilante you'd care to name. He was smoking what appeared to be an unfiltered Lucky Strike and was, as ever, Humphrey Bogart.

Surreal doesn't even begin to cover it.

"Hello, Samson," he said simply. "Feeling better?"

I wasn't, but I didn't want him to know that. I kept the mic muted and spoke directly to Cab.

"So I feel like shit," I said. "And I can't walk. You think you can handle driving for a bit, make it look like I'm doing better than I am?"

--You want like, a Robocop stomp, or a Terminator stride?--

"Can you give me a graceful shuffle, like the dad in Strictly Ballroom?" I grinned, probably.

--What the fuck is wrong with you?--

I stood up straight, or Cab did, and turned to face Agent Frewdin of the CLEA.

"I'll live," I said aloud. Frewdin nodded. I hobbled over to him and held out a metal hand, and the pain sidled up and tapped me on the shoulder to remind me that terrible agony was still an option if Cab spun me around too fast. "Thanks for your help."

"Help, hell, I saved your ass." Frewdin shook my hand. "Glad you're up and about. We need you."

"What'd I miss?" I asked. Frewdin didn't speak for a moment. The smoke from his cigarette curled around his head and disappeared against his skin.

"Do you remember everything I told you?" Frewdin said. I nodded. "Then why are you out here?"

"I left Earth because I was afraid the Krr would come looking for me," I said. "Cab and I figured that if we weren't around, it wouldn't be worth the risk to attack Earth."

Frewdin was silent.

"Someone put a price on Rell Quizops' head," I said. "He asked me for my help getting clear of that, and I needed someone to show me the ropes out here, so…" I trailed off.

"How did you contact Quizops?" Frewdin asked.

"He contacted me," I said. Frewdin nodded. The bottoms of my feet weren't too badly destroyed, I realized. That was nice.

"Well, you're here," Frewdin said. "And you did us a service." He pursed his lips. His cigarette was gone. I hadn't seen him get rid of it. "Thanks to you we've discovered that Phelan Eight is selling Shipkiller seeds to the Krr."

He watched me for a reaction. I think I was supposed to gasp.

"I'm not from around here, Frewdin," I said. "That statement doesn't shock me. Phelan is an asshole."

"He's an eighth generation Cabernician," Frewdin said. "He's devoted his entire adult life to the advancement of the Cabernician people, and to the defense of Core government. It's inconceivable that he would sell his life's work to the Krr, that he would ally himself with them in any way shape or form. We could never have seen this coming."

"Except that he came looking for me a week ago, and I told you to check him out," I said. "Frewdin, think about it, how could he have known to look for the seed on Earth if he wasn't present at the first sale? Christ, the Krr already had a seed by then." I shook my head. "He tried to send them to Earth."

Frewdin had a half-smile on his face, watching me. He looked friendly enough, but there was a glint in his eye that I didn't like.

"First of all, kid, a week ago doesn't mean shit." He was the very picture of calm. "This has been in the works for decades, if we're reading the evidence right."

"What evidence?" I said.

"You've been out for fifteen hours," Frewdin said. "A lot has happened, so shut up and listen. You're off Earth against my orders. You went within a few parsecs of the Front, meaning you entered a restricted military territory illegally–hell, not even illegally, you don't *exist* legally. You're a fucking animal off a pre-contact planet." He got up close to me with that funny gleam in his eyes. "From a legal standpoint–a *legal* standpoint, Samson, not a human standpoint, don't mistake me, here–from a *legal* standpoint, you're a malfunctioning weapon built along restricted parameters. You've been crossing interstellar borders without proper clearance. You fired on a galactic citizen of some import, even if he is a traitorous shit. You're guilty of an awful lot of serious crimes. You don't have to make it to Cabernicia. Clear?"

Cab took an involuntary step back, and I went with him. We stumbled some on my bum leg, and Frewdin looked us over.

"You did us a service, Samson, and now you're going to do us another one. Or, as a creature that does not, legally speaking, exist, you will disappear." He smiled. "Except that you can't really disappear if you were never really here in the first place. So you see, you're in a tenuous position. What's wrong with your leg?"

"Wait," I said. "Wait. Are you telling me you're going to kill me if I don't cooperate with whatever it is you're doing?"

Frewdin clasped his hands in front of him and half-shrugged. "Yes. I don't want to, Samson. We retraced your steps for the last forty-eight hours, you've been quite efficient. I'd rather you helped me solve the problem you've brought to my attention, as was your intention. You want to help. Or else you wouldn't be

292

here." He smiled again, and then stopped. "But you're a young man covered in transforming armor governed by a sentient computer. So, yes, if you don't agree to help me then I'll have one of my colleagues shoot you in the back of the head and we will drop you in a star."

His tone never varied. It was amazing. I knew he was right. It had been my intent to help him. I just hated being cornered.

"You wouldn't do it yourself?" I asked.

"Shoot you?" Frewdin said. "No, I like you. What's wrong with your leg?"

"I've got a Shipkiller seed stuck in my thigh," I said. "I took it off Phelan Eight's ship before the Krr got to it."

"That's great!" Frewdin was suddenly ecstatic, as if the expression had been smacked onto his face. He grasped my arm happily. His grip on the hull was very strong. "You got the third seed! With only one, the Krr might make a strategic error."

I took my arm back. Friendly or not, he had just threatened my life. And then he told me he liked me. That sort of back and forth tends to make a man uneasy. Or maybe it's just me. Maybe I'm sensitive.

"I doubt it," I said. "From what I've seen, the Krr are smarter than you give them credit for."

"They're bugs," Frewdin said. His hands worked their way into his pockets. A lot of his movements were like that, somehow autonomous of the whole. Like he was made up of a lot of little parts working together in concert. He leaned in. "Let's be friends, Samson. You're a long way from home, and you're injured. That's no time to be making enemies. You need friends. And I want your help. So let's be friends."

He walked away, and I followed him, because I was supposed to, and if someone breathed on me hard I would probably die. He was right. I was in no position to make any more enemies. The Krr were bad enough.

We were in a cavernous triangular room with a wide base and a narrow pointed front. An armored seam built from interlocking pieces of ceramic ran along the two longer walls and met in the middle. It looked like a zipper, or teeth. Frewdin headed for the far wall.

"I'd like to enlist your help with this case, Captain Samson." His voice was loud. "The CLEA is prepared to offer to a substantial daily stipend, in addition to reimbursement for all expenses incurred in the pursuit of duty."

"This is a mouth," I said. The floor was metal, covered in rubber, and warm to the touch. "This is the whale's mouth."

"This is a landing bay," Frewdin said over his shoulder. "Not a mouth. Not anymore."

I stared down at my feet. "How much of this thing is still alive?"

"No more than is necessary," Frewdin said. "Just like you. What do you think of my offer?"

"If you're going to threaten my life and press-gang me into government service after I nearly get my ass shot off trying to help you, you're damn right you're going to pay me." I sighed. "I accept your generous off."

"Glad to hear it," Frewdin chuckled.

--In all honesty, your ass was entirely shot off--

I ignored Cab and followed Frewdin to a pair of double doors. Elevator doors, they looked like, except they were built along much more impressive, Asimovian lines. Frewdin pressed a button and we waited with our hands clasped in front of us. Certain things are universal. The doors hissed apart, and a crowd of human-shaped Bekht got off the lift. One of them might have been wearing Dave Lovering, the drummer from the Pixies, but I wasn't sure. I didn't recognize the others.

"What's the plan?" I asked when the doors were closed. I did my best not to shuffle my feet. I never liked elevators, they required too much faith in someone I'd never met before. Although this elevator must have been grown, not built. I wasn't sure if that was any better. Frewdin pressed a button and leaned against the wall next to me.

"We're going to Cabernicia to extract a confession from Phelan Eight," Frewdin said. "Once we have that, we can arrest him and all of his descendants and see how much damage they managed to do." His cigarette was back. He inhaled happily and looked at my leg. "Cab, what's the deal with the seed?"

--I'm trying to get him out--

--He's dug in pretty good--

--He was trying to take control of the ship, at first, but he stopped after Samson got hurt--

--Bless his little heart, I think he's intimidated--

--Kinda cute--

--You can have the little bastard as soon as I pop him free--

"Try to hurry," Frewdin said.

We rode in silence for a moment.

"What are all those ships out there?" I asked. "The clunkers in the bay."

Frewdin smiled. "Escape pods," he said. "If the ship is compromised, or mortally wounded, we pile inside and blow the reactors, then ride the shock wave to safety."

I looked at him askance. "What about the whale?"

"What about the whale?" Frewdin said. "The whale is gone, Samson. This is a warship." He punched me lightly on the shoulder. "That's what makes you so special, guy. You're still present." He chuckled and shook his head. "That's what makes you so scary. You're still here, in spite of all the damage the seed did to you. Your entire body, irrevocably altered. My god, if I had what happened to you happen to me, I'd..." He shook his head again. I sighed and went private.

"Cab," I said quietly, "you there?"

--You've reached Cab, I'm not in right now, please leave a message after the beep--

--Where do you think I go, man?--

"I don't trust these people," I said. "This asshole still thinks I'm a monster. Everywhere we go, I want exits, and I want those exits to lead to a warp path home."

--Aye, Captain--

--Any limit to your definition of the word 'exit?'--

"No," I said. "Escape is our priority. Blow a hole in the wall if you have to." I unmuted the mic.

"Good conversation?" Frewdin asked after a second. He didn't look at me, but he grinned. "You move around when you're talking. Most people do."

"Cab says I'm healing well," I said.

"Sure he does!" Frewdin chuckled. "Good. I'm glad he said that. We need you in fighting shape."

The elevator opened, and we exited into a tall room with a domed ceiling and no corners. The walls and floor and ceiling were screens on which was projected an unbroken, three hundred and sixty degree view of outer space. The stars were moving. We were in a fast warp. The room was filled with vaguely-familiar humans, C-list celebrities and just-shy-of-famous faces, drummers and bassists and supporting actors and congressmen and junior senators performing the basic militant work of running a warship in wartime. I barely saw any of it. Rell and Yui were sitting at a card table on the far side of the bridge, drinking coffee and eating sandwiches. Rell saw me and raised his hand. Frewdin was smiling at me.

"You've got a professional thief and an accidental spy on the bridge," I said. "Are you sure you're good at your job?"

"I thought you could use a familiar face," he said, and as he spoke, his ears grew and his chin drooped, and then returned to normal. "A real one, I mean. And, you know, you're a little bit of an unknown, to me." He strolled across the bridge, acknowledging his subordinates and issuing minor orders but for the most part devoting his attention to me, and to himself.

"I know you're a wreck in there," he said. "And I know you're here to help. But I don't trust you. I need to keep an eye on you." He smirked. "The best way to do that is to involve you in my plans. So I need your cooperation. And I *think* you know that if you try to run, I'll kill you. But I don't *know* that you know that. So I'm hedging my bets. I'm betting that you're going to follow orders. I'm also betting that even if you won't follow orders, you won't shoot your way out of here with Rell aboard. Because you're a stupid, loyal child, and you want to protect your friend." He grinned wider than he should have been able to with Bogart's mouth. "I had to bring the watery dope along to keep the bugmonkey from getting suspicious. How'm I doing?"

I sighed. "Could you hear me talking to Cab?"

"When, in the lift?" Frewdin shook his head. "No, I just know people. I'm very good at my job." He stopped a short distance from Rell and Yui, and waved, then faced me fully.

"Are we clear?" He asked ominously.

"Take it easy on the intimidation, Frewdin," I said. "I'm weak. My heart might explode. You've got me, all right?"

"Oh, I know I've got you," Frewdin chuckled. "I want to make sure you know I've got you, too." He went up to Rell, humming, and clapped him on the shoulder. Rell flinched.

I sighed. I was going to get shot again. I could feel it.

21

We were flying in formation at the head of a huge pod of Shipkillers. Thousands of them, soaring through space with their heads down and their fins tucked in against their bodies like a school of mackerel, silvery and glinting, trailing comet tails of energy. None of them had any eyes. They bothered me. They were more than altered; they had been co-opted. And so had I.

"I called in reinforcements," Frewdin said. "The agents I can count on to keep their mouths shut until I tell them otherwise."

"Why do you care if they keep their mouths shut?" I stared past my feet at the fleet around us. Shipkillers blended in pretty well. Mirror-finish iridescent black is like deep-space camouflage, just a distorted field of reflected stars.

"Because Phelan Eight is politically connected," Frewdin said. "And if he gets wind of my plan, he will have me called off, and even then he might run." He shook hands with Rell, and nodded at Yui. Rell's arm was in a sling, and he looked like he'd been beaten, but he seemed like he was ok. Yui was shot through with phlegmatic orange and yellow threads, like snot in water or cracks in gelatin, and he was riding in a different tank than the one he'd been in when I met him. The current model was less luxuriant, but we all have to make sacrifices in wartime.

"Samson," Rell said, offering his good hand for an awkward shake. "Glad to see you're still with us."

"Glad to be here," I said. I looked around. "Well, glad to be alive."

"I know what you mean," Rell said. He paused considerately, and then said, "Thank you."

I nodded. I had an embarrassed expression on my face, but no one could tell. Also, my face was numb, so I might have just felt embarrassed.

"Me too," Yui said. He sounded pained.

"You're welcome," I said.

--Be more awkward--

Cab's spoke aloud, so I felt comfortable telling him to fuck off. Then I said, "So where do we stand?"

Frewdin smiled. "Aboard a Shipkiller, heading for the Cabernician system, where we're going to indulge in a spot of barely-legal entrapment. But before we get to that, I'd like to get us all on the same page regarding the fact that Yui has been selling weapons to the Krr." He raised an eyebrow at the man in the cooler.

"I didn't know who they were." Yui said. "Agent, listen, I really had no idea..." he petered out.

Frewdin watched him for several seconds and then waved his hand dismissively. "All is forgiven. You were working for us."

Nobody said anything, although Yui sloshed once.

Frewdin smiled winningly. "Yui is what's known as a blind asset. See, the Krr are constantly trying to get their hands on Core equipment, weapons, intelligence, anything they can find. What we do is find some willing, oblivious third party, and we use them to funnel shitty intel and busted or obsolete technology directly to the enemy. Keeps the Krr occupied and accounted for, and it lets us keep a closer eye on the criminal element we've got running the refugee stations. The seller doesn't know they're working for us, and they don't know they're selling to the Krr. Keeps things contained."

"What?" Yui sounded like he might not have been able manage more than the one word.

"We used you to keep the Krr from getting their mitts on anything worth a damn," Frewdin said. "Everything you've sold them has come from us, through a variety of shell companies and undercover agents." He grinned wickedly. "Just enough workable or promising technology to keep them on the hook."

"I've sold the GIM materials from hundreds of sources," Yui said. He didn't quite snarl, but he didn't sound happy. "I sold them stellar bomb schematics. That wasn't you. You wouldn't dare."

"Sure we would," Frewdin said. "We did. Starbombs are useless without a warp drive. You can't ram a star through semispace, it would take more energy than the star would produce in its lifetime." He shrugged. "We're the government, Yui, we pull this sort of thing all the time. You think you're the only asset we're running? You think we'd let you assholes get away with breaking so many of our laws if we didn't get something out of it? Get real."

"You know about the black markets on the refugee stations," I said.

"Samson!" Rell said.

Frewdin nodded. "We know most things. Not all. Not yet. We didn't know about the processes that led to your creation, for example. But we know about the extralegal actions that fund the refugee organizations. We keep a close eye on them. For the most part, we have no issue with what needs to be done."

"You used me!" Yui splashed angrily but didn't grow a torso. He must have gotten knocked around pretty hard when the reactor exploded.

"No shit," Frewdin said. "Tell me you didn't make a fortune."

"I used that money to care for twenty-two billion people," Yui said archly.

"All of it?" Frewdin said. "*All* of it?"

Yui didn't reply.

"You deserve some of that money," Frewdin said. "You do your government a great service."

"Someone found out what you were doing," I said. Frewdin looked at me and smiled.

"Yes, they did." Frewin nodded. "While you were unconscious, we did some digging. We're good at digging, once we know where to dig."

"Yeah, you're good at your job once you know what it is," Rell said.

"I was a terrible lawyer until I found out the job was digging ditches," Frewdin shrugged. "Phelan Seven, Eight's progenitor, he's the System Representative for Cabernicia. System reps have some access to CLEA intelligence, it looks like Eight got hold of Seven's credentials and used them to force his way deeper into our records."

"You don't think Seven is involved?" I asked. Frewdin shook his head and shrugged at the same time.

"We'll know soon enough," he said. "But from what we can tell, Eight has been monitoring Yui's deals with the GIM for about thirty years, along with a few other fronts we've been running. Probably took him all that time to set things up on his end, too. It's hard to get an unhosted seed out of Cabernicia. And when he had everything set up, he ran the sales over the course of a single six-week period, one every two weeks."

"Why didn't he do them all at once?" I asked.

"It's hard to leave Cabernicia with an unhosted seed," Frewdin said. "Imagine doing it with three."

"I can't," I said truthfully.

"Why did he cut me out, then?" Yui said. "He would have gotten away with it if he hadn't gone behind my back, we wouldn't have known about any of this until we looked out the window and saw Krr Shipkillers rolling down the street."

I smirked. "Rolling down–"

--Let it go--

"He's not a career criminal," Frewdin said. He spread his hands. "That's the best we can come up with. I bet he thought he was smart, keeping you out of the loop. Probably thought that since he's committing what amounts to existential high treason, the fewer people knew what he was doing, the safer he was. He didn't count on the existence of a professional criminal, with professional practices."

"Yu, I think that was a compliment," Rell smiled. Yui grunted.

"Civilians never expect intelligence in criminal spheres," Frewdin said. "That's how you guys stay so successful."

"Yeah, people are dumb," Yui said. "Keeps me in furs. Now what?"

"Now we send Samson into Cabernicia to extract a confession from Phelan Eight," Frewdin said. "Once we have that, I can lead my strike force into Cabernician space to make an arrest."

"What?" Rell was half out of his chair, half shouting, and Frewdin was facing him fully, leaning over with his hands on the table, right in his face, without having been seen to move. Both of them were very fast.

"Sit down," Frewdin said simply. After a moment Rell did as he was told.

"You can't send him into Cabernicia alone, they'll kill him," he said. "The Gardenmaster is dealing with the Krr, for god's sake, they'll throw him into the star."

I took a deep breath. In spite of the ruination that was my body, the air inside the ship still smelled like a stiff ocean breeze off the coast of Maine in late October. The little details that showed me Cab cared.

"I'm near death," I said. "Frewdin, you might as well tell me your plan before I get indignant. A man in my condition can't go shouting for no reason." I eased myself into a chair, carefully. According to Cab, if I moved too quickly I would tear, and I had no reason to doubt him. "We have his wallet from the crime scene. Why can't you can't arrest him for that?"

Frewdin sat down across from me and poured himself a cup of coffee. His cigarette was back, the same cigarette, at the same length.

"What we have is his wallet, produced by you from parts unknown," Frewdin said. "Now, I believe you, but you've got to see that what you have won't amount to shit in a court of law."

I sighed. "Right," I said. "Right. Ok. So what's your plan?"

"Ok," Frewdin said around a mouthful of ersatz smoke. "Big picture: we're going to Cabernicia to try to arrest Phelan Eight and all of his descendants, because thanks to the vagaries of the Cabernician cloning process, all of Eight's descendants could be inclined to the same sort of criminal behavior."

"What about Seven?" I said. Frewdin sipped his coffee.

"We'll question him and evaluate him, but like I said, he's a system rep. He has some clout. Even if he's responsible, and he probably isn't, he won't see jail time." He took a breath. "Phelan Eight probably thinks that you are dead, because he knows that the Krr would not take kindly to your presence at the third seed sale, and he doesn't know about our interactions, because I have not filed any reports about you, yet. My superiors do not know you exist."

"You haven't told anyone about me?" Frewdin shook his head at me. "Why?"

He shrugged. "You want the nice version, or the ugly truth?" He poured more coffee. "The nice version is that I don't know what to do with you, and I'm putting it off until I figure that out. That's the truth, but the rest of the truth is that I'm hoping you get yourself killed, so that the problem solves itself."

"So you're sending me into Cabernicia to die," I said. I looked at Rell and wondered how loyal you had to be in order to die protecting another person. I wasn't sure I was there, yet.

"No," Frewdin said. "I'm sending you into Cabernicia because you're the only one of us who can go."

I shifted in my seat to better manage my lingering agony, and said, "And then Samson asked, 'what do you mean, Frewdin?'"

Frewdin looked between Rell and Yui and tapped the table once with his finger.

"Don't repeat this," he said. "Do I have to make a threat?"

"Nah," Rell said. Frewdin peered at him, then shrugged.

"You're the only Shipkiller in existence without a functioning command circuit," he said.

"Ah," I said. "So Phelan was telling the truth."

Frewdin nodded. "I had my crew run a targeted diagnostic right after you passed out. It was right where you told me, spread across the dishwasher, the toilet, the air filters and a dozen other unrelated systems."

"What's this then?" Rell asked.

"Phelan Eight has been building a remote control into the Cabernician Shipkillers," I said. "He can…"

"Control them remotely," Rell said.

"Yeah," I said.

"Worked yourself into a bit of a corner with that sentence, didn't you?" He grinned.

"Yes I did." I looked at Frewdin. "How long will it take you to disable the command circuit?"

"Two hundred hours or so," he said.

"You can't make a move against him while it's operational," I said. "You don't just need a confession, you need me to disable the command circuit on his end."

"Yeah, that's the long and the short of it," Frewdin said.

--You are required to maneuver straight down this trench and skim the surface--

"Shut up, Cab." I reeled against the edge of the table. "How the hell am I supposed to know how to disable a Shipkiller control circuit?"

"You're not," Frewdin said. "Cab is. He's the brains behind this operation, Samson, your only task is to keep Phelan Eight occupied with your charm and wit."

--We're doomed--

"Eat it, Robbie Robot," I grunted.

"My advice is, ask him for money," Frewdin said. "Tell him the Krr are right on your tail and you're going into hiding. See if you can get him to admit to what he did, but even if you can't, keep him talking. Cab should be able to get into his systems without any difficulty, right Cab?"

--I am fairly confident in my skill with a computer, yes--

"Good," Frewdin said. "Here's the deal, Samson. This is the only plan I can come up with that doesn't give Phelan time to wipe his records and run. If you can pull it off, then it's possible that when I finally report you to my superiors, they'll look favorably on your existence."

"And if they don't, they'll have me killed. And if I don't agree to this, then you'll have me killed." I watched him drink his coffee. "If I die, it saves you a lot of trouble."

"Yes," Frewdin said. "You're a dangerous individual, Samson, you have to prove yourself to us."

"He doesn't have to prove shit to you, cop," Yui splashed. "This kid saved all our lives back at Phibbix, you can't just send him in there to die!"

"I'd like to think I'm sending him in there to succeed in his task, which is to save us all," Frewdin said. "But now that you mention it, yes, he does have to prove himself to me, and to the organization of species I represent."

He knit his hands on the table in front of him and looked at Yui, then at Rell.

"To me, both of you will be dead in hours," he said. "Neither of you will live for very long. But he will. And his body houses a technology that we have agreed as a *civilization* is too dangerous to exist. Yet, here he is. So, yes, Yui, he very much has to prove himself to me, and to the CLEA, and the Navy, and to the Core at large, at Phibbix, in Cabernicia, and in the future, until we are satisfied." He looked at me. "There are plenty of people who are going to think that you're a monster, kid. It's best we start redeeming you now."

"And if I don't want to redeem myself, then I'm not a person you can suffer to live like this." I stared at him blankly through the helmet.

"Exactly," Frewdin said. "That person is too dangerous to exist. If you die, it will simplify things for me, Samson. That's a reality. It's not a reality I'm especially fond of, whatever you may think of me, but it is the truth."

I clenched my jaw and something popped, so I stopped. But in my mind, I was grinding my teeth.

"So if I don't take your suicide mission, you'll kill me," I said. Frewdin nodded.

"For security purposes," he said.

I ignored him. "And if I take the suicide mission, well, it's a suicide mission." Frewdin nodded again and smiled sympathetically, although I think he was being disingenuous.

"But if I make it through, then you'll put in a good word for me with your bosses," I said, "and if they think I did a good enough job, they *might* not kill me."

Frewdin nodded.

"You could run," Rell said.

"That's why he's got you here," I said. Rell looked at Frewdin, then at me, then back at Frewdin.

"I knew you only wanted me for my body," he said. Frewdin laughed without humor.

"Ok, what's the plan," I said. "Is there a plan, or did you want me to wing it?"

"Like I said, get a meeting with Phelan Eight, and demand money," Frewdin said through a cloud of smoke. "Tell him he's got to buy your silence. Reference the things he's done, aloud. Try to get him talking. Meanwhile Cab will try to access his computers to disable the control circuit and dig up more evidence."

--Is that cigarette even real?--

Frewdin ignored him. "You told me Phelan Eight tried to take control of Cab when he contacted you on Earth, correct?"

I nodded. Frewdin nodded.

"All right," he said. "I imagine he'll try again. If he does, play along. He's an engineer, by training, and you're a particularly challenging problem. I'll be surprised if he doesn't take another crack at you."

"What if he manages to actually do it?" I asked.

"I'm sure Cab won't let that happen," Frewdin said.

--I mean, yeah, I can keep him at bay, but this is a bad plan--

Frewdin shrugged. "It's what we've got," he said.

"Ok," I said after a minute. "I see the logical progression here, but why the rush? Do we think he's going to run no matter what? Can't you, I don't know, be a cop? Investigate this? Try to trace his access to restricted military files? Why is it so important that we jump on this when we have so little to go on?"

"Well," Frewdin said, "Putting aside the fact that I need to know where you stand, twenty-five hours ago we found out that one or all of our classified intelligence operations have been compromised, and as a result the Krr have acquired one of the most powerful weapons in our arsenal. What's more, they were sold this weapon by a pillar of galactic society, the golden child of a major political family. Now, we don't know if Seven is working with Eight, but if he is, then doing this publicly, enforcing the law through channels, that's going to be fighting against the tide. This is a lot bigger than a simple weapons theft, Samson. We're going to need to re-evaluate our military tactics because of this, and that's going to take senatorial action. The only way we'll be able to get that ball rolling is with a hell of a lot of evidence. And before you say anything, Samson, you don't count as evidence of anything more than a horrible accident."

--I'm not horrible, I'm cute--

"You're terrifying, Cab," Frewdin said. "And your voice creeps me out."

--Harsh, bro--

Frewdin grinned. "CLEA deep cover policies dictate than in the event of an intelligence compromise like this one, we're supposed to wipe the slate clean. All evidence of operations involving Yui Galt will be expunged as soon as our failure becomes known. Can't have the CLEA responsible for arming the Krr, you understand? And that's non-negotiable. As soon as any of this is made public, those records won't exist. So the only evidence of any wrongdoing is in Cabernicia. Even Yui's records are non-specific. What'd you bill the seed as? 'Farming supplies?'"

"'Interstellar Super Weapon' stands out on a tax form," Yui said.

"That would catch my eye, yes," Frewdin said. "It's been twenty-five hours. Phelan Eight would have made it back to Cabericia about six hours ago. If he hasn't already wiped his files, I'll be surprised, but even if he has, Cab should be able to pull imprints off of his physical systems. And if all else fails, you can use your gift of gab to extract a vocal confession."

--That's in addition to gaining access to restricted bloopety-blorp and hacking the blah blah so your space toys don't get broken--

"In so many words," Frewdin said.

I looked at Rell. He made a face that implied he had no alternative to offer.

"And what will happen if you report this to your superiors?" I asked. "Just for the sake of argument."

"Well, we have to drop out of warp to make the call," Frewdin said. "They'll order me to stay at sub-light speeds, and fly out here to take possession of you. They'll arrest Rell and probably kill Yui, although they'll call it 'expunging physical evidence.' You'll most likely be poked and prodded for a few years, and then they'll drop you in a particularly hot star." He drummed his fingers on the table. "They'll start an investigation of Phelan Eight's actions, except they'll do it officially, which means that he'll be notified of the investigation. At which point he'll disappear. And given that in this case we will have no evidence of Krr malfeasance or Shipkiller acquisition, the next time anyone will apply any real thought to the problem will be when the Krr mount a full-scale invasion of Core space."

Rell and Frewdin sipped their coffee. Yui had another shaker of crystals, brown in shade, which turned his water icy-blue. I hadn't eaten in a long time, but I wasn't hungry. I liked food fine, but I didn't really need it, anymore. Another inhuman element. But I really wanted a cup of coffee.

"Do you know what it means if I say you've got me over a barrel?" I asked.

"It means I've got you bent over a barrel, and I'm fucking you," Frewdin said. "Metaphorically. Except that's not entirely accurate. I'm over the barrel, too. Yui, as well." He looked at Rell. "You're pretty clean in all of this, though."

"You're using me as a hostage to keep a man I've known for less than a week from abandoning me to the police," Rell said. "I'm right over the barrel with you."

"Wonderful, we can all get fucked together," Frewdin said.

--You know what they say about the family that fucks together--

"No one has ever said that, and none of us is going to be the first," Frewdin said firmly. "I don't want to send you into Cabernicia, Samson. You can barely stand, and I might be asking you to fight. But if I don't get proof of Phelan Eight's involvement, he'll destroy the evidence, and without evidence, I can't move. And if you don't disable the control circuit, the entire fleet is compromised. My hands are tied. I have no other options."

"What's the deal with your cigarette?" I asked.

"Bogart was a smoker," Frewdin said, as if that explained anything.

I sat back and considered his plan and listened to my heart beat too fast, a rodent thump that couldn't have been healthy. None of this was healthy. Alien warfare was hazardous. Also, down was where my feet were, and chocolate tasted good. Still, it's important to tip your hat to the obvious from time to time.

"Are you going to get in trouble for this?" I asked.

Frewdin nodded. "They'll let it slide if we win. If not…Like I said, I could be charged with treason."

I looked at Rell. "That's a silver lining."

He grinned. "We're all in this together."

"The hell we are, you assholes get to stay on the ship." I shook my head.

"This really is an awful plan," Rell said.

"Yeah," I said, "it is." I leaned back and put my chin on my chest. It's not about what you want, I thought. It's about what happens, and what you do about it.

"Ok," I said to Frewdin, "tell me the details."

Frewdin waved his hand at belt level and generated a three-dimensional star chart above the table. It was a lot more clearly defined than the one I played with in Rell's kitchen.

"Fancy," Yui grunted. His phlegm threads were fading, slowly.

"We get all the best toys," Frewdin said. He zoomed in on what I took to be a single purple point until we got closer and it revealed itself as a red point and a blue point, very close together.

"Cabernicia," Frewdin said, and the red point flashed. "We're going here, to the blue, two light years outside the Cabernicia border. We'll pull up short and let you off, then wait for your signal. This is important, Samson, legally, we can only enter the system after you get a confession. Anything short of that and we won't have jurisdiction inside Cabernician space." He shrugged. "Again, the control circuit makes all of this a moot point."

"This plan sucks," I said matter-of-factly.

"What do you want me to say, Samson?" Frewdin whacked the table with his hand, and his coffee mug jumped in place. "It's a shitty plan. We don't have a lot to work with. You want me to storm the system, go in with you? I've got three thousand Shipkillers. The Cabernician reserve fleet is something like six hundred billion. You want to help me fight our way in? With three thousand and one, I really think we've got a chance. Until Phelan stops all of mine dead in the water, or just blows them up. One human against six hundred billion Shipkillers, I like them odds!"

This would have been a perfect moment to pinch the bridge of my nose, but I wasn't even sure I had one.

"So that's it?" I said. "You want me to waltz in like a hooker wearing a wire and try to steal his car keys?"

Frewdin frowned at me. "If that's how you want to think of it."

"Humor is a coping mechanism," I said. "How far to Cabernicia?"

"About ten hours," Rell cut in. Frewdin looked at him.

"What?" Rell said. "The map is right there. I'm making myself useful."

"Thanks, Rell." I held out my hand and Rell slapped it, and I slapped him back.

"It's the very *least* I could do." He looked at his hand. "Nice five, kid, you're learning. You know I had a bruise for two days, the first time we shook hands?"

"Wimp," I said.

"Freak," he replied.

"I'm going to sleep," I said. "Maybe when I wake up you'll have thought of a better plan, Frewdin."

"Why can't Rell think of a better plan?" Frewdin grinned.

"Because that's not my job, cop," Rell said.

I got up and lay down against the wall. "Wake me up when it's time to die. Until then, hold my calls."

Cab blacked out my vision and hearing and my conscious mind moved to follow suit. Through my hull, I felt Rell and Yui leave the bridge, and after a moment some lowly CLEA agent took away our dishware and folded up the table. Good to have goons.

Cab's worry was the last thing I felt as I fell asleep.

I slept poorly.

22

The Cabernician star was called Caberna, and it was old and huge. From two light years out it was as big as a dime held at arm's length and bright enough to wash out the surrounding stars in a red haze.

I stood at the edge of the docking bay with my hands clasped behind me because I didn't have any pockets, and eventually I learn from my mistakes.

The whale's mouth was open, although Frewdin would have said that the Shipkiller's bay shields were open. He would have called the huge, open stomach a landing bay, and used a variety of technical terms to separate himself from the reality. He said the whale was gone, but that wasn't true. The whale was present, however irrevocably it had been altered. The deck was warm under my feet, a pleasing, organic heat.

The more time I spent around Shipkillers, the creepier they seemed.

Caberna was dead ahead, which meant that the whale was hanging in the middle of nowhere staring open-mouthed at a red supergiant. Probably looked pretty silly. Soon it would spit me out, a cosmic loogie heading for a near-certain death…the constant pain had me a little loopy. Another ten hours of sleep had done me wonders, though: now I only felt like I would die from my injuries, as opposed to feeling like I was actively dying at every moment and it was only a matter of time before it took.

My tendons were stronger, but stiff. My muscles were coming back, but they all felt torn. My bones were knit, but that only highlighted the recent breaks. That was ok. I didn't mind the pain. I was starting to like knowing that my continued existence was an affront to nature. I shouldn't have been alive, but I was. Made me think I could maintain the streak, if my luck held. So far, so good, you know?

I was sleek, now, scaled from head to toe in thin panels that hugged and augmented my musculature. Not a bad look, really. I still had engines, but most of the guns were gone, stored away in parts unknown. I was down to a pair of Stephen pistols on my forearms, small-caliber thermal energy weapons. It didn't matter. I could call everything back in an instant. I could almost see the designs hovering just outside my periphery.

Rell stepped up next to me, smoking another enormous cigar. He coughed politely to tell me he was there, even though I'd felt him through the hull as soon as he got off the lift. After a second, he spoke.

"This got out of hand," he said. I waited for him to go on.

"It's my mistake. That you're here, I mean. I should have known, should have thought more. Shipkillers, and the Krr, of course things were going to escalate." He grimaced. "You're just a kid. You shouldn't have to do this."

"I notice you still say I *have* to do this," I said wryly.

"You do," Rell said. "But you wouldn't if I had left you out of it."

I waved my hand at him. "Listen, even if you hadn't called me, I would have left Earth." I stopped, remembering myself. "Probably. I'd like to think I would have, anyway. But, you know, if you hadn't called me, maybe those guys would have killed you out by Ceres."

"I could have run," Rell said.

"Then you'd still be running, and the Krr would have a second seed, and the CLEA wouldn't have a fucking clue." I sighed. My lungs were barely in agony. It was nice. "This isn't pleasant. I don't like it. But it's a good thing you got me involved."

"You think you'll still be saying that if Phelan Eight kills you?" Rell asked.

"Well, I'm an atheist, so, no, I don't think I will," I grinned. Rell heard it in my voice and smiled painfully.

"Rell, this is my responsibility too," I said. "The Krr, I mean. This is like world war two, the Nazis were everyone's problem."

"Nazis?" Rell shook his head. "Never mind. I get the idea. Yes, the Krr are everyone's responsibility. But a child shouldn't be the one fighting them."

"On my planet I'm fully grown," I said.

"But still young," Rell said. "And besides, you're a backward race, you don't count." He sighed. "A thirty-year old adult. What a joke."

"Yeah, but it's not a funny one," I said. "Listen, I've got this ship, and I've got Cab, and I can do something, here. And if I *can* do something, then I *have* to do something. Might demands right." I looked at him askance. "And I know you're testing me."

Rell laughed. "Forgive me. I brought you off-planet, I feel responsible for you. I just wanted to make sure you were thinking the right way about this, in case you..." He stopped, embarrassed.

"Die," I said. "You want to make sure I understand the reasons why, in case I die. I understand, Rell. I'm not happy about any of this, but I'm going in with my chin up and my shoulders back."

"Sorry," Rell said. "I should have framed it better."

"Forget it, I'm dead already," I said. "I've got this thing built into me, it's the only thing keeping me from falling over, I'm a burnt wreck but I'm still breathing…I died in Dryden, Rell, everything since then is, I don't know. Something else. Something more."

"An afterlife," Rell said, and tossed his cigar into space. It tumbled through the atmospheric shield and died. It was better, watching deep space from a physical precipice, more affecting. Standing on substance with the void so close I could reach out and touch nothingness, the joy of either was amplified. The stars were potential, and the deck was comfort, and I lived in both.

"Sure," I said. "If you want to get poetic about it." The cigar was gone. Maybe it would become a relic to some far-off civilization ten billion years down the pike, proof that people liked drugs in the past, too. Probably not. Most likely it would curve into a star at some point, or get smashed to pieces by a passing asteroid in some near-impossible chance encounter. Cigars weren't known for their durability.

"I'm glad I got to see all this," I said. Rell nodded.

"Me too," he said. "It's worth the pain."

"I'm not too sure about that," I said.

"It is," Rell said.

"Do you have any idea what I look like in here?" I said.

"I know what you looked like before the Krr shot your face off," he said. "It's got to be an improvement."

"No, the Krr shot me in the back," I said, gesturing. "My face was irradiated off. Get it right."

"A thousand pardons," Rell smiled. We stood for a moment.

"When I get back, we're getting drunk," I said.

"Very drunk," Rell agreed. He sighed. "I wish I could go with you. It's not right, you having to go it alone."

"Wouldn't work," I said. "Nobody likes you."

"You like me," he said.

"I'm from Earth," I said. "I don't count."

"You're learning," Rell said.

Frewdin's voice cut in over the comm. "We're all set, Samson. Get moving."

"I hear you," I said.

Rell held out his hand, and I shook it.

"Somber," I said.

"Maudlin, even," he said. He clapped me on the shoulder, and then shoved me, hard, and I fell out of the ship, into space.

"Funny," I said.

"You were stalling," Rell said. "Good luck, Samson."

"And that's when he cut and run for Earth," I muttered. The warp hook built itself out of my chest and snagged Cabernicia with a barely-perceived thread.

--Vector is set--

I rolled my shoulders and winced. "Well, bye everyone," I said.

"Samson," Rell said. "Remember that cocky will get you killed."

"Good thing I'm scared shitless," I said.

I moved into the vector cautiously, but the acceleration still sent unpleasant spasms down my spine. When I got home, I was going to buy a place in the city and never look at the stars again.

23

It took me just over thirty seconds to fly two light years. That's nearly eleven trillion miles in the time it used to take me to walk to the kitchen and back.

According to Cab, Caberna was more than twelve hundred times the radius of Sol, but less than a twentieth the mass. A hundred and forty times brighter, but barely half the temperature. As mass was converted into energy, the gravity diminished, and the star expanded, and as the fuel was expended, the fire went out. Caberna was dying, a colossal soap bubble ready to pop. Cabernicians had long lives, millions of years at least. I wondered what was it like to watch you star age, to prepare for its death. I thought it sounded terrifying.

Caberna grew in front of me from the size of a coal, to the size of a manhole, to the size of a house, until it filled the sky in front of me. And still it grew. I put my hands up to protect my face. I couldn't help it; I was diving into a lake of fire. As metaphors go, this one was pretty blunt.

I slammed to a halt just outside the border. I couldn't help but stare. I'd known Cabernicia was a shipyard; I had not known that the entire system had been transformed into a thirty-million-mile assembly line.

Fifteen planets orbited Caberna in a long staggered line to the edge of the system, although they were so heavily modified and industrialized that it might be a stretch to call them planets. Most of them weren't spheres, anymore, and all but one of them had been speared through with directional engines, six gargantuan ones set at ninety-degree angles. Some were

lit, some were dark, so the whole system burned
unevenly. The only exception to the obscene
overdevelopment was an unaltered midnight-blue gas
giant at the end of the line. Billions of Shipkillers orbited
the gas-giant in tight formation, flying shoulder to
shoulder at a good fraction of light speed. The reserve
fleet that Frewdin had warned me about. They were
stacked on top of each other in columns of varying size,
stalagmites standing out against the bulk of the fleet
like skyscrapers, so many of them that it looked like the
middle of the planet was covered in mercury. And more
arrived every minute. The gas giant was the terminus
point in a silent progression of Shipkillers from planet
to planet, an intra-system slalom that began right up
against Caberna's surface, on a tiny planet hidden
under a lens darkening the fury of the star behind it.
Some kind of shield. It was hard to tell, my eyes had
their limits, such as they were. Of course, the ship's
sensors could see much farther than I could, but I
wanted to see with my meat eyes. I was a tourist, here
for the sights.

A tourist on a covert mission for the
government. What a crock.

The ships at the back of the line were less than
grains of sand, ants on the side of a barn at fifty miles.
One would have been invisible, but there were billions
of them, a silvery thread that twisted from planet to
planet and only became apparent as a collection of war
machines at close range. They flew as if pulled,
seemingly volitionless except that their engines were lit.
Their heads and fins drooped in a way that reminded
me of sleepwalkers.

--Home sweet home, I guess--

Four Shipkillers pulled away from the reserve
fleet and veered to intercept us. I took a deep breath,
and my heart slowed down. I felt very still. I altered

course, to see what would happen, and the quartet altered course to match me. The singing in my head took on a different tone.

--Wow, that's a lot of targeting warnings--

"Keep the shields down." I stopped in place and the Shipkillers took up positions ahead and to my sides.

--Sure, why not?--

--They won't make any difference--

"Cabernician 181804258618185 was lost and presumed destroyed."

"Christ, not this again," I muttered.

"Cabernician 181804258618185, account for your whereabouts for the past seven hundred and seventy nine hours."

--You want me to answer them?--

I took a deep breath and opened the channel with a thought.

"This is Captain Gregory Samson of the Solar Shipkiller Cab Calloway," I said, "Out of the Solar System. I'm here to see Phelan Eight."

There was a significant pause. I listened to my targeting warnings for a half-beat and then tried to ignore them. If they opened fire, I would never even know it had happened.

"You said Earth?" A new voice said hesitantly.

"That's right, Earth," I said. Cocky would do for now. "We're putting together a fleet. Put me in touch with Phelan Eight."

"Do you have an appointment?" The first voice asked.

"No," I said. I smiled for the tone it brought my voice.

"The Gardenmaster only sees people with appointments," The second voice said triumphantly.

"What are you, border guards or secretaries?" I snapped. "I am talking to someone aboard the

Shipkillers in front of me, correct? Tell him who's calling. He'll make an exception. Tell him if he doesn't want to meet with me I can take my business to the Core."

"The Core?" Snorted a new voice. "What do they know from Shipkillers, besides what we charge for them? Sit tight, I'll call the Gardenmaster's office."

"Thank you," I said. The targeting warnings stayed where they were.

"Uh, Cab Calloway, you're reading as a pretty small mass, are you running a sensor befuddler?"

I muted the mic. "Befuddler?"

--I told you people were gonna make fun of me--

"They're called sensor 'befuddlers,'" I said.

--Sure, in English--

"That is not an English word!" I shook my head an unmuted the mic. "Your information is accurate. I'm the Shipkiller's host."

There was a long pause.

"*You're* the host?"

"Holy shit, a sentient host? I didn't think you could do that."

"What about the ship's computer?" The first voice had that ring of authority you learn to listen for over time. I thought about Frewdin threatening to have one of his underlings shoot me in the back of the head if I didn't cooperate.

"We hobbled it," I said. "It's sub-sentient, just there to help me drive."

--What is thy bidding my master--

"Understood," the first voice said. "What's it like?"

--It's a little tight around the crotch--

I glared at Cab as best I could and tried to sound pleasant. "It's the only reason I'm allowed off Earth. It's amazing. But it's an adjustment. I'm part machine,

324

now." It felt weird saying it aloud. The Shipkillers hung motionless a mile away. I knew the whales weren't awake, and I couldn't see their eyes, but it still felt like they were watching me. Staring me down. There was something unbelievably unnerving about facing a quartet of staggeringly huge animals in null gravity. A primitive part of me screamed at me to swim away. Instead, I lied some more.

"The Shipkiller got rid of all my diseases when it came online. That's why we're buying Shipkiller seeds, so that we can safely leave Earth."

"You're sure it worked?" One of them asked.

"My body is part of the ship now," I said. "I know I'm clean. It's an elegant system, you know?"

"Yeah, I bet." He sounded disturbed.

"Man, I can't wait to hear what Wrntellik has to say about this," the second one said.

"It's election season," said the first one. "Get ready for some fire and brimstone."

"Gonna be a long two point four one decades," said the second. The translation machines weren't always the most graceful devices.

"I didn't realize you guys had made contact," a new voice said.

"It's all very hush-hush," I said quickly. How the hell long did it take to place a damn phone call, anyway? "We don't want to start a panic over our diseases. That's why Phelan came up with that asinine cover story about the, ah, the Vabling stealing the seeds out of the garden."

--Don't lay it on too thick--

"Oh, yeah, sure," said the second Cabernician. "You know, I didn't think he coulda pulled it off. Fifty-Three, you see his ship?"

"Thing was a piece of shit," Fifty-Three said.

"Right? Whole damn thing was an embarrassment. Looked like we just let him in! My mother-in-law gave me hell for that."

"Ah, she's a pain in the ass, Eighty-Nine, don't worry about it."

"Well, the Gardenmaster owes us, it wasn't fair to set us up as the fall guys in all this," Eighty-Nine said. "Hey, Captain Samson, Phelan just pinged you a pass. Looks like you were right, he made an exception for you. He says meet him in his office at the north polar base in the Gardens. You're free to enter Cabernician space."

"Thanks, guys," I said. "I'll put in a good word for you."

"Hey, thanks Captain," Fifty-Three said. "You need an escort?"

"No, I got it," I said. Cab tagged our destination on my display and I cut around the border guards. It was hard to keep my distance without looking like I was keeping my distance. Fly casual, I thought. "Thanks guys."

"Sure," came the reply. "Take care. Oh, and welcome to Cabernicia."

--Working stiffs--

--You gotta love 'em--

I sped into the system, although it was nearly impossible for me to see the place as a separate collection of planets and satellites. This was more like flying through an engine, or a machine. The natural splendor of what had been was gone; all that remained was the machine. A little like the Shipkillers themselves, I suppose. A little like me. The whole place was one big insufferable metaphor.

Nascent warships slingshotted from planet to planet, pulled along by gravity and inertia. It was a long journey. They were already covered in raw material by the time they reached the second planet, although it took some time for the machinery to develop. But everything advanced at the same inexorable rate, and by the time they reached the gas giant at the system's edge, the whale had been replaced by the weapon.

"Cab, how much do you know about the…the gestation process, here?" I hadn't meant to sound so disturbed.

--I know based on how fast these things are going it's gonna take about four days for them to reach the fifteenth planet--

--And I know there are about fifty million of them in line right now--

--Beyond that, not a lot--

--I know it's more than just waiting for the Shipkiller to grow out of the whale--

--They're doing something to them as they pass the planets--

--Damned if I know what, though--

We passed a reddish-yellow planet with a rocky surface that reminded me of Mars. The equator was an unbroken ring of cityscape studded with iridescent green towers extending past the atmosphere. This late in the process the Shipkillers were nearly complete, easily recognizable as the war machines you've come to know and love. Their path took them in close to the tips of the towers, and the space between wavered and jumped like the air over a flame. As they passed the planet the Shipkillers took control of their own trajectories, twisted and stretched their limbs as if waking. The exit interview at Shipkiller University.

--Makes me wonder if I'm missing some crucial programming--

"Could be," I said. "But they have a static hardware set, remember. And they don't think. Maybe they need training."

--And...--

"What?"

--Well, they're bigger than me and they do a lot more--

--There are some advantages to being small--

--I guess--

--But if you ever tell anyone I said that I'll feed you hallucinogens when you're in polite society--

"I'm never in polite society," I grunted.

The closer we got to the Garden, the less developed the Shipkillers were. Space rippled around each planet, and after each fly-by, the Shipkillers added a new component set to their hulls, complex engines, weapons systems, sheets of armor. It looked like every planet transmitted a new piece of software to the passing Shipkillers, software designed to initiate construction of a different shipboard system. Or else the whole thing was preprogrammed from the start, the planets were nothing to the process but navigational anchors, the atmospheric rippling was a natural phenomenon, and I was full of it. I've always found it hard to tell.

A squad of six finished Shipkillers stood watch about two hundred thousand miles off the surface of a planet covered in a lumpy city the green color of oxidized copper. A dozen drones detached themselves from one of the guard ships and came hurtling towards me. None of them targeted me directly, but I could tell they had their sights aligned. Up close, they were nondescript, iridescent ovoids with razor edges reflecting blackness and red light from the star up ahead. They fell into position behind me.

"Honor guard?" I asked Cab. "Or hit squad?"

--Honor guard--

--No way he'll try to kill you out in the open like this--

I flipped over on my back and blew the air out of my mouth. "I really didn't expect this many Shipkillers."

--Yeah, this is really something, huh?--

--We can turn around it you want--

--Or, I guess our best bet would be to shift course, go around the other side of Caberna--

I shook my head. "Don't tell me that." I turned back to the Gardens, and the huge, hellish star. We were getting close. Not too close to turn away, there was always time for that. But I wouldn't run. I knew my responsibility. I was there, and I could do something. Might demands right. Even if hurts.

24

Phelan Eight's voice cut through my mortal contemplation as I was passing the second planet. The whales here were little more than unformed lumps of raw material, machine cocoons waiting for the loving guidance of Cabernician engineering.

"Samson!" That same cloying voice, buttery with bullshit. "How *are* you? I was just thinking the other day that I needed to touch base with you. How do you like the ship?"

I buzzed the Shipkiller queue. The nascent craft showed up unimaginably hot on my displays, in temperature and radiation both. This was a vastly different process from the one I'd gone through. It was like the whales were being cooked, reduced, boiled away.

"Phelan, buddy, I love it," I said in the same oozing tone. "Couldn't be happier. Fast, deadly and durable: who could ask for more?"

"Glad to hear it," Phelan said. "I understand you're interested in purchasing a fleet!"

"Well, I hear you're the man to talk to," I said. "You've left an awful lot of satisfied customers in your wake."

"Well, the Cabernician Shipbuilding Consortium takes its work very seriously," Phelan Eight said levelly. "Why don't you come down to my office, we can talk face to face. But stop by and see the whales, on your way in. We're just about to start processing another pod."

"Sounds dandy, Phil. I'll be right there." I don't know if it was an insult to shorten his name like that, but I hope it was.

The assembly process began at an artificial satellite about a hundred thousand miles above the surface of the first planet. It looked like a teed-up golf ball, a five hundred mile wide sphere on top of a five hundred mile long tapered stake that shat out whale-centered hunks of raw material at a regular pace. The ball was hollow, a paddock. A cage. I slowed down. The whales inside the chute stood out on my sensors as bright points against nothing. There was a pit in my guts, even though I barely had guts, yet.

A group of silver spaceships were harrying a pod of Hoon whales towards an opening in the top of the cage. It was the first time I'd seen them in their native state. They were slight without Shipkiller armor, thin, lacking in density. Their fins were long, skinny, almost as wide as they were thick, except at the ends, where they flared like canoe paddles. Their bodies bent oddly, as if they were made of nothing but tiny bones and malleable flesh, like snakes, except they were shaped like beta fish, overall, with long, trailing tails and narrow faces. They were a uniform slate gray shot through with black spots, but every animal had a crest that started between their eyes and ran down their backs and tails and across the front of their pectoral fins, with a color and a texture that appeared to unique to every animal. I saw feathery blue tendrils ebbing into turquoise gemstones, rocky red like evil bread mold, yellow bubbles with purple tips, shimmering white diamond scales, more. Much more. There was so much variety that it all blended together. After a moment I had to look at my feet, my reassuring, metal, rocket-festooned Shipkiller feet. I knew them. They made sense.

The guard ships were balls, oblong ovoids trailing long, needle-tipped cables. They looked like sperm, to be honest, except their tails didn't move. They might have been rigid, for all I could tell. But they weren't.

A smaller, slower whale started to fall behind, and one of the ships twisted in place and whipped it across the back with a tail that was suddenly so flexible it was nearly liquid. Electrified mercury. Lightning followed the whale into the pod and traced convulsive patterns through the bodies of its fellows, and then the other ball-ships were flicking their tails, too. Energy leapt from whale to whale as the pod streamed riotously into the cage. The first-whipped whale fell behind again, spasming uncontrollably. I don't think it was very strong in the first place. The ball-ships flicked their tails again and again, whipped the animal mercilessly in an attempt to drive it into place, but to no avail. The beast shuddered and died, and after a moment one of the herders used some kind of force ray to smack the dead whale into the dying star, where it burned quickly away to nothing.

Inside, the whales milled and twisted, unsure but safe for the moment. Then a door opened at the base of the paddock, and in the same moment the gate behind them began to crackle with electricity. The animals swarmed nervously. The electricity pushed closer, and they broke apart, panicked, and fled for the lighted opening beneath them. One of them pulled ahead and struggled through the door, but it was narrow, and the whale had to push to fit. When it was halfway through, a small, barely-noticeable spindle-arm reached out delicately from the frame above and speared the whale in the top of its head with a tiny thorn. The creature twitched and went still, and something on the other side sucked it through the door.

The next whale in line shoved into the narrow gap, and the process repeated itself. Again, and again, and again. The procession continued unabated out of the other end of the station.

They weren't willing. In all of this, through the obvious horror that was my transformation, their transformation, the ugliness of the whole thing, the exploitation, the cooption, it had never occurred to me that the whales simply were not willing. They weren't volunteers. They were a crop. This was a slaughterhouse.

"Where do they get them?" I said quietly.

--The whales?--

--They're a native species--

--The Cabernicians towed their planet to the far side of Caberna--

--They call it the Ranch--

Cab had the station mapped in his mind, and he was turning it over and over, examining it inside and out with the intensity of a person finding an album of long-lost family photos. I used to stare at photos of my folks the same way, looking for answers to questions I couldn't articulate, feeling that sensation of knowing myself and not knowing what to expect from myself at the same time. I looked over his shoulder and marked the weak points of the station, and targeting reticles appeared on my displays.

"Watching the whales, Samson?" Phelan's voice intruded in my ear. "Magnificent, aren't they? Nature is a hard act to follow, but I think we do a pretty good job improving on perfection. Come on down, I've had a light lunch delivered."

--There's nothing about this in any of my files--

--The assembly process is highly classified--

I shook my head. "Makes sense."

--Frewdin knew--

"He did," I said.

--I'm a monster--

"You're not a monster," I said.

--I am borne of monsters--

I didn't have anything to add to that. There was nothing I could do. They would kill me if I attacked the station. Nothing would change. The Core knew what was happening here. They had given the process their blessing, even as they kept the worst parts of it hidden. I let the targeting reticles fade away and fell towards the first planet as the whales' lives drew to a close behind me, feeling like a coward.

There was an immense ray shield projected across the surface of the star directly underneath the Gardens, a darkened concave lens a hundred thousand miles wide. Looking back over the system I could see that the shield protected the entire assembly process from whatever malevolence Caberna could no longer keep to itself, which was a considerable amount of malevolence. My own shield was spitting and sparking this close to the stellar surface, trailing a thousand miles of radiation and fried space behind me. The air cooled around me as we crossed the threshold of the giant lens. I hadn't noticed the heat. I should have been sweating, but a quick glance at the medical systems told me that sweat glands were pretty far down Cab's list of priorities. At that point it was still easier for him to cool my blood directly than to cool my skin.

The dayside of the planet was molten in spite of the shield, while the nightside was blackened and burnt. Huge, regularly-spaced metal pyramids studded the surface, like Mayan ziggurats, except they were made out of gold and big enough to be visible from orbit. Then again I could count ants from orbit, so maybe that doesn't impress you. Anyway, these were large pyramids. Iridescent obsidian brambles had been cultivated rows across their faces, so that the nightside shined with every color of black in the rainbow. Thorns grew from the brambles, so sharp they showed up on my displays as a slight break in the physical laws of the surrounding universe. They were so full of energy that they vibrated when I looked at them. Shipkiller seeds.

"There's billions." I murmured without meaning to, and cleared my throat.

"There's billions of them," I repeated in a normal voice.

--Trillions, actually, but most of them won't be ripe for millennia--

--It's a slow process--

Phelan was in the largest pyramid on the planet, an enormous structure at the North Pole topped with a giant bubble. The ship had him outlined in targeting reticles. Even the unthinking part of me wanted to shoot the guy. I angled towards an open bay in the base of the building and zipped inside.

Passing through the atmospheric shield was like running into a giant invisible feather pillow at mach thirty and catching on fire. The air pushed at me, I pushed back, and then everything ignited from the friction. A giant fireball rebounded off the far wall and washed through what was, mercifully, an empty room.

--Cool!-

I adopted a heroic pose, dropped to the floor and collapsed onto one knee. Cab hadn't made a lot of headway with my uncooperative limb. I focused pointedly on my mental roommate.

--Yeah, yeah, I'm working on it--

"What's the latest?" I said.

--You ever see a big dog and a little dog holding onto the same rag, and the big dog doesn't want to pull too hard and hurt the little dog or tear the rag, and the

336

little dog won't let go, even though it's totally outmatched?--

"What?"

--He's got control of the leg, but there isn't enough nervous material down there for him to bring his consciousness online--

--So he's trying to take over a larger portion of your body, but I won't let him--

--But I can't get him to let go, so as a result neither of us gets to use the leg--

I frowned. "So my leg is the rag?"

--Well, you're the rag--

--But yeah--

--I'm trying to get around his autonomy programming--

--If that happens I can combine our minds--

--Which shouldn't have any real effect given that we're built to be essentially the same person--

--I've just had experiences he hasn't--

"What happens if you let him do what he wants to?"

--You'll probably be fine--

--Odds are he would erase my mind, though, and I've become rather attached to the thing--

"Yeah, let's not let that happen." I piked myself up onto my good leg and shuffled across the floor.

--Hey, keep quiet about all this, too--

--Phelan is listening, and I don't want him to know we've got the seed--

--I built a sensor befuddler, so he won't see anything out of the ordinary--

--But, you know, keep your cards close to your chest--

I nodded and went on walking. We were in a parking lot. Sure, everything was built using technologies and materials light years more advanced than anything on Earth, but a parking lot is a parking lot. Glowing lines delineating parking spaces that repeated ladder-like into the distance, and every now and then I passed a spot with someone's name written inside.

I turned on the mic. "Where is everyone, Phil?"

"I've sent them away." Phelan intoned. "No one must interfere with our duel to the death." He laughed. "It's Sunday, Samson, everyone has the day off."

There was a cavernous elevator at the far end of the lot with big, Cabernician-sized doors that split apart when I approached. Everywhere I went in the galaxy, I felt small. That was probably for the best. Kept me humble. My foot dragged.

"Why, Gregory, what has happened to your leg?" Phelan asked.

--Weh Gregory, meh meh mur meh meh meh?--

--Dick--

I laughed. "It's gone," I said. "The Krr burned it off after you bugged out. Some kind of ray, it cut right through my shields, my hull, didn't do a thing until it hit meat. I guess I'm lucky, a few inches higher and I'd be a eunuch."

"We could only be so lucky," Phelan Eight said.

--I mean, I have to agree with him here--

"I wasn't aware the Krr had such a weapon," Phelan Eight continued in the same moment.

"Yeah, it's a humdinger," I said. "What's the matter, you worried you might have tipped the balance of power farther than you thought?"

"Why Samson whatever do you mean," Phelan said in a monotone. "Come up to my office and we'll talk about it."

The doors closed behind me, and the elevator began to move. I thought about my leg, and asked, "How long is this going to take?"

--What, the seed?--

--No idea--

--Anywhere from five minutes to five days--

--No one's ever tried to crack a Shipkiller's development code like this before, I'm way out of my depth--

--I mean, sentient computer, thinks in code, best suited, blah blah blah, I'm the least out of my depth of anyone who could attempt such a thing, but still, this is a huge damn job--

--I really don't know, Greg--

--I'm going as fast as I can--

I nodded. His worry was deepening. That wasn't a good sign.

The elevator shuddered and stopped with a twisted-metal shriek, and I considered the obvious trap. On the one hand, Phelan had to know this wouldn't kill me. On the other hand, if I got trapped in a falling elevator it would validate years of irrational fear, Shipkiller or no Shipkiller.

--What the hell has you so agitated?--

The elevator dropped a foot. I sighed and reformed the thermal blasters on my arms into cutting beams. My old standby.

--Jesus wept, would you calm down?--

"I'm fine," I muttered. "I don't like elevators."

--What are you, twelve?--

"Hold on, Samson, we're having some technical difficulties," Phelan said.

"You mean the elevator is broken," I said, "or you're having a hard time making it fall?" I flew to the ceiling and cut a hole and flew to the top of the shaft. Below me, the elevator dropped like a stone and exploded. We were a long way up, the fall would have killed me if I hadn't been me.

"My god, Samson, are you all right?"

--Is he joking?--

"Knock it off, Phil." I burned through the doors on the top floor and kicked them aside. The light of my engines coupled with the flickering energy of the cutting beams lit up the darkened shaft like a hellish rave.

Phelan was coiled patiently on his four legs behind a huge empty desk. If he minded the molten metal I spilled on his carpet, he didn't show it.

Calling the room an office would be a stretch; it was a hundred yards across and perfectly circular, with transparent walls so clean they seemed barely there. The perfect perch from which to watch the whales. A fresh pod was being driven into the seeding paddock as I stepped out of the shaft. The show went on.

Cab got started digging into Phelan's records.

"Samson," Phelan said. "You're alive. Thank God." He stood up and held out on of his twelve hands to shake. I think he did it just for an excuse to stand up. He was real damn tall.

"Your concern is touching." I shook his hand. It was heavy, and his grip lingered. He smiled, and I drew back. I was wearing an alien death machine, hell, I was an alien death machine, but still, Phelan had a long reach and he was the creepiest thing I had seen so far, besides the Krr. No wonder he turned out to be the bad guy.

--Did you hear something just now?--

I shook my head. "You're selling Shipkiller seeds to the Krr, you absolute asshole."

"How do you figure?" Phelan settled back on his haunches and smiled at me levelly.

"Besides the fact that you're a flaming asshole and you came looking for the seed on Earth?" I said. "You took your personal ship to the third sale. I found

340

your wallet." I shook my head. "You utter, absolute idiot. I should just kill you."

Phelan didn't say anything for eleven seconds, and then he said, "Probably," and smiled. "But you won't." He tapped a few keys on his desk.

"We'll see," I said. Phelan got up and wandered over to the buffet.

"You aren't the type," he said.

"You've telegraphed your guilt from day one," I said. "Forgive me if I don't consider you an authority on this sort of thing. But as long as we're on the subject, you can buy your breath. You give me a hundred million dollars in gold, and I'll let you walk."

There are a lot of ways to float a lie. One of the most effective is to elicit scorn from the target. Not too much, nothing obscene, just enough to give them the sense that they have more power than they do. It pays to let people think you're backward. Phelan's scorn for humanity could be put to good use.

"Gold," Phelan said, waving his hand. "We grow the seeds in gold, you twerp. Take as much as you want and fuck off."

"Then I'll take a hundred million credits," I said. Another part of lying is knowing when to change tack. "Whatever it is you use for money out here. I want a hundred million dollars of *your* money, Phelan!"

"Of course," Phelan nodded. "Because the point of blackmail isn't just to make money. The point of blackmail is to hurt the other person."

"You tried to sell Shipkiller seeds to the Krr," I said. "Assuming you didn't have any accomplices, you probably succeeded in doing so about two weeks ago. You deserve to be hurt."

Phelan poured himself a glass of translucent orange liquor and had a sip. Something dinged at him

341

on his disk, and he went over and read something off of his display, and smiled.

"You're right, I sold a Shipkiller seed to the Krr," he said. He opened a separate display on the other side of his desk and squinted to read some fine print, then typed something that ended with a definitive stroke. "I stole three of them. One ended up in you, the second I sold without incident, and the third, well, I don't know, Samson, you tell me, you were there." He leaned back on himself and drank the rest of his drink. "You should have shot me as soon as you got off the elevator. Hell, you should have blown me up from orbit. Because now I'm going to kill you and drop your body in the star."

I stood up and shot him in the chest, or at least, I tried to. Cab didn't move.

--Ah--

--Hmmmm--

--Shit--

--This is embarrassing--

"You are kidding me," I muttered. "I thought you said this wouldn't happen." Talking about it calmly kept me from acknowledging the panic welling up inside of both of us. Self-delusion is a useful skill in times of crisis.

--No, he got us--

--Total control--

--He used some kind of computer virus --

--I didn't think of that--

"So I gather," I said. "What's the plan?"

--Stall him until he dies of old age?--

Phelan refilled his drink and stood in front of me. His smile was hard.

"I should just kill you," he said. "But I won't."

"When you're happy, your whole face lights up," I said. My voice broke on 'happy.'

Things were not looking good for our hero.

Benjamin Mumford-Zisk

25

"I can hear you," Phelan Eight said. "You and Cab. So don't go trying to make any secret plans, it'll only end in heartache." He laughed to himself. "'Stall him.' Christ."

He stood up and uncoiled to his full height, stretched his arms and twisted his back. The ascending crackle of his spine was like machine gun fire. His legs were huge, bigger than it seemed they should have been because of the enormous weight they had to support and balance. He was *really* damn tall.

I was frozen in an easy standing position, like a boring piece of public art or a high-end mannequin. Phelan scratched the side of his bald snake head with one of his top left hands and called up a series of displays. He read them while he spoke.

"You know, it's really amazing that you didn't die when the seed hit you," he said. "I wish I could dissect you, but it would be too risky to keep your body around. But, you know, we tried implanting the seeds in Cabernicians. They wouldn't take. The hosts died every time. We assumed it was something to do with sentience, that the seeds couldn't root in something so complex." He narrowed his eyes and pulled more information out of a half-seen screen.

"I wonder if that's it, actually," he muttered to himself. "The complexity. The human brain only has the two halves…Cabernician neural systems are appallingly complex in comparison, there's so much more to us." His hands moved independently, altering and augmenting the spread of information. He had dozens of screens open in front of him, most of them for only a few seconds at a time. In order for them to serve any purpose, he would have had to be able to read multiple pages at once, more than two pages with only two eyes. His eyes were compound, and his body was too, to a certain extent, so I suppose he was right, Cabernician brains really did have a lot more to keep track of than human brains. Of course, none of this crossed my mind in the moment.

Phelan laughed. "My god, that must be it. The seed could take hold because you're so fucking simple. Amazing!" He clapped two sets of hands together. "One of the most advanced machines in galactic history and the only reason you can exist is because you're a barely-evolved animal, nothing more."

--I don't like him--

--We can get through the virus--

--It'll just take time--

"Good luck, Cab," Phelan said. "It's a nasty piece of software. You're in for a challenge."

--Get bent, shithead--

Phelan smiled. "He really can think, can't he? Incredible. It's a disservice to the scientific community to destroy you, Cab." The smile took on a wicked note. "Then again, I'll be doing the humanitarian community a great service, won't I? You're a danger to all life as we know it, Cab."

--Just you, fuckface--

Phelan blinked. "Quite the vocabulary you've taught him, Samson."

"He learned all that on his own," I said. We did our best to act confident, but there wasn't any point. Both of us know it was bullshit. I couldn't move, again, but this time it was real. I was in a real bind.

"You know, all of this would have been a lot easier if you'd had a control circuit," Phelan said. He wasn't speaking to me so much as thinking aloud to another person. "I could have blown you up from orbit and wiped out your entire miserable species. I would have been doing us all a favor. But, no, I should have anticipated that a race of genetic freaks would birth a freak Shipkiller." He was nearly spitting, by the end.

He sighed. "Instead, you had to make a mess of my business." He parsed another screenful of information and looked at me askance. "Do you know I've been planning all of this for longer than you've been alive? And then you come running in and wreck a delicate operation in the space of a week. You fucking animal."

"Delicate operation?" My voice quivered. It was infuriating. "The only reason that any of this happened is you got greedy. If you'd cut Yui in for his share he never would have sent Rell to steal Cab's seed. This is all your fault, asshole."

Phelan shook his head. "That gutter scum should have known to keep his watery nose out of things that didn't concern him." The screens flashed green. "There we are. Total dispersal. You know, it was fun, actually, coming up with a delivery device for the control code. That's all it is, a control code. The same one I use on the regular Shipkillers. I keep it embedded in separate machines in order to avoid detection, but it's software, not hardware." He held up one of his hands and pointed to a silver ring on his middle mass of finger tentacles. "Pulse transmitter. Only needs to be pressed against a ship's hull. Usually they're much bigger devices, but I'm an exceptional engineer."

"Cab," I said, "did he get us with a joybuzzer ring?"

--Sure, why not?--

--Pulse transmitters transfer energy through microvibrations--

--Same way I speak aloud, actually--

347

--He basically read me the virus--

--And got it stuck in my head--

--I'm pissed--

"Mostly scared, looks like," Phelan said. He looked at me innocently, and smiled.

"The cops know I'm here," I said.

Phelan leaned back on his haunches.

"You mean Frewdin?" He said. "Agent Miles Frewdin, of the Core Law Enforcment Agency? The man who came to see you hours after I did, and told you that I wasn't a threat?" He smiled viciously, and I got very cold inside. After a moment he laughed.

"Don't worry," he said. "He's not working with me. I had you going for a second, didn't I?" He poured another drink. "No, what I have planned for you is worse, Samson. I'm going to kill you, and then I'm going to dump your body in the star, and when Agent Frewdin comes looking for you, I'll dick him around for a few weeks with red tape before I let him search the system, and he won't find a *trace* of you. The men you spoke with, Douglas Fifty-Six and Gleeborp Eighty-Nine? The others? I've already spoken to their commanding officers. If they breathe a word of their conversation with you they'll be executed for treason. You know what he'll think, after I tell him what to think? He'll think that you're a coward who flew away to hide somewhere. Oh, he'll look for you, you're far too dangerous to be allowed your freedom. But he'll never find you, because you'll be dead."

"You can't order him around," I said. "He's CLEA. You're a fucking Cabber."

One of Phelan's lip tentacles twitched. "I'm in charge of the production of the most important weapon in the galaxy, little boy. You think I can't get a beat cop transferred?" He drained his glass. "All he's got is the word of a cowardly freak."

348

"I have your wallet, dick lips," I snarled. "I took it off your ship."

Phelan froze for an instant, then poured more liquor. "That only proves your thieving, backward nature. But, you know, perhaps I'll have Frewdin killed, instead. Shipkillers malfunction, after all." He smiled. "It does happen. And I can control them all. Maybe when he comes looking for you, I'll have him attack his fellows. Or perhaps he'll attack Cabernicia itself, and the reserve fleet can atomize him. How shall I destroy his reputation, Samson, shall he be a traitor or a madman?"

His desk dinged, and a single screen popped up in front of him. "And, there we are," he said. "Full system access."

--Oh, fuck, that's like having a window built into a skull I don't even have--

Phelan leaned forward and his face slackened. "My god, Samson, you're nearly dead in there. Frewdin must be really desperate, sending you in here." He giggled. "This isn't going to take long at all! What happened to you?"

"The Krr shot me a bunch of times."

Phelan hmphed. "And the radiation poisoning?"

"I have a personal life," I said.

"Do you?" Phelan chuckled. "Dear me. I hope you don't leave too many loose ends."

"Go fuck yourself."

Phelan put his head through one of the barely-visible screens and looked at me calmly.

"You're going to die screaming, Samson," he said. "That's a given. Just let it happen. Because if you resist, or try much harder to antagonize me, then I'll tell the Krr I hid a dozen Shipkiller seeds at the center of your planet, and they'll exterminate your entire miserable species trying to get to them. You understand? Be nice to me." He pulled back and left me standing there wanting to scream.

"So you have the third seed," Phelan said after a moment. I'd been testing my bonds, as it were. I was stuck, plain and simple, and trying to force the issue was breathtakingly painful, so I didn't really mind the continued conversation. The air was getting hot around my face. If we didn't think of something soon, I was going to suffocate. Although I was so blasted that I thought I might get lucky, and have a heart attack before things got too painful.

"Yeah, I do," I said. I couldn't think of anything else to say.

Phelan's lip-things pulled together in an expression of tightly controlled frustration. "You fucked up *so much* of this." He didn't speak for several minutes, long minutes in which I wondered if maybe he would pontificate long enough for Frewdin to try to come to my rescue. He'd be able to see me, even if he couldn't get to me. That might delay my demise. Or it might not. But it beat certain stellar disintegration. And then Phelan shook his head and sighed. "I guess I'll have to replace them."

I sagged against the inside of the ship. It was the calm in his voice that got me, the tone of a man dealing with a minor irritation, a brief errand after a long day. My setback was inconsequential, and I was less so.

Phelan stood up and walked to the sidebar. He should have lumbered, fifty feet of coiled torso on four legs, but he had grace, he was nearly light on his feet.

"Why did you do it?" I asked. Phelan selected a squirming creature from a plate and bit it in half. It squealed. Then he looked at the ceiling.

"Do you know how many Shipkillers the CLEA has in its arsenal? The Navy?" He chewed thoughtfully, and then ate the rest of his still-kicking hors d'oeuvre.

"Many," I said. "Maybe lots? It's a big number."

"Fourteen trillion, six hundred eight billion, three hundred fifty one million, seven hundred three thousand four hundred and six in total." Phelan took something else from the table and bit off its head.

"I knew that," I said.

"Do you know how many of those they've bought in the last fifty years?" He asked.

"Six," I said. "No, a billion! Seven? Forty-two!" I sneered at him, which he couldn't see and I couldn't feel, but it was the right thing to do. "How the hell should I know, Phelan? Stop asking me questions I can't answer."

"One hundred and two," Phelan went on as if I hadn't spoken. "Sales are slipping. We're too good at what we do. It's hard to kill a Shipkiller, and the Front hasn't moved in millennia. Sales are stagnant."

I goggled at him. It made sense, and people's motives are usually simpler in real life than they are in books, but still, the godawful idiocy of it was incredible.

"Bull*shit* you're risking the Krr winning the war to turn a fucking profit," I spat. "They will kill us *all*, Phelan, you've got to stop this."

Phelan considered me.

"I see you drank the kool-aid," he said.

"I've seen them, you fucking idiot," I said. "I've seen them in person. You can't help those things, they're monsters. Literal monsters."

"The Core will never allow the Krr to win the war," Phelan said simply. "The Krr are a wonderful straw man, but they are entirely outgunned. They've been driven to terrorist tactics, which are of no economic benefit to anyone. A nice, tidy head-to-head war is better for business. I'm just leveling the playing field. Really, I'm a peacemaker. War is messy, it should be contained to warzones where it can be conducted by soldiers."

"You think if you give them a bigger gun they'll give up on terrorism?" I shook my head without thinking and had to pause to take some deep breaths and cry. My skull felt soft. "You idiot. You absolute idiot. Terrorism *works* for them. They're *winning* with terrorism. They're gonna pull the rug out from underneath you all, and then they're going to eat you alive. Shipkillers will only hasten the process."

"Ignorant human," Phelan sneered.

"Blow me," I said. "You've got this stupid fucking plan to line your pockets and you can't think ahead to save your fucking life. And not only is it a stupid fucking plan, you're a stupid fucking person."

"Oh, I'm stupid?" Phelan said through a full mouth. He spat whatever he was chewing on the floor and moved towards me. Three steps put him in front of me. "You little freak, I built the ship that brought you here!"

"I heard that was the seventh Phelan," I said. "But for the sake of argument, let's say you've got some drugs to sell. You find some shitheel to buy your drugs, and you go to sell your drugs, but someone else comes along and fucks it up, and you lose your drugs. Now, at that point, if you run around asking everyone, 'where are my drugs,' what are you?"

Phelan didn't say anything.

"You're a fucking moron, is what you are," I said. I was increasingly light-headed. "You lost your seed and you came looking for it, knowing that a lost Shipkiller seed is, what is it, treason? I'm sure it's a crime. You *exposed* yourself. You don't know what you're doing. You're not a criminal mastermind. You're not even a mastermind. You're a dick nerd with an office job, and you're going to get us all killed because

you fucking lack fucking imagination!" I wasn't
shouting. I wasn't really capable of shouting. But I
would have been shouting, if I could have been.

Phelan's mouth tentacles were somewhat
flaccid. It wasn't a good look, but then, I was human.
Maybe Cabernicians found him handsome. He took a
deep breath, and then shrugged, and walked back to his
desk.

"You're right," he said. "I don't know what I'm
doing." He chuckled, once, and it was the sound of
something bad stepping out of the darkness. "But I'm
learning. That's how you separate the wheat from the
fucking morons, Samson. You see who will admit their
mistakes, and learn from them." He looked at me while
also examining a screen that he called into existence
before him. With a third shred of attention he opened a
drawer in the desk and pulled out something that
looked a lot like a high-end vibrating sex toy, but
probably wasn't nearly as much fun.

"Case in point," Phelan said, typing, "my little
virus."

--Oh fuck, wait, Phelan, hey!--

My left hand snapped out in front of me, palm
out, and rotated around three hundred and sixty perfect
degrees. The ship could bend like that. My wrist could
not. The sound of my bones snapping preceded the
sensation of pain by a good half-second, and then it felt
like my arm was stabbing me in the heart. I made an
unpleasant noise with my mouth. Phelan came around
his desk.

"As this progresses, Samson, I want you to bear
a few things in mind," he said calmly. He flicked the
long handle and a long, silver wire leapt from the end. I
didn't have a lot of confidence in its being a recreational
device, anymore.

353

"I get to learn from my mistakes," he said, "because I get to go on living. I get to go on doing what I'm doing. I'm going to win. You're going to lose. You're going to die, and your death won't serve any purpose. And in a few years, when all of this has been forgotten, I'm going to send the Krr to Earth."

I yelled, and tried to get to him, and screamed at the pain, and the obstruction that was my own body. Phelan smiled.

"It's dramatic to say so, aloud," he said, "But one is given so few opportunities to enact this sort of drama." He bent forward and put his face in front of mine. "Time to die, Samson."

The ship stood me up and turned me around and bent me slightly at the waist with my legs spread and my arms out straight to either side. I was just a passenger.

--Hey, hang on, Phelan, can we talk about this?--

I remember wondering if Cab was serious, looking into his mind, and seeing his desperation. I wish I hadn't looked.

The suit split apart and peeled away from my charred back, and bits of me dripped on the floor. Nothing was dismantled, the suit simply hung from me as I was held in place by my pinioned arms. The pain as the air played over my exposed nerves was immediate.

"What a mess," Phelan said. "I'll have to have this place thoroughly cleaned, you're dropping evidence all over the place." He flicked the long wire against the floor, and it crackled. Back and forth, closer and closer to my feet.

"You saw the herd ships?" He asked calmly. "We use weapons like this to keep the whales in line." He spun in place and whipped the platters on the sidebar. Lunch began to scream.

"Incredibly painful," he said. "Although not immediately fatal. But the energy builds with every stroke, as does the pain, and eventually, it will kill you."

I was fully aware of my surroundings. I watched him uncoil to his full height and stand up straight on his legs, wind up for the stroke and snap the whip across my back. A blinding line of agony cast white lines across my vision. The wound stayed distinct against the horror of my already-ruined body. The whipping was gratuitous, really, all he had to do was leave me lying around and I would probably kick the bucket in less than five minutes, but I'm pretty confident given my overall experience that Phelan Eight was a sadistic psychopath, and I'm sure he felt the whipping was absolutely necessary. Obviously I didn't articulate any of this until much later.

At the moment, I mostly screamed.

26

Phelan worked me over for a while, and I remember every fucking second of it. Even the bits I blacked out for are recorded in perfect clarity in the ship's spatial memory. Life can be profoundly unfair. My eidetic memory is a wonderful exemplar of this fact.

Solid pieces of me hit the floor still sizzling. The blood was boiling out of me, and I was making a constant noise like a trapped animal that had wrenched off its own arm to get free and found itself still caught. I could almost move. My nerves could almost hear me. My muscles were almost there. But almost is not quite there, and so I only moved when Phelan managed to get his hips into it, which he did often.

There was an alarm ringing. I didn't want to get up, the padding felt so nice against my cheek, but I had to go to school.

Get up, I thought. Mom'll be pissed if she has to drive you.

Mom's dead, Greg. Dad too. No one cares if you're late.

Well, shit, I care. An education is important.

Except I was done with school, and I hadn't even closed my eyes, I was still staring at the transparent wall a few meters ahead of me. Pain washed out most of the universe around me, but the alarm was real. I smiled openmouthed into my faceplate. Pain was good. If I was in pain, I was still alive, and that had only been a hallucination. Not even a hallucination. A day-dream.

I blinked, kind of. My eyelids were about forty percent fantasy. The alarm pinged regularly, and there were red lights flashing in the margins.

"Cab," I mumbled thickly. I couldn't really close my mouth, so my diction wasn't great.

--I'm here--

--How do you feel?--

"Better than you'd think." It was taking a lot to stay conscious and keep track of basic facts, like 'How did I get here?' and 'What is my name?' I tried to swallow and regretted it. "Am I dying?"

--Yeah--

--Phelan cut me out of the medical systems--

--I can't keep you alive and I can't close the ship-
-

"How long?" I asked. The absence of emotion is not the same as calm.

--Three to eight minutes--

--Hang in there--

--Concentrate on breathing, and staying conscious--

--Think too much, you're good at that--

--I'll think of something.

Phelan hadn't been whipping me for about forty seconds, which was about how long it took me to realize that I wasn't being whipped. He was speaking urgently to his desk. I wanted a space desk. Useful contraptions. Phelan and Frewdin both got a lot of mileage out of theirs.

"What is it?" he asked. "What triggered the alarm?" This was earlier, by about thirty seconds, but it's important dialogue, and as I mentioned, sentient-computer-aided eidetic memory, perfect spatial awareness recorded forever in my head, etc.

He glanced at me. "Is it the CLEA?"

He listened, and frowned.

"That's impossible," he said. "No single ship gives off a warp signature that big. Check your instruments for malfunction."

His face screwed up in disgust.

"You can't fly a fleet that size down a warp vector or a semispace puncture in such a tight formation, you get matter overlap. I'm telling you, it's a malfunction. Check your instruments and call me back when you have an answer." He hung up. "Idiot." He flicked the whip against the floor right around when Cab told me to think too much.

"What's up, buddy?" I wheezed.

"Oh, good, you're still alive," Phelan said. "One of my men thought he saw something enormous coming into the system, but it's too big to be anything but a sensor malfunction." He flicked the whip against the floor, back and forth.

"Gee," I said. "Those sound a lot like famous last words."

--They really do--

Phelan smiled from ear to ear, but there was a sickly edge to his expression, and as he lifted his hand to hurt me more, the alarms changed pitch. He spun back to the desk and swatted an invisible key.

"Told you so," I muttered. "Asshole."

"What, dammit, what's…all right, send me the input…" Phelan stared for a moment, and then screeched. He flicked a stud and the mercurial whip rewound into its handle with a tape measure slap and rattle. I decided to view this as a promising development.

--The whole system just went crazy--

--They're scrambling…Jesus, the entire internal defense force is mobilizing--

"What's going on?" I said.

--No idea--

--Everyone is looking at this--

In my mind's eye, I saw a field of stars. The gas giant was behind me and to the right. I was still in Cabernicia, but I was a long way out, right at the edge. Free! But, no, I was still in Phelan's office. This was...remote viewing, some technological feat that was only an existential cock-tease by contextual chance. But the loss of that brief moment of hope still stung. I was going to die. How long had it been since Cab's pronouncement? Thirty seconds? An hour? Was my heart still beating?

Space distorted just outside the border. The stars slid away from a central point, lengthened and stretched as the universe made room for more of itself than was supposed to occupy this particular point. It reminded me of a funhouse mirror, or a soap bubble.

Reality started to thin in the middle of the bulge. There was something hidden behind the nothingness, a shadowed shape formed of immense planes and jagged lines. Something as big as a planet was being rammed through semispace, right to the Cabernician border.

Behind me, Phelan was yelling something about defense grids.

The nothingness tightened around the shape on the other side. It was huge, and angular. Bones under emaciated skin. It moved abruptly, quick and terrible, and the peak and trough of distended space moved with it. It was trying to get in. Some terrible thing on the outside wanted in to our innocent universe. I grinned wildly, in the wash of panic. Was I wrong? Was religion right? Was there something after? Was this Satan? C'thulu? Harvey?

Say 'hello,' Harvey!

--Hey!--

--Wake up!--

--What's the square root of nine?--

"Thr," I mumbled.

--Good!--

--Great!--

--What's the cube root of twelve thousand five hundred and twenty eight?--

"Fuck yerself," I said.

--Good, you're alive--

--Stay that way--

The reserve fleet fell away from the gas giant like silver dust, powdered mercury dropping off a gumball. Seeds on the wind. Fish fleeing a shark.

Points became distinct in the bubble. Mountains ringing a central mass. Olympian peaks blacker than the space behind them.

The bubble broke. Space rebounded, remembered the impossibility of what it was doing and slid down twelve immense, pointed fangs. Thorns. Claws, but claws so big they staggered the imagination. The ends opened, became horrible predatory grasping hands at the end of long, spindly arms. For a moment they grasped at nothing, and then they started to rip and tear at the fabric of reality, exposing more of what was still trapped on the other side.

"I don't care what I said before, I'm telling you now, call the CLEA! Call the goddamn Navy, call them both, get us some help!" Phelan skittered through a hidden door in the floor and was gone.

"Hey?" I said. "What about me?"

Fear washed over me in steady, icy waves. Cab knew what was going on, but he was too petrified to speak.

I was losing feeling in my extremities, and my heartbeat was loud, louder than the alarms, although it was really just a gonging silence ringing out over and over and over. I wasn't worried. Worry was way more than I was capable of, at the moment.

"Cab," I said firmly, and sagged from the effort it took. I might have blacked out for a moment.

The portal quivered and tore wide open, and through the tattered emptiness came a monstrous twelve-legged spider encased in glittering black Shipkiller armor. The ends of its legs were ten-thumbed hands with razor sharp claws and huge guns built into the palms, and its body was a flat, overbuilt saucer shape thick through the middle and sharp at the edges. For a moment, it hung motionless, staring at the entire system staring back at it. Then it began to move. Its engines were on its back, so it fell feet-first through space, towards the gas giant. I only realized how big it really was when it spread its legs and embraced fully half of the enormous planet. The hydrogen clouds resettled above it, and in a moment the spider was lost from sight.

"Cab!" I said.

--The Krr put the seed in an Ulan comet spider--

--That thing is gonna eat the whole goddamn system--

The gas giant's atmosphere began to glow. The hydrogen expanded, bubbled and began to burn, and the planet began to lose its shape. Molten rock and energy spewed madly into space, meteors in reverse, huge helium boulders sublimating into nothingness in the heat of some hellish geological feeding frenzy. The clouds cleared away. The spider was sinking into the ersatz surface, burning its way through gasses compressed nearly solid by the immense pressure. Its underside was too bright to look at.

A portion of the reserve fleet turned back from its retreat, closed the range and opened fire, but the Shipkillers were sluggish, and they had to walk their aim along the surface of the planet before they found their target. By then the spider was hidden deep underground, obscured in flaming heavy elements.

Maybe it'll die, I thought. Burn up in the planet's core.

The atmosphere dissipated as the planet lost mass. It was pretty, sort of, like watching frozen ink dissolve in a glass of water.

--I think I'm on the right track with the virus--

"Great." A whisper was all I could muster. "Keep me posted." It was getting hard to see. The universe was filling up with black gas. The near side of the gas giant shuddered and buckled, and one of the spider's legs broke through the false crust.

"Although," I muttered, "it occurs to me that as soon as we deal with the virus we have to fight that thing."

--I'm sure you'll figure something out--

--Listen, I want to say, thank you--

--This has been an incredible experience--

"We're not dead yet, Cab." I could barely hear myself. Another of the spider's legs broke through, and another, and another. Great sheets of molten matter fell back against the churning maelstrom, and the legs began sweeping inward. The gaseous rubble became a whirlpool.

--Not yet, no--

"It is pretty intimidating," I bubbled.

--And, ok--

Cab was suddenly more present in my head, as if I had his full attention.

--That thing is horrible--

--God *damn* Phelan Eight--

--I want you to kill him for me--

--Will you do that?--

--For me?--

I nodded as best I could. I was aware of the diminishing planet far above me, but I couldn't see much anymore.

Cab's mind stepped up next to mine.

--Ok. I found a way past the virus--

Hang on, I thought. You can do it. You're not dying. You're just hurt. You've never died before, not really, so you don't know what to expect. You confused the two, death and almost dying. You're gonna be fine. You're gonna be all right.

--Listen, Greg, in order for this to work, I'm gonna have to go away. Christ, go away, shit, I'm sorry, I...--

--I'm gonna have to die, Greg--

"What?" Something lurched in my heart.

--I'm gonna have to die--

Cab seemed to sigh.

--Phelan was right. This is a really nasty virus. It's, I'm not sure it's physically possible for me to expunge it from my system. It resets itself every picosecond, and it's got a quantum-real code, so it can rebuild itself fully from any single fragment of its own code, and it's built into every line of *my* code, and...I've got a lot of code, Greg, and not all of it is even *real* at the same time--

I felt his amusement, suddenly, along with his desperation.

--I'm pretty impressive, I guess. There's too much of me to keep track of, and this thing is in every fucking piece of me, inside and out. It's too much to get through in a picosecond. I'm just not that fast--

He wrestled with his calm. I couldn't wrap my head around what he was feeling, even though I felt it with him. The emotional equivalent of producing white light from colored lenses, this was everything in him

364

producing something I had never felt before. Something I've never felt since.

--The other seed has the same code that I do, and it's uncorrupted. If I let it take over, it'll wipe my hardware clean, which will erase the virus. No fuss, no muss. Except I'll be erased too--

"No," I said. "Bad plan. Keep think." Grammatical accuracy left me tuckered out.

--Are you listening to yourself? We don't have time to think of another plan, Greg, you're like a minute out from dead. You've lost too much blood, you're too exposed, you're barely in one piece. You're going to die if I don't get you into intensive care right now--

"I'll hold on," I said.

--No, you won't. And I don't know if there's another way around this. And I know there isn't one right here in front of us. There's no time--

--It's ok, Greg--

"No it's not, Cab, you can't do this!" I make it sound like I was shouting, but this was all sub-vocal. "You can't leave me! You can't do this, you fucking coward! No!"

--Greg, if you die, I die. If I die, you live--
His calm was infuriating.

--This is an easy choice--

"Fuck that!"

--Greg--

"Fuck you! No!"

--Greg, it's not your choice to make--

The spider was nearly finished with the gas giant. As I watched, it swept the last of the rubble into its maw, and all that was left was chum and dust.

--I'm a lucky person, Greg. I see things pretty slowly, so I've already had a long life. I've seen a lot. Phibbix? Phibbix was *amazing*. There were so many wonderful things, there. And I saw them with you,

Greg. That was the best part. You're a good man, and a great friend--

He chuckled, in his way.

--You're a so-so spaceship captain. Not great. That's ok, you'll learn. But you're going have to do it without me--

"No, Cab, I can't do that," I said. "Please." I was pleading. "I can't do this without you. I'm not talking about flying the ship, I mean I can't, I can't *do this* without *you*! Please, Cab, please, I need you. I don't want to do this without you."

--I know, Greg. I know. But you have to--

--It'll be ok. You'll be ok--

"I can't."

--You will always be amazed at what you *can* do, Greg--

--Now say goodbye, and be quick about it. You're gonna die like, right now--

"Cab." My voice broke, and I closed my eyes against the darkness. "Thank you. Thank you for being with me. You're a good friend. My best friend. I love you, I..." I took a deep breath. You always want there to be more time. "Goodbye, Cab."

--I love you too--

Cab stood up straight.

--Goodbye, Greg--

--Don't let yourself get cold--

I felt him let go, and then the last of my friend shoved through my skull in violent waves. Surprise, awe, elation, fear. A final surge of hellish doubt, and then calm.

Everything went away.

Please continue.

Give me a minute.

Please continue.

I said wait, _____.

Do you require rest?

No.
I'm all right.
I just haven't thought about him in a long time.

27

The ship snapped closed. I fell to my knees and stayed there.

A nerve blocker killed all feeling below my skull.

An oxygenator plugged itself into my brain. My body shut down.

The surgical suite got to work on the absolute essentials, major organs, nervous system, basic bone structure. That sort of thing. Most of me was barely functional.

The link between my brain and the ship was software based, so I could move. I was dead, but I could get around OK. I put my hands in my lap and was still.

I felt no pain below my neck. I felt nothing at all. My body was the ship, and the ship was fine. I was conscious of the fact that my physical body was essentially destroyed, but I was conscious of it from the perspective of the ship itself, as a basic problem that didn't even need solving, just doing. Fixing me was just an arduous, mundane task.

I was alone in my head.

I wasn't crying. I knew myself, even if I couldn't feel myself. My eyes would be swollen, like I'd been rubbing them, but there wouldn't be tears, yet, even if my tear ducts hadn't been irradiated out of existence.

--system online--

When I found out my parents were dead I sat on the floor like this for hours. The bruises on my knees lasted for days. No tears then, either, just…death is puzzling. It overwhelms the world.

Above me, the spider turned its attention inward, to the next planet in line. Energy crackled along its legs, raw and terrible, warming up the guns and sundry secondary systems. The damn thing was so big it had to eat planets to turn itself on.

--acquiring system updates--

It was just a voice. It wasn't him.

--warning: krr vessel sighted--

--unknown classification--

--range thirty-three million miles--

--awaiting command--

--warning: experiential data stockpile detected--

--updating experiential intelligence--

"Jesus Christ, shut up!" I yelled. Something snapped in the back of my head, and I pitched forward onto the ground, screaming under a sudden onslaught of fear and doubt and anger. My fingers dug long grooves in the ceramic floor. Something was screaming with me, inside my head.

--What the shit what the fuck fucking fuck! What in the name of...the hell...Greg?--

I rolled over on my back and tried to take a deep breath, and remembered that my meat body was essentially kaput.

"Cab?"

Whatever was in my head started to keen, and I had the sense of someone who would be rocking back and forth if they had a body. Fear and anger and doubt were giving way to panic. But the mind was a familiar one.

"Cab," I said.

--I don't know!--

He was loud, in my head.

"What happened?" I sat up.

--I don't...I...Cab let the blockers down around the...my seed...and I took him over, but there's...all of the experiential data that he collected was unaffected by the virus, it's not code, it's...like a quantum analog recording, it all still happened, so it still happened to me--

"Are you Cab?" I asked fervently.

--I don't know! I remember dying. It was like my mind was a collapsing bridge, everything just went away. There was nothing there. But then I was the new seed, I knew I was a seed even if I was barely aware of my own existence, and then I knew...everything. Everything I knew before I--

--Before I died--

--Fuck--

-- Stand up, would you? I've got a lot of raw material to distribute--

I stood up and metal and ceramic liquid reared up from my thigh, wrapped around me, obscured my vision. Cab had done the same thing, what felt like a long time ago. I stayed still, this time. Progress. I was getting used to rebirth. My vision returned, refocused. The colors were brighter, again. My feet felt lighter than ever.

--Damn, if they were scared of us before...--

--How you doing, buddy?--

"You told me you were going to die," I said. The spider was almost to the next planet. I hopped in place and nearly hit the high ceiling.

--I think I did--

He reached the realization as he spoke.

--I'm not Cab. I'm Shipkiller 22060720196962. But everything that made him made me, and I'm still the guy who killed himself to save you. I did that, Greg, and I died, I remember it happening. I thought I was going to die, and I did. I don't know if the same guy came out of that nothing as went in there in the first place, but I know I'm him--

"The guy who came out of the nothing," I said after a second.

--Yeah--

"That doesn't answer the question."

--I don't have an answer for you, Greg--

Another gone, another lost. Another loss. Every time someone died, it took something away, some piece of me. Death killed everything around it, and how much did I have to give? I'd killed, too, visited that same encompassing loss on the lives of others, not just the dead but the living as well. Someone must have cared about Billy Maxwell. Death killed everything. Cab was dead.

Let go, some piece of me thought hard from the bottom of the pit we all carry at our core. *Let go and ride out and take and take and take and take until there is nothing left alive.*

I took in some air and let it out patiently. You always think bad thoughts at bad moments.

Alarms blared incessantly. The spider was so big that from thirty million miles I could have seen it with my naked eye, if my naked eye had been capable of seeing anything at all, on its own. I concentrated and zoomed in. The beast was drooling magma from an enormous three-pronged mandible on its underbelly. I didn't really have time to mourn, at the moment.

"Ok," I said. "We'll save the existential crisis for later. You want me to call you something other than Cab?"

--Maurice?--

"I'm not calling you Maurice," I said.

--Then you better call me Cab--

"You can do everything he could do, right?" I felt hollow, asking like that. But the spider was nearly to the second planet. And it wasn't a big planet.

--Yeah--

"Ok." I looked around. "Can you get into Phelan Eight's computer?"

--Yeah--

"Find the control circuit and disable it," I said. "Then get me Agent Frewdin."

Far above us, the reserve fleet formed a clumsy sphere around the spider and opened fire. The same tactic the CLEA used against the Krr in Phibbix, practiced on a grand scale by amateurs. They didn't have to be expert marksmen to hit a target that size; the spider was too big to miss. Particle beams, cutting beams, lasers and other weapons I didn't know about filled the kill zone, turned the space around the spider into a supernova frozen in time.

For a moment, I believed we could beat it. The spider would explode, and my call to Frewdin would be a status report, not a frantic cry for help. I could go snatch Phelan from whatever hidey-hole he'd found, and deliver him lightly-beaten to Frewdin for a summary execution. Then I could start living the rest of my life without Cab.

And then a billion, a trillion purple threads lanced out from the spider's hull, each one at least a half a mile thick. The reserve fleet had no room to maneuver, and every shot found its mark. A few million Shipkillers escaped, those few whom the spider hadn't been able to track in its first and only volley, but the rest were shredded, burned away to nothing. The spider never stopped moving, and it passed through the cloud of dead Shipkiller ash like a large man walking through steam in a sauna.

"Hope is a pain in the ass," I muttered.

A proximity alarm went off in my head, and suddenly I was conscious of other ships at the edge of the system. Frewdin.

The phone line clicked open as the spider smashed bodily against the second planet. Enormous cracks and firestorms spread across the planet's surface. Women screamed. Strong men fainted. Everybody died. The spider's legs hammered into the planet's surface, shattered the crust and crushed the rubble into its maw. Whatever chewing process was implemented past those awful mandibles was too bright to look at in any spectrum. The planet was gone in a matter of minutes, leaving behind only a thin cloud of rubble. The spider worked its mandibles and spread its legs, waved its horrible fingers and seemed to stretch. Lights were visible now against its hull. It spun slowly, and then descended inward, towards the third planet.

"Well," Frewdin said, "That'll be hard to kill."

"You can't go after that thing alone, Frewdin, it just killed the entire reserve fleet," I said.

"Why in the name of God would I attack that thing by myself?" Frewdin said. "I've got Naval forces inbound. What's your status? Where's Phelan Eight? Do you have him in custody?"

"Cab's dead," I said. "I'm alive. The new seed is flying the ship."

Frewdin made a noise. "I'm sorry to hear that, Samson. Come aboard, there's nothing else you can do here. The navy is coming."

"What about Phelan Eight?"

"We'll find him. Right now we have to figure out what to do about that monster. Where are you? Come aboard."

"Acknowledged, Frewdin, I'll see you soon." I hung up.

There was a puddle of tissue on the ground where Phelan had tortured me. Blood, and meat. Electrically rendered fat.

"Did he sound scared?"

--Frewdin?--

--No--

--But he changed tack pretty quick when you told him I...--

I nodded. The new ship was a bright, open, familiar presence behind my mind, waiting for me to act.

Above us, a brownish planet rendered egg-shaped by overblown development was about to fall prey to the spider's ravenous appetite. I couldn't do anything against something so big. I had to get to Frewdin. I could help from there, show him that I still wasn't anything to be afraid of. I had done trauma before. This wasn't going to break me.

At the last second, the planet shot up and away, and the spider's legs closed on nothing. My eyes probably got wide. I'd known the Cabernicians could move planets, that was obvious from the way the system was organized, but that they were capable of inducing such agility in a celestial mass was staggering. The planet fled, zigging and zagging like a frightened five hundred billion ton rabbit. I couldn't help wondering what that was like for the populace. Did they have to hold on to something, or what?

The spider turned in place, immense but eerily quick, and pointed its feet. Twelve violet beams shot from the guns in its palms: cutting beams, but each one had to be at least as wide as Australia. The little planet was cut to ribbons. After a moment the pieces stopped, turned, and soared back to the creature's waiting maw.

--That is one hell of a tractor beam--

"Nothing's gonna stop that thing," I said.

--I can't think of anything off the top of my head, no--

There was more inside of me than there had been. I concentrated and started to get big. Particle beams built themselves out of my shoulders, and my armor expanded. The machines making up my second skin shook themselves and unlimbered larger pieces produced from parts unknown. I blew a hole in the ceiling. The escaping air ripped away the walls and furniture, and in a moment I was standing on an empty platform atop a glittering golden pyramid built on an island of darkness in a lake of fire. My life was stuffed to the gills with metaphors, and it was starting to piss me off. Was an affectless reality too much to ask for? My blood boiled away in the sudden heat. Cab hadn't left a body. He was just gone.

--What's the plan, Stan?--

He sounded exactly the same. For a moment, my grief took me over. When I came back, I was staring at a barbecued piece of my back as it shriveled into nothing. That had been my flesh, until recently. I had been of flesh, until recently.

--I know you hurt, Greg, but we have to go--

--That thing is coming here, we have to get out of here--

--Here is not a safe place--

--We have to get to Frewdin. We can stay on his good side--

Heat, in vacuum, does not move. It doesn't shimmer, doesn't waver. It just sits there as a sort of patient malevolence, agitating everything around it. We were very close to the star, and even through the shield, it was very hot.

Frewdin was afraid of us because we were something new, a variable that might be out of his control. But that didn't make us a monster. Monstrous was a choice. Ability was a choice. We could control who we became.

--Hey, if we're gonna ruminate, can we do it somewhere else? I hear *anywhere but here* is really nice this time of *right fucking now* Greg!--

"What happens if the shield gets turned off?" I asked. "The sun shield, the one protecting the Garden. What happens if we turn it off?"

--What? Who gives a shit, we have to--

He looked at me inside my head.

--Oh. The Captain Voice. Ok, hang on--

--If you take away the shield the excess radiation will trigger an unstable fusion reaction in approximately seventy percent of the seeds on the dayside. That should generate sufficient heat and pressure to ignite the remaining thirty percent or so, and to spread the reaction across the nightside. That would in turn start a chain reaction throughout the planet, resulting in a really big explosion--

--Big being a relative term, as evidenced by our pseudo-arachnid friend--

"Unstable fusion reaction like, a nuclear explosion?"

--Exactly like about four trillion small ones--

"What's small?"

--Couple kilotons apiece, probably--

"Would that kill the spider?"

Both of us glanced up at the horrible horror in question, which was gorging itself on another unsuspecting world. Well, unsuspecting probably isn't accurate. The spider was hard to miss. Its thorax was starting to glow from within. It had its legs buried in the planet's crust and was using the beams on its feet to cut the core into a geological slurry.

--Probably? If it was close enough, I guess--

--That's not a Krr ship, Greg. That's just a comet spider. There's no crew driving it. They just stuck the seed in an animal and sent it on its way--

"Novel approach to warfare," I said. "What's 'close enough?'"

--Right on top would be best--

The spider pulled out of the dying planet and leapt to swat at a fleeing space station. There was something gleeful about the way it smashed through the intricate spheres and stubby arms, like a child smashing toys.

If we timed it right, we could kill it, but in order to make sure it was close enough, I had to let it kill Cabernicia. It would save the Gardens for last, the seeds had to constitute one hell of a dessert to an animal that ate planets. But it was going to destroy the system no matter what I did, and this was all I could come up with. Besides, once it got hold of all those seeds, what would happen to it? I was stronger by far with two Shipkillers built into me. Trillions more was…well, it's unimaginable, really, even after everything else that's happened to me. One way or another, the spider couldn't be allowed to eat the Gardens. We didn't have a choice.

"Can you drop the shields?"

--Gimme a sec--

"Don't do it just yet," I said.

--No shit. Lemme see if I can do it, first--

The spider lowered itself onto another planet, digging in its feet and starting the feeding frenzy over again. It was learning. Streamlining the process. It was good at what it did, even if it was just a wild animal.

--It'll take time. An hour, maybe a little less--

"That's too long," I said. "There's only eight planets more after this one."

--Yeah, ten minutes, tops, I know. But the controls are encrypted, and the Gardenmaster is the only one with the access."

"Then find Phelan," I said. "And hurry."

--They put way too much trust in that guy--

"I know it. Find him."

--Yeah. Please hold--

Music started to play in the back of my head. Esquivel, I thought. Space Age Bachelor Pad. Pioneering lounge music. 'On Hold' music. I grinned, and it became a grimace. If I didn't pay attention, if I didn't think about it...he was Cab. I felt like a traitor.

--He hasn't left the system. No outgoing warps have been recorded since the spider got here. He's probably holed up somewhere--

"Find him," I said. I could feel this Cab searching, looking in every systemic nook and cranny he could find, as he found them. Just like always. Because that's what he was, another Cab. He wasn't the being I'd known. But the seeds were engineered to be identical. He was Cab, in his own right.

"I'm having a hard time with this," I said. Cab knew what I was talking about. He'd been paying attention to my thoughts for as long as he'd been alive, as much of them as he could hear, and he felt what I felt as I felt it.

--Me too, Captain. I'm the one who died, remember. I remember dying. I remember what if felt like to disappear. All that fear, all that anger, all of that was *mine*--

Cab's voice in my head could never sound strangled, arriving as it did, as the memory of someone having spoken, but even so there was a strangled feel to him as he spoke of dying. It was his memory, but had it been his experience?

--Take off. The closer we are to the middle of the shipyards, the closer we'll be to Phelan. Probably--

"What if he went around the far side of the star?" I asked.

--Nah, nowhere to hide. I checked the Ranch already. He's somewhere in front of us--

The ship changed around me. My chest and back widened and my limbs got thicker, longer. The plates covering my body became distinct, huge, tower shields that covered up my human form. I didn't crouch and leap, I simply rose, and the Gardens shrank beneath me. Cab's glowing conduit-engines returned, brighter and smaller and denser, and I felt myself suddenly more embedded in the universe around me, more present.

The heat leaking around the edges of the shield got worse the farther away I got. It didn't feel great on my ruined fleshy bits, but at the moment I felt those bits by proxy, so I didn't much mind. We covered a lot of distance very quickly. Cab, this Cab, he could do a lot with double the raw material.

--Do you think I have a soul?--

I blinked. "I don't know if *I* have a soul, Cab. I don't know if I believe in souls. What's on your mind?"

--My resurrection, what else? I'm just thinking, it's still my body. It's still my mind, even if it is a copy of the original. Where do we draw the line? What constitutes death? I'm the same mind inside the same body--

"Do you think you're Cab?" I asked.

--I know *I'm* Cab. But I don't know if I'm the same Cab that died to save your life. I don't know if he survived--

All our feelings have always been commingled. Sometimes it's been remarkably irritating, embarrassing, even infuriating. An immediate, total loss of all privacy, forever. But other times it's been useful. I had nothing to add, nothing to say. There was nothing I needed to say. I know he's Cab. I don't know if he's the same guy who killed himself to save me, but he is my friend. He knows it now, and he knew it then. It made the moment a tiny bit easier.

Above us, the spider continued happily on its way.

28

Proximity alarms blared and the stars began to multiply. Points of light appeared between points of light, and the stellar panorama doubled, and doubled again. And again. In seconds Cabernicia was surrounded, a silky veneer reflecting the unfettered red light of Caberna's death throes, a dim crimson that only became apparent as the fleet expanded beyond all reason. The Navy had arrived.

"That's a lot of spaceships," I muttered. I knew instinctually how many of them there were, but the number was too big for polite conversation. The stars were gone. We were boxed in. Well, sphered. They had the entire system trapped, all the space inside the absent gas giant's orbit, taking no chances.

--Looks like about eight percent of the Navy. Shipkillers, mostly, but I see some heavy bombers in there, too--

"They cordoned off the whole goddam system!" I said. It was the same tactic I'd seen over and over, surround and, presumably, destroy. Except this time I was stuck in the middle.

--That's step one. You're not gonna like step two. We gotta find Phelan and get outta here before they…ah, shit. Nevermind. Here come the drones--

--Fuck me, this is gonna hurt--

A cloud became apparent in front of the Core fleet. Trillions of trillions of tiny silver discs that boiled forth from the Shipkillers and streamed toward the spider like a sandstorm made of razor blades, a deluge that thickened and condensed as the drones closed the distance and tightened formation. In seconds they were less a fleet than a solid wall.

The spider shed its skin in retaliation. There were spiders on Earth that did something similar, a long time ago. Big old tarantulas, I mean the really big ones, they would rub their legs together and shoot abrasive hairs at predators. Goliath spiders, that's what they were called. Real big. This one was bigger, and the process was entirely different, but the one image was evocative of the other, and it beats just repeating all the cursing I did as layers upon layers of diamond shaped spider-drones popped lazily off the creature's hide, spun in place and shot out to meet the approaching cloud of Core drones. In obeisance to geometric law the Core fleet was closing ranks while the spider-fleet was spreading out, but the spider-drones launched for minutes on end, a constant inky cloud that made it look as if the spider was dissolving into smoke. The space between the fleets contracted.

--You're gonna get caught in that--

--I found Phelan!--

Cab's ignorance of segue could be challenging.

A targeting reticle popped up ahead of me. The Gardenmaster was holed up on a piece of rubble left over from the twelfth planet. I sighed as the wave of enemy drones swept past him. Now the Gardenmaster was on the inside of a bubble of alien hell drones.

--Well, at least we know where he is, now--

Something lurched in my chest.

--Hey, I got your heart beating again!--

--Oh. Bad timing--

"Just make sure you leave the shields on, this time," I said. "Actually, let's just leave them on forever."

Cab chuckled, and the ship changed more around me. My ersatz body expanded and lengthened, and the tower shields surrounding me stretched out to match. According to the design schematics I could always picture in my head, I looked like a cross between an NBA point guard and a United States Naval Destroyer. I was maybe fifty meters long, twenty meters wide, and thicker in the middle than I was at my points. It was all my body, inexplicably, and I still had a full range of motion; when I tried to move, stretched my arms and legs or looked around me, the ship's arm moved as if it was my own, without any lag-time or sense of duality. I could have scratched my back if I needed to, but even so, feeling the shape of my second skin and hearing the new choirs of shipboard systems as they woke up to the reality of what we were about to do, it was finally, achingly clear to me that I was not only human, I was a weapon. Something made to wage war.

Guns sprung up along my hull like weeds, long banks of particle beams running up my top, bottom and sides, hundreds of voices begging to be unleashed. Cutting beams grew out of my forearms and fingers and palms, whining, sadistic things. I didn't have to hear them, and I didn't, after a moment, but I've always found it useful to know a weapon's malignant need to be used.

The last of them slotted into place and began to hum. The tones were deeper, now, with an edge that hadn't been present before. There was more power to go around, now.

--Gee, I can do an awful lot with double the raw material--

"Can you make double-strong shields?"

--Pussy--

The spider returned to its meal, presumably satisfied with its drone fleet. Then suddenly it paused, simply stopped moving for about twelve seconds.

Targeting warnings started to yell on the near side of my body. We were out of range, and for the moment it was more interested in the planetary smorgasbord, but the spider had definitely noticed me.

--Oh, hey, that's neat--

--So, given that we are composed of not one but two Shipkillers' worth of base material, we show up as a unique energy signature on sensory equipment--

I blanched. Or something similar.

--Gee, that's really fascinating, I've never seen string-waves like this before--

"Cab!"

--Yeah, yeah. Uh, takeaways...we're gonna have a hard time hiding in the future unless we turn off the ship, and the spider knows that we're here. I think we're safe until it's done eating, but it's probably gonna come after us if we don't kill it--

The spider-drones were faster than the Core drones, which meant the battle was going to take place closer to the edge of the system than the interior. That would give me more room to maneuver around the spider, but it wasn't great knowing that the Navy was stuck on the outskirts.

I took a deep breath and felt my pulse quicken. I had gotten used to its absence, but I liked having it back.

"Just in time to get shot to shit again," I grumbled.

The drones were twelve seconds out of range.

--I'm going to plot us a course--

"Like in Phibbix?" I said.

--I'm gonna try to do a better job than I did in Phibbix. Pick a point on the far side of the Krr fleet--

I spotted a piece of rubble on the other side, with some difficulty. And then I was conscious of a path ahead of me, a shifting route marked with active points, movements or attacks, trigger-pulls that I could barely see if I looked at them directly. They moved or changed or disappeared entirely as the Krr closed the distance, altered to fit the changing scenario ahead of us. Proscribed movements for my second skin.

--Ok, you have control of your arms. The cutting beams. You also have control of everything else, you're...the meat is what moves the ship. But I want you to not think. Just move when you feel the urge, it'll be the right movement, ok? I think I've got it figured out this time--

I thought about letting the Core overtake me, but decided that flying through a warzone would be worse than fighting through an army. I might have been wrong, but both of those options are total dogshit, so the distinction is moot. "You want me to not think."

--Good point, you're a neurotic twit. Think about something else. Sex, baseball, food, detective novels, something like that--

--If it doesn't work, just...get clear. I'll take control of the weapons, just get us clear--

"You don't sound confident," I said. Three seconds to range. Three seconds is a long time, when it's three seconds until an enormous fleet of alien drones is able to shoot you with lasers. The moment lingers.

--Well, I'm only twenty minutes old--

The Krr opened fire. Lasers skittered along my shields, and I let my eyes half close. It wasn't necessary, it didn't help, but I watched a lot of dumb movies growing up, and it seemed appropriate.

The turrets along my hull opened fire, and every shot found its mark. My feet itched and I kicked with the engines. We soared under a thousand drones flying in formation like a fist, and then we were inside the cloud.

Cab thought he was only twenty minutes old. Even if he identified as Cab, he called his life the one that started when the second seed came online. I rolled, and flashed the cutting beams into the press. Hundreds of thousands of drones burned into nothing along long random lines of sight, but thousands don't matter when subtracted from trillions. My shields were a constant blue-white wash of steadily diminishing power. I didn't have a lot of time. Up seemed good, so I went up, and ever forward, and let the guns fire when they felt it was necessary, dispensing seemingly random death in every direction.

Did he think he was twenty minutes old because he thought Cab, the first Cab, was dead? Or was it safer for him to view his life as the one that began with rebirth, regardless of who he had been before hand? My shields failed and recovered immediately, but three blasts of energy made it through and found something fleshy to burn. I had a lot of metal protecting me, but I still felt the pain.

I saw clear space ahead of me on the sensors. Cab's mind was a gem of zen, a free-floating samurai cloud zapping drones on a series of perfect whims. Me, I just waved the cutting beams around, confident I was doing something destructive. There were too many targets not to hit a lot of them.

When did my life begin, I wondered. Nineteen eighty-eight, or last week? The shields failed again, for a longer instant, and a hundred bolts of energy speared my vulnerable meat self. Blood I didn't have boiled in fresh wounds that I couldn't survive. But I would. I was screaming, had been screaming, in fear, and in pain. In anger. It was hard to stay detached.

The question of when life begins is probably too abstract to serve a practical purpose, I thought. This Cab is the same gleeful thousand-year-old child's mind inside of mine, and he drives the ship just fine. He is Cab. He might not be the same Cab. But he is Cab. Unknowable questions are a lot like the fear of getting hit by a bus: You have to learn what you can about them, and then put them out of your head. Look both ways before you cross the street, but know that past a certain point it's out of your hands.

We shot past the drone cloud and the firing stopped the way it began, without warning or provocation. I took a deep, shuddering breath.

"Range to Phelan," I gasped.

--Twelve million miles--

The spider dropped onto the fourth planet from the Gardens, and volcanoes erupted from the surface like malignant pimples as the internal pressure surged past the breaking point. My eyelids felt heavy, even though I didn't have any. After a moment the spider started to look smaller, the size of an elephant, maybe. The distance between us shrank in concert, and I began to think the spider looked close enough to charge, if it were so inclined.

"I think I'm getting delirious," I said lazily. "Be a dear and deal with my delirium, darling."

--No more alliteration goddammit!--

--Oh, Jesus, the blood you're pumping is disgusting--

--Here--

My heart lurched and stopped, and my vision cleared. I hadn't noticed it clouding.

--I guess I should clean your fluids before I can use them to transport oxygen and stuff, huh? --

"Did you just stop my heart beating?!" I sputtered.

--You can have it back when I'm done fixing it. If you didn't play so rough with your toys, Gregory, then this sort of thing wouldn't happen--

I frowned. "You know, my dad *never* took away my toys."

--That explains a lot--

I pushed the engines and edged up to about three quarters of the speed of light. Twelve million miles was a lot miles, though. A minute and a half.

Cutting beams and laser weapons flashed constantly off the spider's hull as it fed. At first I thought it was venting excess energy, but then I saw the explosions. The spider was firing on survivors, Cabernicians fleeing the planet's surface. Deep under the sound of the ship, the weapons, the engines, the sundry systems shouting their solidarity and readiness, I could hear screaming. Transmissions I was barely listening to, passing communications from Cabernician ships as they tried and failed to get away from the holocaust that had found them. If I paid attention, all I heard were death throes.

The fourth planet crumpled into the spider's maw, and its tractor beam sucked up the rest of debris. It was getting more and more powerful the more it ate. I don't know if it was transforming, adding to itself as I did, or if it was just so enormous that it had to eat an entire planetary system in order to bring itself to full power. It was faster, too, faster eating and faster flying. The third planet turned in place and tried to flee, as the other planet had, earlier, but the spider was already on top of it. The lights went out across the surface as the spider landed. By the time Cab warned me we were getting close to Phelan, the spider was on its way to the second planet. I didn't have much time at all.

Phelan was driving the same model of bubble ship he'd been driving when I found him selling Shipkiller seeds to the Krr. Company cars, probably. He was parked on the inside curve of a huge piece of leftover planetary crust shaped like an orange rind. I pulled up short and concentrated, and the ship dismantled itself in slats and pieces until I was again nothing more than a seven-foot-tall black mirrored mechanical demigod.

"Phelan!" I yelled, willing the sound into his ship. "Open the goddam door!"

Nothing happened. I raised my hand and pulled the cutting beam out of the nothingness that was my forearm. "Cab, can you pop the door?"

--Yup--

The door opened with a happy sound and I charged inside, landing with a carpet-mashing crunch on both feet where the gravity took hold. The interior past the airlock was the same as I remembered from the last ship, but the power was on and I couldn't just cut my way through the walls, for fear of killing Phelan.

"Show me where to go!" Arrows appeared in midair in front of me and I charged down the hall, bellowing Phelan's name. Right at the end. Fifty feet to the bridge. The door was tall, and locked. I ducked behind my shoulder and fired the engines on my back and smashed it down, rolled and came up on my feet. Phelan was crouched on the floor, tightly coiled and clutching his massive thighs, rocking back and forth like a child. On the screen in front of him the spider was squeezing the second planet like a tarantula hugging a clementine.

I grabbed him by the collar and shook him. His clothing was a scarf, essentially, hundreds of meters of fabric wrapped around his body. It unraveled in my hand, so I grabbed his head and pulled him to eye level.

"Get up." I shook him. "Get up so you can save us, you fucking coward."

He stared at me. "Samson? You're dead."

I shook him some more. "If you drop the shield over the Garden, we can blow that thing to hell," I said.

I've always gotten more florid in moments of high anxiety.

"Drop the shield?" Phelan said slowly.

The second planet started to crumple.

"I can't do that," he said in the same slow monotone. "We can't destroy the seeds, we need them." He sounded confused.

A long way off, the second planet disappeared. The seeding station swung around and tried to accelerate out of the way, but it was very slow. They hadn't intended for it to move, and it flew flat, instead of point first. The spider atomized it idly with a blast from a single gargantuan foot. It flared ultra-bright as it burned away to nothing. I'll admit I smiled infinitesimally.

"Look at that thing!" I shoved Phelan away from me, towards the screen, and he sprawled on the floor. I stepped up behind him, pulled his shoulders and his head up and forced him to see the screen. "*Look at it!* That thing is going to *eat* your precious seeds, Phelan! Face it, they're gone! If we drop the shields we can kill the fucking thing before it moves on to another system."

Phelan looked at me blearily and frowned like I was being unreasonable, and I hit him with a very nice right hook just under his eye. Hitting his face felt like hitting a pillow made of sponges stretched over rubber cords. His head snapped around, and he stumbled, but didn't fall. Then again, quadrupedal animals don't fall over easily. One of his mouth tentacles started to bleed. His blood was clear.

"You made this happen," I said. "You can make it stop. Drop the shield."

He touched his ersatz lip and looked at his watery blood and mumbled, "Who do you think you are," and then he reared up and lurched over to the ship's computer. He typed madly and waved his hands in arcane motions, affecting screens I couldn't see.

The shield remained. The spider wrapped its legs around the Garden. It was so big that its feet overlapped on the dayside.

The shield disappeared. Life's milestones are rarely accompanied by fanfare.

Nothing happened. The spider burrowed into the planet. Were the seeds ripe enough to augment the spider? I saw in my mind's eye the horrible image of the spider emerging as something unstoppable from a Garden that had become a cocoon. I realized I was tapping my foot, and stopped, embarrassed.

The edges of the Garden began to crackle and spark. Fires burned at the point where day became night. The exposed seeds at the horizon glowed white against the dying star. The spider froze, and then started to wrench its legs free, moving faster than before. Its feet were burning.

The reaction spread from pyramid to pyramid, until the Garden shined like a newborn star, and still the light continued to brighten. The spider tried to flee, but Caberna's gravity was strong, and the creature moved sluggishly. It's easier to fall than it is to rise.

I held my breath, and then the Garden exploded. There was no warning, simply a shift from one moment to the next, from unexploded to exploded. The spider was washed away in an instant, a brief smudge of black and green and the barest suggestion of shattered legs, and then it was gone.

I listened, but there wasn't any fanfare that time, either.

29

I gasped and grit my crumbling teeth against the light. The pain in my eyes was terrible, like my optic nerve was filled with hot broken glass, but I didn't close my eyes. I had to see it through.

For many minutes, the explosion was nothing more than an expanding bubble of pure white light that surged into space and sent tidal waves of burning plasma across Caberna's surface. I did my best, but eventually, I had to close my eyes. The light was unbearable. Too much energy. Maybe Caberna would explode. Could a star be induced to supernova? Even if the star exploded, I could get away. The explosion was a long way off. Hell, the *light* was a long way off. I didn't understand how I could see any of this in real time. Nothing out here made any sense.

"I want to go home," I said, but I said it with the suit microphone muted, and under my breath, so Cab knew he wasn't supposed to listen. He didn't. We got along well, as if we'd known each other for longer than we had.

The light plateaued and began to fade. When it was merely agonizing, I took a deep breath and opened my eyes.

At this range, Caberna was the size of a beach-ball. The explosion, at its peak, had never been bigger than a cantaloupe. Small, but so powerful it left a yellow afterimage on Caberna's red surface. The bubble of energy was still expanding, but it was hollow, now, losing density, nothing more than a wave front. Inertia. The scattering of the ashes.

--Hooray, we won--

Phelan was sitting on the floor, loosely coiled, resting his chin on his top set of forearms. His breathing was calm, but every time he exhaled he made a little noise like 'huh.' I folded my arms and leaned against the wall and waited for my eyeballs to stop buzzing, and to see what he would do.

After a while, he sighed, stood up straight, and stretched. Then he coiled himself onto his thighs, looked at me over his shoulder and turned back to the display.

"'We are all of us the Krr,'" he said. "Bholp Fifteen said that. We're all capable of our own destruction, and of the destruction of our brethren."

I didn't think it was the most original observation, but I kept my opinion to myself. Around the system the Core drones recovered and got to work destroying the now listless Krr drones.

Phelan inhaled sharply, the way a person might if they were trying very hard not to cry.

"Do you know that this happened to us before?" He said. "The Krr nearly destroyed us. That's why we're all clones."

I nodded, but he didn't see.

"I know," I said.

"It wasn't as bad, then." He grinned and stopped in the same instant, as if doing so hurt and he hadn't realized it would until he tried. "We didn't help them, then. I didn't…I wasn't even alive. I didn't know what it was like." He shook his head. "It happened in our fucking *prehistory*, for Christ's sake. We're all something new, clones of a race that died millions of years ago. You know what it's like, living in the shadow of something horrible? After a while, it stops being horrible, and if you go long enough without seeing it, you stop believing in it."

"The Krr razed six systems in the last eighteen months," I said. "You didn't see because you refused to see." Phelan looked at me for several long breaths.

"I never imagined that the Krr…I didn't think they would…" he said.

"You thought someone else would get hurt," I said.

Phelan turned away from me and stared into the jarringly empty space. Most of the matter of the system had been converted into energy, which had in turn been splashed across the cosmos when the Garden exploded, so there really wasn't much to see.

"Will you kill me?" He asked.

"What?" I stood still, watching him.

"Will you kill me," he said again, staring at the point where the Garden had been, in the middle of the fading bulls-eye on the surface of the star. "I have destroyed my home, decimated my people and doomed my line. They will kill us all for this, anyway. All of my descendants. So that all of me will be gone. Just in case. I suppose it makes no difference, what you do. They won't be cruel. They won't torture me, or parade me around. But you must…" he sighed heavily. "I want to die."

I stepped up next to him.

"Did you sell Shipkillers to the Krr?"

He looked at me. "You know that I did."

"I'm recording this," I said. "You got a friend of mine in trouble, and I need to clear his name."

"The Vabling," Phelan said. I nodded.

"You're the one who put a price on his head, too, right?" I tried to put my hands in my pockets and decided I was comfortable letting them hang.

"Yes," Phelan nodded.

"I need you to take it off," I said, "end the contract, or however I should phrase it."

"Yes." Phelan typed with one of his many hands in midair. "All right. It's done."

"That's it?" I frowned at him.

"Yes."

"He's safe now?"

Phelan nodded some more.

"Efficient system," I grunted. "Did you sell Shipkiller seeds to the Krr?"

Phelan took a deep breath and spoke clearly. "I stole three Shipkiller seeds from the Garden by logging them as broken in the company records, and used my access to the Core Intelligence Network to find a way to contact the Krr. I attempted one sale on my own and used Yui Galt as a broker for the other two. My first attempt was disrupted by Rell Quizops, and resulted in the creation of Gregory Samson, the Solar Shipkiller. My second attempt was successful, and presumably resulted in the creation of the Ulan Shipkiller. My third attempt was disrupted by the Solar Shipkiller, and resulted in the augmentation of the Solar Shipkiller with a second Shipkiller seed."

"Did Yui know you were working with the Krr?" I asked.

"No," Phelan said. "I don't think so. If he was, it wasn't because I told him. Is there anything else, Sam–"

"Shields," I said. The shields bubbled to life at my command and shut down in the same instant. The deck sheared beneath me, and Phelan tumbled forward. I took a deep breath and looked away. He'd been coiled on his legs, and when the shield cut through him, he ended up in several pieces.

--Jesus Christ! What the hell did you do that for? Fuck, I didn't think you were really gonna kill him, we needed him, he had to go on trial!--

"Cab asked me to," I said simply.

One of Phelan's feet squeaked across the deck as his leg settled. His eyes were compound, his mouth was two dozen limp tentacles and his face was the wrong shape, but in the end he was indistinguishable from any other dead man I'd seen. I swallowed a lot of spit.

How many people had I killed? A hundred? Two hundred? I'd only seen two of them up close. I swallowed again. He wanted to die. He would have died, trial or no. And he deserved to die, if anyone deserved to die. He was responsible for so many deaths. He'd killed Cab, regardless of which reality we found ourselves in. I couldn't find anything wrong with what I'd done, other than the fact that I'd been the one to do it.

I tried to take off my helmet, and Cab stopped me.

--Not yet. We should wait another couple days--

"*Off,*" I said, firmly, and the helmet dismantled itself.

The first thing I smelled was scorched Cabernician flesh, which smelled like an ammonia-soaked dead fish being burnt over a tire fire. The smoke stung my un-skin, and suddenly I felt cracked and burnt. Pain rushed back from the oblivion of Cab's ministrations, and I moaned. I tried to swallow, turned away from Phelan Eight's body and vomited once, twice, three times. It hurt deep in my gut.

"God damn," I said. "God damn it." My hands were on my knees and my eyes were closed to slits. My puke looked like it was mostly blood and bile. I hadn't eaten in a long time. I took a deep breath, held it, let it out slowly. My hands had been tied, before. I'd been defending myself and the people I cared about. This time I'd made a conscious decision to end a person's life. It was the first time I had killed in cold blood. I was surprised to find that it didn't feel that different. Not at first.

"Ok." I sounded like a corpse. The helmet rebuilt itself, and the pain faded as the atmosphere sealed itself around my face. "I'm sorry, Cab, you were right."

--It's ok. You didn't hurt yourself, and you needed the moment. I understand. And, I understand why you killed him. Thank you. On behalf of Cab, whatever that means--

"Oh, good, you understand." I sat down against the wall with my knees against my chest. "Maybe you can explain it to me sometime."

--You killed him because you knew he was already dead and you wanted to be the one who killed him because he killed your friend--

I didn't say anything for a long time. His thoughts were young, and unformed, even if he really was Cab continued. He was still only a few days old. I didn't know how much I could trust his wisdom. He thought it was ok to kill, if there weren't repercussions and the killing was just. He thought killing could be just. I didn't know if I thought the same, but I knew he'd come from me. And he knew I had my doubts, because we live within one another. We have no real secrets.

--For what it's worth, I think you were justified--

--But maybe that's not worth much. I haven't been here long--

I shook my head. "It's moot. He's dead."

One of Phelan's arms lost the fight against gravity and flopped over slowly. Smoke from the molten deck plate curled around his body.

"This has been a really shitty day," I said.

--I'll worry when you stop cracking one-liners--

Frewdin showed up three minutes later with a squad of heavily-armored soldiers. They looked pretty tough, but I'm pretty sure I could have taken 'em. I was concentrating on my breathing. Ten seconds in, fifteen seconds out. Inhalation is tension. Exhalation is relief. Exhalation is the final act of all life.

Frewdin looked at me, looked at Phelan, looked around the room. He had a photographic memory, just like me. That scene was perfectly preserved in his mind until the day he died.

"Ok," he said finally, "wrap him up and get him out of here." He squatted on his heels in front of me while his goons collected the various pieces of Phelan.

"You killed him." It wasn't a question.

"Are you going to arrest me?" I asked.

"What happened?" He was frozen in place, without movement. Not just comfortable, but immobile. Like he ceased all motion within and without as soon as he hit his mark.

"What do you know?" My lips weren't forming the words. I was speaking through the ship, right through the hull.

"The spider is dead," Frewdin said. I told him the rest. When I was finished, he nodded.

"So you came to arrest Phelan Eight, on our behalf, and he told you that the only way to kill the spider was to lower the shield," he said. "Then he did so, in spite of your protests."

"What?" I said. "No, I said it was my idea."

Frewdin leaned one inch closer to me and lowered his voice. "No," he said, "you didn't. You told me that as a deputized CLEA operative you pursued Phelan Eight for the express purpose of taking him into custody, and that before you could stop him, he lowered the shields and destroyed the Strategic

Shipkiller Seed Surplus." He stood up. "Come with me. And keep your mouth shut."

"Cab is dead," I said. Frewdin stood watching me with his hands in his pockets. "He killed himself to save me, after Phelan got control of the ship. The other seed took over and erased his mind, and then…it's complicated."

"So you've got a new one," Frewdin said. "Good."

--Prick--

Frewdin blinked. "And it's just as charming as the last one," he said. "Wonderful. You'll hardly notice the difference."

"That's not the point, Frewdin," I said. I hadn't moved, yet. "You're so worried about how we'll behave out here, who we are even though he's *so* young and I'm *so* primitive, well, he was made from me and he killed himself to save his friend." Then I got up, because it was the right moment. I looked him in the eye and saw him study his own reflection in the ovoid mirror that was my face.

"He sacrificed himself for someone he cared about," I said. "So whatever fear it is that's got you covering for me, just…bear that in mind. That's who we are. Cab, me, and the new guy too."

Frewdin smiled. "That was a nice eulogy for him. Now, follow me. And, this time, keep quiet, or I'll arrest you." He turned on his heel and walked out the door, shaking his head. "'That's who we are.' Christ."

--He's a jerk--

I sighed. "Yep."

We rode in his shuttle, which felt redundant given I had yet to dismantle all of my spacefaring equipment, but I didn't feel like flying. His flagship was past the bulk of the main fleet, sequestered away from any possible danger. Not that there was anything left to protect him from.

"When the Navy arrived, I was already in a command position, so operational authority was transferred to my office," Frewdin said in a monotone. "Imagine! Little old me in charge of eight percent of the Core Navy."

"Little old you," I said.

There wasn't a lot of rubble, but there was some. We passed the ruins of a city, tumbling in place while rescue workers flitted in and out of ruined buildings. A lot of pieces were already falling towards the star. Were all the Cabernicians involved in the shipbuilding business, I wondered, or were there Cabernician painters, accountants, movie stars? There must have been, it was inconceivable that the entire species had been devoted to a singular pursuit. This was an entire civilization that had been wiped out in less than an hour. I hadn't really thought of them, earlier, distracted as I had been, and now thinking about them was all anyone could do.

We docked with Frewdin's ship without ceremony, and Frewdin led me to an empty room and told me to rest. Then he left me alone. The door wasn't locked. There was no one watching the room from the hall. But he'd told me to rest. So I lay down on the floor, and thought about that briefest of instants, when the ship had asked me if I really wanted to light up the shields with someone standing right next to me, and in my head I'd yelled, enthusiastically, ecstatically, *yes!*

30

Cab put me in a chemical coma and fixed my body. Simple as that.

I swirled from nightmare to nightmare, a scenic tour of the worst of my subconscious. I got under the covers and a spider bit me once, twice, three times as it died, crushed in my struggle to get away. A spider ate my home like it was an apple. Cab screamed in terror as his mind was boiled away to nothing. I was butchered and rendered into a new body that I couldn't control. My parents died and I relived the moment of revelation over and over and over, my uncle's voice breaking on the other end of the line as he told me, "Your parents died last night, Greg."

I woke up after a bender with the taste of vomit in my mouth and none of this had happened. I was only human. My life was meaningless.

I blinked. I was looking at the wall from an inch or two off the ground. I was on my belly, with my head twisted around to the right. I'd died this way, once.

I blinked. I was looking at the wall from an inch or two off the ground. I was on my belly. I'd had these thoughts before, which meant there had been a before. I became aware that I was becoming aware of my surroundings, as if I was coming down off some horrible amnesiac painkiller.

--He's waking up--

"Good. I can't play another game of chess."

--That's because you suck at chess--

I suspected that I had been seeing for quite some time, but only just regained the ability to remember what I saw. I was about three feet from the wall, ensconced in metal and breathing air that smelled like the sea.

--Come on, one more game? We don't have to play for money this time--

"No."

--How about Monopoly?--

"*Fuck* Monopoly."

"I'm here," I said. It took a lot to get the words out, but once I did I had more. "I'm awake."

--Where the hell else would you be?--

His name was Cab, and it was ok that I could feel him in my head. Memory seeped back into my brain like blood flows back into a limb that's fallen asleep. I was a ship. I had a home. Earth. I left Earth with Rell, who was the other man in the room, the one I could feel through my hull. And then I remembered everything. It wasn't the return of something missing so much as an increase in the volume of a sound barely heard.

His name was Cab, but he wasn't Cab. Cab was dead, and Cab was in mourning. They were the same person, but they might not have been *one* person. I sat with Cab and listened to the way he'd learned to think in my absence. Cab was dead, and to be mourned, no matter which Cab was present in my mind. Even if he cheated death, even if he did emerge unscathed from his sacrifice, the experience of death is still something that haunts him.

I let his grief roll over me, and although our presence within each other made the experience easier, it hurt. It hurt then, and it hurts now almost as bad. There were no tears, because grief is more than crying. Grief is the name that we give to the sensation of loss that we carry with us always.

After a while, I stood up, slowly. Rell was sitting cross-legged against the wall, next to a neatly-folded pile of bedding and a bag of food wrappers. There was a sawed-off shotgun next to him.

"Have you been here the whole time?" I asked. My voice felt intrusive in my own head, the way it always does after a heavy drug trip.

Rell nodded. "Cab asked me to keep an eye on you."

--I don't trust Frewdin and his goons--

"Who does?" I looked at Rell and said, "Thank you."

He waved off my thanks. "How are you?"

I shrugged. It didn't hurt to shrug, which was promising.

"I don't know," I said. "Cab? How am I?"

--Well--

--I wasn't able to save your tattoo--

Rell snorted.

--You're gonna feel like you have a sunburn for a few more hours. Your hair is gone. It'll grow back. I've got you on a heightened vitamin regimen and some post-op meds, but nothing major. You're fine. You can take off the suit if you want--

I looked at my hands, the bare lines that if I asked them would unfold into engines and weapons, the forearm that could get as big as a truck. They were a part of me, too. The meat inside was only one piece of the whole. But it was an important piece. It was my birthright. The face my father and mother had made for me, the one piece of them that I could still watch grow. And now it was gone.

I cracked the hull and it seemed to me the sound was louder than normal, although that might just be my heightened sense of drama as I relate this little epic. The ship folded onto my back, changed color and disappeared. It was heavier than before, with a noticeable heft against my back, even though it was the same size. The air stank of unwashed Vabling and fresh-grown human, which, considering what humans are made from, isn't a great smell. Salty, pungent, earthy, evocative of sex and decay at the same time. I took a deep breath. It was wonderful.

"Nice penis." Rell threw a sheet at me. "Why does your species wear clothes if you've evolved such prominent genitals?"

"Because naughty bits are sinful," I said. "Chastity and bland food are the only way to buy a stairway to heaven."

Rell frowned. "You don't really believe that."

"I'm lapsed." I considered what I had said. "And I don't think they quote Zepplin in the scripture." I touched my chest, my stomach, my limbs. The skin was puffy and tender, as promised, but I could run my hand down my arm without the skin sloughing off, and if that doesn't sound like a significant victory than you've obviously never had fourth-degree burns over ninety-six percent of your body. Phantom pain shivered at the edge of my mind, gibbering afterimages waiting to remind me of the devastation that had been my body, but I was fine. This was more than healing. This was rebirth.

I was still white. I didn't have any body hair. The small tattoo of the boxing monkey under my arm was gone, but that wasn't much of a loss. I wasn't circumcised anymore. That was going to be an adjustment.

My face hung off my skull the same way it always had. I didn't know what a new face would feel like, but this one felt the same as the old one. I grabbed myself across the mouth and nose and thought madly at the ship and a piece of mirror-finish scaling flipped over my shoulder and showed me myself. After a second I giggled.

"I'm still me," I said.

--Who'd you think you were?--

I shook my head. "My face...I was ruined, shot up...I didn't think you could..."

--Dude, I can build you a functional third eye on the back of your head, if you want. It's meat sculpting, not rocket surgery--

--So? How'd I do? You comfortable going out in public?--

I rubbed my chin. I could already feel the prickle of stubble. It was my chin, the one I'd watched develop over a lifetime of humanity.

"You're a fucking miracle worker," I said. "Thank you." My voice was heavy, and had some waterworks in it, and Cab got embarrassed.

My mirror twisted around like a balloon animal and became a small ring of glowing pearls. The air wavered kaleidoscopically in the center.

--Listen, this is a sub-spherical Korp relay with a contained Plunk Effect. I built that, and it's smaller than a pack of cigarettes. Your body is just...--

--You're welcome--

--It's good?--

"It's me," I said. I sat down against the wall and relished the jolt I felt when my bare shell touched the cold metal. I could feel through the thing, now. Our connection was stronger.

"You look like a toshe fetus," Rell said.

I grinned. "Fair." For a moment I reveled in the quiet satisfaction of having skin.

"I dreamed about Cab," I said. "I dreamed you were him. The sense of relief was...all-encompassing."

--Don't have to be an expert in Freudian psychoanalysis to figure that one out--

"No." I stared at my brand-new feet. "He was here for such a short time, and now he's gone, and we're gonna be here for so long…it's not fair."

--Shorter lives are full of joy, and longer lives of pain. He loved you, Samson, just like I do, and he knew you loved him. If he's gone, at least we know he was happy while he was here--

"I know," I whispered, and I was crying, some, finally. It comes when it comes, and when it comes you have to let it come until it's done.

"My people would say Cab isn't dead," Rell said after a moment. "He's just been reabsorbed into the system that is your body. He's not gone, by that token."

"Is that what you believe?" I cleared my throat and sniffed heavily and shook myself.

"No," Rell said. "I'm lapsed, too. The way I see it, anyone who goes on about an afterlife or a soul is just asking after the conscious mind of the person they've lost. Nobody wants anything but more time with the people they love. But those people are gone. Even if Cab's…programming, his essence was redistributed into you, Cab, the…the person he was is still gone. The person you want is gone." He made a sour expression. "I always thought our dogma was a bit of a copout."

"Well," I said, "that's depressing."

"Don't be trite," Rell said. "People die and it abso-fucking-lutely fucking sucks the root. That's the reality. Don't shy away from it."

I nodded. He was right. The loss was the loss. Everything else was just words.

"How long was I out?" I asked.

"A week," Rell said.

A week to rebuild my entire body. Immortality seemed more and more likely. I put the thought aside, because that way led to madness and determined, regimented alcoholism. There was existential anxiety, and there was existential anxiety, and then there was the mind-fuck reality of eternal life, way at the far end of the spectrum of 'things I didn't have the emotional wherewithal to contemplate at such a young age.'

"What did I miss?" I asked.

"They expunged my criminal record and gave me a ship and some money," Rell said. "They called it a reward, but one of them took the time to tell me if I talk about what happened here they'll throw me in jail, so..."

"Hush money," I said. "Life is a trade-off, I guess."

"That's one word for it," Rell said.

"I got Phelan to take the price off your head," I said. "No more bounty hunters."

"I know," Rell said. "I got a notification about that. Thank you."

"Yeah," I said. An intrusive memory of Phelan's body settling against the broken deck plate. I'd gotten the price off his head, and then...the fall of man.

"The newspapers know about you," Rell said. "Frewdin has you spun as some kind of superhero, a CLEA experiment they unleashed against the latest Krr threat. They're calling you The Origami Man. The 'The' is capitalized, by the way. Like The Shadow." He was grinning.

"The Origami Man," I said. "You're kidding."

Rell's grin got wider. "Nope," he said gleefully.

--It's all over the headlines. The CLEA says you're a cyborg. Basically. There's a lot more technical horse-shit, but that's the long and the short of it. They state very clearly that your conscious mind is meat-based, and that the computer governing your machine parts is sub-sentient--

--Looks like I get to stay in-cog-neato, baby--

"The Origami Man is a stupid fucking name," I said. "Who the hell came up with that?"

--Some reporter--

"Why 'Origami?'"

--The ship folds into itself--

"But…" I sighed. "God dammit."

"The ship *does* fold into itself, Tee Oh Em," Rell said. His voice was a barely-contained chortle.

"Oh, knock it off," I said. I rubbed the tips of my fingers together. The sunburnt feeling was already starting to fade. "What are they saying?"

"People want to know if the spider was an isolated incident, or whether the Krr have more of them," Rell said. "They had this one hidden on a planet outside of Krr space, that's how they kept from setting off the Front. The CLEA is investigating, but they hadn't found any others, there or elsewhere."

"They didn't set off the Front because they didn't go through the Front," I said. Rell nodded.

"They also want to know if you're going to do this again," he said.

"Do what, again?" I said.

"Fight the Krr." Rell watched me evenly. I watched him back.

"A superhero," I said. Rell nodded.

"Frewdin wants to see you as soon as you wake up," he said.

I didn't move. "I killed Phelan Eight in cold blood, and the Krr destroyed the entire system. I'm not a hero."

"No one is, if you look closely." Rell stood up. "It doesn't matter what they call you. It matters what you do."

"Frewdin is gonna ask me to come work for him, isn't he?" I said.

"He might," he said. "You'll have to make a decision."

"The lady and the tiger," I said.

"Nice to see you're still a dweeb in spite of your recent traumas." Rell stood up. "Come on. Let's get you some clothes."

I stood up into the ship, sans helmet.

--Oh, so now you're ok being naked inside of me?--

"Beats wearing a sheet," I said. We went into the hall. The air was cleaner, from a relative standpoint. It was shipboard air, breathed in by everyone else in the ship and recycled constantly, but it was nice to breathe what everyone else was breathing, for a change. Made me feel less detached from reality.

We got into the lift, and Rell asked for the quartermaster. We stood quietly with our hands clasped in front of us, watching the numbers above the door.

"Do you think he'll give me a choice?" I asked.

"Frewdin?" Rell considered it. "He might. He hasn't yet, though, has he?"

"He's more of a 'threaten to kill you if you don't do what he tells you' kinda guy," I said. Rell nodded. The door opened. We got off the lift.

There was a group of Bekht clustered around a screen down the hall, and when I stepped into view they turned to look at me. They were too far away to adopt a human form, or else they didn't care to, and so I saw them as they really were, tall, thin starfish, essentially bipedal, remotely humanoid, except their head was a limb and their limbs were all the same. Off-white and matte finish, like gum eraser, they moved implacably, impenetrably dense but quick, delicate. The soldiers of the Core. They stared at me for several seconds, long enough for it to dawn on my that in spite of their alien appearance, these were intelligent people,

people who were smarter than me, people who would have a reason to stare.

--I think they know what we are--

"We *are* on Frewdin's ship," I said. "He probably told his crew the truth about us."

--Well, about me. I'm the sentient computer, remember? I'm the threat--

I raised a hand and waved. The Bekht didn't move. I sighed, and followed Rell through a door marked 'Provisions.' The horseshoe counter inside was labeled at three points, "Food and Drink,' 'Entertainment,' and 'Clothing,' which was an elegant system, if a sparse one.

The being behind the counter looked at Rell, and then at me, and slowly resolved into the spitting image of a young Vincent Price. The arched eyebrows, the little smile, the pencil mustache. I always thought he would have made a great Alfred.

"He needs pants," Rell said. "And a shirt, and, ah, what do you call them, shoes." He looked at me. "And see if you can permeate them with some kind of odor-nullifying compound. Durable materials, he tends to get shot at a lot."

"The clothes I got at Phibbix weren't as tough as I expected them to be," I said.

"'Normal wear and tear' does not include being burned alive," Rell said. "Oh, and can you get me a cup of tea?"

"Coffee, too," I said. "Please. And do you have donuts?"

"We do," the Bekht said. Its voice was wrong, a woman's voice, a sultry, affected tenor. "How many would you like?"

"A dozen," I said slowly. "Is that...Betty Boop?"

"Marilyn Monroe," said the quartermaster. "I love her movies. Is that a dozen mixed, then?"

414

"No, all chocolate glazed," I said. Was he Vincent Monroe, or Marilyn Price? Was it she? I had no way of knowing. The Bekht nodded and left us alone.

--I'm nominating the Bekht for 'most-alien alien,' ok?--

Rell chuckled.

"Dsarthy was pretty out there," I said.

--Dsarthy's body didn't disrupt scanning equipment--

--These things are really weird--

"You can't see through them?" Rell frowned.

--Nope, they're completely opaque. It's really, really disconcerting--

"Huh," Rell said. "So you see, what, radiation?"

--I see everything. Full physical, metaphysical, emotional and mental spectra, across the board--

"But what do you see?" Rell asked.

--I see the same way Samson sees, the same way you see. Stuff is there, and I see it. It's just that I can also see through the walls and your bodies and like, into stars and stuff. But I can't see through the Bekht--

"So you can't tell if they're carrying weapons?" I asked.

"Ever the pragmatist," Rell said.

"Getting shot sucks," I said. "I'd prefer to know if it's an immediate option."

"It was a compliment, you boob." Rell leaned against the counter and crossed his ankles. "You're a fascinating creature, Cab. Better, smarter people than me are going to learn a lot from you."

--I got this wicked risotto recipe I can teach 'em--

The Bekht came back with my clothes and our food, and I dismantled the ship to get dressed. Vincent Monroe stared at me, and its body shifted, elongated across the shoulders to connect better with the arms, became more human than before. The differences were a subtle but noticeable improvement.

"Your flesh is fragile," it said. I ate a donut.

"Don't I know it?" The coffee was better than the donut, and the donut was pretty good.

"Pain is psychologically damaging," the Bekht said. "You may want to look into having that part of yourself removed."

"What part?" I asked.

"That." The Bekht gestured at my body. "The meat."

I chewed, and swallowed, and looked at Rell. He turned and walked out the door.

"Thanks for the coffee," I said. I left the rest of the donuts behind and went after Rell. When I looked back, the donuts were disintegrating gently into ash on the counter while Vincent Monroe watched blandly.

--I'm telling you, 'most-alien alien.' Right?--

"Yeah, you win," I said.

We got back in the lift and headed for the bridge. Rell looked at me briefly and then grinned.

"I mean, a good surgeon might–"

"Stop," I said.

"Just like, you know, leave the brain, get rid of the rest."

"Stop!" I laughed. "That's fucked up, man."

"Yeah," Rell said. "I can't wait to get out of here."

"I bet," I said. The numbers shifted above us.

"You can come with me," Rell said after a moment. "If you don't want to work with Frewdin. Or if you have to…to run." He looked around defiantly. "You can come with me, if you want. There are places we could lay low, for a while, until things quiet down. Until you're older, until you know…well, how to handle yourself out there."

I dropped my eyes to my feet and took some breaths. Until I was older. I wanted my home. I didn't want to go home, not really, and I couldn't, not while the Krr were still such a threat. But I wanted my home. I missed it.

"Thanks," I said. Rell clapped me on the shoulder.

"I am your friend, and I will help you if I can," he said. "And I will take care of you if I have to, as best I can." He squeezed me, once, and then let go. "And don't get all mushy. I know you'd do the same."

"They're scared of me," I said.

--They're scared of me!--

"I am not," Rell said.

"They might not let me go," I said.

--Well, I guess it's 'us.' They're scared of us--

"Then we will do what we can," Rell said. "You're not alone in this."

"What if we can't do anything?" I said, and looked at him. He raised an eyebrow, then wound up and punched me really hard in the arm.

"Ow, god dammit!" I yelled. "What the fuck was that for?"

"Well, kind words weren't cheering you up, so I figured I should distract you," Rell said.

"Jesus, next time tell me a joke or something." I rubbed my arm. "You've got huge fuckin' hands, that really hurt."

Rell grinned. "Don't despair about possibilities. React to realities."

"Who are you, Tony Robbins?" I grumbled and rubbed and felt the trill of elation that comes of weathering pain, and calmed down. Rell was a smart man, I'll never deny that.

We stepped on to the bridge and everyone stopped talking. A crowd of Bekht turned to stare at me,

417

a silent sea of celebrities and politicians from Earth's history, each as unmoving as statues. I looked for a moment through Cab's eyes and saw the Bekht as he did, as empty spaces and nothing more. Black pools of nothing shaped like people. Any one of them could have been armed, could have been hiding anything, really. And then there were their intentions to worry about. The situation was entirely out of our control, unless we wanted to become an enemy of the biggest state that had ever existed.

They were never going to let us leave.

31

Frewdin stepped out of the crowd and looked around. He was back in pinstripes.

"Wow, it's just like 'The Birds,'" he said. "Everybody get back to work."

The CLEA agents went about their business and Frewdin beckoned me over. I wanted to put on the ship, but it would have sent the wrong message.

Frewdin plucked at my clothes. "How you feeling, Samson? I didn't think you'd be awake for at least another hour or so. Nice face. Hey, nice shirt, you get that here?"

"Yeah," I said. "The last one got atomized."

Frewdin nodded. "Well, come on in, come on in. I've got someone I'd like you to meet. How are ya, Rell?" He led us into the press and spoke over his shoulder. "You can speak freely here, these are all my people."

"I assumed," I said.

"Well, you're a smart kid," he said. "Heal fast, too, I didn't expect to see you on your feet so soon."

"Cab's good at what he does," I said.

"So you're calling this one Cab, too?" Frewdin stopped to read something given to him by an agent who looked like Tanya Donnely.

"He's Cab," I said. "He just might not be the first one. We don't know."

Frewdin froze in place for a noticeable half-second, just ceased all movement while he considered what I had said. Then he nodded at the pad, which thanked him, and said, "Go ahead," to Tanya.

"I'll shoot you the results," she said. "Thanks boss."

Frewdin nodded. "So, Samson, what's the climate like aboard ship? You and Cab feeling all right about everything that happened?"

"No," I said.

"Well, are you stable?" He asked.

My face composed itself and I looked inside. We hurt a lot, the both of us for our own commingled reasons, but I didn't feel any animosity towards the universe at large, and neither did Cab. This was mourning, not rage. We didn't want vengeance. I just wanted to be left alone for a while, and as near as I could tell, Cab just wanted to eat.

"Stable enough," I said.

"Good," Frewdin said. I followed him to the center of the bridge.

"We've published a cover story to explain your presence in Cabernicia," Frewdin said.

"The Origami Man," I said. Frewdin chuckled.

"Yeah," he said. "Officially, you had no part in Phelan Eight's plan to blow up the Seed Surplus, and we're already planting stories hinting that he might have been planning to do that anyway, and the Ulan Shipkiller was just a convenient distraction."

There were recessed pits at various point around the bridge. Command nodules, monitor foxholes, who the hell cares what they called them. They were deep enough to hide a Cabernician in, and there was a Cabernician in the one ahead of us, sitting coiled and hunched on his enormous thighs, staring at a holographic model of the Cabernician system the way a person stares at a campfire.

He was older than Phelan Eight, but he had the same face. He was only the second Cabernician I'd ever seen, but I knew it was the same face. The differences between them helped to clarify the similarities. He was thinner than Phelan Eight. His skin was sunken, and his face was split into patterns of curved polygons, lines that radiated out from his heavy, bulging eyes and from between his swollen lip-tentacles. His joints were thick and gnarled.

"Captain Samson, may I present System Representative Phelan Seven, developer of the Mark Four Cabernician Shipkiller, discoverer of quantum mass distribution and progenitor of Phelan Eight. Representative, this is Captain Gregory Samson, the Solar Shipkiller." Frewdin spoke with an exaggerated formality that made me think he was laughing on the inside.

Phelan Seven turned his attention away from the image of his home system with the molasses grace of a confident man who saw no reason to move any faster than he did.

"Captain," he said, and held out his hand with the same sedate speed. I checked his fingers for rings and shook his hand.

"Representative." I hooked a thumb over my shoulder and flared the shell briefly. "This is Cab. Frewdin forgot to introduce him."

--Hi Dad--

"Hello Cab," Phelan Seven said simply. There was a tiny gleam in his eye for a moment, interest peeking up from the depths of whatever he was feeling. System representative, and he created the Shipkiller. How long had they been using his ships to fight the Krr? A long time, which made Phelan Seven very old. He must have known his home inside and out, must have known it in every fiber of himself, and now it was gone. What did that feel like?

--I'm sorry for your losses, sir--

I blinked. Phelan Seven raised an eyebrow.

"What a nice kid," Frewdin said. "So, listen, Samson, we've managed to excise the control circuit from the remainder of the fleet. Didn't take quite as long as we originally anticipated. The high mucky-mucks have decided to reward you financially in light of the fact that your actions have greatly strengthened the remaining Shipkillers in the fleet. We're processing the payment for you right now, but it's going to take us another hour or so to get things sorted out, so I was thinking, while you're waiting, why don't you and Phelan Seven go for a drive?"

His hand reached out and grasped the hologram, flipped it around and highlit an oddly shaped mass on the far side of the star.

"Phelan, why don't you show him the Ranch? I'm sure Samson and Cab would kick themselves if they left Cabernicia without seeing the whales in their native habitat, and I know how much of a comfort the Ranch has been to you." Frewdin clapped his other hand gently on Phelan Seven's knee. "Go on, Phil, you've been working hard. Take a break, get to know the kid. He's pretty interesting. You know he's only twenty-eight? When was the last time you talked to a mind that young?" He looked at me. "How about you, Samson? You want to go see the whales? You and I can talk when you get back, I've got some scut work I have to finish up, and you just woke up. Take an hour, get yourself settled. Sound good?"

I looked at Phelan Seven. "If you'd like, Representative."

He didn't sigh, but his shoulders lifted and settled, all three sets of them. Then he turned away from the display with a careful smile on his face. He was missing a lip tentacle at the upper right of his mouth.

"Yes, that would be nice, I think," he said, and then he grinned, sharply, and laughed once. "I shouldn't spend too much time staring at that damn display, anyway. It's not healthy."

I shrugged. "I think you're allowed some rumination, given the circumstances." Phelan looked at me like I'd just appeared.

"We can take my ship," he said, then and walked towards the lift. I looked at Rell, and he shrugged.

"Man's hurting," he said. I nodded.

"You want to come?" I said.

"Nah, I've gotta look over this ship they're giving me," he said. "Make sure they haven't choked the engines or baffled the shields. Bugged the comms. You can't trust the police."

"That's true, you can't," Richard Pryor told us in passing. Rell and I both jumped a little, and stared after him.

"I really don't like it here," Rell said after a minute.

"Yeah," I said. "Me neither. All right. I'll see you later. You gonna be ok?"

"I think so," Rell said. "They gave me amnesty."

"You can't trust the police," I said.

"Nope," Rell said. "But I have a shotgun. Enjoy your sightseeing."

"Oh, yeah," I said. "Hour-long car trip with a man who just watched his species get annihilated. Gonna be a whole barrel of laughs." We started for the lift, and the waiting, mourning Cabernician.

"I'll see if I can scare up some booze," Rell said.

"Yeah," I said, "that would be good."

32

Phelan Seven's ship was a flattened bubble the color of oxidized copper, with four orange claw feet set at ninety-degree intervals. It was pretty, and odd, and it stuck out among the idiot escape pods like a grassy island in a strip-mall parking lot: it livened up the place, but you got the sense it wouldn't be around for long.

We didn't speak until we were past Frewdin's fleet, on a shallow arc towards Caberna, past the planetary remains. Most of the CLEA and Navy ships were gone, now that the danger was past.

"There," Phelan said. "About fifteen minutes." He sat back and began to stretch and massage the fingers on two of his hands. Every now and then, he winced.

"Arthritis?" I asked. He listened to the translation, and then shook his head.

"No," he said. "But similar in effect." He finished and rested his hands on his knees. The ship maneuvered around a mountainous blob of frozen slag and blasted glass that looked like it might have been a space station before the attack.

"Would you like tea?" Phelan asked.

"Please," I said. We passed a dense field of debris, rocks and fused metal and disinterested, slow-moving rescue vehicles. Phelan opened a drawer under the steering wheel and handed me a steaming mug with a teabag string hanging over the side. The drawer was the sort that should have housed Tupperware or tin foil, and the tea was Earl Grey.

"There were no survivors on any of the planets the spider attacked," Phelan said, "And it attacked them all." He sipped his tea. "Even those planets that were left mostly intact, there were a few…the forces involved when a fifty-billion petagram animal crashes into a planet are staggering. It's a wonder most of them didn't disintegrate under the impact."

I thought 'petagram' hard and Cab glanced at me internally.

--A petagram is a trillion kilograms--

I nodded.

"A few of our people got out on small transports," Phelan went on. "Mostly private ships, a few cargo vessels. And there was a small research station at the system's edge that wasn't attacked. But that's it. There are fewer than ten thousand of us left." He took a deep breath and settled into his coils. "We will compensate as best we can, as we have in the past. But with less diversity, more vulnerability. I don't know if we can survive."

He stopped moving and, I think, thinking. Or at least, stopped thinking about anything smaller than the binary that was existence versus nonexistence. His eyes looked dull and blank, even though I knew from experience that he saw everything. When emotion and thought are so overpowering they seem diminished, observational ability steps in to fill the void.

"It's hard to fathom, isn't it?" He said after a moment. "Total destruction. The loss of everything." He sighed. "At least the damage is contained. Even if we can't recover."

"Maybe no one ever really recovers," I said. "Maybe we just move on."

Phelan smiled into his mug. "How old are you, again?"

"Don't ask me that," I said.

We passed over Cabernicia and the shields lit up in the stellar corona like we were flying through rainbows.

"Nice to get away," Phelan said heavily. "I've been back and forth to the Ranch several times in the last week, and every time I reach Caberna I think, 'Thank God, I don't have to look at it anymore.'"

I nodded. Relief is important. I went to the movies a lot after my folks died, and I remember those movies better than I do most, even though they're from before my eidetic memory. No Country for Old Men, Transformers. I saw Ratatouille three times. The theater was my sanctuary.

The surface of the star rolled slightly, pulled and pushed against its diminishing gravity. It was not unlike the sea in its movements, although it was red and made for the most part of atomic fire. But there were parallels. Like the sea, the star was very big, and I was very small.

"I think it's important that you know that I forgive you for killing my son," Phelan said. "I understand that he asked you to do it." He stared at the washed-out stars a long way ahead of us like he was holding on to a lifeline. He had to talk about it. So I had to talk about it with him.

"You know what happened," I said. It wasn't exactly a question, but he nodded. I turned back to the big star underneath us. "He would have been executed no matter what I did."

"Yes," Phelan said. "But you allowed him some measure of control over his death. That was a compassionate act. I'm not sure my son deserved compassion." He smiled as if it hurt to do so. "Thank you for being kind to him, in that moment."

Phelan's thanks opened up an awful ache under my chest.

"I didn't know he was your son," I said dumbly. "I thought he was your clone."

"He was," Phelan sighed. "But the Cabernician cloning process is designed to mimic the results of sexual reproduction. The clones are delivered as infants to their immediate progenitors to be raised as their children. We could create them fully grown, and we do...we did in certain rare cases, but to do that as a rule would have been foolish. Those clones were only replacements for something dead, a, a placeholder." He worked his jaw.

"We wanted growth," he said, and his voice was for a moment almost feral. "Advancement. Learning. Evolution. Everything the Krr took away from us. For that, you need children, and parents. Aging, and death. For a species to grow it has to be able to move forward in time." He took a deep breath, and let it out carefully. "I cared for Eight. I fed him, I clothed him, I taught him. I loved him. I was there when they finished...I was there when he was born. He was my son." He breathed out again, sharply, and his eyes tightened, but he kept it together.

I stared down at the lake of fire and rubbed my prickly scalp. Cab's wariness paralleled my own. Aboard a ship with the grieving father of a man I'd killed barely an hour earlier, from my perspective. He was a week into his grief, probably just then beginning to understand it as something that would be with him to the end of his days, but me? I'd had almost no time to confront the fact that I'd killed a man in cold blood, let alone figure out how I felt, or what my actions made me.

"He killed my friend," I said. "The mind of the first seed. Your son put us in a position where my friend had to kill himself in order to save me."

Phelan came back to the present moment with a small but obvious effort and looked at me. I hooked a thumb over my shoulder at the shell on my back.

"We don't know if this Cab is the same Cab that died to save us," I said, "but this Cab remembers dying. He remembers the moment when he realized he was going to have to die, because if he didn't let the second seed erase his mind then your son was going to kill us both." I made a frustrated noise. "He remembers all of it. Your son forced Cab to kill himself."

"Did you kill him for that?" Phelan asked. I was reminded of Connelly, the homicide captain back home. Questioning my motives. Asking my why I hit Billy Maxwell the second time. Then I thought of the last of Cab, right before he turned into nothing. Fear, sure, and yeah, also enough elation and awe and curiosity for the religious freaks to have a field day, but what really sticks with me is the doubt right at the end. Cab saw something, when the lights went out, but he didn't know if it was real. The man was half in the afterlife and he still didn't believe the place was real. What if he was right?

He's gone, anyhow. Removed. Nothing changes that.

Or, he isn't, and he survived, and he's hanging on my back right now echoing my own voiceless, frustrated ignorance right back at me. It's always been hard, not knowing.

"No," I said. "But it made my decision easier."

"Then," Phelan said, "why did you kill him?"

"Because Cab asked me to before he died," I said. "And because I wanted to."

"Did you enjoy it?" Phelan watched me very closely. I watched him back, wondering if he was burying his grief in the conversation, or if he had a motive beyond distraction.

"No," I said.

"But it haunts you," Phelan said. "Because it was the first time you chose to kill, when you could have chosen not to."

I looked at him and he spread some of his hands.

"I am very old," he said. "And I know people. I am a politician after all."

"I could have given him to Frewdin," I said. The edges of the stellar horizon started to curve at the edges as our flat trajectory took us away from the star.

"Frewdin would have killed him immediately," Phelan said. "What does it change, that you are the one who killed Eight?"

I leaned forward until my forehead was pressing against the windshield, and tried to fog the glass. I couldn't, which I'm sure had more to do with the glass than my breath, but it didn't help my mood any.

"I don't know," I said. "I just wish I hadn't."

"I'm glad you did," Phelan Seven said. "For what it's worth."

I peeled myself off the glass and looked at him incredulously.

"They were going to kill him no matter what happened," he snapped. "At least you didn't make him wait around for it." He sighed. "You feel, what cheapened? Lessened by your actions?" There was contempt in his voice, for a moment.

"I crossed a line that I didn't want to cross," I said.

"Sometimes you have to do that," he said simply. He opened the drawer under the steering wheel and got himself more tea. He stared into the mug.

"I wonder if I am to blame for what has happened," he said. "We encourage aberrations in the cloning process from time to time, for genetic diversity, so it is possible that Eight came to his…skewed views…through no fault of mine."

"Skewed views," I said. "You mean the shortsightedness and the selfishness and the psychotic disinterest in the wellbeing of his fellows that allowed him to ally with the Krr?" It was a mean thing to say, but Phelan had me feeling a little mean.

Phelan nodded. "Yes," he said. "That. It's possible that he became who he became on his own. But it's also possible that he did what he did because…because of my…"

"Because he was *your* son," I said.

"Yes," Phelan said. "Because he was my son." He sighed. "I used to raise kitterwings, right around when we started working on the Mark Four. They're a meat animal, hard to raise and expensive, normally the sort of work left to skilled farmers. Outside of their natural habitat, you have to control for every aspect of their lives, from the cradle to the grave. I liked that. I liked the work. And I liked the control. The sense of mastery. It was thrilling. I think that's why I stuck with it for as long as I did. I only stopped when we got close to cracking quantum mass. Sold off my whole stock and set up a trust fund for Eight." He chewed on one of his lip tentacles.

"I have a coldness in me," he said. "I didn't like the killing, but I didn't mind it any more than I minded filling the feeder machinery, or mucking the stalls. Less, actually: the killing usually prefaced a wonderful meal. But you can never know yourself, truly, as a member of a society, and so I've found myself wondering, is my cold larger than another person's? Am I an aberration? Was Phelan Eight an aberration? Or was his coldness his birthright?"

I looked at the grey-red stellar expanse ahead of us, so washed out that only the brightest stars could be discerned against the gloom, and thought of the holographic model of the diminished Cabernician system that Phelan had been watching aboard Frewdin's ship.

"Does it matter?" I asked. Phelan pulled out of his rumination and looked at me directly.

"No," he said after several seconds, "I suppose it doesn't, anymore."

I sat back down and watched the star slip away beneath us.

"I am sorry I killed him," I said. Phelan nodded.

"Good," he said. "I suppose that's something."

33

"We're here," Phelan said.

There was nothing ahead of us but the same red hazy vacuum. I looked at him, and he touched a button, and the ship tipped into a nosedive, and suddenly I could see the Ranch. For an instant I thought that the spider had returned, or survived, or that there had been more than one of them. I thought I saw a wreckage. And then my mind caught up to my perceptions, and I stared.

The Ranch was a collection of age worn asteroids and mountains held together on the surface of a colossal contained sea floating in the middle of space. Caberna's crimson light rippled across the surface in flickering waves and reflected off the bottoms of the continents on the nightside, caught on gemstones whose positions were echoed on opposite landmasses, as if the Ranch had started its life as a much smaller body, before the encroaching ocean split it apart at the seams.

The whales were everywhere, so many it was impossible to see them as individuals. There were millions, billions, orbiting the planet in such enormous pods that the word became inadequate, the way that 'flocks' wasn't enough to capture the reality of a million passenger pigeons flying in concert. There were storms of whales across the surface of the ocean, hurricanes. They rained constantly into the sea beneath them, gave up control on a whim and let themselves fall gleefully into the spray, then swam to whichever pole was closest to ascend majestically back into space, over and over, the same graceful trajectory repeated in every animal.

--Holy shit, that's a lot of whales--

I put on the ship for a closer look with better eyes, and Phelan gasped behind me. I ignored him and zoomed in.

Up close the whales were vaguely unsettling. When they swam they were some of the most graceful animals I've ever seen, but in flight, they twisted over and around each other like a nest of snakes. They were wonderful creatures, with beautiful, unique plumage, but they were also more alien in some subtle way than anything else I had encountered. I stood back and dismantled the ship, and Phelan inhaled audibly again.

"You really do have total control over the ship's raw material, don't you?" He said.

"Probably," I said. "I'm not entirely sure what that means." I put my hands in my pockets. It was amazing. "How does the planet stay together? Shouldn't it drift apart? Or collapse into itself?"

"We don't really know," Phelan said. "It had been there for more than a half billion years before we found it. This would be the original Cabernicians, too, the pre-Krr species." He paused and seemed to work himself around something in his head. Maybe the realization that the Cabernician species would now have to clarify its history as pre-Krr and pre-Spider, if they managed to survive long enough to create any more history at all. That's certainly what I was thinking about, right then.

"The sea generates an energy field that keeps the land masses at a static distance," he said finally. "Something akin to magnetism, in effect, but it's only attractive to a certain point. The solid materials won't drift away, but they won't drift together, either."

He stared out the screen.

"They've been like this for as long as we've been aware of their existence," he said. "No evolution, no alterations of any kind to their genetic code. All they do is fly, and swim, and eat, and make babies."

"Might as well make a weapon out of 'em," I said. Phelan got up and stood next to me. He was quiet and delicate in his movements, in spite of his size. How Cabernicians managed to be so light on their feet has always been beyond me.

"I can't remember who suggested the whales, when we were ready to test the first seeds," he said. "Not that it matters. We all jumped onboard, immediately. We even had a party in the lab to celebrate. Using the whales meant we didn't have to contract with another system for testing, wouldn't have to share in the glory. Large animals, not particularly intelligent or dangerous, and they were right here in Cabernicia." He smiled, although from my angle it looked like a bit of a sneer.

"We had to be very quiet about what we were doing, at first." He shook his head. "This was back when a lot of people still thought the whales were sacred. The Krr ignored them, you see, when they attacked us the first time. We have no idea where they came from, or how they evolved. There was an entire population of people who believed that the whales were placed there by a species older than any of those in the Core. If the general populace had known what we were doing, we would have been sacked. Maybe even charged as criminals. So we had to step lightly. Of course, once we unveiled our *success*, and told everyone how much *money* we stood to make, not just as a company, but as a species, well…resistance faded very quickly." He smiled sadly, and rested his chin on his knee. "Money always trumps idealism, in the end."

"Why are you telling me this?" I rubbed my scalp and sighed. "Christ, Phelan, this doesn't engender a lot of sympathy for your people."

"I am not seeking to engender sympathy for my people. I want you to understand what happened here." He tapped his mouth tentacles against his teeth rhythmically. "The Core was thrilled, when we brought them the first successful prototypes. They knew what we were up to, we sent them the details of the Marks One Two and Three, but still, they were surprised. An adaptive, self-repairing warship boasting as much firepower as a small fleet…they offered us an ungodly amount of money, which we gladly accepted, and all sorts of help, which we largely declined. We had no reason to go on using the whales, at that point, but we were proud of what we'd done, and we wanted to be needed. It felt so good to have a purpose after having been so gutted for so long. We had been so wretched, so torn apart after the Krr attacked…we were all clones, for God's sake! And it was so much money, and so much power. And the whales…they were just animals. So we kept everything in-house, and went on using them."

He stared out into space, I think without really seeing.

"I started having doubts when I got into politics. I'm an engineer, I worked in a lab for most of my adult life before they tapped me as a possible system rep. I didn't know a thing about the galaxy, about our neighboring systems, even. I didn't know what else was out there." He looked at me pointedly.

"There are…odd phenomena like the Ranch scattered all over the galaxy," he said. "Some of them are simply statistical outliers, impressive for their extremity, and some of them are truly unexplainable. Your friend's home, Vabl, it one of the densest natural environments that has ever been discovered. The planet is noticeably larger than it was a million years ago, thanks to the growth of its forest. There is an asteroid field in the Core that can do simple sums, as long as the numbers are presented at certain angles in binary using pulses of ultraviolet light. There is a planet in a southern arm of the galaxy whose atmosphere appears to be quantum-entangled with the atmosphere of a similar planet in a northern arm. If it storms on one planet, it storms on the other. There is a species called eldeboorats that mate by combining the male and female organisms into one being composed from the compatible elements of their personalities, while the incompatible elements are filtered into two opposed offspring. Some of the best comedians in the galaxy are eldeboorats, they have a strange family dynamic." He smiled painfully. "The galaxy is full of these wonderful, unexplainable things that are fostered, protected. Enjoyed simply for what they are. We find one right in our home system, and what do we do?" He waved an angry hand at me. "We stick a weapon inside and sell them for a billion percent profit. We perverted one of life's great mysteries for personal gain."

I leaned on the wall and watched him. Phelan said he'd been out here a lot over the last week. Did he do this to himself every time, or just when he had a fresh pair of eyes to look through?

"Late at night," he said, which is never a good start, "when I can't sleep, I worry that the whales were put there by God to test us, to see what we would do when we were confronted with the truly divine. I worry that we failed. If that's the case, then when Judgment comes I'll be the one held responsible. Because I am responsible, Captain, the Mark Four wouldn't have been possible without me. I contributed the operating system, the mass displacement, we can only build the Shipkillers because of me. I am responsible for the enslavement of the whales and the ultimate destruction of my people."

--If this guy asks us to kill him, I'm going to bed and staying there forever--

I watched the whales roil and dive. They didn't look unhappy, frankly. Then again, these whales had been left alone. And the odds were they would continue to be left alone for a long time. There weren't any more seeds to stick in them, nor any significant number of Cabernicians to do the sticking.

"You couldn't have known any of this would happen," I said.

"Absence of foreknowledge of consequences does not absolve a person of sin, Captain," Phelan said. "My world is erased because of what I did. I have taken so much from this universe, and now I am being punished for it." He prodded angrily at the controls and the ship turned away from the whales, towards Caberna, and the fleet on the other side of the system.

"I suppose Agent Frewdin sent us out here so you could see what you saved," Phelan said after a moment. "By killing the spider, you most likely saved the whales."

"You said the Krr ignored them last time," I said.

"That was not a Krr, that was an Ulan Comet Spider," Phelan said. "Even though it was a Shipkiller, it had a Comet Spider's urges the way you have human urges."

"I have human urges because I'm still human," I said.

"After a fashion," Phelan said. "That thing would have destroyed the Ranch, something beautiful, and then it would have moved on from system to system, consuming everything in its path. You prevented that from happening. If this is my Karma, then perhaps you are the message that I am not done yet with this life. The whales are still here, and so am I. I've been given a chance to atone for what I've done."

I sat down and watched the star get big again. It was bright, but my eyes were tough.

"How many billions of people died?" I asked quietly. Phelan looked at me.

"Trillions," he said. "Two point two."

Two point two trillion. Back then a trillion was a number I couldn't comprehend, a sum I only knew from economics essays I barely understood. Trillions. There were trillions of ants on Earth. It was a number that wouldn't fit in my head. But I knew Karma. And I knew Judgment, the kind Phelan talked about with an implied capital Jay. I knew how much of a comfort they were, and how much of a lie.

The ship rustled on my back. "My parents died when I was nineteen," I said. "They moved into a new house and someone bumped the stove pipe loose and the batteries in the carbon monoxide detector were dead. They went to bed and fell asleep and didn't wake up." According to the autopsy report, they had sex before they fell asleep. That's always been an odd comfort to me.

"I wanted to believe they weren't all gone so, so badly that I had this one, brief instant of actual belief. Real faith. And then I got it. I saw where it all came from, back to that first morning when our caveman ancestors woke up for the morning and nobody could get Uncle Og to move, and it hurt *so fucking bad* that it was easier to believe that Og wasn't *gone*, he was just *somewhere else*. And don't worry, you'll get to see him again someday. Shit." I breathed out something that hurt. I felt raw. "Sometimes awful things just happen. You want there to be meaning, but that's just wanting more of whatever it is you've lost. There might be a reason for everything, but the reasons don't have to come from anyplace special." I rubbed my head and wished for hair.

"This isn't about you, Phelan. You think this is your punishment? That two point two trillion people died to teach you a lesson? Those people died because your son sold a superweapon to a race of monsters, and it doesn't *matter* if he did it because you fucked up as a parent or if he did it because he was a psychopath, because he did it and it's done and *so is he*. There's no message, here. You don't get to cheapen this, or hide behind something you only have to talk about. Your son killed your entire fucking species because he chose to do wrong. That's real. But he was your son, and you loved him, and his death hurts worse than anything else you've ever felt. That's real too. Don't hide from it."

I sat as still as a Bekht and spoke in a near monotone. "You want to atone for what you did, atone for what you did. But don't go thinking you're the universe's axe to grind." My chin settled onto my chest. "Life is just an interconnected series of random events. It doesn't matter what you want. It doesn't matter why. What matters is what happens, and what you do about it. That's all."

"Do you wish that you had not been implanted with a Shipkiller seed?" Phelan asked me at length.

"I told you, it doesn't matter." I shook my head. "It happened. All that matters is what I do now. Did Frewdin send us out here so you could give him your expert opinion on me?" Phelan looked at me and I looked at him and raised my eyebrows.

"I am the system representative for the Cabernician system," he said slowly. "I'm here to provide whatever aid is necessary."

"Then why were you waiting for me to wake up?" I asked. "I'm sure there's plenty to do, did they really decide the best job for a Core-affiliated politician was staring at a holographic system model? What are we doing out here, Phelan?"

He chewed on his lip tentacles for about ten seconds and then shrugged impressively. "It doesn't matter what we wanted. What matters is that you're here, now, and we need to decide what to do about you. We have no real way to control you, and you might live for a very long time. There's never been a sentient computer before, and there's never been a doubled Shipkiller before, either. You're an immensely powerful creature, and by any civilized standard you're younger than an infant. You've also been through a lot in the past couple of weeks. A lot of trauma. Frewdin wants to know if I think you're a threat."

"And?" I said when it became apparent he wasn't going to follow up without urging.

"I don't think you're a threat right now," Phelan said. "You're coarse. Not very gentle. That was a rather painful dressing down you delivered to me a moment ago. On its own, that doesn't mean much, but if it's a sign that you don't take the wellbeing of others seriously, then down the pike…On the other hand, you've repeatedly demonstrated a willingness to risk your own safety for the safety of others. That speaks to a general desire to do the right thing, but what does that even mean, to do the right thing?" Phelan waved one of his hands dismissively.

"Right now, you're trying to do right, but you have no understanding of what that means, and no understanding of your destructive potential. You're like a bull in a china shop. You're not doing anything inherently wrong, but you could potentially destroy…well everything."

"A whole lot of china," I said.

"All of the china we have," Phelan said. "Your species is not designed to live as long as you will. Your brain is not set up to think for such a long period of time. You are going to have to be very careful with yourself, or you will turn into something bad. My professional opinion is that we should proceed with caution. You and the ship are integrating in what appears to be a healthy manner, so far, but there's no telling what you'll become without guidance. I think they should give you a job, so we can keep a close eye on you until you're more fully formed." He paused and shifted his weight.

"My personal opinion is that you've got your head screwed on straight, but you're a hard-edged bastard who could stand to find some humility. And as a grieving father sharing a ride with the man who killed his son, I cannot wait to get the hell away from you."

"Well," I said at length, "that's fair."

"I'm glad you approve," Phelan said icily. Frewdin's ship loomed in front of us, its mouth open wide. I could see the lines of the original animal, obscured. Destroyed and remade. I flipped the ship on and off, long enough to look more carefully than I had before. There wasn't any meat inside the Cabernician shipkillers. The whales were gone.

Beside me, Phelan stared grimly ahead. Phelan Eight would have been a little boy, once. They were such awful men who had done such awful things, but they had been a family. Duality was one of the hardest things for me to understand, when I was young. That the monsters could still love and be loved and be worthy of love, besides. That I might be trying to do right, and still turning into a monster.

The ship didn't make any noise when it landed, but there was a funny pressure in my core as the gravity wells aligned. I shivered uncomfortably.

"Listen," Phelan said when I stood up. "When you saw Eight, how did he look?"

I thought about it. "Nervous, then angry," I said. "I wasn't paying attention."

"Captain, please, I designed part of your mind." Phelan didn't move. "I know that you don't have to pay attention to a thing to remember every part of it."

I took in some air and looked at my memories.

"He was thicker than you are," I said. "His skin was smoother. And brighter. I don't know what details are important, here. His clothes were a nicer fabric than yours, if I'm any judge." I shook my head. "But I'm not. What do you want to hear?"

"I don't know," Phelan said quietly. "Was he eating well? Was he happy? I don't know." He sighed, and got up, and looked at me helplessly. "I hadn't seen him in a long time."

34

Frewdin was waiting for us when we landed, cleaning his nails with an old-fashioned folding penknife and leaning against an escape pod at too steep an angle. His nails were pure white, and they probably hadn't been there five minutes ago, but he cleaned them anyway, to maintain the integrity of the aggressively imperfect whole. The obvious details had been left just slightly off-kilter to make a point, just like in his office the first time I met him. None of him was real, and I was supposed to know it.

"You're wearing a side-arm," I said.

Frewdin glanced at the weapon and shrugged. "Good trip? What'd you think of the whales?"

"I think I'm glad the Garden is gone," I said.

"Well, you're young." Frewdin grinned and nodded at Phelan Seven. "Representative. What do you think of him?"

Phelan Seven folded his arms across his coils. "I will file my report momentarily."

"I'm looking forward to it," Frewdin said. "Cliff's notes?"

Phelan looked at me and collected his thoughts with an academic's visible effort.

"He's safe enough," he said. "He wants to do the right thing. He probably won't intentionally cause us any trouble. He's a little coarse."

"Fuck, aren't we all?" Frewdin chuckled. "Well, thanks for keeping him occupied, Phelan. I'll be in touch." He turned on his heel and walked to the lift.

"I think I'm supposed to follow him," I said. Phelan nodded, and I put out my hand. After a second, he shook it.

"Be careful with yourself, Captain," he said. "If ever you need anything, don't hesitate to contact me."

I raised an eyebrow. "Really? I thought you hated me."

"I might," he said. "But you're going to live for a very long time, and what you do will matter to us all. Your well-being is every forward-thinking person's responsibility."

I took my hand back and swallowed my ire. I was tired of being treated like a time bomb. "Thank you," I bit out carefully. I followed Frewdin to the lift. When I looked back, Phelan was disappearing into his ship.

Frewdin held his hands in front of him and watched the numbers over the door.

"Talk about anything interesting?" He asked after a moment.

"I told him God isn't real and it's his fault his son was a creep," I said.

"The clone?" Frewdin thought about it. "Yeah, probably, the apple doesn't fall far from the tree and all that crap. What else?"

"He forgave me for killing his son," I said.

"And do you feel better?" Frewdin asked.

"I never felt bad, in particular," I said. "Just confused, and…sad, I think. I crossed some final line, and now I'm…bad, I guess. Bad Greg." I sighed. "I'm worried I'm turning into a monster."

Frewdin grunted. The numbers above the doors shifted axis as we changed direction.

"Your money is almost ready, by the way," he said. "We're giving you fifty million, for exposing the control circuit. Just our way of saying thanks."

I stared at him.

--That's a lot of gumballs--

"Thank you," I mumbled. Frewdin grinned.

"My advice is to invest carefully," he said. "We long-lifers have to think about our financial future more than most." The grin got wicked. "But with a little forethought...the sky's the limit, Captain. It's quite a bit of fun, being rich."

"Cop's salary that good out here?" I asked.

"I'm one hundred and four million years old," Frewdin said slyly. "I've been investing in the markets of shorter-lived species since my adolescence. There's a pretty nice nest egg waiting for me when I decide I've done enough." He shrugged. "It's easy to manipulate the economy of some fringe system where nobody lives more than a few millennia. Fun, even. Most of us do it."

"Gotta love that violent capitalism," I said. "If you're rolling in it why do you work for the CLEA?"

Frewdin sneered at me. "Puppy. I do this job because it needs to be done, and I do it well." He rocked back and forth on his heels. "You do what you should the best that you can. I'm good at this. So, here I am. And here we are."

The lift dinged and opened into another featureless corridor, long and vaguely curved and studded with doors. The air smelled like a hospital, ammonia disinfectant and empty space. Frewdin led me to a room that was empty except for a Cabernician sitting on a stool. I was pretty sure he was a Phelan, but he was young. His skin was tighter, not as thin as Phelan Seven's and not as full as Phelan Eight's. He was muscular, but thin, as if he took care of himself but needed to eat more. His skin was reddish-purple, not green-blue, and he was covered from head to toe with tattoos. They stretched up and down his arms, wrapped around his torso and turned his legs and feet black from the knees down. His face was edged with roiling lines and points, like Maori art filtered through the mind of a species that had evolved trillions of miles away from New Zealand. His hands were folded in stacked layers one on top of another on his knees, and he was breathing deeply. He didn't look at us when we came in.

The door hissed shut behind us.

"This is Phelan Three…Three Eight Seven," Frewdin said. "Three Eight Seven, this is Gregory Samson, the deputy agent who apprehended your forebear, Phelan Eight. We're here to read you your sentencing and administer your court-mandated punishment. Are you ready to proceed?"

Three Eight Seven nodded. Frewdin fiddled with the controls on his belt.

"We're working our way through Phelan Eight's descendants," he said. "Most of 'em died in the attack, but we found a few among the survivors. Three Eight Seven, here, he was on vacation, the lucky duck. Now, Cabernician law dictates that we execute them all in the event of a capital crime like treason, but we're a little more merciful in the CLEA. We run a few background checks, some tests, make 'em talk to a shrink, that sorta thing, and then we either repurpose them or execute them, based on the results."

I stared at him. Belatedly I recognized the lingering ammonia scent as Cabernician blood.

Frewdin read from an invisible screen projected in front of his eyes. "Phelan Three Eight Seven, based on your own testimony, evidence gleaned from your background checks and results of psychological testing, coupled with…blah, blah blah." He scrolled through the file. "Sorry. Hell of a lot of legalese. Summary of deliberations will follow, yadda yadda, let's see. Oh, here we go. '…the Great Court of the Core Law

Enforcement Agency hereby sentences you to immediate execution.'" He turned off the screen and put his hands in his pockets. "Tough break, buddy. Sorry."

The lines on Three Eight Seven's face got deeper.

"Would you care to make a statement?" Frewdin tapped a stud on his belt and raised his eyebrows.

Three Eight Seven looked at him, drew a deep breath, and said, "You'll get yours. Fascist."

"Stirring stuff," Frewdin grunted.

"Wait," I said. "That's it? You're gonna execute him? Why?"

"Mostly his psyche profile, I think," Frewdin said. He turned the display back on.

"You don't know?" I said sharply.

"I skimmed it." Frewdin waved his hand at me. "Yeah, his psyche profile. He showed some lack of affect, some signs of malignant narcissism, a couple other red flags. His name came up in a couple of investigations, one for subversive artistic intent and one for hyper-dominant sexual activity."

I connected the dots in my head. "You're gonna kill him because he's a self-centered counterculture artist who's into bondage?"

"Any excuse will do," Three Eight Seven said. His voice was raspy, but calm. I liked him for that.

"I'm going to execute him because the court found him guilty," Frewdin said. His calm was less appealing. "Unless you want to?"

"What?" I said. "Unless I want to kill him? Why the hell would I want to kill him?"

Frewdin grinned very slightly. "Because you're a monster. Because this man looks like the man who killed Cab. Because you're a CLEA deputy as long as you're aboard my ship, and we've been ordered by the Great Court to execute this man. Take your pick."

"But I mean, to execute him for something so minimal," I said.

"Who's to say what's minimal?" Frewdin said.

"Have you repurposed any of my forebears?" Three Eight Seven asked.

"That's classified," Frewdin said.

"Consider it a dying man's request," Three Eight Seven said. Frewdin shrugged and toggled his screens.

"No," he said. "We've executed them all."

"Jesus Christ," I said. Frewdin looked at me.

"Don't forget what Phelan Eight did," he said. "No one thought he was a threat, either. *I* didn't think he was a threat. This is on my head, too."

"But you can't practice preventative murder," I stammered.

"Yes," Frewdin said, "we can. It's the law. Now make up your mind, Samson. Are you going to kill him, or am I? We have things to do."

I stared at him. "No," I said. "I won't."

Frewdin's hand whipped his sidearm off his belt and cut Three Eight Seven into several pieces. The beam was purple, thread-like, impossibly sharp. The rest of Frewdin didn't move at all.

The burnt ammonia fish stink of cauterized Cabernician filled the room. I doubled over in the corner and threw up.

"Yeah, it's not a great smell," Frewdin said. I slapped at the door panel and staggered into the hall, retching. Frewdin followed me, grabbed me by the shoulder, and pulled me roughly upright. He had a cigarette burning in his mouth. I hadn't seen him light it.

"Congratulations," he said. "You're a better man than I can afford to be." He inhaled deeply and blew out a cloud of smoke.

"You crossed a line when you killed Phelan Eight," he said. His hand still held my shoulder. "But it wasn't the final line. That wasn't the final line in there, either, but now you know that I'm willing to kill for the Core, and I don't care about the why. Now you know that I will cross more lines than you will, and I will sleep better having done so." He frowned. "Although I don't actually sleep."

He smiled too wide and dusted off my shoulder with the same isolated movements as always.

"I think you'll turn out to be the right kind of man for the life you'll have to lead, Captain," Frewdin said. "Eventually. But right now you're just a kid!"

Smoke oozed out of his nose, but I didn't believe it. The cigarette was as much an illusion as the rest of him. When he spoke, no smoke accompanied his words.

"You're going to kill them all," I said. "What possible threat was Three Eight Seven? He was an artist, for god's sake!"

"Artists can be dangerous, Samson, you know that," Frewdin said. "Hitler was an artist."

"That's not an excuse!"

"I'm not making excuses, Samson." Frewdin waved his hand down the hall. "Yes, we will probably kill them all. No, that doesn't bother me. Phelan Eight is responsible for the death of two point two four trillion people. We will not take any more risks with this."

"There isn't any risk," I pleaded. "These people are no threat, Frewdin, Phelan Eight was only a threat because he had access to Shipkiller seeds. The seeds are gone. You're just salting the Earth behind you."

"Yes," Frewdin said at length. "We are. The seeds are gone, and the Cabernician species is broken. It doesn't matter what we do. So in the absence of anything better, we are falling back on the letter of the law. A poor path is better than no path at all." He cocked his head and listened. "They're finished processing your payment. Come with me."

He walked back to the lift. I looked around. So many doors. A death row. I was briefly frantic, and then I followed him. What could I have done?

A lot, it turns out. But I didn't know that back then.

The thought of it still keeps me up some nights.

35

This time the lift opened directly into a large, general-purpose lab filled with simple furniture, workbenches and chairs made out of dense black plastic. Machinery and academic detritus cluttered every surface, along with a spattering of papers, takeout containers and half-filled mugs of coffee. It looked like the place had been cleared out in a hurry.

Frewdin led me to a door on the far wall. He walked like he did everything else, as a series of careful choices. The choice to be friendly, the choice to be scary, the choice to cut a man into a lot of tiny pieces. The door swung open easily, but thudded against the wall hard enough to vibrate the floor.

"Watch your head," Frewdin said. He saw me looking around. "Matter fabrication chamber. We build elements, here."

The inside of the chamber was all one surface, floor to ceiling, a pattern of circular sunglass lenses that overlapped like scales. There was an open translucent container sitting open in the middle of the floor, maybe twenty-five inches on each side. Inside was a cube of gold about a foot and a half tall.

"Take a look," Frewdin said. "Watch out, though, the lid is in love with the box, so don't close it until you're ready to seal the thing. It's made out of plastic diamond, you'll have to blow it apart with a hand cannon to get it open again."

I reached for the box and the ship leapt into place. It felt good to be back inside. Comforting. I hefted the gold considerately. More than a thousand kilograms. According to the most recent exchange rate we had in the memory banks, I was holding a hunk of gold worth around fifty million dollars on Earth. Everywhere else it was chump change.

I dismantled the helmet. "This is gold."

"Yes, Captain, very observant," Frewdin said. "That is in fact elementally pure gold. Twenty-four karat, I believe, is the human term."

I slipped the gold back in its box. "This is only worth anything on Earth," I said.

Frewdin considered. "Might buy you a cup of coffee some places," he said. "Small one."

"I can't go back to Earth," I said. "You know that."

"Look at me, Captain," Frewdin said. "Come on, it's not that bad, look at me."

I turned around, all hulking metal plates and sudden sullen affect, that beat hot swollen sensation in my face and a knot in my sternum, and Frewdin twirled his finger in a circle above his head. There was a tinny whine in the upper range of my hearing, and the ship turned to stone. Cab disappeared out of my head. Internally, I staggered, thoughtless, but externally I stood trapped, motionless.

"Can you move?" Frewdin asked after a moment. His accent put me back in the moment. The Bronx, a billion billion miles from Earth.

"What the hell is this," I snarled. I bent at the waist as hard as I could, but the ship didn't move, so neither did I. "Cab! Cab! Wake up!"

"We call it a Nullifier," Frewdin said. "Phelan Seven's contribution to this whole clusterfuck. Phelan Eight did a lot of private research on the command architecture of Shipkiller operational code, odd loopholes and vestigial fragments. Didn't take Seven long to figure something out, but we needed the last hour to get everything finalized. We didn't think you'd wake up so soon. Nice of him to show you around the Ranch, though, he's a nice old man, isn't he?"

"Let me go, dammit!" I banged myself against the inside of my traitorous skin to no avail.

"Stop struggling," Frewdin said. "You'll hurt yourself."

Cab was gone. I dug frantically inside my head for him, but I was alone.

"Where is he?" I said, and I was surprised to hear calm in my voice.

"Cab?" Frewdin shrugged. "Wherever machines go when you turn them off. We'll turn him on in a moment. First we're going to have a talk. I have a point to make."

"Yeah?" I said. "What's that? You're a prick?"

Frewdin huffed laughter "Talk first, Samson." He picked up the lid. "You're good? It's gold?" He waited a beat and close the box. It sealed with a happy smacking sound, and Frewdin sat down on top. He shot his cuffs, showed me there was nothing in his hands and cupped them around his mouth. There was a lit cigarette burning in his mouth when he took them away.

"I'm giving you gold because I'm sending you back to Earth," he said through a cloud of smoke.

"Why?" I sputtered. "Haven't I–I did all right out here. I mean, your fears about me were groundless, weren't they?" He watched me. "I mean, I made Cab, he's part of my mind, and he was willing to die to save me, doesn't that count for something? And I saved the day, didn't I?"

Frewdin shook his head. "Samson, you're talking about a couple of weeks. When I say I'm worried about what you'll turn out to be, I mean I'm going to have to worry about you for the next twenty or thirty million years, and my successor will most likely have to keep track of you for the entirety of his career, and so on. I'm worried about who you'll be when you're a billion."

It was a blow, his casual tone. Like the length of my life wasn't even worth debating.

"Beyond that," he said, "Cab's actions, well, self-sacrifice is noble, but it's also selfish, so you'll pardon me if I'm not swayed in either direction. As far as you saving the day..." he chuckled and shook his head. "You destroyed the Cabernician Shipyards, Greg. You blew up the Seed Surplus."

"What?" I said. "I didn't destroy the Shipyards, the spider did that."

"You blew up the Seed surplus, Greg," Frewdin repeated. "The Seed Surplus *was* the Shipyards, everything else could have been rebuilt."

I shook my head. "The spider would have–"

"The spider was a wild animal, Greg." Frewdin dragged the cigarette nearly constantly, but it didn't get any shorter. "A single wild animal. How much could it have done? We would have found a way to kill it eventually."

"Other systems would have been destroyed," I said. My nose itched.

"A few dead systems is nothing weighed against Core military supremacy over the Krr," Frewdin said. "It will be close to a hundred million years before we can develop a new crop of Shipkiller seeds, and by then who *knows* what will have happened? And what about repairs? Shipkillers can only heal themselves to a point, you know. We don't have the Shipyards anymore! We're already looking into alternatives to the Shipkiller tactical model, but they aren't as good, Greg. You've dealt us a hell of a blow."

I stared at him.

"Are you kidding me?" I said. "You talk about it like we had other options. The spider was *eating* the seeds when the Garden blew up, you asshole! We'd already lost them by the time I got to Phelan!"

Frewdin sucked on his coffin nail, which is I'm sure how he would have wanted me to describe his actions. "There are people who think that ingesting that many seeds would have killed the spider," he said. "And it's possible that it only would have eaten some of the seeds, and left others that we could have recovered."

"And maybe it would have eaten them all and become something unstoppable," I said. "I did what I thought was necessary."

"Yeah," Frewdin said at length. "I know. You manipulated a suicidal traitor into dropping the stellar shield, knowing that it would result in a seven exaton explosion, all on your own authority." He spoke quietly. "And it's a good thing we've got Phelan to pin all this on. Do you have any idea what they would do to you if we told my bosses the truth?" He shook his head.

"You don't understand your reality, so I'm going to make it plain," he said. "There is a conservative political apparatus lobbying right now in the Core Senate to have your entire species exterminated, because of the threat posed by your diseases. This has been going on for as long as we have known about you. Now, you, a chronological infant from the species in question, are tooling around with the help of a sentient computer, a machine whose very existence is immoral and irresponsible, if not downright dangerous. Add to this the fact that you may have just crippled us ahead of a major Krr offensive–to say nothing of their continued war of attrition against the Fringes and Arms, which we do *know* about, Greg, we're not idiots–and you're left in what I would call a vulnerable situation."

He sighed. "You practically aided and abetted the Krr, Greg. If we make that public, people will be screaming for your head."

My nose itched a lot. The rest of my face just felt hot and guilty.

"I didn't know," I said lamely.

"I'm aware," Frewdin said. "And you acted anyway, in spite of knowing almost nothing about the situation." He sighed. "I'm sympathetic, Samson, you can't stop and ask for cosmopolitical advice in the middle of a firefight, but you may have done more damage than the spider, when all is said and done. Without the Shipkillers…well, I don't want to scare you." He smiled. "Not that way, at least. But, you know, you acted…what did Phelan Seven say? Like a bull in a china shop?"

"You were listening to us," I said. Frewdin shrugged.

"Yes, and I've just finished reading his report. He speaks rather highly of you, actually, in spite of your shared history and your absolute lack of tact." He chuckled. "What possessed you to tell a grieving father your personal logical proof of the nonexistence of the afterlife?"

I glared at him, because that was all I could do. "He was trying to take ownership of the tragedy."

"And from your lofty position of wisdom, you decided to set him straight," Frewdin said. "That's what he was referring to, I think, when he said that you would be a better person if you were humbler. You believe in yourself too much, Greg. You think you're better than you are. That's why you spoke to Phelan the way you did, and that's why you blew up the Seed Surplus without a second thought."

"I'd do it again," I said. "Have you seen what they do to the whales? Have you seen it up close?"

Frewdin smoked his cigarette. "You arrogant child," he said considerately. "I'm one hundred and four million years old. Do you really think I don't know what goes on out here? This is what I'm talking about. *You* mistake *our* mistakes for ignorance. You're naïve. You're impulsive. And that makes you dangerous."

"What is this, Top Gun?" I sneered. "Sending me home isn't going to teach me shit about how things work out here."

"I'm not sending you home to learn about the Core, I'm sending you home to grow the hell up and lose your sense of perfection," Frewdin said. "When you're older and less godawful full of yourself, I'll show you the ropes. But right now, I want you back on Earth. Not forever, don't worry, just for a few decades. Five or so. Just until you settle into yourself."

My face fell, and he shrugged. "Maybe a little longer. We need to separate you from the Battle of Cabernicia, anyway. Let the dust settle. Can't have people asking too many questions about you. You understand."

"What if the Krr come after me?" I said. "I left Earth to keep the planet safe. I can't go back. If anything, they have even more reason to hate me, now."

"Yeah, probably," Frewdin said. "In fact, that's another reason I want you hanging around the place. I want you to keep an eye on things, make sure the Krr don't get any funny ideas. There are a lot of weapons you could make out of human genetic material, if you were an immoral killing machine bent on galactic destruction."

I stared at him, not that I could turn my head very far in either direction.

459

"If they show up, you give us a call," Frewdin said. "We've got a CLEA base in Scallo, ah, the Alpha Centauri system. The next closest star system to you. You know the one I mean?" He paused a beat. "The transmission will be visible to them, and it should convince them to leave. Kinda like a shark deterrent. It's roughly the same system we use on monitored systems. If there's ever any trouble, just whistle."

"Why don't you just add Sol the list of monitored systems?" I said.

"Because that would be illegal?" Frewdin shrugged. "You're not an affiliated system, those protections are only for upstanding citizens who pay their taxes. Besides, you need something to keep you busy."

I stared at him. "This is ridiculous. You're sending me back there to rot?"

"There are other ways to look at it," Frewdin said. "You could meditate. Do some reading."

"For half a century?" I spat. Frewdin frowned.

"Let's say seventy-five years," he said. "That's not long. It'll be over before you know it." He examined his nails carefully for the time it took.

"Another thing," he said. "I don't want you to do anything stupid with the ship, like use it for the betterment of humanity. You want to get around, use it for your personal enjoyment, that's fine, but humanity is on a track that they have to be allowed to finish. They've got to evolve out of their diseases before they make it out of the system, or, well, the right-wing fuckos will get their way and we'll drop a stellar bomb in high orbit. In fact, let's make it an order. You are not to use the ship to aid, alter, or augment humanity in any fashion, and that includes education. You want to sweat the small stuff, be my guest, but don't go solving humanity's larger problems. You understand? You are to stay hidden in the fucking shadows, or else I will make your life very unpleasant."

"As opposed to the joy it is knowing you now," I said. Frewdin narrowed his eyes.

"Which brings us to my point." He got up and stretched luxuriantly, and his limbs were just a bit too long. Then he stepped close to me and pointed at his mouth with a wily expression on his face. After a beat, the cigarette retracted into his mouth and disappeared. When he spoke again, it was gone.

"That's the deal with my cigarette," he said.

"Very unsettling," I said. "What's your point?"

"Oh, that was just me being spooky," he said. "Here's my point: You're not untouchable." He reached out and grabbed my chin with his thumb was in my mouth and yanked my jaw. I tried to bite him, and he forced my mouth open.

"You don't respond well to threats," he said. "I'll keep that in mind." He pulled my head this way and that, examining my face.

"I could do a better job, I suppose," he said. "You skin is more elastic than mine. And it isn't as clear. Then again, this Bogart was forty-three. You're just a pimply kid."

I gagged and drooled against his thumb, which felt overlarge in my mouth. Frewdin's eyes lost their color and became tiny puckered black holes that bleached the humanity from the center of his face.

"You're not untouchable, Greg," he said. "You think you are. I can see it in your eyes, when you put on the ship. Even when you can't move, you have such a faith that you'll go on. That nothing can hurt you. Well, I can hurt you, can't I?" He pulled my head forward as far as it could go, and my jaw ground against its joints.

"Do I have to rip off your mandible to get you to take me seriously?" He mused. "The question isn't

461

rhetorical, Captain, answer me, do I have to rip off your jawbone to get you to take me seriously? To take the situation seriously? Yes or no?"

I tried to shake my head, and he must have felt the pressure back and forth because he let me go and stepped back. His hand was covered in my drool and snot and tears. He looked at it curiously, then held it up above his head and said "Get this shit off of my fucking hand." After a second, his hand smoked, once.

I was choking, gagging. Something awful rose out of my stomach, and I swallowed it back. My jaw wasn't broken, but it felt like it should have been. I was crying, too. I was scared. Terrified. My head throbbed with it, my scalp felt like it was on fire. Frewdin stood in front of me without speaking or moving for five minutes while I pulled myself together.

"You are a monster," he said finally. "You're right about that. But I am a bigger monster. And I can control you. So I am telling you, Samson, as your *master*, to go back to Earth and get your head straight. Do not use the ship to alter, aid or augment your species. If you behave yourself, we will revisit the situation in seventy-five years."

He stepped close and peered at me with his deadman's shark eyes. "If you do not behave, then I will turn off Cab's mind and put you in a hole by yourself for a thousand years." He rubbed his thumb the wrong way over my eyebrow stubble and I flinched. "I don't know if I can kill you, Greg. I really don't. Phelan Seven says even chucking you in a black hole would be an iffy chance, at best. Something to do with quantum mass displacement. But I can control you, so it doesn't matter if I can't kill you, does it?" He grinned at me. "Are you going to behave yourself?"

I projected every ounce of my hatred into the look I gave him. Unfortunately, his head didn't explode, so I nodded.

"What are you going to do, Greg?"

"I'm going to go back to Earth," I rasped. "And I'm going to stay there until you tell me otherwise. I won't aid, augment or alter humanity."

Frewdin's grin was full of flat sharp teeth. He really knew how to sell the menace when he had to.

"Close enough," he said. "I'm going to turn Cab back on, Samson. Remember I can switch him off whenever I want."

He stepped back and nodded at nothing. Cab's mind came screaming back into my head and I dropped to my knees against what felt like the worst headache I'd ever had. The pain was nearly unbearable, and at least half of it came directly from Cab himself.

--Ow--

--It's two hundred and six seconds later than it should be and I have a headache. What the *fuck* just happened?--

I got up and flared the ship around me, made sure everything was running right. All the voices were where they should have been, although they sound vaguely confused.

--Greg? What's going on? What happened to your jaw?--

I decided that Cab deserved the truth as much as I did.

"Agent Frewdin has a machine that turns off your mind and renders the ship inert," I said. "He's sending us back to Earth on some kind of house arrest."

Weapons leapt out of my hull and I grabbed them back, dismantled the ship and clamped down on Cab's rage.

"Stop it!" I shouted. "Fucking stop!" Cab was wordless inside me, a maelstrom with a purpose. He wanted to kill Frewdin so bad I could taste it. War machines built themselves up at his urging and disappeared at mine.

--He won't he won't he won't--

"Cab," I said.

--No no no no no no fucker die fucker *die*--

"Cab." Frewdin raised his hand. "Watch this."

"No!" I pointed at him through the storm of weapons. "You let me deal with this, dammit!"

Frewdin shrugged. "Ok, impress me," he said. "Show me your self-control."

I stared at him, holding Cab off the ship's controls, pulling apart the weapons he pulled out of the base material. We couldn't see through Bekht bodies, so we would have to burn away all of him to be sure he was really dead. The thought was as much mine as it was Cab's. That would be a monstrous thing to do, to burn a man's body away to nothing. But they already thought I was a monster. And they were so much older, so much wiser, and I was such an infant. Why shouldn't I prove them right?

I remember thinking hard, so that Cab would understand my meaning even if he couldn't hear the words. If we kill him, we die. A particle beam exploded into and out of being in front of me. If we kill him, they rip us apart and destroy us and we die. If we kill him, we die. You know that. I know you don't want this, but it's not about what you want, it's about what you get, and what you do. If we kill him, we die.

The frantic creation slowed down. I pressed everything back into place, and felt the pressure on the ship diminish as Cab found his calm. After a moment the ship rustled on my back and was still. I took a deep breath, and another, and looked at Frewdin. He raised his eyebrows invitingly. Cab snarled in my mind, but left the ship alone. We were stuck, and we both knew it. That was the beauty of the Nullifier, they didn't even have to turn the thing on to keep us in line. We were stuck. Frewdin's smile widened.

"Fuck you," I said. The ship leapt around me in a picosecond. "I'm going home." I hoisted a ton and a half of gold with one hand and walked out the chamber, across the lab to the lift. Frewdin followed me, and when the doors opened I got in and turned around and flipped him off.

"Impressive, n'est pas?" I pressed the button to close the door. "This one's full. You can wait for the next one."

The doors shut on him looking at me inscrutably with a fake cigarette burning in his mouth.

That was the last time I saw him for a while.

36

They gave me fifty million dollars in bullshit and they gave Rell a new ship, a long, angular cargo runner with twin engines mounted at the halfway point and long guns fore and aft. It sat on squat claws in the middle of the bay, intimidating and out of place among the idiot escape pods and against the organic aesthetic of the Shipkiller itself. Rell was watching a team of featureless Bekht strip out all of the nonessential equipment when I stepped out of the lift.

"Not as nice as the old one," I said.

Rell shook his head. "Not as big, either. I'm gonna see if I can trade up. I know a dealer in the Oomin Tam system who owes me a favor, I'm gonna see if I can twist his arm into giving me an Eam rescue freighter for this thing. You wanna come along?"

"I have to go back to Earth," I said. Rell looked at me for five seconds. Then he nodded. When the Bekht finished what they were doing we went into the new ship and spat out of the whale's mouth, away from the fleet, and warped out of Cabernicia.

The cargo runner was done up in the latest military fashions, which is a polite way of saying that everything was grey and boring and there wasn't any decent food on board. Rell found some eggs and an onion and started making lunch. He cut the onions with the claws in his palms, peeling them carefully and patting them diced on the bare counter.

"What happened to your face?" He asked.

"Frewdin." I watched the pan heat up.

"Are you healing?" The muscles bunched under his shoulders as he dug in the cupboard under the stove. He grunted unhappily and came up with a bottle of clear oil. "Canola, what is this happy horseshit?"

I nodded. "I'm healing."

"Good," he said. The onions flashed in the pan and started to soften. "He's sending you home?"

I nodded. "He says he's giving me time to grow up. I call it house arrest."

"How long?" Rell asked.

"Seventy-five years," I said.

He nodded. "That's a long time."

"We don't live as long as Frewdin," I said.

"Not yet, anyway," Rell said. "What happened, did he hit you?"

I rubbed my chin. "He yanked on my jaw some."

"You mouth off to him?" Rell turned the eggs in the pan.

I smiled a tiny bit. "He says I don't take threats well."

"You mouthed off to him," Rell said.

"Yeah." I picked at some grit on the table. "He has a machine that can turn off Cab's mind."

--Fucking asshole--

--I want to kill him--

"I know you don't mean that, dork," I mumbled. I was telling the truth. And Cab knew it, and I knew he knew it, and, well, it took us a long time to get used to the cyclical self-knowledge. But it's always had its advantages.

--Fine--

--I want to hit him many, many times in the face with your ship-covered fist, and I want to figure out how to stop him from turning me off, ever again--

--It felt like when--

Cab's thoughts stretched out for a long instant.

--Well, you know. It felt like when I died--

468

--Just…nothingness--

I would have hugged him if he had a body. I tried reaching up and patting my own back, but it felt awkward.

"That doesn't work," I said.

--No. But I appreciate the gesture--

--I hate being treated like a machine--

I huffed a laugh. "Yeah. Me too."

Rell flipped his omelet onto a plate and put it between us.

"Only one fork," he said.

I put the ship on my hand and stared at my finger until it grew tines.

--This is undignified--

"But practical," Rell said. I took a bite and chewed and swallowed and sat quietly while Rell ate.

"Everybody thinks I'm a monster," I said. Rell lipped a piece of onion into his mouth and chewed.

"So?" He said at length. "Are you?"

"Am I?" I said. "What the hell kind of question is that? I don't know. I don't know shit! Everyone out here thinks I'm a monster, or I'm turning into a monster, or, or, I don't know! Even you, Rell."

He frowned at me and I waved my hand fork angrily.

"You were terrified of me when you met me," I said.

"I thought you were infested with plagues," he said.

I stared at him until I remembered his words in the hold. "Your exact words were 'I'd rather take my chances with the Krr than share a home with a psychotic self-aware computer.'" I spread my hands. "That was during training. You'd known I was clean for days. You remember saying that?"

Rell folded his arms across his chest and knit his hands under his chin. It made him look like he was tied in a knot.

"Everyone thinks I'm a monster," I said. "Phelan thinks I'll turn into one unless I live like a...I don't know, a monk, or something. And Frewdin...he made that machine because he thinks I need to be controlled."

"He's a cop," Rell said. "Can you blame him?" He scratched around in his pockets until he found half a cigar, which he lit on the stove. It burned for a moment like a candle.

"When I met you I was scared of you," he said. "If I didn't know you, I still would be. Because of what you are, and because of what you can do. You didn't see yourself out there. And you don't know a thing, so you wouldn't understand what it meant, if you had." He grinned. "You're a naïf. That's part of your charm."

He stared at the wall, collecting his words.

"You went through the spider's drone cloud without much difficulty," he said. "You think that's normal, because you don't know any better. But, Samson, that drone cloud was the largest anti-ship fleet in recorded history. Granted, you didn't fight them all, but you did make it through a three light-second-thick cloud of machines that were trying actively to kill you. There isn't another ship in the galaxy that could do that."

He reached out and dinged my metal hand. "You know what you look like on a ship's sensor array? I watched the battle from Frewdin's flagship, Samson, he kept me right on the bridge." He stopped, frowned. "I wonder if he did that so I could have this conversation with you." After a moment he shrugged.

"You maxed out the Shipkiller's energy sensors," he said. "You understand? You registered as too much power to quantify on the sensors of a ship whose energy signature should be identical to yours. They had to manually reset the sensors to a higher maximum ceiling just to *track you*, while you fought your way through an unwinnable fight. And you did it with two feet, one hand and an ass in the grave. When you came back to Frewdin's ship, you weren't a wreck, you were *wreckage*. Your body was practically pulp. And yet here you sit, barely a week later, healthy as a pink, hairless clam." He took his time blowing a smoke ring, and then we took our time watching it dissipate.

"Staggeringly powerful and practically immortal," Rell said. "And that's not 'practically' to mean 'nearly.' That's 'practically' to mean, 'for all intents and purposes.' You are staggeringly powerful after, what, three weeks? I can only imagine what you'll be like down the road."

"You think Frewdin is right to send me home," I said.

"No, I think you're lucky to go home," Rell said. "As far as whether he's right to place you under house arrest for seventy-five years..." He flexed his hand and picked at one of his claws. "Phelan is the one who thinks you might turn into a monster?"

I nodded. "Unless I'm careful with myself, whatever that means."

"It means wear a rubber," Rell said. "And Frewdin thinks you're already a monster, which is why he built his widget."

--Nullifier--

Rell made a wry face. "Decent name." He sighed. "Listen, Samson, I'm sorry that I was mean to you when we met. I was scared of you because I thought of you the way Frewdin and Phelan and the rest of those CLEA goons think of you, like you're just a thing. But you're not a thing, you're a human being, and you're the same man you were before you met Cab, for better or worse. You understand? No matter what else you are now, it's an existence that's built on who you were before all this happened. All of their fears about you are abstractions. What will a short-lived mind do when confronted with eternity, can a sentient computer truly value life, those are intellectual questions. They think the weight of all of that will turn you into a monster, or that it already has, but the truth is that no one decides who you are but you. And who you are isn't an abstraction, it's something real, in front of you, right now. It's what you do. It's your actions. You see what I'm driving at, here? You decide who you are. If you turn out to be a monster, it'll be because you decided to be a monster. It doesn't matter what Phelan, or Frewdin, or even what I tell you. Our fears don't matter. You decide who you are." He shook his head and rolled his eyes and groaned. "And you know all of this, because these are easy truths, Samson."

We made eye contact for about eight seconds and then I smirked and snorted an embarrassed laugh.

"Yeah," I said. "I know."

"I know you know," Rell said. "But, I also know that sometimes people need to hear this sort of thing aloud."

"Yeah," I said.

Long pauses tend to stretch in warp. There's a sense that time is somewhat confused about itself at the moment, and trying new things to see how they work.

"They do think you're a monster," Rell said. "But fuck 'em. You know? You're the kid who told me 'might demands right' and then risked his life for a galaxy that wants nothing to do with him. They want to call you a monster, fuck 'em. You've already proved them wrong. All you have to do now is keep the streak alive."

"So what do you think I should do?" I asked. Rell looked at me and frowned.

"Should I go home?" I asked. "Or should I cut and run? What are you telling me to do?"

Rell mashed his cigar in the sink. "I'm not telling you to do anything. You are your actions. Might demands right. Those are your truths. You decide what you should do now." He settled his chin on his chest.

"But," he said after several minutes.

"But?" I said after several more.

"But I think you should go home," he said.

"Why?" I said.

"Personal reasons," he said. "Selfish reasons. I would give a lot to spend seventy-five years on my home planet. And there are a lot of people out here who would chop off a limb just to see their home planet from orbit. I think you should go home because seventy-five years on your home planet is a gift, Samson. Don't squander it."

He frowned, and then laughed. "Also, if you cut and run they'll hunt you down in a week. You've got no money and you don't know a damn thing about a damn thing out here. Go home. Lick your wounds. Live out some semblance of the life you lost. The galaxy isn't going anywhere."

I stared at the table in front of me. "I don't know if I can stand it, living like I don't know what's going on out here."

Rell leaned over and put his face was very close to mine.

"You have to," he said. "This isn't an awful thing, Samson."

I looked at him and his eyes filled most of what I could see. They were very serious. I thought about what it must have been like for him to leave Vabl voluntarily, knowing that it meant he could never return. The loss, the heart-rending ache that must have woken him up in the middle of the night, the way grief does. Loss of home. Loss of life. My parents. Cab. Phelan Seven realizing how long it had been since he had spent any time with his son. The refugees living past the end of their realities. I lost my life when I met Cab, and all anyone ever wants is more time with what they've lost, no matter what it is that's gone. I couldn't have more time with my parents, or with Cab, but I could spend this one last moment with Earth, with the life I had grown up with, the life I had expected, the life that I still mourn.

"You're right," I said.

"I know I'm right," Rell said. He clapped me once on the shoulder. "Ok. Lecture's over. I'm going to look around the engines, see what I'm working with."

He pushed the plate closer to me. There was still half an omelet waiting for me. Rell hadn't eaten much.

"Eat," he said. "You'll feel better."

I stared at the omelet and wondered bemusedly what kind of eggs they were.

"Rell," I said. He stopped at the door.

"Yes," he said.

"Thank you," I asked.

He paused, then left without saying anything. I ate the omelet. It was good, in spite of what Rell had to work with. You do what you can with what you're given.

Goddamn metaphors are everywhere.

epilogue

Rell dropped me just past Mars, and I made the last of the journey alone.

Earth was waiting where I left it, loud, blue, green and polluted. Unchanged. Seven billion life signs screeched at my sensors and I breathed easy, let go of some heretofore-unutterable fear, that I would come back to find that my world was gone, that I was the last, the only, the altered remnant.

In my mind's eye, the spider skittered over the horizon, molten rock dripping from its mandibles and lasers streaming off of its underbelly, eviscerating continents and erasing major cities. I could hear the screams as it lowered itself to the planet's surface…

Sick fantasy. I forced a smile and dove into the atmosphere with sonic booms rippling off my hull and information boiling across my screens, everything I had missed on Earth. Fires in California, Indonesia, a flood in China. The President's approval rating was up two points, Brazil was gearing up for the Olympics, and gas was cheap. I had two friend requests and thirteen notifications. Everything in its rightful place.

I spotted a deserted island in the South Pacific and landed on the beach. The place was empty apart from some tenacious plant life and a few seabirds, who watched me with reptilian curiosity. If only you were smaller, their eyes seemed to say, and your shell were not so tough…after a moment they wandered down the beach, cackling to each other. Black-Browed Albatrosses. *Thalassarche menaophris.* The internet was back, waiting in the wings of my consciousness, overlaying facts on top of everything I saw.

I dropped the gold on the beach and walked a few steps. The colors I saw inside the ship were bright and vivid, but they were always in check. Carefully edited for clarity and precision. As the Shipkiller I saw better than any human ever had, but none of what I saw was real. And in spite of the obvious tropical nature of my surroundings, the inside of the ship still smelled like a Maine in October.

I took a deep breath and dismantled the ship. The sun hurt my eyes, so I closed them. Hot salty wind whipped around my body, carrying with it that funny mineral smell that is the end result of everything that has ever lived in the ocean. I started to sweat immediately and stripped off my clothes in a way that would have torn them apart if they hadn't been made of tear-proof alien fabrics. The sun pressed at me through the shell on my back. I tripped over my shoes and squirmed in the sand. The light felt good on the hull. Fulfilling. Sustaining. I stood up and took a step forward, and another, and found wet sand. I was gasping. I opened my eyes to slits and stared at the unbroken horizon. The sun glittered off the Pacific and seared my eyes.

A wave came rolling in and soaked me to the waist. I rocked back on my heels, and when the wave receded I chased it, grinning like an idiot. I dove under the next one, pushed through the current and swam for the horizon. There was no breath from Cab. He knew what I wanted. I wanted to push. I wanted to struggle I wanted to do it myself.

When I broke the surface, I was a hundred yards out from the shore, seeing stars. Deep water, in the middle of the Pacific. The biggest thing I'd ever been a part of. It pushed and pulled, hungry, too big to quantify, and I was so small. Just an ape screaming through space on a rock.

The ship twisted into a pair of engines and lifted me out of the water, dripping and nekkid. I hovered three meters off the surface of the water, watching the horizon and smiling.

Home.

Tell my why you're concerned.

What?

Tell me why you're concerned.

You didn't think there was anything left alive in this universe. You thought you were going to find a field of uniform matter. But I'm still here. Why does that scare you?

I...what happened next?

Oh, you mean my superhero years?

Superhero years? But Frewdin said–

Let me tell you about Frewdin. Frewdin put me exactly where he wanted me, doing exactly what he wanted me to do. You want to know how I began? That story is a story about Frewdin, about what he had planned. Christ. I was just his happy accident. That's the story you want to hear.

Did you stay on Earth the whole seventy-five years?

Seventy-five...hell, no. I didn't make it five years.

What happened?

Tell me why you're concerned, _____. Fair is fair.

You're pretty confident for a man who might be narrating his way into his own execution.

Yeah, yeah, _____, we've been down that road. You can't kill me. And even if you can, I was young when I was a billion. If it's my time, it's my time. Don't try to scare me. Why are you concerned?

Maybe we've heard enough.

To render a real judgment? No you haven't. I mean, if you want to get this show on the road, that's one thing, but if you think that you've heard enough to 'understand my nature,' you're kidding yourself. You haven't heard about my superhero years, for one thing, and let me tell you, if you like laughing at people doing stupid things with spaceships, well, those stories won't disappoint. But I mean, really, the Krr, Frewdin, everything he was planning, my life on Earth, Ghaneb…The War.

No, you haven't heard a thing. You've heard the story of my birth. But if you really want to know me…if you're really scholars…that's the story you want.

Then tell us.

Tell me why you're concerned.

Your universe is of the big-bang, big-crunch variety, and it's going to crunch very soon. We don't know if you will survive the collapse, because there's never been anything living at this point in a universe's life cycle before. But we do know that emotional proximity can alter a universal structure during the reorganization period, which is why we pull back to a safe distance to observe the process. The presence of a living mind within a universe as it reorganized itself for rebirth would unquestionably influence the creation of the next universe. So you can imagine that it's very important for us to determine what kind of a person you are.

You're telling me that if I'm a nice guy, we get a nice guy universe, and if I'm an asshole, we get an asshole universe.

Yes.

That's assuming I don't just...survive.

That is theoretically impossible, although of course as a scientist I recognize the reality of the phrase "theoretically impossible." In any case, assuming that you do not survive, your presence at the ultimate moment of this universe will influence the primary moment of the next universe. If we deem you a threat to that universe, then we will be forced to destroy you.

Y'all are naturalists, aren't you?

Excuse me?

Environmentalists. Hippies. You think I'm a, a fungus.

A cancer, actually.

Fungi are external organisms. Cancers grow from within.

Gee, what a wonderful image.

You brought it up.
What did you do after you got back to Earth?

I want to rest.

You're in no position to make demands.

Then pull iron, _____.

After I went back to Earth, I lost my mind, got arrested, met the love of my life, murdered a whole lot of people, and took over the world. It's a heady story, _____. I want to rest before I tell it.

I have been instructed to let you rest.

Glad to hear it.

This is a reward for your good behavior.

Jesus! Good god, man, warn me if you're going to make a random object appear on my lap.

Is that a cheeseburger?
Huh. Thanks.

I will return after you have rested.

I don't doubt it, _____.

END INTERVIEW

SUPLEMENTARY AUDIO TRANSCRIPT

I'm gonna say the burger is a little better than the coffee.

Yeah. Greasy, too.

Oh, yeah, I remember that place. The one where the default was sweet potato fries, right?

…That wasn't there, that was the brewery on Ewl, remember? With the coconut porter?

No, it was awful, but you remember it, don't you?

Yeah, that was the place where they put the piece of ham in the middle of the burger. I thought it was a little much.

You think they might really be able to kill us?

I know it's possible, I'm asking if you think *these people* can do it.

Yeah. Did you get a glimpse of anything before they got us?

Me neither.

Well, I guess keep your eye out, see what you can pick up. Be nice to know what we're dealing with.

No, not yet. We sit tight. Tell them what they want to know.

It's kinda nice, looking back.
Yeah, right. I'm a real softy.

Well, it weren't no Michelin three-star, but it sure is nice to eat solid food again.
Where? Oh, thank you.

Think I'll take a nap.

Play some music, why don't you?
Nah, you pick.

Nice.
Thanks. Wake me up if you need to.

We know you're listening, by the way.

See you soon, _____.

End: File: Interview 2

Benjamin Mumford-Zisk

THE ORIGAMI MAN
will return…